Th

on the
Beach

The Boy
on the
Beach

Mary Towne

Library of Congress Cataloging-in-Publication Data
Towne, Mary.
[Dive through the wave]
The boy on the beach / by Mary Towne.
—1st Paperback ed.
        p.   cm.
Summary: During her family's visits to the beach on Long
Island, Ruth makes friends with a lifeguard who helps her handle
her worries about the war, an outbreak of polio, and being the
youngest girl in sixth grade.
ISBN 0-8167-3479-8 (pbk.)
1. World War, 1939–1945—United States—Juvenile fiction.
[1. World War, 1939–1945—United States—Fiction.   2. Family
life—Fiction.   3. Friendship—Fiction.]   I. Title.
PZ7.T6495Di   1994   [Fic]—dc20   93-40999

The Boy on the Beach

CHAPTER

ONE

It was an almost perfect beach day, Ruth thought dreamily, floating in a trough of blue water between two white flurries of foam—the wave that had just slid away beneath her and the wave she could see gathering itself ahead. Only two things would make it better. One would be if Joan were here instead of away at some boring lake up in New Hampshire. The other—here Ruth let her feet down hastily and waded forward to join the rising wave, letting it lift her to the sky—would be if it were still July instead of August.

But no, she wasn't going to think about that today.

"Ruth! Ruthie!"

As the wave set her down again, Ruth turned to see her mother beckoning from the beach. Was it lunchtime already? She hoped not, because they had a rule that you couldn't go in the water again for an hour after you ate.

A whole hour! It always seemed endless to Ruth, no matter how many poems or multiplication tables she recited in her head during the first half hour, when they had to stay lying down. During the second half hour she could sit up and read, if it wasn't too bright or too windy, or dig boring tunnels in the sand with her younger sisters. Ruth didn't really like getting all sandy anymore, the way Betsy and Carol did. Sometimes Carol would let them bury her, all the way up to her dimpled chin.

But no, it wasn't lunchtime yet. Ruth had just let the current carry her too far down the beach. Her parents liked her to stay opposite the place where they'd spread out their steamer rug and towels, so they could keep an eye on her.

Ruth waded into shallow water, keeping her side to the waves the way her father had taught her—one thing you never did was turn your back on the ocean—and splashed back along the shore.

It was funny: even on days when you could barely feel that sideways current, it could still pull you a long way from where you started out. Sometimes Ruth would come up out of the water onto the dazzle of the beach and head toward what she thought was her family, only to find a group of strangers—the wrong color towels, a fancy picnic hamper instead of their frayed old basket, a father with a potbelly instead of her tall, skinny dad.

Of course it didn't help that she was near-sighted. Ruth frowned and kicked at a tangle of seaweed. That was another thing not to think about today.

She saw Betsy up ahead, so she must be almost back to her starting place. Betsy was tossing a tennis ball in the air, spinning around twice with her eyes closed, and trying to catch it before it bounced. As Ruth came up, Betsy missed, grabbed the ball before it could roll into the surf, and said, "Do you want to play Spud?"

Ruth shook her head. "I'm going back in the water. Anyway, you can't play Spud with only two people."

Betsy looked around for their father, but he was helping Carol build a sand castle above the tide line. Their mother had returned to her towel and book.

"I wish we didn't always have to come to Number Nine," Betsy grumbled. "There's nothing to *do* here. Why can't we go to Number Two sometime? We never get to go there anymore."

Jones Beach State Park, on the south shore of Long Island, was divided into numbered sections along its wide white miles of sand. Number Nine was at the far end, with a modest, flat-roofed pavilion and a small parking lot that hardly ever got filled up, even on weekends. That was partly because of gas rationing, of course. But Ruth couldn't remember it being crowded even before the war, the summer before last.

Number Two, by contrast, was one of the big pavilions near the start of the beach road. It had a huge swimming pool, a playground with slides and swings, and a boardwalk where you could buy thin hamburgers in fresh, damp buns oozing catsup and pickle relish.

Ruth's mouth watered at the thought of those hamburgers, but she said, "You know why—it's too crowded." When Betsy opened her mouth to argue, she said, "There were zillions of cars in the parking lot, didn't you see? We would've had a really long walk to the beach."

Betsy said, "Well, we could go on a weekday sometime. That's what the Thomases do, and it's hardly crowded at all." Cindy Thomas was Betsy's best friend, the way Joan Decker was Ruth's. "Cindy says there isn't even any line for the slide."

The tall slide into the swimming pool, she meant. Ruth stared at her. "You mean they go in the *pool*?"

"Well, sure."

But Betsy's blue eyes avoided hers. They both knew that public swimming pools were where you could get polio, especially late in the summer. Polio was infantile paralysis. That sounded like only little kids could get it, but the President had had it—that was why he was always sitting in a wheelchair—and so had a girl at school who wore a metal brace on her leg and got to be excused from gym.

Ruth didn't have much use for Cindy Thomas, and Cindy's little brother Jimmy was a brat. Still, she didn't want them to get sick and maybe end up being crippled. She said, "Doesn't Mrs. Thomas worry?"

Betsy shrugged uneasily. "I guess she thinks if the pool isn't crowded . . . Anyway, the doctors don't know for sure how people get it."

Ruth shivered, in spite of the sunlight and the warm blue air that seemed to pulse and quiver with the motion of the waves. She imagined a germ floating in a giant swimming pool, like a tiny, transparent jellyfish. But of course you couldn't actually see a germ, no matter how hard you looked, unless maybe you had a microscope. Betsy had a pretend microscope at home, made of cardboard. She wanted to be a scientist or a doctor when she grew up. Anyway, Ruth thought, you couldn't take a microscope into a pool.

Maybe Betsy was thinking the same thing, because she said with sudden fierceness, "If I was a doctor, I'd find out. I'd stay up all night, every night, until I found out."

Ruth nodded. Betsy would, too. You wouldn't think it to look at her, with her snub nose and soft, honey-blond curls, but Betsy was amazingly stubborn. Once she'd spent a whole afternoon trying to win at solitaire, dealing the cards over and over and never cheating. By the time the game finally worked out, Ruth and Carol were halfway through supper. Betsy had to have cold macaroni-and-cheese and didn't get any dessert.

Ruth said, "Well, anyway, I'd rather swim in the

ocean than in a pool any day. Something's always *happening* in the ocean."

She stood surveying it with satisfaction, her fists on her hips. The waves were medium-high today, just the way she liked them—long combers rolling in to break near the shore in lacy, dancing flakes of light.

"I'm going back in from farther up the beach this time," she told Betsy, pointing toward the distant lifeguard's chair. "Then I won't have to keep coming out all the time. Tell Mom, okay?"

Before Betsy could say they were supposed to stay even with their parents, not go in swimming off by themselves, Ruth splashed rapidly away.

CHAPTER

~~~~~~~~~~~~~~~~~~~~~~~~~~~~~~~~~~~~~

TWO

A couple of older boys were trying to ride a big wave all the way in to shore, holding their prone bodies stiff as boards amid the rushing tumble of white water. As Ruth dodged out of their way, something banged into her ankle—a wooden beach pail. She grabbed the handle before the pail could be sucked away into the receding wave and handed it to its owner, a little kid about Carol's age.

Then she angled up the slope of the beach toward the tall, white lifeguard's chair, intending to get a running start back into the water.

"Thanks," said a voice high above her head.

Ruth squinted up into the face of the lifeguard, a bronzed young man in orange trunks with a sailor's hat perched on top of his curly, salt-stiffened blond hair. "What for?" she said, shading her eyes.

"For catching that pail. I've been keeping an eye on that little boy—his folks aren't paying any attention to him." He nodded over his shoulder at some people playing cards around a square of oilcloth. "If I had my way," he added, "kids wouldn't be allowed to take anything in the water with them until they knew how to swim. The pail or the ball or whatever it is gets caught in a wave, and next thing you know they've gone in after it."

Despite his friendly tone, the lifeguard didn't look at Ruth as he spoke. His gaze was on the ocean, sweeping slowly from left to right and back again.

Ruth moved around to the other side of the chair where the sun wasn't in her eyes and said shyly, "I guess that's why they don't allow rafts or inner tubes—little kids could get carried out too far."

"Right, and not just little kids. Stuff like that can be a real headache for a lifeguard, rafts especially. They're fun to ride in the surf, though, if you've ever tried it." He grinned, showing teeth as white as his sailor's hat.

Ruth was about to say she had, just once, at a private club farther out on the island that friends of her parents belonged to, when the lifeguard blew a shrill blast on his whistle and made a series of beckoning motions with his muscular arm.

She turned to see who he was looking at and finally spotted two small bathing-capped heads bobbing in the blue water out beyond the breakers.

"Are they all right?" she asked anxiously,

hitching herself partway up the ladderlike side of **the chair** in order to see better.

"Oh, sure—a couple of ladies, got talking and lost **track of** where they were. It's a light surf today, and **no rips** to worry about in this area. Still, I don't like to see anyone drifting too far out unless they're strong swimmers."

The two women had turned and seemed to be breaststroking slowly toward shore. After a minute, they stopped and began treading water again, but the lifeguard seemed satisfied.

"You must have really good eyesight," Ruth said, impressed.

"Yeah, that's one thing you can't do without on this job—twenty-twenty vision."

"I'm probably going to have to get glasses in the fall," Ruth said glumly, hooking an arm around one of the white-painted rungs. "When school starts."

"Well, hey, they'll probably look good on you." The lifeguard shot her a quick glance. His eyes were hazel green like her own, only with blond lashes and eyebrows bleached almost white by the sun. "Anyhow, you gotta be able to see the blackboard, right?"

Ruth nodded. If they even use the blackboard in sixth grade, she thought, and felt the familiar quake in the pit of her stomach. She'd almost rather think about wearing glasses and how awful they were going to make her look. It just wasn't fair that she had to be the one in her family who needed glasses. Both of her sisters were cute, with rounded, sturdy limbs and naturally curly hair and faces people smiled at. But Ruth was skinny and plain and uninteresting-looking, with straight, mouse-colored hair and a gap between her two front teeth.

Well, of course, her father wore glasses, but that was different—they were like a part of his face.

"I bet you're smart in school," the lifeguard offered, when Ruth didn't say anything more. "I can tell by the way you swim."

"Really?" Ruth felt herself flush, surprised that he'd noticed her.

"Yeah. I've only been working here about a month, but I noticed your family right off because of the way you three girls all wear the same bathing suits."

"That's so our parents can keep track of us better," Ruth muttered. This year's suit wasn't too bad—blue, with yellow zigzag stripes that reminded her of Captain Marvel in the comic books. "Shazam!" she'd said when she first tried hers on, making her sisters giggle. But Ruth hated wearing matching clothes, even when there was a good reason for it.

"Anyway," the lifeguard said, "I could tell right off you were a good, smart swimmer, just like your dad. You don't take a lot of dumb chances the way some kids do, but you're not scared of the ocean, either."

"I'm scared of it sometimes," Ruth felt honor-bound to say. "When it's really rough, or right after I get boiled."

"Boiled" meant catching a wave wrong and being

rolled around inside hard, bumpy knots of foam that didn't even feel like water, with sand getting in your eyes and nasty little shells scraping your knees and elbows.

"Well, sure, and you're right to be. Unless you respect the ocean, it can't be your friend. That's not the kind of scared I mean. Your sister, now, the one with the blond hair—is she older or younger?"

"Younger." Ruth scowled, though it was a familiar question. Betsy was big for her age, Ruth small for hers.

"She never has any fun in the water because she's always tensing up. By the time she decides if she's going to ride a wave or jump it or dive through it— wham! It's already on top of her."

"But Betsy's the good athlete in our family," Ruth said in surprise. "She's really well coordinated. Daddy always says so."

The lifeguard shrugged. "Maybe so. But not when it comes to swimming in the ocean."

Ruth had never really thought about it, but it was true that although Betsy usually beat her into the water when they first arrived—just as their mother was usually the rotten egg—she never stayed in very long unless their father stayed in, too. It was almost as if she still needed him nearby to catch her or tell her where to stand. She said she got cold, but maybe that wasn't the reason.

"My parents call me their water rat," Ruth confided. "I never like to come out of the ocean, even after my lips turn blue."

She leaned out from the chair and gave a sigh of contentment as she surveyed the scene around her—the dimpled expanse of sand dotted with the bright colors of towels and bathing suits and an occasional striped umbrella, the sparkling blue water crisped with white beneath a paler blue sky.

"I wish I could always be at the beach," she told the lifeguard. "It's my favorite place in the whole world."

"And you'd like it always to be summer, too, right?" He chuckled. "Yeah, I know what you mean."

Something in his voice made Ruth swing around to look up at his face. But just then he noticed a bunch of big boys trying to duck each other in the surf—or maybe he'd been watching them all along, Ruth thought humbly, aware that his attention had been only partly focused on her.

He picked up his megaphone and called through it, "Enough horsing around there!" The boys looked around, startled. Sheepishly, they separated, then made a show of racing each other out into deeper water, whooping and bellyflopping through the waves.

Ruth dropped down onto the sand, feeling a little sheepish, too. She'd been ready to tell the lifeguard about her special reason for wishing fall would never come this year—because of skipping a grade in school and having to make a whole lot of new friends, something she was afraid she wouldn't be any good at, especially if she had to wear glasses.

But probably he wouldn't be interested; probably he'd just been talking to her to pass the time. It must get lonely, Ruth thought, sitting up in that tall chair all day, while the people on the beach were free to chat and wander around and toss beach balls back and forth and run races along the hard sand at the water's edge.

She had turned away and was squaring her shoulders for her dash into the ocean when the lifeguard called down, "Say, what's your name? I need to know what to call you next time."

"It's Ruth," she said, feeling a little glow of pleasure. Next time. So he really was being friendly, not just feeling bored, or worse, sorry for her, a funny-looking girl who might be a good swimmer but who was also shrimpy and skinny and not as cute as her sisters.

"Mine's Russell," he told her. "Russ, for short. I guess you don't need a nickname, though—not with a short name like Ruth."

It was funny, the way he had of picking on things that bothered her. Ruth wished she *did* have a nickname, the way Betsy was short for Elizabeth and Carol was sometimes called Carrie or Caro. But there was nothing you could do with a plain name like Ruth.

"People call me Ruthie sometimes," she said reluctantly. "Even my mother, if she forgets. But I hate it."

"Ruthie for long, hey? Okay, I'll remember—just Ruth."

He smiled, but his eyes were scanning the ocean again. Ruth hesitated a moment, then took a deep breath and sprinted for the water, knowing how cold it was going to feel after such a long time out in the sun. Without pausing, she splashed through the foam, dove through a small wave, swam hard, and did a porpoise dive under another, bigger wave, aiming deep for its powerful, gleaming roots.

Then she couldn't help turning her head to see if Russ had been watching. But there was no way to tell. He was sitting back in the chair with his arms folded, his head swiveling slowly from side to side, keeping all the swimmers safe.

CHAPTER

THREE

Ruth knew she was lucky that her family lived only fifteen miles from the ocean, an easy drive along the flat Long Island roads in their old gray Ford. It was lucky, too, that her father could take the train every day to his job in the city, so they could save their gasoline for the beach.

Still, she always dreaded the trip home, with everyone crammed together in the hot car, all sticky and sandy and cross. Today it was Ruth's turn to sit in the middle of the backseat. Carol was a sleepy, heavy lump on one side of her, while Betsy kept crowding her on the other, chanting, "Ruthie has a crush, Ruthie has a crush," even after their parents told her to stop. They'd all noticed her talking to the lifeguard.

"I hope you weren't bothering him, Ruth," her

father said. "That job takes full-time concentration, you know." He had been a lifeguard years ago, at some lake in upstate New York.

"Oh, he was watching the ocean the whole time," Ruth assured him.

"It must get lonely, sitting up on that platform all by himself," her mother remarked. This was what Ruth had thought, but somehow she didn't like her mother saying it.

"Well, it's what he's paid to do," Mr. Owen said grumpily, stamping on the brakes to let a large, sunburned family cross the road in front of them. They were laden with folding chairs and portable radios and other paraphernalia the Owens considered unnecessary for the beach. "He's lucky the draft hasn't caught up with him."

Ruth hadn't thought about that. She frowned, hoping it wouldn't.

Betsy poked her in the ribs. Annoyed, Ruth started to poke her back, then saw what Betsy was looking at: the giant swimming pool at Number Two, clearly visible from the road behind its tall chain-link fence.

Silently, they gazed at all the kids frolicking and splashing and yelling and having fun, when all the time a single drop of water—a drop that looked just like every other drop of water—might land on them, with poison in it.

It was the scariest thought Ruth had ever had, even scarier than thinking about the third rail on the train tracks.

As usual, though, she cheered up once they turned into the leafy streets of their town, where people were outside watering their lawns and throwing balls for their dogs and playing lazy Saturday-afternoon games of badminton in side yards.

After she'd washed away the salt and sand and put on a clean polo shirt and shorts, there was even something magical about going out into her own familiar backyard. The grass felt silky and cool beneath her feet, and the air was deliciously soft against her skin. Tonight they were having an early picnic supper, the way they often did after a day at the beach—potato salad with thin-sliced cold cuts and thicker-sliced tomatoes from the Victory Garden beyond the garage.

Also, it was tonight that Ruth was finally getting to call her friend Joan long-distance in New Hampshire. The Deckers were away for a month, and the two sets of parents had agreed on one telephone call apiece, three minutes at a time.

"Hello, there, Ruthie. My, how brown you're getting!"

Ruth had taken her plate to the glider swing in the corner of the yard and was planning what to say to Joan—three minutes wasn't a whole lot of time when you hadn't seen each other in nearly ten days. She looked up to see their next-door neighbor, Mrs. Buell, beaming at her from the other side of one of the fat snowberry bushes that separated the two yards.

"I don't suppose I could interest anyone over there in a cupcake, could I?" Mrs. Buell inquired in her twinkly way. "I've got some extras I'd hate to let go stale. Some have vanilla icing and some have orange."

Ruth set her empty plate down and scrambled out of the swing. Mrs. Buell was always baking something delicious, in spite of food rationing; Ruth's mother said she must use all her butter and sugar just on desserts. Of course, there were only the two of them, now that their son Jack was in the Army.

Besides, it was always interesting to go into the Buells' yard, so much smaller and tidier than her own—a rectangle of thick, perfect grass with a hole in the middle for the clothesline tree and a rock garden on the far side that enclosed an oval goldfish pond.

While Mrs. Buell was in the kitchen, Ruth inspected the dark surface of the pond. She was relieved to see a flicker of orange in its depths. For a while, the Buells had kept a pair of little alligators instead of goldfish. Or maybe the alligators had eaten the goldfish—Ruth had never felt like asking. Betsy had been fascinated by the alligators, but Ruth thought they were creepy, even after she'd forced herself to touch one and had had to agree with Betsy that they weren't slimy.

She wondered what the Buells had done with them. *The New York Herald Tribune* said some people flushed their pet alligators down the toilet when they got tired of them. That was so disgusting

Ruth didn't even like to think about it. Also, what if the alligators didn't die but kept on growing down in the pipes somewhere?

"Here we are, dear." Mrs. Buell came down the cement step from the kitchen door with a pretty china plate. On it were eight cupcakes in pleated wrappers—four white ones and four orange, Ruth saw in some dismay. She foresaw a fight with her sisters over who got to have two orange cupcakes, assuming her parents took white ones and the girls were allowed to have seconds.

"Fred says to say hello," Mrs. Buell said, referring to her husband, a small, walnut-skinned man who ran a hardware store in a neighboring town. Mr. Buell was also the air-raid warden for their block, doing his rounds in a helmet that came down over his ears and made him look exactly like a picture-book gnome wearing a toadstool hat. Ruth and her sisters never giggled when they saw him, though—they were much too fond of him for that.

"He's got his feet up, listening to the radio," Mrs. Buell explained. "Feeling the heat, I expect."

For a moment, her kindly, soft features seemed to pucker. Ruth hadn't thought it was especially hot, not now at the end of the day, with the sun just a golden shimmer through the trees. Maybe Mrs. Buell didn't either, because she added with a sigh, "And of course he worries about Jack. He's on his way to the Pacific now, we think."

Ruth looked at her in alarm. "I thought Jack was at that camp, down in . . . in . . ."

"Georgia," Mrs. Buell supplied with a nod. "Well, he was, dear, but that was just for training, you know. They don't keep them there very long these days, I'm afraid. We hoped he might get a few days' leave, but . . ."

She shrugged her plump shoulders under her flower-sprigged housedress. "It does seem hard that they can't say where they're going. But then, I don't suppose they know themselves until the last minute."

She gazed down at the plate of cupcakes for a moment, then blinked and smiled, handing it to Ruth. "Well, now, you run along, dear, and give your family our love."

Ruth thanked her and went slowly back into her own yard. A ripe snowberry popped under her heel, but the sensation didn't give her its usual pleasure.

Jack Buell had always been an important person in her life—a lanky, slow-moving boy who towered over his parents and who always had a smile and a humorous word of greeting for the three little Owen girls next door. Secretly, Ruth had thought of him as a kind of older brother, someone she'd get to know better when she grew up.

Until now, she'd pictured Jack's being in the Army in terms of the cartoons in *The Saturday Evening Post* and songs on the radio like "You're in the Army, Mr. Jones" and "Oh, How I Hate to Get Up in the Morning"—that one especially, since Mr. Buell used to grumble that it practically took a cannon to get Jack out of bed on a school morning.

But now it seemed that instead of worrying about pulling his blanket so tight a mean-looking sergeant could bounce a coin on it, or getting his boots so shiny the same sergeant could see his face in them, Jack might be worrying about a torpedo hitting the ship he was on. And if that didn't happen, he'd have to worry about landing on some little island where sneaky Japanese soldiers would shoot at him from behind palm trees.

"Oh, how nice of Mrs. Buell," her mother said as Ruth set the plate of cupcakes on the round metal table her father repainted white each spring.

Instantly, Betsy dropped the paddle and ball she'd been playing with, trying to see if she could hit to a hundred without missing, and said, "Dibs on orange icing for firsts and seconds."

"No fair," Ruth protested, coming back to herself. "I was the one who brought them!"

Their father sighed. "Pick a number between one and thirty."

"Seven," said Carol in her funny, gruff voice, looking up from the doll she was undressing, its arms twisted backward over its head.

"You always say seven," Betsy told her scornfully. "And Daddy hasn't even had time to think of the number yet."

. As Carol's face fell, Mrs. Owen said firmly, "One cupcake each is enough for now. We've all had plenty to eat. Don't argue, Betsy. We'll put the rest in the icebox and have them tomorrow. I hope you remembered to say thank you to Mrs. Buell, Ruth."

Ruth nodded. While they ate their cupcakes, she told them about Jack. Both her parents were silent for a moment. Then her father crumpled up his cupcake wrapper, tossed it into the trash can beside the table, and said, "Well, now, who's going to help me find a four-leaf clover? We haven't looked over by the jungle gym in a long time, and I bet there's at least one there."

"To bring Jack good luck," Carol said with a nod, setting her doll aside. "If we find one, we can send it to him. In a nenvelope, with a red stamp."

"*Envelope*, dummy," Betsy said, but added, "Yes, could we do that, Daddy?" as she followed her father over to the small wooden jungle gym at the rear of the yard.

"I don't see why not," Mr. Owen said. He took off his glasses and stretched out on the grass, propping his chin in his hands. He loved looking for four-leaf clovers and usually found one. This was partly because it was one of the few things he was patient about. It was also because he was so nearsighted that he could see small, close-up things very clearly. He didn't paw the grass the way most people did, just searched it methodically with his eyes.

Ruth lingered by the table, eyeing the remaining cupcakes and wondering if there was any more potato salad in the kitchen. She was still hungry. Even though she was skinny and small for her age, Ruth was always the first to clean her plate, and always felt that she never got quite enough to eat.

Her father was the same way. Sometimes they

met in the kitchen at night, looking into the icebox for something to nibble on. He would shake his head at her because of her mother's rule about not eating between meals, but if he was making a cheese sandwich for himself, usually he'd give Ruth a corner of it.

Ruth hoped she'd never be as nearsighted as her father, though, even if it meant she'd be good at finding four-leaf clovers. Maybe she couldn't quite read the blackboard from the back row, but at least she could tell a cow from a horse through a train window, which was more than her father could without his glasses.

CHAPTER

~~~~~~~~~~~~~~~~~~~~~~~~~~~

FOUR

Thinking of this, she turned to her mother and said, keeping her voice low so her father wouldn't hear, "Do you think Daddy still minds about not being in the Navy?"

He'd been offered a commission, she knew—although she didn't know what a commission was, exactly—but then had been turned down because of his eyesight.

Mrs. Owen was gathering up glasses and silverware to take back to the kitchen. She hesitated, looking down at the cluster of forks she held in one hand, and said, "Yes, I'm afraid he does. He'd like to feel he was doing his part."

It was rare for her mother to look troubled or uncertain, but Ruth thought she did now, for just a moment.

Then she squared her shoulders and said briskly, "Of course, he wouldn't have been *in* the war, dear, just working in an office, pretty much the way he does now." Mr. Owen was an engineer who made plans for machines and electrical systems.

"And we would have had to move to Washington, D.C.," Ruth said, remembering the discussions she'd overheard.

"Well, maybe. It's terribly crowded there these days, and we might have had trouble finding a place to live. Probably Daddy would have stayed in a hotel and just come home on weekends whenever he could."

"You mean he wouldn't really live with us anymore?" Ruth stared at her mother in consternation. "I'm glad the Navy wouldn't let him in, then."

Her mother gave her shoulders a squeeze. That was unusual, too. Mostly it was Betsy and Carol she hugged, as if Ruth, being the oldest, didn't need to be hugged as often. "So am I, to be honest. A lot of other families aren't so lucky, you know. . . . Well, now, if you're not going to join the clover hunt, you can give me a hand with these things and then"— she looked at her small gold wristwatch, last year's Christmas present from all of them—"it'll be just about time to make your call to Joan."

Ruth helped her carry the trash can over to its place against the garage wall.

She said, "I think it's dumb, though, if the Navy turned Daddy down just because he has to wear glasses. If he was only going to be in an office, not on a ship or anything, what difference would being nearsighted make?"

Did wearing glasses mean you got left out of things somehow, as if other people assumed you weren't as strong or quick or capable as they were? That was what Ruth really wanted to ask, but she knew her mother wouldn't understand the question. If your eyesight needed fixing, you wore glasses and were grateful to have them, and that was that. You certainly didn't fuss about how they made you look. After all, you were still the same person underneath, weren't you?

"Oh, it's just one of their rules," Mrs. Owen said as they went in the back door. "The way the Army won't take people with flat feet, even if they're going to be cooks or supply sergeants or something and probably never have to do any marching. Whew, it's hot in here! Turn on the fan, would you, Ruth?"

Ruth grinned in spite of herself. " 'The Flat Foot Floogee with the Floy, Floy,' " she sang, switching on the fan that stood on the kitchen table and watching the petal-shaped blades whir into a figure eight and then vanish altogether in a silvery blur.

"Really, the nonsense that comes over the radio these days," her mother said, but she was smiling as she reached up into a cupboard and took down the egg timer.

"Now, Ruth, you're to talk for three minutes exactly, no more." She gave the little hourglass a shake so that all the fine sand settled in the bottom part. "When the operator connects you, you're to turn the timer over and keep an eye on the three-minute line there. Is that understood?"

Ruth nodded solemnly. As she went into the hall and pulled a chair up to the telephone table, she decided it might be a good idea to write down a list of all the things she wanted to tell Joan in three minutes—or rather in the minute and a half that would be her share. It wasn't only the cost of telephoning long distance, she knew, but also the fact that the call was just for fun, not a necessary one like the war posters said. "Is This Call Necessary?" they demanded in big, reproachful letters.

But although she and Joan had a good connection, with hardly any static, the call didn't turn out to be much fun, after all.

For one thing, Joan sounded almost surprised to find that it was Ruth on the phone, as if she'd forgotten all about their arrangement. For another, she was so full of all the things she was doing up at the lake that Ruth was barely able to get a word in edgewise.

With almost half their precious time used up, Ruth crumpled up the list she'd made and blurted out the most important item on it—her continuing dread of going into sixth grade in the fall.

"But remember how bored you were last year?" Joan said reasonably. "Mrs. Chapman had to give you a special reading list and make up extra arithmetic problems—either that or keep sending you out of the room on some dumb errand. And it would be worse next year, because now you already know all the stuff we'll be learning."

"I'd rather be bored and still be with all my friends," Ruth protested. "I don't even know any of those sixth-grade girls, except for Mary Jo Douglas, and you know what *she's* like."

Mary Jo lived on the next block. She had a loud voice and greasy hair and always tried to cheat when they played Beckon, saying she'd seen someone beckoning to her when she hadn't.

Joan said, "I know, but they won't all be that way. Anyhow, Ruth, I don't think you should worry so much about age. This girl I was telling you about, Ann Reeves, the one who has a pony and goes to private school—well, she's a year younger than us, but she's really fun. She reads a lot, like you do. In fact she likes a lot of the same books—*My Friend Flicka* and *Lassie Come Home* and *Swiss Family Robinson.* Oh, I forgot to say she's learning the recorder too, and sometimes we play duets."

She giggled. "The hardest part is finding a place to practice. Usually we go down in the boathouse where no one can hear us. Once we tried playing in the field where Ann's pony is, only he got spooked by the high notes. Ann says—"

"Listen, Joan, our three minutes are almost up," Ruth interrupted unhappily, watching the sand trickling silently, unstoppably, into the bottom of the timer.

"Already? Okay, I guess we better hang up, then."

"Next time it's your turn to call," Ruth reminded her. "Two weeks from tonight."

"Sure. Only maybe we should make it three weeks. We might be staying longer," Joan explained rapidly, "because of the polio scare. My parents think it's safer up here in the country, where there aren't any crowds, so they're going to see if we can have the cottage till the end of August."

The receiver felt cold and heavy in Ruth's hand as she replaced it in its black cradle—as cold and heavy as her heart. Now she wouldn't see Joan until September. Worse, it didn't sound as if Joan even cared, happy with her new friend Ann (whom Ruth decided she hated) and not really minding any more about their being separated at school.

They'd agreed they wouldn't let Ruth's being a grade ahead make any difference. They'd still eat their lunches together and walk each other home from school. On winter weekends they'd still go ice-skating and sledding together. As often as their mothers would allow, they'd still stay over at each other's houses on Saturday nights, sneaking on the radio to listen to *Your Hit Parade* long after they were supposed to be asleep.

Now Ruth wondered if things would really work out that way. She thought of Joan's sparkling dark eyes and smooth cap of black hair, her infectious laugh and quick, confident movements, and knew there were plenty of fifth-grade girls who'd jump at the chance to be Joan's best friend. Boys liked her, too—Joan was always one of the first to be chosen for teams, and usually got the most valentines of anyone in their homeroom.

"Ruth?"

Carol was standing in the kitchen doorway, clutching her grubby doll. Ruth scowled at her. The worst thing about being the oldest was that someone was always following you around and watching what you did and listening in if they could.

"What?" she said, in her most forbidding voice.

"We found one. A four-leaf clover." Carol's brown eyes were shining. "*I* found it," she said proudly. "Daddy says that means I'm lucky."

Ruth looked at her cute little sister, whose chestnut curls were haloed by the late sunlight streaming through the kitchen window behind her.

"Yes," she said bitterly. "You probably are."

CHAPTER

~~~~~~~~~~~~~~~~~~~~~~~~~~~~~~

FIVE

Except for having to get dressed up and wear a hat that looked stupid on her, Ruth didn't mind the church part of Sunday morning too much. What she minded was Sunday school, especially in summer.

The rest of the year they were divided into regular classes, and sometimes it could be sort of interesting to learn about people like the Good Samaritan and the man who took up his bed and walked.

In summer, though, they were all herded together in the parish hall and made to sit at a long table furnished with coloring books and crayons and dumb follow-the-dot puzzles. Soon the littlest kids would get bored and restless, and since there were only two teachers in charge, Ruth—as one of the older girls—had to spend most of her time chasing small boys around the room and dragging them back to their chairs.

This morning, sitting with her sisters at the end of a pew where they could be excused quietly before the sermon, Ruth viewed this prospect even more darkly than usual. Last night's conversation with Joan still rankled. Besides that, her parents had decided against going to the beach again today. It was Communion Sunday, which meant the service would be longer than usual. By the time they got home and changed, her father said, there'd be a lot of traffic heading for the beach—to say nothing of crowds when they got there, what with all the buses carrying people out of the hot city.

Ruth had heard on the radio that the temperature in New York City was supposed to get up to one hundred degrees today. The radio announcer also said the police were going to arrest anyone they caught turning on a fire hydrant, because the water might be needed to put out a fire. Ruth had seen city kids playing in the gush of rusty-looking water from the hydrants and thought it looked like fun— much more fun than just going under the garden hose, except maybe for all the icky stuff that might be floating in the gutter.

Here inside the tall, gray Episcopal church, though, the air felt almost shivery, with heavy blocks of stone walling off the outside air and colored windows filtering out the sun. Ruth shifted uncomfortably on the thin pew cushion and tugged at the waistband of her second-best summer dress, which was too tight under the arms.

At least that proved she'd grown some since last year. Unfortunately, Betsy had grown, too, meaning she couldn't always wear Ruth's hand-me-downs anymore. In fact, it was Betsy who'd gotten to have a new dress this summer, instead of Ruth— buttercup yellow, with crisp little tucks down the front and a floppy white collar. Ruth eyed it enviously, though the dress probably would have looked dumb on her.

Even her hand-me-downs usually looked better on Betsy than they had on Ruth, making her wonder if it was really Betsy her mother had in mind when they went shopping at Loeser's or Arnold Constable. This blue, for instance, was exactly the color of Betsy's eyes. Too bad she'd gotten too big to wear it, Ruth thought meanly.

The minister had climbed into the pulpit and was reading out some announcements. Ruth found herself thinking about Joan again—how Joan's clothes always fitted her perfectly and looked exactly right. Her red plaid skirt with the knife pleats, for instance, and her new penny loafers. Ruth's mother wouldn't let her have loafers. She said they were bad for her feet, so Ruth was still stuck with lace-up brown oxfords.

Of course, Joan was an only child, and the Deckers were richer than the Owens. For a long time Ruth had thought that was because their money just had to be divided among three people instead of five. Gradually, though, she'd understood that things like Mrs. Decker's fur coat and their big Buick and the new Frigidaire that made ice cubes in little trays cost a lot of extra money—more than her own parents would have been able to afford, even without Betsy and Carol to feed and buy clothes and shoes for.

The Deckers had a maid as well—Nora, a tall, rawboned woman who always seemed to be ironing something and who smelled, not unpleasantly, of blueing and starch. Last winter Ruth had heard Dr. Decker grumbling about having to pay Nora more money to stop her from going off to do war work in a factory. In the end, though, he must have paid it because Nora was still with them. Dr. Decker was a dentist, not an ordinary dentist, but the kind that straightened people's teeth.

Ruth's family might have been rich, too, at least on her mother's side, if it hadn't been for the Crash that had happened a few years before Ruth was born. (Ruth pictured this as a kind of earthquake that toppled people's best china off even the highest, safest shelves, though she knew it really had to do with something called the stock market.) Grandfather Prescott had had to close the doors of his bank, and by the time he paid everyone what the bank owed them, there was hardly any money left for him and Grandmother.

Now, instead of living in the big stone house in Brooklyn Heights where Ruth's mother and brothers had grown up, they lived in a three-room apartment crowded with dark furniture, and cooked their meals on a hot plate—or rather heated up food from cans, because Grandmother had never really learned to cook.

More bad luck, Ruth thought moodily. She'd been thinking a lot about luck recently. Not that her grandparents seemed particularly cast down. On the contrary, they joked about bumping their shins on the sideboard and having to go single file in the hallway because of the bookshelves on either side. When Ruth went to visit, they played Chinese checkers and always had a good dessert from the bakery around the corner—cream puffs or chocolate eclairs. Also, it was fascinating to explore her grandfather's closet, filled with smooth, dark suits and hand-stitched shoes that had been made for him in England. He still kept the shoes polished, too.

Maybe it made a difference that the Crash had been a lot of people's bad luck, Ruth thought. Like the war now, and the polio epidemic.

The minister had finished his announcements and was leading them in a special prayer for their fighting men overseas, reading out the names of all the sons and brothers and husbands. From her kneeling position, Ruth found herself thinking suddenly of what Joan had said about crowds. Did that mean it wasn't just swimming pool crowds you could get polio from, but any kind of crowd?

She sneaked an uneasy look at the bowed heads and shoulders around her. The congregation was a small one on this summer Sunday, but maybe it was big enough to be called a crowd. It was hard to imagine a polio germ lurking here among all these sober, well-dressed people. But if you could get a cold from someone like dignified old Mr. Murray, now blowing his nose loudly into a snowy handkerchief, maybe you could get polio, too.

Would her own parents have taken them to the country this summer if they could have afforded it?

The organ thundered out the opening bars of a hymn, and there was a rustle as the congregation rose to its feet.

"Eternal Father, strong to save, Whose arm hath bound the restless wave . . ." The hymn was one of Ruth's favorites because it was about the ocean. Although she wasn't musical like Joan, who played the piano as well as the recorder, she sang the words out heartily:

> "O hear us when we cry to thee
> For those in peril on the sea."

Ruth frowned down at the hymnal she was sharing with Betsy and almost lost her place. Until today, she'd pictured those in peril as reckless swimmers who'd gone out beyond the breakers on a rough day, or else as old-time sailors in striped jerseys pulling at the oars of a pitching boat with a tattered sail.

But all at once the picture in her mind was of Jack Buell in his soldier's uniform, standing at the rail of a gray battleship in a crowd of other soldiers. They were looking back at the land—at America and the houses they'd grown up in, with their parents standing on the front steps and the grass growing tall and thick in the yards they used to mow every Saturday afternoon.

As Ruth watched, or seemed to watch, the soldiers got smaller and smaller in the distance, until they were just tiny matchstick figures caught between the enormous sky and the endless, rolling miles of waves.

Looking at the faces of the adults around her, at the somber profiles of her own parents as they sang, Ruth understood for the first time that it was the war they were thinking about. That was why they were always singing this hymn lately—because of the war and its peril.

Betsy was nudging her. "Go on, Ruth," she whispered. "It's time!"

Ruth blinked, returning to herself with a start. The hymn had ended, and the minister was clearing his throat, ready to begin his sermon. Hastily she scrambled out of the pew, ducked her head toward the altar as she'd been taught, and led her sisters down the aisle to the tall, carved doors and the shimmer of the August day beyond.

CHAPTER

~~~~~~~~~~~~~~~~~~~~~~~~~~~~~~~~

SIX

One good thing about Sunday school—at least Ruth got to take off her hat.

She and her sisters wore identical Scotch caps with jaunty, peaked crowns and grosgrain ribbons hanging down the back, a gift from their Owen grandmother in Ohio. Their mother's friends were always saying how darling the three little girls looked in their matching hats, but Ruth knew it was Betsy and Carol who looked darling. The perky shape of the hat was all wrong for the shape of her own face, making it look even narrower and thinner than usual. Somehow it made her hair look straighter, too.

But actually, Sunday school turned out to be almost fun today, thanks to the heat. It was so stifling in the low-roofed parish hall, even with all the windows open, that after about ten minutes, Mrs. Morgan and Mrs. Graham decided to let them go outside and play on the side lawn of the church.

"*Quietly*, though, children," Mrs. Graham cautioned in the doorway, holding a finger to her lips in her silly way. "We don't want to disturb the service. Now who can think of a nice, quiet game we can all play?"

Ruth sorted rapidly through a mental list of possibilities—she was used to organizing games for her sisters and the other kids in the neighborhood. "How about Green Light?" she suggested.

"Or Giant Steps," said a large, freckle-faced girl Ruth had never seen before. She had thick blond braids that reached below her shoulder blades, and wore a ruffled, pink-checked dress that looked too young for her. But maybe that was just because she was so tall—as tall as a junior-high girl, with big hands and feet.

Mrs. Graham beamed at both of them. "Very good, Ruth and—Laura, isn't it? Yes, Laura King, whose family has just moved to town. And this is her brother, Billy." She indicated a stocky, towheaded boy standing off to one side with his hands in his pockets and a sulky look on his face. "I'm sure we'll all do our best to make them feel welcome."

She turned back to Ruth and said distractedly, "Now, let me see, dear, I suppose we'll need someone to be 'it' . . ."

Some of the little boys were already tussling on the lawn, getting grass stains on their good pants.

Ruth said quickly, "Maybe we should divide into two groups. One group could play Green Light, and the other could go over on the other side of those trees and play Giant Steps." She turned to Mrs. Morgan, whom she considered the more sensible of the two women, and explained, "I could start out being 'it' with one group and she—Laura—could take the other."

"How come Ruth gets to be 'it'?" Betsy grumbled as Mrs. Morgan began counting them off into two groups.

"Yeah, and how come Laura does?" demanded the towheaded boy.

Ruth met Laura's eye; they shrugged and smiled at each other.

"Because it was their idea," Mrs. Morgan said briskly. "And anyway, isn't the whole point of the game to *keep* from being 'it'?"

Well, it was and it wasn't, Ruth thought, but you couldn't explain that to a grown-up.

The games weren't as quiet as they might have been, mainly because of a tendency to squeal whenever the person who was "it" got tagged and gave chase to the others. But at least there weren't any fights, and when it was time for juice and crackers in the shade of one of the big elm trees, everyone lined up in an orderly fashion.

Standing at the back of the line, Ruth got talking to Laura King and found out she came from

Nebraska and was in sixth grade, too. Not only that, she was going to be in Miss Amory's homeroom, like Ruth. The other sixth-grade teacher was grouchy old Mr. Burnside, who was always confiscating things and was said to have a locked drawer in his desk crammed full of marbles and slingshots and comic books and hundreds of bubble-gum wrappers.

"I'm really supposed to be in fifth," Ruth told Laura, her mood darkening again, "but I got skipped. They do that quite a lot here."

"Do they keep people back, too?" Laura sounded so eager that Ruth gave her a puzzled look. "I just thought if they did, maybe I wouldn't be the tallest one in the class, for once."

Ruth was so used to being short and skinny that she'd never really imagined what it must feel like to be so big for your age that you towered over all your classmates. Thinking of this, she said, "Well, at least you don't have to wear glasses." It was Laura's turn to look puzzled. "I'm probably going to have to," Ruth explained with a scowl. "I'm nearsighted."

"So is my brother." Laura sighed. "Only he hardly ever wears his glasses. Either he breaks them, accidentally on purpose, or he pretends he's lost them. My mom gets really mad at him. She didn't make him wear them today, though, because of being new."

Ruth thought Laura's mother sounded very understanding. She also thought that maybe she herself could get away with wearing her glasses only part of the time. Of course, she wouldn't break them—glasses cost a lot, she knew—but there was nothing that said she had to wear them after school, or even at recess.

This was such a cheering thought that she was surprised to find Laura still looking downcast.

"Billy really hates it here," she said. "He misses the sky."

"The sky?" Ruth looked up at the vivid patches of summer blue tangled in the leaves of the elm tree.

"It's not *big* here, like it is at home." Laura swept her arms wide to demonstrate. Mrs. Graham was just reaching over Ruth's shoulder to hand Laura a little paper cup of apple juice, and Laura almost knocked her hat off. She mumbled an apology, flushing under her freckles.

"I'm always doing clumsy things like that," she muttered as she and Ruth took their juice and crackers around to the other side of the tree.

Ruth was thinking maybe she understood what Laura meant about the sky. It was something she loved about the beach—that feeling of being able to see as far as you could in all directions. "If you like a whole lot of sky," she said, "you should go to the ocean. To Jones Beach—that's where my family always goes."

"I've never even seen the ocean, except in the movies," Laura confessed, brightening a little. "It looks like it would be scary to go swimming in, but fun." Her face fell again. "But that wouldn't be the same, though—a place you have to drive to. At home, you just walk out the back door, and there's the prairie and the sky going on forever and ever. You know, like in the song—'amber waves of grain.'"

It didn't sound very exciting to Ruth, but then, she'd only seen pictures of the prairie, just as Laura had only seen pictures of the ocean. She nodded politely.

"I think it's sort of pretty here," Laura conceded, "with all the trees and the green grass and the houses being so close together and everything, but Billy . . . well, he feels sort of cooped up. He wants to be a farmer when he grows up. All my dad's brothers are farmers," Laura explained, "and my granddad, too. We've always lived on my grand-parents' farm, even though my dad's an engineer and had to drive to Omaha every day. But now he has a new job at Sperry, on account of the war, so we had to move here."

Ruth was about to say that her father was an engineer, too, when Laura's brother Billy, crossing the lawn with another boy, came to a sudden halt and burst out laughing.

"Boy, do you two look funny together," he said, pointing at Laura and Ruth. "Like Mutt and Jeff in the funny papers." He punched the other boy in the arm, and they both doubled over. Some of the other kids looked around to see what the joke was.

"Shut up, Billy," Laura said angrily. As he ran off, still laughing, she said to Ruth, "My brother can be a real dope sometimes. And I was just feeling sorry for him!"

Ruth glared at Betsy and Carol, who'd been giggling, too. "You must really hate having a younger brother," she said, trying not to notice that the top of her head only came up to Laura's shoulder. "Sometimes I can't stand my little sisters, either. I've decided what I'd really like to have is an older brother. Either that or be an only child."

"I don't know." Laura looked thoughtful. "Only children can be really spoiled. I have a baby brother at home," she added, "and he's just as cute as can be. Sometimes I get to give him his pabulum and look after him when my mom's busy."

Pabulum—ugh! Ruth could still remember how Carol used to smear it all over her face, even on her eyebrows, and then bang her spoon on the tray of her high chair so everyone would look at her and laugh. When Carol misbehaved, her parents thought she was cute. When Ruth misbehaved, she got sent to her room.

Ruth heard organ music and looked over at the church. People were filing out of the big doors, shaking the minister's hand and stopping to chat on the steps while they fanned themselves with their programs.

A few minutes ago, Ruth had been on the point of asking Laura where she lived and inviting her to go to the beach with them sometime. Now she hesitated, telling herself she ought to ask her mother first.

50

But it wasn't just that. She'd had a sudden dismaying picture of herself and Laura, two new sixth-grade girls, on the first day of school. If she made friends with Laura, it would be only natural for them to stick together, and what if people laughed? They probably *did* look pretty funny side by side, she thought, almost like members of different species. A horse, say, and a squirrel . . . worse, a squirrel wearing glasses.

Besides, no one Ruth knew thought babies were cute. No one wore their hair in braids, either, except for Hilda Gutterson, whose father spoke English with an accent and who some kids said was a German spy. Ruth thought Laura's braids were kind of pretty, not stiff like Hilda's but golden and shiny like cornsilk in the sunlight. Still—

"I see my mom looking for me," she told Laura quickly. "See you next week."

She tossed her paper cup into the wire basket beside the tree. Then, feeling the space between her shoulder blades begin to prickle with the lie, she hurried along the walk to the parish hall to retrieve her hated hat.

CHAPTER

SEVEN

Ruth weighed down her towel against the wind with her sandals and her library book. The fourth corner still flapped, so she dumped some sand on it. Then she straightened, holding back the strands of hair blowing across her face, and squinted along the beach to see if Russ was in the lifeguard's chair today. But it was too far—she couldn't tell for sure.

"There's that nice lifeguard again," her mother said, answering the question for her. Ruth thought resignedly that she really did need glasses. "And there's another lifeguard with him. I'm glad to see they're doubling up today."

It hadn't seemed very windy at home, just a pleasant breeze ruffling the crowns of the maple trees along Kempton Road. But there'd been whitecaps on Great South Bay, and when they turned onto the beach road, they'd seen the flag that meant swimming would be restricted in some areas today.

Even though such restrictions didn't usually apply to Number Nine, where the sand shelved away very gradually and there weren't any dangerous currents, Mrs. Owen had slowed the car and almost turned back. Then Betsy pointed out that they had to eat their picnic lunch somewhere, and it might as well be at the beach. They wouldn't even have to go in the water, she said, if it was too rough.

Ruth, of course, planned to, whatever the water was like, though she'd had to promise her mother not to go in over her head without her father there. Mrs. Owen was a stylish swimmer, with a smooth Australian crawl, but she hadn't taken a course in lifesaving like Mr. Owen.

"Come on, Betsy," Ruth urged now, turning to face the ocean. "We'll hold hands and just jump the waves. Look, it's low tide now, and they aren't even very big."

Betsy eyed the choppy blue water while the wind flattened her curls against her head. "Maybe I'll go in later," she said. "Right now I want to go look for shells and crabs and things."

"Take me, Ruth!" Carol begged as Betsy set off along the hard sand at the water's edge, carrying a pail in which to store her finds. Ruth hoped she wouldn't bring back any dead fish. "Can Ruth take me in the water, Mommy?"

"Well, all right, but just wading," their mother said.

The tide was so low that Ruth barely got wet as she wandered around with Carol's hand in hers. Carol was delighted by all the shallow water, though, and said she wanted to practice her swimming. She had just learned the dog paddle.

Mindful of her promise, Ruth sent her back up onto the beach to get permission. Their mother was standing talking to a large woman wearing a flowered bathing suit and a white bandanna around her head. Carol had to tug her hand several times to get her attention. Mrs. Owen nodded distractedly, and Carol scampered back to where Ruth stood hugging herself against the breeze. She'd probably be warmer in the water than out of it.

"Now remember," Carol said, "you have to keep your hand under my tummy—not holding me up, but *touching*."

"Who's Mom talking to?" Ruth asked curiously.

"Oh, some lady she knows. She's friends with the Stewarts, only they're sick. They had to have the doctor come. Wait, I better get my face wet first."

Carol screwed up her eyes, bent over at the waist, and dipped her face in the water. As she raised it again, gasping and spitting, Ruth said, "Who had to have the doctor?"

The Stewarts were friends of their parents. They had three boys who were almost the same ages as Ruth and her sisters, and they were always inviting them to the boys' birthday parties.

"I don't know. Randy, I guess."

Carol said this with an air of satisfaction. She and Randy Stewart always fought when the two families got together, though Ruth herself liked him the best of the three boys. David, the one nearest her own age, was a handsome boy with an aloof, superior manner, polite but never really friendly. Ruth dreaded going to David's birthday parties, in spite of the fact that they'd had a magician once and always showed cartoons down in the basement rec room after the ice cream and cake—Mickey Mouse and Porky Pig and (Ruth's favorite) Felix the Cat.

"Come on, Ruth, I'm ready," Carol said. She was stretched out in the water, kicking her feet.

"No fair holding on to the bottom," Ruth told her, crouching down and turning her face away from Carol's splashing.

"I won't if you'll keep your hand under me, like Daddy does."

Ruth slid the flat of her hand under Carol's barrel-like stomach. Carol took a big breath, tensed her body, and paddled furiously for about five seconds. Then she looked over her shoulder and said disappointedly, "I didn't go anywhere. You were holding on!"

"No, I wasn't. You just forgot to kick."

In fact, Carol was so buoyant in the water, it would have been hard to hold her down. Ruth envied people who could float easily. She herself sank like a stone in fresh water. Even in salt water she couldn't float for more than half a minute without having to move her arms or legs. One of her ambitions was to go swimming in Great Salt Lake. She'd seen pictures of people bobbing around in the water there, reading newspapers.

This gave her an idea. "Listen, Carol, forget about using your arms. Just do the dead man's float—you know, with your hands straight out in front—and kick your feet. That way, you'll really move."

Carol disliked putting her face in the water for more than a few seconds, but finally Ruth persuaded her to take a deep breath and try. Unfortunately, the tide was coming in, and just as Carol raised her head to get another breath, a small wave smacked her in the face. She swallowed water, spluttered, and started to cry.

"You're all right," Ruth told her encouragingly. "And look how far you went! Come on, try it again."

Carol shook her head. "I like it better the other way."

Ruth sighed. "Okay, but that's not really learning how to swim."

"It is, too! I bet that's how you learned."

But she looked up at her older sister uncertainly, her wet dark ringlets clinging to her cheeks. Actually, Ruth couldn't remember learning to swim, any more than she could remember learning to read. It seemed like something she'd always known how to do.

"All right," Carol said suddenly, to Ruth's

surprise. "I might try it one more time. Only you watch and tell me if there's a wave coming."

Ten minutes later, Carol was almost swimming—kicking and paddling with her face in the water, raising her head to suck in a noisy breath, then kicking and paddling some more.

"Okay," Ruth said at last. "That's enough of a lesson for now."

She needed to go for a swim herself before she got any colder. Besides, the strip of shallow water was shrinking by the moment, beginning to swirl with sand and foam and little shells.

To her relief, Carol didn't argue, only nodded solemnly. Then her face split into an enormous grin. She dashed up onto the beach, windmilling her arms and yelling, "Mommy! Mommy, did you see me? I was really swimming!"

CHAPTER

~~~~~~~~~~~~~~~~~~~~~~~~~~~~~~~~~~~~~

EIGHT

Smiling to herself, Ruth pushed forward into the waves. They were unexpectedly strong, and so choppy you couldn't really jump them or dive through them, let alone ride one in to shore. Remembering she wasn't supposed to go in over her head, she tried to stay where the water was only up to her chin. But the sand was bumpy and uneven under her feet, and the waves kept lifting her over hollows where she couldn't quite touch bottom.

Ruth turned and tried swimming parallel to the shore, using the overarm sidestroke her father had taught her, so she could keep an eye on the waves. It was hard going, though, with the water so churned up. After a long, bristly cord of seaweed wrapped itself around her wrist, Ruth gave up and let the waves push her back into shallow water.

"Hi, there, Ruth!"

Ruth looked up to see Russ waving at her from his tall, white chair. She'd swum farther up the beach than she'd realized. Russ was alone in the chair now, she was glad to see. She'd been hoping to talk to him again but had felt shy about approaching him when he was with another lifeguard.

As she scuffed through the warm, powdery sand, she saw the other lifeguard down by the high-tide line, leaning against the big rowboat they used for rescues. He was a grizzled older man with burly shoulders burned mahogany by the sun. Russ was more of a golden color, with a fuzz of blond hair on his arms and legs. Today he'd smeared a white triangle of sunburn cream over his nose, giving him a clownish look that made Ruth smile.

"I look like Emmett Kelly, don't I?" he called down.

Emmett Kelly was a famous clown with the Ringling Brothers Circus, Ruth knew, even though she'd never been to the circus. Her parents were waiting until Carol was old enough to appreciate it.

Sometimes it seemed to Ruth that she was always waiting to do things until her sisters got old enough. Joan had already been to the circus twice, and to the ballet *The Nutcracker Suite* at Christmastime. She was always getting to go to Radio City Music Hall, too, and not just to see baby movies like *Dumbo* and *Bambi.*

"Say, I saw you teaching your little sister to

swim," Russ said in his friendly way. "You must be a good teacher—she was really making progress."

"She can be a terrible crybaby sometimes," Ruth told him offhandedly, trying not to show how pleased she felt. "But I guess maybe she's starting to grow up a little."

"Give her time," Russ advised with a grin, returning his gaze to the ocean. "Speaking as the youngest of five kids, I can promise you it'll happen."

"Five kids!" That was a big family, like her parents said people used to have before the Crash. Ruth knew hardly any families that even had three children, like her own.

"Three sisters, one brother. It wasn't easy, I can tell you." Russ shook his head. "The mashed potatoes were always cold by the time they got passed to me, and I was just a tagalong when it came to playing Kick the Can or going to the candy store."

Ruth thought about this. Did Carol ever feel like a tagalong? It seemed to her that Carol got the most attention of anyone in the family, but maybe that was just because she needed taking care of the most. She also thought about Carol getting big, as big as Betsy. What if she, Ruth, ended up being the smallest sister in spite of being the oldest?

Russ glanced down at her. "Hey, you're covered with goose bumps. Have a towel." He tossed one down, a stiff white towel with an official-looking laundry mark on it. As Ruth rubbed her sticky, wet hair, he added, with that way he had of guessing her thoughts, "You know, you may be kind of small for your age now, but I bet you're going to shoot up one of these days and wind up being tall, like your dad."

That was what Ruth's mother was always saying, too. But it was right now that Ruth cared about.

She sat down on the sand with the towel around her shoulders and stared moodily at her skinny outstretched legs. After a while, drifting a handful of sand over one bony kneecap, she said, "Did you ever have to skip a grade in school?"

Russ laughed. "Me? Listen, I was lucky to get promoted from one year to the next. The only subject I was ever any good at was science."

"Like my sister Betsy," Ruth said, nodding. "She wants to be a doctor when she grows up."

"That right? So did I, until . . . when I was younger." Ruth looked up at him quickly, wondering what he'd been about to say. Until what? Until he found out he wasn't smart enough? But she couldn't tell anything from his profile, especially with all that silly white gunk on his nose.

"Either that or be an explorer," Russ went on, shifting his weight and crossing one ankle over the other. It must get uncomfortable sitting for so long, Ruth thought, even though the seat had a padded boat cushion on it. "I was going to hunt dinosaur bones in the desert, or maybe climb Mount Everest, just for fun." He gave a wry chuckle.

"Well, you still can," Ruth said. "I mean, you

won't always be a lifeguard, will you?" For the first time, she wondered what Russ did in the wintertime. Maybe he went to college, she thought. He seemed about the right age for that, a couple of years older than Jack Buell.

Russ didn't answer her question. Maybe he hadn't heard it. Instead he said, "Hey, see that sailboat there, the one drifting this way? Looks like it's in some kind of trouble." He picked up the big pair of binoculars he kept beside him on the seat.

Ruth had been watching a fat man in baggy red trunks trying to set up an oversized striped umbrella in the damp tidal sand below her. Meanwhile his wife and little boy had unfolded a pair of canvas deck chairs and were opening a large picnic hamper that had a whole set of silverware fitted cunningly into the underside of the lid. There was even a checked tablecloth which the wife started to unfold but stuffed hastily back in the hamper when the wind almost snatched it away.

Now Ruth transferred her gaze to the ocean, where she could see a scattering of white sails in the distance, all leaning at the same angle. The sailboat Russ must mean was closer to shore, though, closer than boats usually came, and it was moving oddly. One moment it would tip way over, so the sail almost touched the water. The next moment, the mast would be upright again, with the sail flapping in the wind. Ruth could make out someone moving around on deck, but she couldn't see if there was more than one person on board.

"Right, we'd better lend a hand," Russ decided, and blew a short blast on his whistle.

Down by the rowboat, the other lifeguard looked around, nodded, and motioned to a couple of boys playing catch nearby to help him push the heavy boat into the water. In seconds, it seemed, he'd buckled on his orange life jacket, scrambled aboard, and started rowing strongly toward the struggling sailboat.

"A job after Pete's heart," Russ said with a grin. "He'd give his eyeteeth to join the Coast Guard, but they turned him down—too old."

He studied the sailboat again through his binoculars. "Probably just a fouled rudder from all the seaweed," he said, and lowered the glasses. "That's tough to handle if you're alone, though. Well, now"—he relaxed and sat back, glancing down at Ruth—"what was all that about skipping a grade? Hey, I guess you're even smarter than I thought."

Ruth had stood up to get a better view. A lot of other people on the beach were standing too, shading their eyes to look out to sea, the way they always did when the lifeboat went out. When she didn't say anything, Russ dropped his teasing tone and said, "You don't seem too happy about it."

"They never even asked me if I wanted to," Ruth muttered, twisting the ends of the towel between her fingers.

"Who didn't ask you? Your parents?"

"My parents, and the principal, and the lady at

school who gave me a lot of tests. They just told me I'd be going into sixth grade instead of fifth next year. They expected me to be glad about it, but I'm not." Ruth swallowed over the lump that had risen in her throat. "I'll always be younger than everyone else in my class, and I'll never fit in."

"Sure you will," Russ told her. "Listen, Ruth, I'm pretty sure they don't skip people just because they're smart. They look at other things, too, like how well you get along with other kids and whether you're a leader and—" He broke off suddenly. "Watch it!"

Ruth had half-turned to look up at Russ. She turned back just in time to dodge the spokes of the big, striped umbrella, which had pulled out of the sand and was being blown up the beach by the wind.

It bumped past her like a giant tumbleweed, picked up speed, and started to cartwheel. Ruth ran after it and managed to grab the center pole before the umbrella smashed into a pair of sunbathers lying prone on the sand. It was surprisingly heavy, even after she'd dragged it around to face the wind.

"Thanks, girlie." The fat man came puffing up, red-faced. "Thought I finally had it in deep enough, but this blasted wind. . . . Brand-new umbrella, too—hope nothing got busted."

Ruth took the end of the pole and helped him carry the umbrella back down toward the water.

As they passed the lifeguard's chair, Russ looked down and said sharply, "You're lucky that didn't hurt someone, mister." In a milder voice, he added,

"You'll do better with it up this way, where the sand's drier. Besides, the tide's coming in."

The fat man followed his glance and saw that the water was already lapping at one of the folding chairs, unnoticed by his wife and son, who were watching the boats. His face went even redder. He muttered something under his breath and changed direction, plodding off to one side with the umbrella and dragging Ruth with him. She hung on to her end, feeling the wind tug at the striped canvas.

"Husky young fella like that," the man said, stabbing the pole into the sand. "Why isn't he in uniform, I'd like to know?" He scowled over his shoulder at Russ, then yelled at his wife to start moving their things. "Can't you see the tide's coming in?"

The sailboat was moving freely now, skimming away to join the other white sails on the horizon. Ruth looked from it to Russ, who was watching the lifeboat maneuver back through the choppy waves.

"He's doing an important job," she said with a frown. "Just as important as being in the Army or Navy."

"A nice, safe job, anyway," the man said with a grunt. "High and dry in that chair of his. Didn't even take the lifeboat out himself, you notice—just sent the old guy to do the dirty work."

Ruth started to say that Pete had been down by the boat in the first place, and also that he liked taking it out. But the fat man was already trudging away from her, yelling to his son to grab his shoes before a wave got them.

Had Russ heard what he'd said? Ruth didn't think so. Still, she felt awkward somehow. As she retraced her steps, she saw the towel he'd lent her lying on the sand behind the chair. It must have slipped from her shoulders when she ran after the umbrella.

She hesitated, looking up at Russ's head and shoulders outlined against the sky. She didn't really feel like going back to the conversation they'd been having before. Why had she gotten started talking about school, anyway? That was the last thing she needed to think about on this breezy, blue beach day, when it was still summer, when nothing really bad could happen to her for at least a few more weeks. Besides, the way her stomach was growling, it must be almost lunchtime.

Quickly, Ruth picked up the towel, shook it out, and hung it over a back rung of the chair. As she broke into a trot, heading back to her family down the beach, she gave Russ a wave over her shoulder. But she didn't know if he saw.

CHAPTER

~~~~~~~~~~~~~~~~~~~~~~

NINE

Dear Joan,

I was glad to get your letter. It sounds neat there with canoes and horseback riding and everything. What color pony is Peanuts? Mom took us to see the movie *Lassie Come Home*. It was super! There's a girl in it named Elizabeth Taylor. I'm going to send away for her picture.

We've been going to the beach quite a lot, but today it's raining and also everything is sad here. Do you remember Alan Selby down the street? He used to set off firecrackers to scare the Fosters' dog. One time he dared Betsy to climb a big tree and when she couldn't get back down he just laughed and went away.

Well, he got killed in the war, over in Italy. At first they said he was Missing in Action, but now they know he's dead. The Selbys have a gold star in the window and they keep their blackout shades down in the daytime. It's hard to believe. I know I never liked Alan very much, but still.

The other sad thing is that a family we know got polio, all three boys. You met the oldest one at my birthday party, David Stewart. He had it the worst and almost died because he couldn't breathe, but now he's all right. The middle boy whose name is Jonathan was really sick too, but he's home now and they think he'll be able to walk okay, only with a limp. But the littlest one, Randy—

Ruth put down her fountain pen and stared at the windowpane, where drops of rain were sliding down like tears. Her mother had talked to Mrs. Stewart on the phone this morning, and when she hung up she couldn't speak. She'd put her arms around Ruth and her sisters and held them pressed against her like that for what seemed like a long time. Then she'd tied a scarf around her head and gone out for a walk, even though it was raining.

—Randy is still in the hospital and he'll probably have to stay there until

Thanksgiving at least. His legs won't move at all. They think he'll have to be in a wheelchair till his arms get strong enough so he can use crutches. I guess the braces they put on are really heavy.

Well, I'm sorry this is such a sad letter but that's the way things are right now. Maybe it won't seem so sad up in New Hampshire with all the fun you're having. Don't forget to call me a week from Saturday. By then I'll probably have some better things to tell you.

Love, Ruth

Ruth read the letter over and gave a sigh. It certainly wasn't anything like Joan's letter, which had been full of jokes and funny drawings. She had also enclosed a snapshot of her and her friend Ann standing on a narrow wooden dock. Ann was as tall as Joan, even though she was younger, with straight blond hair and what Ruth had to admit was a nice smile.

Maybe she could add a P.S. about how she'd made friends with one of the lifeguards at Number Nine, and how he was really nice, not mean and bossy the way they'd always thought lifeguards had to be.

But Ruth had been feeling uneasy about Russ. In spite of what she'd said to the fat man, was it really fair that Russ got to stay out of the war, when so many other boys and young men had to go and get shot at and maybe even killed, like Alan?

Of course, Russ might have tried to join and been turned down, like her father. But there was nothing wrong with his eyesight, Ruth knew. She didn't think he had flat feet, either. Russ's feet were at her eye level when she stood beside the lifeguard chair, so she could picture them clearly—high-arched and strong-looking, with short, straight toes.

Or she could tell Joan about the new girl, Laura. But that might sound as if Laura was her friend, and Ruth was guiltily aware that she hadn't done anything about inviting Laura over. She hadn't even talked to her again in a friendly kind of way. Yesterday at Sunday school, she'd sat at the opposite end of the long table from Laura and only said "hi" to her quickly when they were getting in line for refreshments. Then one of the little boys had spilled his juice, which gave Ruth an excuse not to say anything else while she went to get a dishrag.

"What're you doing?" Betsy appeared in the doorway of Ruth's room, looking bored and out-of-sorts.

"What does it look like I'm doing?" Carefully, Ruth printed Joan's address on an envelope.

Betsy and Carol shared a room at the other end of the hall, bigger and lighter than her own. Still, Ruth was glad she had a room to herself. It was one of the few good things about being the oldest.

"I was playing pickup sticks with Carol," Betsy

said sulkily, "but she isn't any good at it. The only ones she can pick up are the ones that are already loose. Now she's lying on her bed, pretending to read. I said I'd read to her from *The Five Little Peppers And How They Grew,* but she didn't even want to do that. She says she has a sore throat."

They looked at each other. "Did Mom take her temperature?" Ruth asked.

"Yes, and she doesn't have any fever, or a stiff neck or anything. Mom thinks it's just a cold, or maybe her tonsils."

Ruth and Betsy had had their tonsils out two years ago. That was the one time they'd shared a room, with Carol's crib moved into Ruth's room. It had been kind of fun, once their throats stopped hurting so much. They'd gotten to eat a lot of orange ice and listen to serials on the radio, like *Our Gal Sunday* and *Young Doctor Malone* and *Mary Noble, Backstage Wife.*

The hospital part of it was only a blur in Ruth's memory, except for the smells and the squeak of the nurses' rubber-soled shoes on the linoleum floors. She thought of little Randy Stewart lying in one of those beds with rails around it, like a cage, looking up at the ceiling and trying not to cry. Once when they were having a snowball fight in the vacant lot down the street, Carol had thrown a chunk of ice at Randy and cut his forehead open, but he hadn't cried, even though it must have hurt a lot.

Ruth hated the way polio was making everything so scary. The minute Betsy'd said that about Carol's sore throat, Ruth had found herself trying to remember if they'd been in any crowds lately. All she could think of was going to the movies in Hempstead, but their mother had taken them to the late-morning show, and there'd been hardly anyone else in the theater.

"Anyway," Betsy said, "now I don't have anything to do." She'd been wandering restlessly around the room. Suddenly she came to a halt in front of Ruth's bureau. "Those are my scissors!" she said, snatching them up.

"No, they're not," Ruth said automatically.

"Yes, they are. Here's my mark, see?" She showed Ruth a tiny red dot on one of the handles, made with their mother's nail polish.

Ruth could see her deciding whether to get really mad or not. Betsy was very possessive about her things, even dumb things like dried-up palm crosses left over from Palm Sunday and broken balsa-wood wings of model airplanes. Their father said it came from being the middle child. Right now, though, Ruth could tell Betsy needed someone to do something with more than she needed to get mad.

Sure enough, she dropped the scissors into the pocket of her scruffy blue overalls—Ruth's old overalls, with the straps let out all the way—and said, "Do you want to play jacks?"

Ruth shook her head, though it was one of the few games she could usually beat Betsy at. "We can't, unless we put the puzzle away."

It was too wet to play jacks on the front porch, and the floor of the little sunroom they used as a playroom was covered by a large jigsaw puzzle they were all working on.

"We better not," Betsy decided. "Daddy said he might finish the sky part tonight."

Their father was almost as good at doing jigsaw puzzles as he was at finding four-leaf clovers. Thinking of this reminded Ruth of Jack Buell. As Carol had suggested, they'd sent Jack a clover, carefully pressed between two tiny pieces of cardboard, along with a card Ruth had bought at the ten-cent store with part of her allowance. It said "Wishing You the Best of Luck!" in fancy gold letters, and they'd all signed their names.

Ruth hoped the clover wouldn't dry out too much by the time Jack got it. The Buells didn't have a real address for him, just an Army box number. Although they wrote him every day, they knew he only got their letters in batches, the way they got his, usually several weeks after the date on the last one.

Ruth looked down at her own letter to Joan and decided to go mail it now at the box over on Spaulding Avenue. It was the middle of the afternoon, and Chip the mailman had long since come and gone. First, though, she needed to get a stamp from her mother.

"Can I come with you?" Betsy asked, trailing her down the stairs.

Ruth shrugged. "If you want. It's still raining, though."

"I'll get our slickers," Betsy offered. "We don't need our boots—we can just go barefoot."

Mrs. Owen was in the kitchen, slicing a banana into a glass bowl to mix with the raspberry Jell-O she was making. She glanced at the envelope in Ruth's hand and said, "Oh, Ruth, there was something else in the mail for you besides Joan's letter. A little envelope—I put it on the desk. It looks like an invitation."

Ruth frowned. She couldn't think of anyone she knew who had a birthday in August. She said, "Can I get a stamp, if you have any?"

"In the pigeonhole on the right." Her mother gave a stir to the saucepan and looked back at Ruth. "Oh, heavens, Ruth, look at your fingers! Get that ink off first, please. I hope it's the washable kind."

Ruth could never use a pen, even one that didn't leak, without getting ink all over her fingers. She thought it had something to do with being left-handed and trying to write straight up and down in the awkward way Mrs. Chapman had taught her, instead of curving her hand around the top of the paper. That was another thing that made her different in her family. Even her father was right-handed.

As she stood at the sink rinsing off the ink—Scripto's Washable Blue—and gazing at the can of Dutch cleanser with its fascinating repeating picture of the woman holding the can with a picture on it of the same woman holding the same can, and so on, her mother said, "When are the

Deckers coming back, do you know? I need to make an appointment for Betsy with Dr. Decker."

"Betsy?" Ruth turned to stare at her mother. "Betsy doesn't need to get her teeth straightened— she has the best teeth of any of us. I'm the one that needs braces, for my front teeth."

Mrs. Owen sighed. "Now, Ruth, we've been all through that. Dr. Wood says they'll get closer together as you grow older. And braces are terribly expensive, you know."

Dr. Wood was their regular dentist, the one who put fillings in.

"I don't really know how we're going to afford them for Betsy," her mother went on, pouring a thick red stream of Jell-O from the saucepan into the bowl, "but it seems her jaw is too small for the new teeth that are coming in, and something has to be done."

"I'm going to have to wear *braces*?" Betsy was standing in the dining room door, their yellow slickers bunched over her arm.

"That's not fair!" Ruth said in outrage.

"Who said?" Betsy demanded, and added, "I won't!"

"Now calm down, both of you. It's not definite yet, Betsy—we'll have to see what Dr. Decker says."

Mrs. Owen put the bowl of Jell-O in the icebox, took out a package wrapped in butcher paper, and closed the door hard. She got another bowl from the shelf and dumped the meat into it.

"Ugh, meat loaf *again*?" Betsy exclaimed, her teeth momentarily forgotten.

"Yes, meat loaf again, and you'd better be grateful for it! It's a lot more than most children get to eat in this world today. And yes, I could give you lamb chops for supper more often if I were willing to deal with a black-market butcher, like some of the women in this town."

Actually Ruth liked meat loaf, at least the way her mother made it, and thought having it so often was one of the few good things about the war.

"And as for wearing braces on your teeth, or not wearing them, if that's all you two have to worry about, I'd say you're pretty lucky."

This silenced even Betsy. Ruth could see her thinking about the other kind of braces, the ones Randy Stewart would have to wear on his crippled legs.

She also saw that her mother's hands were shaking as she opened a can of tomatoes. That was scary, somehow. It was one thing for Mom to get mad at them. It was another for her to be upset inside herself.

As Ruth went into the living room to get her stamp, she heard Betsy asking in a subdued voice if she could put the empty tomato can in the special press their father had made, to flatten it for the scrap collection. Mrs. Owen said all right, but to wash it out first and be sure not to cut herself. She still sounded cross.

CHAPTER

~~~~~~~~~~~~~~~~~~~~~~~~~~

TEN

After she'd put a stamp on her letter to Joan, Ruth opened the small envelope her mother had mentioned. It contained a folded invitation card with a silly-looking pink frog on the front and filled-in blanks on the inside giving the date, time, and place of the party. Under "place," beneath the address, it said "BRING YOUR BATHING SUIT!" in capital letters. The invitation was from a sixth-grade girl named Vickie Blair. Ruth knew who she was, but that was all.

"Oh, you lucky!" Betsy was looking over her shoulder. "That's Todd Blair's sister. They have a pool in their backyard—a real one, with a diving board and everything. Todd's always bragging about it."

When Ruth didn't say anything, she added

quickly, "It's okay to go in a pool like that, I'm pretty sure. It's not like a public pool."

"Why would she invite me?" Ruth said with a frown. "I don't even know her."

"I think Mom knows Mrs. Blair," Betsy said thoughtfully. "From playing tennis."

They both knew what that meant—an invitation arranged between mothers. Betsy wouldn't have minded, but Ruth did.

Slowly she put the card back in its envelope, already feeling a little sick to her stomach, even though the party wasn't until next Saturday. Unless she really got sick, she'd have to go. If she said she didn't want to, her mother would say firmly, "Now, Ruth, it'll be a good way to meet some of your new classmates before school starts," and Ruth wouldn't be able to argue with that.

"Is it a birthday party?" Betsy asked, handing Ruth her slicker. "Because if it is, you could get her one of those funny animals you blow up and ride around on in the water. That would be a neat present."

"I don't know," Ruth said heavily. "The invitation doesn't say."

"Well, you can ask Vickie when you call her up," Betsy said, opening the front door.

Ruth put on her slicker, slid Joan's letter into one of the big pockets, and followed Betsy out into the warm, rainy afternoon. Just the thought of calling someone she didn't know made her feel sick.

Betsy was brooding about her teeth again. "It's all backwards," she complained as they went down the walk. "You're the one that wants to get braces and I'm the one that doesn't. Why does everything have to be the wrong way around?"

The rain had made a stream in the gutter, a miniature river running the length of Kempton Road. Automatically they both stepped down from the curb to wade in it.

Ruth tried not to see that there were some yellow maple leaves swirling in the water along with the green ones, and even one leaf that had already turned orange. Instead she thought how every night for a whole month, after her parents had kissed her good night, she'd wound a rubber band around her two front teeth, hoping they'd grow closer together while she slept. It hadn't worked, though. Betsy's teeth were like pearls, small and white and even, without any spaces between them.

A gum wrapper glinted in the water ahead of her. Ruth bent down to fish it out, her slicker crackling. Later she'd peel away the paper backing and add the piece of tin foil to the ball they were making. When the ball got to be the size of a grapefruit, her father had said, they'd turn it in to the scrap drive. So far it was only as big as an apple.

The war certainly involved a lot of collecting— not only foil and flattened tin cans and bottle caps, but also newspapers and string and jars of fat. Ruth understood about saving metal and scrap paper. But what could the admirals and generals be planning to do with all those balls of string and people's leftover bacon grease?

Betsy had turned to see what Ruth was doing. "That's another thing that's backwards," she said grumpily as Ruth put the gum wrapper in her pocket. "People with braces aren't allowed to have gum, and you don't even like gum. It's just rotten luck." She sloshed on angrily. "Everything is rotten luck today. The Stewarts and the war and having to have meat loaf, and now *braces*."

Ruth didn't say anything. Privately she agreed, though she would have subtracted the meat loaf and added glasses, sixth grade, and having to go to Vickie Blair's party.

They were coming opposite the Selbys' house. Ruth sneaked a glance at it from under her hood, feeling somehow as if she shouldn't look, and saw that the black shades were still down.

The rain was letting up. In the vacant lot on the next corner, some little boys were playing with capguns, sneaking up on each other through the long, wet grass and yelling things like "Bang, bang, you're dead!" and "Got you, you dirty Hun!" Ruth's parents wouldn't allow them to play with guns, except for water pistols.

Betsy looked over her shoulder at the Selbys' house and said, "Do you think Alan killed any German soldiers before they killed him?"

Ruth shuddered. "I hope not."

"Well, that's what soldiers are supposed to do," Betsy pointed out as they turned the corner onto Spaulding Avenue. "That's why they have guns—to shoot at the other soldiers and kill them if they can.

80

I bet Alan didn't mind, though," she added. "He was mean. He liked to hurt people."

"You shouldn't say that," Ruth told her automatically, though she had an uneasy feeling that Betsy might be right.

"Not like Jack," Betsy said. "Jack liked people to be happy."

Ruth stopped short, staring at her sister's shiny yellow back.

Somehow she'd never thought about that part of it at all. She'd worried about Jack getting wounded or killed, but she hadn't ever imagined him pointing a gun at another person and taking aim and pulling the trigger and watching the person fall down with a bloody hole in him.

How could Jack be made to do such a thing— Jack, who was so easygoing and funny and popular, with friends always honking the horns of their jalopies for him and pretty girls calling him up on the telephone? Mrs. Buell used to shake her head over that, but Ruth didn't think she really minded. Did Jack's gentle, kindly parents ever picture how he'd have to act in the war—how he'd be using bullets and hand grenades and maybe even his bayonet to smash and hurt another human being? A boy his own age, maybe, who might be some other parents' only son?

Betsy had already crossed the strip of grass to the big green mailbox.

"Can I put the letter in?" she asked as Ruth came up. She looked surprised when Ruth nodded. They were fascinated by the way the box almost seemed to snatch at your fingers when you pulled back the heavy steel lip and fed an envelope into the slot. Sometimes they teased Carol by telling her a tiny postman lived down inside the box, ready to reach up and grab her and drag her down into the darkness, where there might be frogs and spiders and even snakes.

Ruth watched Betsy insert the letter and then jump back quickly in spite of herself, looking shamefaced.

She realized Betsy was too young to understand that what she'd just said about Jack Buell added up to the rottenest, most backwards thing of all. Ruth herself had thought she understood the worst thing about the war—that it was ordinary people dying, especially little children who'd had bombs dropped on their houses. But maybe she'd been wrong. Maybe killing was the worst thing.

CHAPTER

ELEVEN

"Telephone for you, Ruth," her mother called. "Someone named Laura."

It was the next morning. Ruth had finally found her skate key and was sitting hunched over on the front steps, trying to adjust the clamp of her left skate so it would stay on without pinching her toes. She already had the right skate on.

"It's all right," her mother said from the doorway behind her, referring to the rule about not wearing roller skates in the house. "Just be careful on the rug."

Ruth set the left skate aside, slung the precious key around her neck, and stood up gingerly. Mrs. Owen looked at her watch and added with a frown, "I can't imagine what's happened to Miss Nitcomb. I told her I wanted to catch the 9:35."

She already had her hat and gloves on, ready to leave for the station. She was going into New York City to visit Randy Stewart in the hospital. First he'd been in a hospital here on Long Island, but then he'd been moved to one in New York. Miss Nitcomb was an elderly lady who lived on the next block with her even older sister and who sometimes took care of Ruth and her sisters when their parents weren't home.

"We'll be okay, Mom," Ruth assured her, clumping past her to the telephone. "We won't get into trouble or anything. And if we need someone before Miss Nitcomb comes, we can always go over to the Buells'."

Her mother hesitated, then looked at her watch again and sighed. "Well, all right. There's tuna fish salad in the icebox for your lunch. And tell Miss Nitcomb that Carol can have another Aspergum at eleven if she needs one."

Carol still had a sore throat, or at least she was pretending to—she loved Aspergum.

Between her mother's departure and the odd, unbalanced feeling of having one skate on and one off, Ruth barely had time to think that it must be Laura King on the phone before she picked up the receiver and said, "Hello."

"Hi, Ruth. This is Laura King. From Sunday school, remember?" She sounded nervous. Before Ruth could say sure, she remembered her, and also apologize for taking so long to answer the phone, Laura said, "What was that bumping sound?"

Ruth laughed. "That was me." She explained about her roller skate.

Laura said, "Oh, I love roller-skating. Only I'm not very good at it, because there weren't any sidewalks where we used to live. I used to skate in the driveway."

Ruth pulled up a chair and sat down, which made her feel less peculiar. When Laura didn't say anything more, she said, "Well, maybe we can skate together sometime"—not knowing if she really meant it—and added quickly, "Only not today, because we have someone taking care of us, and we can't have anyone over when she's here."

"Why not?" Laura asked. She didn't sound offended, just curious.

"Well, she's sort of old and shaky, and if too many things start happening at once, she has to go lie down on the couch and have us bring her a glass of ice water."

As she spoke, Ruth saw Miss Nitcomb hurrying up the front walk. Even though it was a warm morning and was supposed to get really hot later on, Miss Nitcomb was wearing her heavy navy-blue silk dress that looked as though it had been made for someone much larger.

"Excuse me a minute," Ruth said to Laura, and half-hopped, half-rolled to the door. "Hi, Miss Nitcomb," she said rapidly. "I'm on the phone, and Betsy and Carol are out in the backyard. Mom had to go catch her train."

"Oh, I'm so sorry to be late," Miss Nitcomb said

breathlessly. "What *must* your dear mother think of me? But my sister had one of her turns after breakfast—a pear I don't believe was quite ripe—" She broke off to stare distractedly at Ruth's feet. "Ruth, dear, ought you to be roller-skating inside the house? Somehow I don't think . . ."

"It's okay," Ruth told her, and waved her on into the kitchen as she returned to the telephone.

"Miss Nitcomb?" Laura said. Ruth could hear her trying not to laugh, and liked her for it. It *was* sort of a funny name, if you weren't used to it. "It sounds like you should be taking care of her, not the other way around." Now she did laugh.

Ruth grinned. "Well, in a way we are. She and her sister have hardly any money to live on," she explained, lowering her voice. "Also, she loves to play cards, but her sister is almost blind. She's taught Betsy and me some neat card games, like Casino and Russian Bank."

There was a silence. Then Laura cleared her throat and said, "Well, what I called about was to see if you could come over Saturday afternoon and maybe spend the night. My dad's going to cook hamburgers and hot dogs in the backyard, if it doesn't rain, and maybe take us all out for ice-cream cones after. Your parents could get you at church in the morning." She said all this in a rush, as if she'd practiced it.

Saturday was the day of Vickie Blair's party. Ruth would a thousand times rather go to Laura's, but she knew she couldn't, even though she still hadn't called Vickie, as she'd promised her mother she would. Nor could she tell Laura she'd been invited to a party that Laura wasn't invited to. That was practically her mother's number one politeness rule.

"I'd really like to," she told Laura sincerely, "but there's something else I have to do on Saturday."

"Oh. Well, if you can't . . . " Laura's voice trailed off. "I guess I'll see you in Sunday school, then," she said, and added, "I better get off the phone now. I'm calling from our neighbors' house, because we don't have a telephone yet. We were supposed to get one by now, but there's a shortage because of the war."

"The war is always messing things up," Ruth agreed quickly, feeling she shouldn't hang up just yet. She realized she'd hurt Laura's feelings, but she didn't know what to do about it. Without planning to, she found herself confessing, "I worry a lot about the boy that lives next door to us, Jack Buell. He's a soldier, and he might be in the Pacific now."

Laura said, "I know what you mean. One of my uncles is in the Marines, and my best friend at home's older brother is in the Navy. He's a Seabee." She giggled. "I know I shouldn't laugh, because what they do is really important and everything, but that's such a silly name, don't you think?"

Ruth smiled. "Like Kilroy," she said. No one knew who had started it or even what it meant, but all over Europe American soldiers had begun scrawling the message "Kilroy was here" on walls and doors and fences.

"Anyway," Laura went on, "my mom says we should concentrate on feeling proud of them instead of worrying so much. I mean, think how you'd feel if your neighbor was a draft-dodger. There was this one man in our town who pretended to have something wrong with his knee, when he was only double-jointed. And my grandfather had a hired man last year he was sure was hiding out from the draft, the way he'd moved around so much. Granddad was going to report him to the draft board, but before he could, the man quit. He just left, early in the morning, without even milking the cows. I think it's really rotten to be a draft-dodger, don't you?"

"Yes," Ruth said slowly, straightening the fringe of the hall rug with the rollers of her skate. She hated the thought that had sprung into her mind at Laura's words—that Russ, too, might be hiding from the draft. Well, you couldn't say he was hiding exactly, sitting up in his lifeguard's chair every day in full view of all the people on the beach. But what if the draft board had lost his address or something and didn't know where to find him? And what if Russ was glad about that?

Of course, it could be that Russ didn't believe in wars, even when they were to get rid of evil men like Hitler. Ruth knew there were people who refused to fight and would rather be put in jail instead. She'd thought that was just because they were scared. But now, with the ugly new picture in her mind of Jack Buell armed with a loaded rifle and a razor-sharp bayonet and a string of hand grenades on his belt (somehow the grenades were the worst), she understood that it might be because they hated the idea of hurting and killing so much.

"Ruth, are you still there?"

Laura's voice seemed to be coming from a great distance. Ruth discovered she'd let the receiver slide away from her ear. Hastily she slid it back and said, "Yes, but I better go now. See you on Sunday, okay?" Remembering her manners, she added, "And please thank your parents for inviting me over."

As soon as she hung up, she thought she should have asked Laura to go to the beach with them the next time they went. But she didn't know for sure when that would be. And she couldn't call Laura back, because she didn't know the neighbors' name or phone number. In fact, she didn't even know where Laura lived.

"Excuses," said a voice in her inner ear, as distinctly as a telephone voice with a good connection. She was almost glad to be distracted a moment later by Betsy stomping into the hall from the kitchen and declaring, "That's my skate key!"

"No, it isn't," Ruth told her, holding the key out on its cord and turning it over to show her. "There's no red mark."

"Maybe it wore off."

Ruth was happy for an excuse to get mad. "Betsy, I found this key in a shoe box in my closet, with my trading cards and my autograph book. How could it be *your* key?"

Betsy hung her head. "Well, I don't know where mine is." After a moment she mumbled, "Can I use yours when you're done with it?"

"If you give it right back. I don't want to get two blocks away and have my skate come off and not have my key."

Betsy scowled and turned away. "It's too hot to go roller-skating, anyway," she decided. "I'm going to go help Miss Nitcomb and Carol give Elinor a bath." Elinor was Carol's awful doll. "She said maybe we can go under the sprinkler later, as long as we don't get our hair wet."

The strap of Ruth's skate was hurting her ankle, and the little breeze that had been stirring the curtains at the side window seemed to have died away. Now she had to go skating, though, whether she felt like it or not. Besides, going under the sprinkler was for babies.

All the time she'd been sitting at the telephone table, she'd been trying not to see the invitation card tucked into the corner of the mirror above her. The pink frog continued to grin at her from its emerald-green lily pad. Quickly, before her heart could start pounding, telling herself that at least going to a swimming party was a grown-up kind of thing to do, Ruth plucked the card from the mirror and lifted the receiver.

CHAPTER

TWELVE

The first thing Ruth did wrong was to go to the front door instead of heading directly around the back to the swimming pool.

As her father turned the Ford into the Blairs' semicircular driveway, a station wagon ahead of them was letting out a couple of boys. Whooping and yelling, they vanished onto a tree-shaded walk beside the house as the station wagon pulled away. But since she'd never been here before, Ruth thought she ought to ring the doorbell.

"I'll be back at five," her father told her as she got out of the car. "Now, Ruth," he said, looking at her. "You're going to have a good time."

She nodded wordlessly, clutching the rolled-up towel that contained her bathing suit and cap. On the phone Vickie had said to be sure to bring a bathing cap—it was one of their rules that girls couldn't go in the pool without one. She'd also said it wasn't a birthday party or anything, "just a get-together before school starts."

Three whole hours! Ruth tried not to think about that as she turned toward the shallow front steps, whose curve matched the curve of the driveway.

"You look very nice," her father added with an encouraging smile. He gave her the V-for-Victory sign before he drove away, tires crunching on the gravel.

The house was large and white, with two chimneys and a lot of green shutters. The inner door stood open, but Ruth couldn't see inside because the screen door made everything dark.

She took a deep breath, trying to stop the shuddering in her stomach. Before she lifted her hand to the doorbell, she checked to make sure her white blouse was still neatly tucked into her good powder blue shorts from Best & Company with the white stripe running down each side. Vickie had said not to dress up—everyone would just be coming in shorts.

Ruth was glad of that, at least. It was a hot, sultry afternoon, with thunder rumbling in the distance. She'd been watching the sky since early morning, hoping it would rain and they'd have to cancel the party. But the sky had remained smooth and pale, with nothing you could call a cloud.

After what seemed like a long time, a maid answered the doorbell. She was a large black woman wearing a starched blue uniform with a white collar and cuffs.

"You here for the party, honey?" she inquired, looking mildly surprised. "They're all around back, where the pool is."

"I guess I should have taken the path," Ruth stammered. "I'm Ruth Owen," she added, and stuck out her hand. "I hope I'm not late."

"Glad to know you, Ruth Owen," the woman said, shaking her hand gently. "I'm Sophie. Well, now, long as you're here, you might as well come on through the house. Lordy, ain't it hot today?" She fanned herself as she led Ruth through a dim, high-ceilinged hall. "Anyways, you ain't late, child. There's lots of folks still to come."

They went into a dining room, past a big, polished table bristling with chairs that Ruth kept her distance from in case they tripped her. A pair of tall doors opened onto a flagstone terrace. Beyond the terrace was an expanse of green lawn, and beyond that was the pool, a glittering rectangle of pale blue water with a long, low-roofed bathhouse at the far end.

No one was in swimming yet, though Ruth could make out several figures milling around among the chairs and tables in front of the bathhouse. She hesitated, dreading the walk across the lawn with everyone looking at her. If only she'd taken the path, she would have been shielded by trees and bushes until the very last part.

As if Sophie guessed what she was feeling, she gave Ruth's shoulder a little squeeze and observed,

"Got some nice refreshments for later, when you all get tired of swimming. You like those little egg-salad sandwiches with the crusts cut off?"

Ruth nodded. She adored egg sandwiches, at least she did in her other life—her real life, where she was always hungry. Today she hadn't been able to eat any lunch, only a saltine and a sip of milk her mother made her have before she left.

"Well, ain't nobody makes a better egg sandwich than me," Sophie assured her. After a pause, she asked kindly, "You see anyone there you know, honey?"

Ruth shook her head. "I'm nearsighted," she explained miserably. At the moment, she would have been glad to recognize even Mary Jo Douglas, with her loud laugh and stringy hair. She squared her shoulders, said, "Well, I guess I'll see you later, Sophie," tucked her rolled-up towel under her arm, and forced herself to cross the terrace and go down the steps.

She was halfway across the lawn when Mrs. Blair saw her and came hurrying the length of the pool to greet her. She was a thin, blond woman wearing a flowered beach coat and espadrilles and dark glasses, like a movie star.

Ruth's heart sank. The only thing worse than arriving at a party alone was having the mother lead you around and introduce you to everyone, so they all had to stop talking.

Sure enough, Mrs. Blair took Ruth's hand and said brightly, "You must be Ruth. I've seen you from a distance with your mother"—making it plain why Ruth had been invited. "Where's that daughter of mine? Vickie, come say hello to Ruth." She drew Ruth toward the end of the pool and announced, "This is Ruth Owen, everyone. She's going to be in your grade this year. Isn't that right, dear?"

There were six guests at the party so far, already changed into their bathing suits—four girls and the two boys Ruth had seen arriving earlier. They stared at Ruth as Mrs. Blair rattled off their names. Two of the girls said "hi" without enthusiasm.

Vickie was back in a kind of kitchenette that separated the two sides of the bathhouse, opening bottles of soda and bags of pretzels and potato chips. She gave Ruth a friendly smile over her shoulder and said, "Hi, Ruth, glad you could come." Vickie was blond like her mother, with her hair cut in a perfect pageboy. She wore a two-piece white bathing suit that made her skin look the golden color of perfectly done toast.

She added to one of the boys, "Hey, Brian, you better watch out if you still want to be at the head of the class. Ruth skipped a grade, so she must be really smart."

Brian was skinny and redheaded and not much taller than Ruth, which should have made her feel better, but his expression was anything but welcoming. He studied her for a moment with flat, greenish eyes, then shrugged and helped himself to a handful of potato chips.

"Oh, who wants to think about *school*,"

exclaimed one of the girls, tossing a head of short, glossy brown curls. "It's so hot! Can we go in the pool now, Mrs. Blair?"

"Yes, I suppose so," Mrs. Blair said distractedly, as a group of new arrivals appeared along the flagstone path. "My husband promised to be here to help lifeguard, but since it looks as though he's still out on the golf course . . ."

"Oh, Mom, we don't need a lifeguard!" Vickie protested. "Everyone knows how to swim."

"Well, as long as there's no roughhousing, and only one person on the diving board at a time . . ." Mrs. Blair turned to Ruth, still standing awkwardly beside one of the padded lounge chairs with her towel under her arm. "Why don't you run along and change, dear, before things get too crowded. Take the door on the right—that's the girls' side. Your mother tells me you're a fine little swimmer," she added with an encouraging smile.

Ruth cringed, but attention was diverted from her by the other boy, Richard, who ran the length of the diving board, bounced high in the air, and hit the water in a cannonball that produced an enormous splash.

She hurried into the dressing room, hoping it would have separate cubicles. But there was just a bench with a mirror over it and some hooks for people's clothes. Wanting to get changed before anyone else came in, Ruth shucked off her blouse and shorts and tugged on her bathing suit, almost stumbling in her haste.

She avoided her reflection in the mirror, not wanting to see how babyish the suit looked, besides being all stretched out and faded. The bold yellow zigzag was only a faint pattern now against the washed-out blue. Then she thought of all the big waves she'd dived through in this same bathing suit, and felt comforted.

When she came out, Vickie was talking and laughing with some girls who'd just arrived. Ruth knew one of them, Ellen Collier, from air-raid drills at school, but she couldn't think of anything to say to her. She and Ellen had both been homeroom captains last year, in charge of counting kids in and out of the basement and making sure everyone had a kit of quiet things to do. That was in case the air raid turned out to be a real one and they had to stay down in the gloomy cement corridors for more than the usual ten minutes.

The girls went inside to change, and Vickie turned and handed Ruth a Coke. The heavy green bottle was so slick with condensation that Ruth almost let it slip through her fingers. She set it down quickly on a table and told Vickie, "No, thank you."

"We have ginger ale, too, if you'd rather," Vickie said, looking at her curiously.

It was true that Ruth's parents didn't like them to drink Coca-Cola, saying it was bad for their teeth, but that wasn't why Ruth had refused. She said, "Shouldn't we wait to eat until after we've been in swimming?"

Vickie frowned. "Why?"

Ruth realized she'd made another mistake. She looked down at the bathing cap in her hand—a new one, chalky white, made of some thin, stretchy synthetic because of the rubber shortage—and said lamely, "Well, it's just a rule in our family."

The curly-haired girl was sitting on the edge of the pool, munching a pretzel. She looked around and said with a giggle, "What's the matter, are they afraid you'll get a nasty old cramp and drown?"

Richard, the boy who'd jumped off the diving board, was climbing up the ladder at the corner of the pool. Now he flopped back into the water, pretended to sink, and came up crying, "Help, help, Mommy, I've got a tummyache" in a high, squeaky voice. He let himself sink again, while everyone laughed.

The curly-haired girl said teasingly, "Hey, Ruth, I dare you to eat a pretzel."

"Two pretzels," someone said.

"No, no, two might sink her." This was Brian, his green eyes gleaming with malice.

"Come on, you guys," Vickie said reproachfully.

Ruth made herself smile, though her cheeks were burning. "Well, I guess I'll get wet," she said, and walked away to the shallow end of the pool. Behind her she could hear Vickie saying something to the others in a low voice. She went down the shallow steps into the water, sure that all eyes were on her. But when she looked up from fastening the strap of her bathing cap, no one was even facing her way. The new arrivals had come out of the bath-house and were helping themselves to refreshments, while Mrs. Blair was greeting yet another group of guests coming along the flagstone path.

The water was much warmer than Ruth had expected, almost like bathwater from all the hot weather they'd been having. She swam the length of the pool and back again, keeping to the side away from the steps at one end and the ladder at the other. Then, because she couldn't think of anything else to do, she started another lap. This time she almost collided with two girls who were floating on their backs, talking. Changing direction, she struck out on a diagonal toward the corner where the ladder was, and just missed being jumped on by Richard, doing another cannonball off the diving board.

"Hi, Ruth," a voice said in her ear as she clung to the edge of the pool, trying to plot a path back to the shallow end. It was Ellen Collier, almost unrecognizable without her glasses and with her long, dark hair tucked out of sight beneath her cap.

"I just heard you're going to be in our grade this year. That's neat! Do you know what teacher you have?"

"Miss Amory," Ruth told her shyly.

"So do I," Ellen said, looking pleased. Ellen had the right kind of face for glasses, Ruth thought enviously—broad cheekbones and a wide mouth. In fact, she almost looked better with her glasses on than without them. "Let's go down to the other end, okay? It's too crowded here. Unless you want to go on the diving board."

Ruth shook her head. "I don't really know how to dive," she said, "except through waves."

She didn't think Ellen heard that last part, though, because she'd turned her face away to avoid being splashed by a beefy, straw-haired boy who was diving into the pool over their heads. It was getting very noisy. Mr. Blair had arrived and was yelling at two boys to quit ducking each other, standing back from the tiled edge of the pool to keep his plaid golfing pants from getting wet.

"Vickie must have invited the whole sixth grade," Ellen said as they edged their way to the shallow end. "We better not have a thunderstorm like the radio said—we'd never all fit under that little roof." She looked at the bathhouse, adding uneasily, "I guess we shouldn't be near a pool anyway, if there's lightning. I hate thunderstorms, don't you?"

Ruth nodded, though actually she thought they were kind of fun. Ellen sat down on the middle step, hugging her knees, and Ruth sat beside her, though she was so much smaller the water almost came up to her chin.

She, too, felt uneasy, but she wasn't sure just why. Ellen was telling her about some of the other kids— who was okay when you got to know them (Janice, the curly-haired girl) and who was mean (Brian) or stupid (Don, the big boy with the spiky blond hair).

Ruth tried to listen, but somehow she couldn't concentrate. She looked at the pool, which seemed to have shrunk in the half hour since she'd first seen it, clear and shining at the end of the lawn. It was so full of kids now that there wasn't any room for swimming, and the churned-up water had a dull, soapy look.

She stood up abruptly. "I think I'll get out for a while," she told Ellen.

Ellen looked surprised. "Why? At least it's cooler in the water than out of it."

"I know, but—" Ruth shook her head and backed up the steps.

Suddenly all she could think of was how crowded the pool had become, more like a public pool than a private one. The Stewart boys hadn't gotten polio from going in a pool, she was pretty sure. Still, it was David who'd gotten sick first, and then passed the germ to his younger brothers. Now David was all right, and Jonathan would be, too, except for a weak leg that would probably get stronger in time. But Randy wouldn't ever run again, or ride his tricycle around in circles, or do silly somersaults in the snow. What if that should happen to Carol, all because of Ruth and her everlasting rotten luck?

"Oh, there you are, Ruth!"

As Ruth stood dripping on the tiles, tugging at the strap of her bathing cap—which suddenly felt much too tight, almost making her gasp for breath— Mrs. Blair appeared at her elbow, smiling her bright, hostessy smile.

"I thought in a few minutes we might clear the pool and have some relay races, boys against girls. You're such a good little swimmer, perhaps you'd like to be captain of the girls' team?"

But all Ruth wanted now was to get away from the pool with its close-packed, squirming bodies, its warm, cloudy water sloshing back and forth like water in a mop bucket.

The snap on her bathing cap was new and stiff. She yanked the strap free at last, with an effort that almost made her stagger. And that was when the third wrong thing happened. As she stripped off the cap and turned blindly away onto the grass, Ruth crashed headlong into Sophie, coming across the lawn with a tray of sandwiches and two tall glass pitchers of lemonade.

CHAPTER

~~~~~~~~~~~~~~~~~~~~~~~~~~~

THIRTEEN

"And that's how I cut my foot," she told Russ forlornly the next day. "It was just a little piece of glass that didn't go in very far, but it bled a whole lot." She sighed. "At least no one else cut themselves."

Though it might have been easier if someone else had, she couldn't help thinking, remembering the silence that had followed the crash. All the bodies in the pool had stopped moving, except for heads turning to stare. Then some of the kids started laughing. Well, they probably *had* looked pretty funny—Ruth hopping up and down and clutching at Sophie in her spattered uniform, Mrs. Blair on her knees, hands fluttering as she tried to decide which to do first, pick up the broken glass or retrieve the sandwiches from the grass.

"Well, hey, it was just an accident, right?" Russ said. "I mean, it's the kind of thing that could happen to anyone."

Ruth hadn't told him the real reason she'd been in such a hurry to leave the pool. She only said she'd been feeling sick. She was ashamed of her panic now, and thought maybe she really had been kind of sick, from the heat and not eating any lunch and not wanting to be at Vickie's party in the first place.

She bent over and gave a tug to the cotton sock her parents were making her wear over the Band-Aid on her instep. They'd allowed her to go in swimming, saying salt water would be good for the cut, but they didn't want her to get sand in it.

Seeing Ruth hobbling around, Russ had called to her and invited her to sit up in the chair with him for a while. He wasn't supposed to have company, he'd said with a grin, but Ruth wouldn't take up much room, and maybe she could help keep the sand flies off him. It was another hot, windless day—so hot back on Kempton Street that Ruth's parents had decided to skip church that morning and go straight to the beach. The predicted thunderstorm had never happened, and the sky was once again a pale, cloudless blue.

In spite of her confused feelings about Russ maybe being a draft-dodger, Ruth was glad to see him again. Telling him about the party hadn't made her feel better, though. Instead, it made it seem to be happening all over again, even more painfully—

as sharp in her memory as the feeling of the glass sliver piercing her foot.

"I wish I never had to see any of those kids again," she muttered.

"Well, sure, I can see how you might feel that way." Russ shifted on the cushion, and Ruth looked quickly to see if she was crowding him. But there was plenty of room, as long as she held the megaphone and the binoculars on her lap.

"But hey, Ruth, they've probably forgotten all about it by now. It seems like a big, embarrassing thing to you, but to them it's just one of a whole bunch of things that happened at the party. And it's not like you're naturally clumsy. Once they get to know you better—" He shrugged.

Ruth shook her head. "You don't know what they're like, some of them. There's this one boy named Brian . . . "

She swallowed hard and sat staring out at the gleaming steel blue skin of the ocean, rippling like the back of a whale. There were some big waves far out, but otherwise the water was calm, with just a frill of white along the shore.

"The only person I liked at the whole party was Sophie," she said after a while. "And Ellen, I guess."

Another tall girl, she thought morosely, though not quite as tall as Laura King. That reminded her she was missing Sunday school today and wouldn't be seeing Laura as she'd told her she would. Oh, well, Laura would be better off not having Ruth for a friend anyway, now that she'd made a fool of herself in front of practically the whole sixth grade.

"Sophie?" Russ said.

"The maid," Ruth explained. She added, "I found out she has two children down South that she hardly ever gets to see. When they were little, she came up North to work, so she could send them money and keep them in school till they grew up. The boy might even go to college, if the war gets over in time."

It was Sophie who had helped Ruth across the lawn to the house, where she'd removed the sliver of glass with a pair of tweezers, washed out the cut, and wrapped a clean rag around Ruth's foot. While Ruth waited for her father to come get her, she'd sat at the kitchen table with her leg propped on a chair, watching Sophie make more egg sandwiches and squeeze lemons for a new batch of lemonade.

She'd felt bad about that, but Sophie said only one pitcher had broken and that she still had more lemons than she knew what to do with—eggs, too. And although Ruth was sure she'd lost her appetite forever, she'd ended up eating half a dozen of the little sandwiches, which were just as delicious as Sophie had said they'd be. She even had a slice of chocolate layer cake that wasn't supposed to be for the party.

"It's not fair," Ruth said now, sliding down on her spine and glowering out at the ocean. "Why do things have to be so hard for colored people? And now, after all Sophie's work and being so lonely and everything, what if her son has to go in the Army and maybe get killed? It's just rotten luck, that's all."

She hadn't meant to mention the Army to Russ, but he didn't seem disturbed. He said, "Well, maybe none of that will happen," and punched her lightly on the upper arm. "Come on, Ruth, cheer up. You're here at the beach where you love to be, remember? And it's still summer. Another couple of weeks before school starts. A lot can happen in two weeks—good things, I mean."

Ruth nodded, although she couldn't think of any. The only two things she knew were going to happen were that she had an appointment with the eye doctor next Wednesday and that Joan was going to come home and tell her how much fun she'd had in New Hampshire.

She raised Russ's binoculars to her eyes and fiddled with the lenses until the focus cleared. She found herself looking at two small pairs of legs sticking out of the water some distance from shore. A sandbar, she realized after a moment, and a couple of kids standing on their hands. She smiled in spite of herself at how silly they looked.

Then the heads came up, and Ruth saw that one pair of legs belonged to her sister Betsy and the other to Betsy's friend Cindy. She was surprised to see Betsy out so far. Then she realized that the binoculars made the big waves beyond Betsy look much closer than they really were, looming like mountain peaks with snow spilling down their steep slopes.

The binoculars were heavy. After another moment Ruth lowered them again.

"Well, I hope *you* never have to go in the Army," she told Russ, having made up her mind about that much at least. When he didn't say anything, only frowned a little, she explained, "I don't mean just because of being in danger, but because—well, you wouldn't want to hurt someone else, would you, someone you didn't even know? I think it's much better to save people, like you do."

"I guess it would depend on the circumstances," Russ said, taking the binoculars from her. "If someone was trying to kill one of my buddies, or if it was a choice between killing and getting killed—"

He broke off suddenly and thrust the binoculars back into Ruth's lap. "Hold the fort, okay? Looks like I may have a little job to do."

Before Ruth could respond, he'd swung himself down onto the sand and was running toward the water with an odd, lurching gait that Ruth noticed with one part of her mind. The other was busy refocusing the binoculars so that she could see what Russ had been looking at.

There were a number of swimmers in the calm water beyond the sandbar, most of them just floating in the swells or practicing their strokes. One of them, though, seemed to be doing a lot of splashing, twisting and turning and thrashing around as if something had her by the legs.

Ruth froze as the small head came into focus. It was Betsy who was in trouble! Clearly now, seeming so close that Ruth felt she should be able to reach out and touch her sister, Betsy's white, scared face came into view. Her eyes were squinched shut, and her squared-down mouth kept gasping for breath as she swallowed water and tried to spit it out again.

Quickly, Ruth scanned toward shore and saw Betsy's dumb friend Cindy wading through the shallows, patting the small waves with her hands, not even looking over her shoulder. Where was Dad?

CHAPTER

FOURTEEN

Clutching the binoculars, Ruth jumped down from
the chair, barely noticing the jolt to her injured
foot as she hit the sand. Russ was swimming
powerfully on a long diagonal toward Betsy,
swimming faster than anyone Ruth had ever seen
except for Johnny Weissmuller in the newsreels—
and Russ didn't even have his face in the water.
Instead, he was holding his head up in order to
keep Betsy in sight.

Awkwardly, trying to steady the binoculars
against her eyes as she ran, Ruth angled down the
slope of the beach into the water and almost
collided with her mother, who was standing in the
frill of surf gripping Carol by the hand. Through the
binoculars, Ruth saw that her father was out on the
sandbar now, standing up tall while he yelled

something to Betsy through his cupped hands. "Float!" he was calling. "Float, Betsy! Wait for the swell and just let the water carry you."

"It's okay," Ruth said breathlessly over the thudding of her heart. "Russ will get her."

Her mother nodded tensely. Ruth offered the binoculars to her, but she waved them away. "I can see. He's almost there . . . ah, he's got her." Her shoulders sagged, and she let out a long, shuddery breath.

"Ow, Mommy, you're hurting my hand!" Carol complained.

"Sorry," her mother said, releasing it. "Your father was swimming without his glasses," she explained to Ruth. "He probably saw Cindy come in and thought Betsy was with her. But Betsy was so far out—and those enormous waves . . ."

"They're miles away, though," Ruth said.

"I know, but if Betsy got scared . . ." Mrs. Owen shook her head.

So her mother knew about Betsy's being scared of the ocean, Ruth realized in surprise. She raised the binoculars again, then realized she didn't need them. Russ and Betsy had almost reached the sandbar. He wasn't towing her, the way Ruth had sometimes seen lifeguards do, holding the person's chin or wrapping an arm around their chest. Instead, he was swimming on his back with Betsy's hands resting on his shoulders, and they seemed to be talking.

"What's happening?" Cindy demanded, wading over to them and wringing the water from the ruffled skirt of her bathing suit. "Why are you all standing here?"

Ruth exchanged a glance with her mother. She thought how embarrassed Betsy was going to be, and wondered if her mother was thinking the same thing. Before they could say anything, though, Cindy turned and looked out at the sandbar, where Russ was just handing Betsy to her father. "Ooh," she said, "did Betsy have to get *rescued*?"

"She just got a little tired," Mrs. Owen said firmly.

"Ooh," Cindy exclaimed again. "The lucky! I wish that would happen to me sometime. Is the lifeguard gonna have to carry her out of the water and do that thing where they make you lie down on the sand and start pushing on your ribs?"

Not for the first time, Ruth decided Cindy was a real dope. "Oh, Cindy, don't be dumb," she said. "Betsy's fine. Look."

Russ and her father were swimming slowly in from the sandbar now, with Betsy doing the elementary backstroke between them. Mrs. Owen started to wade toward them, then seemed to think better of it. Instead, she said briskly, "All right, Carol, if you're going to have a swim, you'd better do it now. It's almost time for lunch. And Cindy, you look cold. Go on up and dry off. We'll be along in a minute."

After Cindy had turned away, Ruth splashed through a couple of small waves and swam out to join the others. The water felt cold after all the time she'd spent sitting in the sun, and the sock dragged at her foot.

"I think you can touch bottom now, Betsy," her father was saying, standing up himself in waist-high water. He turned to Russ and shook his hand. "Good thing you were keeping an eye out," he said with a grimace. "Ought to know better than to swim without my glasses, but they're a darned nuisance. No matter how I try to tie them on, they're always falling off."

"Oh, I don't think Betsy was in any real danger," Russ said in his easy way. "There might have been a bit of rip current, though. Just as well to play it safe."

Betsy was trying to smile, but her teeth were chattering.

"I got sort of turned around," she said, looking at Ruth. "I meant to be coming back in, but then the water was so deep, and there were all those big waves up in the sky . . ."

Ruth thought how she herself had panicked at Vickie's party.

"Yes," she agreed. "I sure wouldn't want to try and dive through one of *those*."

Russ gave her a quick little nod of approval, as if he knew what she'd been thinking. "Hey, Ruth, I thought I told you to hold the fort," he teased, nodding in the direction of the lifeguard's chair.

She clapped a hand to her mouth. "Oh, your binoculars! I left them on the beach—at least I hope

I did." As she plunged back through the water, she heard her father say to Betsy, "Hey, how about a piggyback ride?" and saw him boost her onto his shoulders. Betsy squealed, sounding more like her usual self.

The binoculars were lying in the wet sand at the water's edge where Ruth had dropped them. Luckily they were too heavy to have been carried off by a wave. She rinsed them off and turned to give them to Russ, who had waded along behind her. He seemed to stumble as he reached for them, steadying himself with a hand on Ruth's shoulder.

"Hey, you didn't cut yourself on something, did you?" she asked in concern. "That's all we need—both of us with a cut foot."

Russ smiled and shook his head, slinging the binoculars around his neck. Now it was Ruth's turn to steady herself against him while she took off her sock, emptied the sand out of it, and pulled it on again. When they came out of the water, though, Russ was still limping.

"Hey—" Ruth said again, and stopped.

Now she could see that there was something wrong with Russ's left leg. It was a little thinner than the other, something she'd never noticed when he was sitting up in the chair. There was something funny about his hip on that side, too—it turned out more than it should.

Ruth stood stunned, watching Russ move up the slope of the beach. His left foot dragged behind

114

him, scuffing against the sand and causing him to put his weight stiffly on his other leg—his good leg.

She hurried to catch up with him, clutching his hand and staring up wide-eyed into his face.

"Yeah, I realized you didn't know," he said gruffly. "You never saw me do anything but sit, right? I should have told you, I guess, but . . ." He shrugged. "It's not such an easy thing to work into a conversation." He gave her hand a little shake and said, "Hey, pal, don't look at me that way! One leg's a bit shorter than the other, that's all. I manage okay—not too gracefully, I guess, but it looks worse than it is."

Still speechless, Ruth trailed after him as he covered the remaining distance to the chair, noticing how people on the beach stared for a moment and then looked quickly away. She wished furiously that the fat man, the one with the murderous umbrella, was here to see him.

With a swift, practiced movement, Russ hoisted himself up into the chair. No wonder his arms were so strong, Ruth thought.

Finding her voice at last, she said, "Is it . . . was it from polio?"

He nodded, settling himself on the seat and looking around for his sailor's hat. "When I was twelve. In fact, the doctors didn't think I was ever going to walk again, so I figure I'm way ahead of the game." He put the cap on at a jaunty angle and grinned down at her. "Also, it keeps me on the home front, as you noticed."

With his white cap tilted against the blue sky, Russ looked exactly like the smiling sailor in one of the posters urging people to buy war bonds.

Ruth said hesitantly, "Do you mind about that?"

He shrugged. "Well, I guess I'd like to be part of it." Like her father, Ruth thought. "But you're right that I'd just as soon not get shot at, let alone have to shoot someone else."

Ruth sank down on the sand in front of the chair, feeling hot with shame that she'd ever supposed Russ could be a draft-dodger. "The way you were swimming just now," she said after a moment. "I never saw anyone swim that fast."

"Water therapy," Russ explained, his eyes scanning the ocean in their steady, methodical way. "You know how the President had a pool put in at the White House?" Ruth nodded. "Well, swimming's one of the best things you can do if you've had polio. The minute I heard that, there was no keeping me out of the big pool at the hospital where I was." He laughed. "I made the nurses roll me down and tip me in, and I never came out until they made me. Talk about blue lips and goose bumps!"

Ruth still couldn't even smile. "Didn't it hurt?" she asked.

"Oh, hurt . . ." Russ shrugged, as if that didn't matter. "Well, sure. But if you want something badly enough, you go after it. My family helped a lot, too, my big brother especially. He'd take me to the pool—this was after I was back home again—

and when he'd see I was getting tired, he'd bet me I couldn't do one more lap." Russ shook his head. "He'd yell stuff about how I was a coward and a sissy, and if I didn't watch out, I'd wind up being a no-good, useless cripple for the rest of my life."

"That's terrible!" Ruth said, staring up at him.

"Yeah, I used to think so too, and I'd get mad as heck at him. But inside . . ." Russ paused. "Well, I guess I knew he just wanted me to be the best I could be. I mean, suppose he'd said, 'Great, Russ, you're doing fine, why don't you take a rest now'? I might never have gotten this far." He grinned. "Tony's in the Air Corps now, a bombardier. I bet his crew never stops hearing it from him."

Ruth was silent, trying to decide if Tony was a person she would have liked. She hoped he hadn't asked to be made a bombardier.

Russ gave her a thoughtful glance and said, "It's sort of like what your parents are doing to you, maybe."

She frowned and looked away. "It's not the same," she said, picking at a scab on her knee. She'd gotten it roller-skating last week, when she'd taken a corner too fast and gone down in a heap. Miss Nitcomb had insisted on painting the scrape with mercurochrome, though Ruth would have preferred iodine—it stung more, but it also worked better.

Russ seemed to be waiting for her to go on. She said haltingly, "They don't know how I feel inside. About being shy and small for my age, I mean, and always having to act like the oldest and be grown-up with my sisters, even when I don't feel like it. Well, maybe my dad understands, but my mom doesn't. She's too different from me."

"I bet she does. Being different doesn't necessarily mean you can't understand." When Ruth didn't say anything, Russ said, "About that party yesterday."

She looked up at him, feeling her skin go clammy again at the thought of all the kids staring at her and laughing—and even worse, at the prospect of having to face them again on the first day of school. She'd been thinking she might be able to hide in the girls' room until the bell rang, and then creep into a chair at the back of the room. At least with her new glasses, she thought bitterly, she'd be able to see the blackboard from there.

Russ said, "Sounds to me like you got boiled."

Ruth smiled reluctantly, because that was exactly what it had felt like—like getting up your nerve and plunging into a big, scary wave, thinking you were going to be okay, and then getting boiled after all.

"So okay," Russ prompted. "What do you do next? Let's say you stand up, you're all dizzy and sore from being knocked around—and right away there's another big wave hanging over you."

Ruth knew what he wanted her to say, but somehow it was hard to get the words out.

"Dive through it, I guess," she said at last.

"You *guess*? Hey, you've got no other choice." Russ grinned at her, shifting in the chair in the way she knew now probably meant that his hip was

118

hurting. "Maybe you'll get boiled again, but you'll get boiled even worse if you don't try."

Ruth thought about this—about all the bad-luck waves that could rise out of nowhere to smash people down, and how Russ had gotten boiled in one of the biggest waves of all.

She wanted to tell him she thought he was as brave as any soldier charging up a hill against enemy fire, any sailor watching a torpedo speed toward his ship. But before she could find the words, he glanced along the beach and said, "Hey, I see your folks waving at you. Time for lunch, maybe?"

Ruth nodded and pushed herself to her feet. "Spam sandwiches," she grumbled, then shrugged a bit sheepishly. "Actually, I kind of like Spam," she confessed, "even if everyone else hates it."

"With plenty of mustard," Russ agreed. "So do I. But then, we're probably both a little peculiar, you and me." This time his smile was as wide as the brim of his sailor's hat, and Ruth noticed for the first time that there was a small gap between his two front teeth. "Better put a new Band-Aid on that cut," he advised. "I don't think that sorry-looking sock can be doing much good any more."

"Aye, aye, sir," Ruth said, smiling back.

She started to turn away, then thought of something. Even though it hurt to put her full weight on her cut foot, she drew herself stiffly to attention and gave Russ a salute—a real salute with a snap to it, like she'd seen Jack Buell practicing before he went away.

CHAPTER

~~~~~~~~~~~~~~~~~~~~

FIFTEEN

As she limped back along the beach, zigzagging around the families on their blankets and the little kids burying each other in the sand, Ruth wondered if the Stewarts knew about swimming, for Randy. If they didn't, she'd get her parents to tell them.

She also found herself wondering if Laura King's family had gotten their telephone by now. If they had, she could probably get the number from Information. It was always fun to tell the operator, "Information, please," and then listen while she rustled through the pages of some special phone book and finally recited the number in a voice that sounded like someone talking through a hole in a tin can.

Yes, Ruth thought with a sudden surge of energy,

maybe she'd try calling Laura when she got home. And if the Kings still didn't have a telephone, she could get their address from Mrs. Morgan or Mrs. Graham and ask her mother to drive her there, if it was too far to walk or ride her bike.

In fact, maybe Laura could come to the beach with them some day next week. That would give them both a chance to get used to the difference in their sizes and see if they really liked each other. Ruth might even tell Laura about Vickie's party. She had a feeling it would make Laura laugh, at least if she told it the right way. Laura would have to watch out for getting sunburned, though, with her light hair and all those freckles. Ruth made a mental note to ask Russ for the name of the white stuff he put on his nose.

"There you are!"

Her mother was pouring milk into the battered metal thermos cups, saving the biggest one for Ruth. She looked up with a smile and said, "I was afraid you'd lost your appetite."

Maybe because of what Russ had said, Ruth saw the concern behind the smile. She smiled back, shaking her head, and reached for a Spam sandwich.

"Careful!" her father said as she flopped down on the old steamer rug between Betsy and Carol. Ruth looked and saw she'd almost sat on his glasses. She handed them to him and watched him hook them carefully over his ears. Immediately they became part of his face again.

As she ate her sandwich, she remembered the page from a ladies' magazine that Joan had enclosed in her last letter. It showed different shapes of faces and a row of differently shaped eyeglass frames. The directions said to trace the frames and then try them on the face whose shape matched your own, to see the kind of glasses that would look best on you. Or you could draw the glasses on a snapshot of yourself, if you had a special kind of grease pencil.

Ruth had barely glanced at the page, telling herself Joan was just trying to rub it in about her having to wear glasses. Now she admitted that Joan was only trying to help. When she got home today—maybe even before she called Laura—she'd take a piece of tracing paper and try out each frame on the face that was the longest and narrowest. The magazine said you could also draw your hair around the face. That would be easy enough in Ruth's case, since all she'd need were a few straight lines.

This reminded her of Ellen Collier, who really did look good in glasses. She thought how Ellen hadn't laughed when Ruth broke the pitcher; instead, she'd scrambled out of the pool to see if she could help, only to be waved away distractedly by Mrs. Blair.

If only Ellen weren't so tall.

Ruth grinned suddenly at the picture that had just formed in her mind. If she made friends with both Laura and Ellen, she'd look even shrimpier than she already did. On the other hand, the three of them together might look funny ha-ha instead of funny peculiar—almost as if Ruth were a kind of mascot. Everyone liked mascots, even in the Army. At least they did in the comic strips, where the short guy was always the spunky one who made the others laugh and who had all the good ideas.

"Feeling better?" Her father patted her on the knee, sprinkling some grains of sand in her cup of milk.

Ruth didn't mind. What was a picnic at the beach without sand? She nodded slowly, knowing he didn't mean just her cut foot, and looked out to sea.

The big waves loomed against the horizon, still keeping their distance from shore. Meanwhile the sun burned hot on the top of Ruth's head and dazzled like a million silver coins on the gently heaving surface of the water. The briny smell of the ocean prickled her nostrils, and her ears were full of the slur and swish of small waves breaking along the miles of sand.

She turned to her mother. "Can I have the other half of Betsy's sandwich if she doesn't want it?" Betsy hated Spam.

Carol said, "I might want it."

Ruth glared at her. Their father said in a resigned voice, "Pick a number between one and twenty."

"No," Carol said suddenly. "Ruth can have it."

"Thanks," Ruth said, and gave her little sister her biggest smile, the one she knew showed the space between her front teeth. She took another bite of

Spam—saltier even than the sea—washed it down with a swallow of sandy milk, and heaved a sigh of contentment.

"I didn't even think I was hungry," she told her family. "But all of a sudden I'm starved!"

nately, the chair next to Lola slid out and Deacon sat down, making it so I'd have the perfect view of him from the corner of my eye no matter how hard I tried to avoid it.

Damn. Damn. Double stuffed damn.

Everyone else took their seats, and the room quickly filled with the chatter of conversation and the clinking of utensils against plates. The food looked absolutely delicious, but unfortunately my appetite seemed to have escaped out the very door Deacon and Leah waltzed through earlier.

What I was feeling wasn't rational, I understood that, but I couldn't shake the instant dislike of the woman on Deacon's arm. It was nothing that she'd done to me personally. If I was being honest with myself—which was something I'd been avoiding like the plague lately—she was actually a really nice girl. But she had what I'd so carelessly tossed away. I was a woman, after all; we tended to be ruled by our emotions the same way men were ruled by their dicks.

It was science. So even though I had no reason to hate Leah other than pure unadulterated jealousy, it was completely unavoidable. The feelings were beyond my control. At least that was my excuse for wanting to stab her in the eye with a turkey leg.

Not that I'd ever act on that impulse.

"So, Fiona, darling. Your father tells me the Fall line was a huge success."

I looked from the frowny face I'd been drawing in my mashed potatoes with my fork down the length of the table to Nolan Lockhart, Grayson and Deacon's father. He and my dad were best friends. That was why I'd grown up so close to the two Lockhart boys. The three of us had been thrust together practically since birth. The Lockharts were basically an extension of the Prentice family, and vice versa.

Pasting a smile on my face, I spoke to the man who was, for

all intents and purposes, a second father to me. "Yes, it was very successful. Everyone's geared up to push the Spring line in a few months. We're hopeful it does just as well."

"We're all so proud of you," Nolan's wife, Cybil, said. My smile turned genuine at the heartfelt compliment. They'd always treated me just like a daughter, so hearing that she was proud of me warmed me from the inside.

"Thanks, Cybil."

"Of course, I'll be thrilled when you stop concentrating so much on work and find a nice young man to settle down with," she continued. "Give us more little babies to keep us old folks feeling young."

I promptly choked on the water I'd just taken a sip of and started coughing uncontrollably.

Sophia and Daphne started patting my back in an effort to help me breathe again while Grayson grumbled, "Jesus, Mom."

"What?" Cybil asked innocently. "I'm just saying. We're getting up there in age, son. And I know Evelyn agrees with me. She's been going on about grandbabies ever since you and Lola announced you were pregnant."

Sweet baby Jesus in a manger. She'd been talking to my mother? That wasn't good.

One of the many curses of being a redhead was my fair skin's tendency to blush a furious shade of pink. And if the way my face was burning at that very moment was anything to go by, by cheeks were currently the color of fire.

"Mom, will you please lay off?" Grayson grunted. "There's nothing wrong with Fee focusing on her career right now."

I shot him a thankful look across the table while silently praying for the floor to open up and swallow me.

"Is there more wine?" I asked, scanning the table for the closest bottle. Sophia's fiancé, Dominic, reached across her, bottle in hand.

"Of course there's nothing wrong with that, dear," Cybil said. I hoped that would be the end of the painful conversation.

No such luck.

"But a woman needs to be mindful once she reaches her thirties. Our eggs are only good for so long."

Dear Merciful Lord who art in Heaven, if you care for me at all, you'll send down a bolt of lightning to kill me right now.

"For shit's sake," Grayson cursed.

"Cybil, darling, that's enough," Nolan stated sternly.

"She could always go to one of those banks that keep all the sperm," Nana Lockhart said loudly. Nana was Grayson and Deacon's eccentric grandmother. I loved the woman to death, but she only had two settings: hilarious and humiliating. There was no middle ground. "You know, the ones that use those turkey baster thingies?"

I turned to Daphne and held out my butter knife. "Will you do me a favor and plunge this into my neck?" I tipped my head and pointed where I wanted to be stabbed. "Right here in the jugular."

Her eyes flashed with genuine concern before something unsettling started working in their depths. I didn't like that look. Not one damn bit. "Um, well... uh, Fiona's actually... what I mean to say is..." I could practically see the light bulb flick on about her head as she finished with, "dating! She's dating!" she said loud enough for everyone to hear. "Or she's going to, anyway. I set her up on a blind date."

Eff my life. Eff it so damn hard.

I gave her a squinty-eyed look and screamed with my eyes, *What the hell are you doing?*

I'm sorry, I panicked! her eyes returned.

Have you lost your mind? my glare asked.

I'm sorry! I didn't know what else to do!

Caleb broke into our mental argument. "Fee's going on a blind date? I didn't know that."

A *thunk* sounded from beneath the table, and Caleb winced at his wife's well-placed kick, muttering a string of curses under his breath.

"She totally is!" Sophia joined in, clearly having taken the same crazy pills as Daphne that morning.

"And he's totally a great guy!" Lola chimed in. My friends were dead. I was smothering all three of them in their sleep. "He's... a surgeon!"

"Yeah!" Sophia added. "He works on babies. And he's totally cute."

Dominic gave Sophia a quizzical look, clearly not buying the shit she was shoveling for a second. "He *works* on babies?"

"Yeah," she replied. I couldn't tell by the back of her head, but I was pretty sure she was giving her man the stink eye. "He's a pediatric surgeon. A *super-hot* pediatric surgeon."

"He sounds like a catch!" The four of us turned our attention to Leah. "Don't you think, babe?" she asked Deacon, wrapping her hands around his arm and leaning against his shoulder. "I mean, a handsome doctor who takes care of teeny tiny babies? He sounds like Prince Charming. Isn't that great?"

"Yeah," Deacon said in a flat, emotionless tone before lifting his beer bottle to his lips and taking a long pull. "Just great."

Something glittered behind his eyes as he stared at me over the amber glass. I couldn't quite understand what I was seeing, but whatever it was twisted my stomach into knots.

"Oh, how lovely," Lola's mother, Elise, stated happily. "Every woman wants to land herself a doctor."

Her husband, Maury, shot his wife a bland look. "Good to know, darling."

Before taking it upon herself to come to Seattle and interfere in her daughter's life, Elise had been a single woman, still bitter over her divorce from Lola and Dominic's father years ago. Then she met the doorman in Lola's building. It was kismet. The two of them married shortly there after, and have been acting like randy teenagers ever since. It was sweet... to anyone who wasn't Lola or Dom.

Elise rolled her eyes at her husband. "Oh, you know what I mean. *Young* women want stuff like that. I'm perfectly content with you, sweetheart." She kissed his cheek, and it was his turn to roll his eyes.

"Just what every man wants to hear, that his wife is *perfectly content*. Warms my heart," he teased good-naturedly. Meanwhile, I was busy aiming deadly eye lasers at each of my girls.

Grayson gave Lola a curious look. "This is the first I'm hearing of it. When did you guys set this up?"

"Uh, recently," she answered quickly. "Like really recently. They're not going on their date for a couple weeks. You know, because of his busy surgery schedule and all."

"Yeah," I deadpanned. "Busy, busy, busy." I emptied my glass and held it out to Dominic for a refill.

What had started as a tiny white lie had quickly snowballed out of control, as was wont to do when it came to those three women.

The more they talked, the more elaborate the lie became until the man they'd dreamed up became some modern-day prince who could do no wrong. I wasn't sure if men like the one they were describing even existed. There was such a thing as *too much* perfection. And they'd really laid that shit on thick.

Everyone seemed to think it was a brilliant idea, excited for what could come from my upcoming date with Dr. Wonderful. All the while I was silently planning my escape from the country before this insanity could actually take place.

Thanksgiving could officially suck it.

CHAPTER THREE

THE PARENTS HAD all cleared out shortly after dinner was over. Talk of my impending date had thankfully died off when the tryptophan started to hit everyone. Lola had laid down for one of her many pregnancy naps, and everyone else scattered to different parts of the house. I'd taken the opportunity to snatch up the baby and escape to the quiet sanctuary of the nursery upstairs to prevent any more questions.

"Your mommy is a nutter," I cooed in a baby voice as I bounced Evie on my hip.

She let out a little baby squeal before shoving her whole fist in her mouth.

I giggled down at her, unable to keep a straight face when the cute, pudgy little girl gave me that gummy grin. "That's right, a nutter. She totally screwed Aunty Fee."

In response, Evie leaned in and tried to suck on my chin while smacking me in the chest with her tiny balled-up fist.

"Who's Auntie Fee's special girl? Who's her little angel?" I baby-talked, nuzzling her neck to make her giggle again. I inhaled deeply, pulling that soothing baby smell into my lungs.

"You're good with her."

My head shot up. Deacon stood in the doorway, watching me and Evie closely.

"Uh, thanks."

He stepped farther into the room, and the air around us grew uncomfortably thick. I hated that being in such close quarters with him felt so weird. Deacon had been the most important person in my life for so long. Growing up, he meant everything to me. Still did, honestly. And now there was this huge chasm keeping us apart. It was like I was standing in front of a stranger. It broke my heart.

"So," he started slowly, "a blind date with a doctor. That's...."

"Insane?" I asked with an awkward laugh. One corner of his mouth hitched up in a crooked smirk, and my belly instantly warmed at the sight of it. In an attempt to keep myself grounded, I held Evie even closer to my chest.

"I was going to say out of character."

My mouth curved into a slight confused frown. "How so?"

Deacon's shoulder lifted in a casual shrug. "It's just... the way they went on about the guy you'd think he created a cure for cancer or something. It was almost like they thought his occupation was the most important thing about him. You just never struck me as the type of woman to give a shit about that kind of stuff."

I couldn't help but feel offended at the implication that I could be that shallow. "I don't," I snapped somewhat bitterly. "I couldn't care less if he was a surgeon or the dude who shoveled roadkill off the highway. Are you saying I'm conceited?"

His head jerked back infinitesimally. "Shit, no. That wasn't what I meant. You know me better than that. I was just surprised is all. You've always been kind of private. A blind date is really out of the ordinary for you."

My shoulders drooped with relief once I realized he wasn't

insulting me. "Oh. Yeah. Well, you know the girls. When they get something in their heads, there's no talking them out of it. All you can do is brace."

He chuckled, and I felt that down to my core. "Yeah. I get that."

Why is this so freaking hard?

It had been more than a year since that night he laid it all on the table. More than a year since I lost him all over again, all because I was scared. Daphne had once told me that the ball was in my court. He'd taken the first step and I shot him down. If there was any hope of having him back in my life, it was up to me to take the next step.

I'd wanted to. God, how I'd wanted to.

I tried my hardest to explain. I wanted him to know that I felt the same way he did, that he was it for me. I wanted to apologize for not seeing it, for being so goddamned blind. I wanted to tell him just how badly I wanted him, how he'd consumed my every thought since that kiss on my porch. I wanted to make it right so I could finally have him.

But when Deacon said he was done, he'd meant it in every way possible. He shut me out completely. Any attempt I made failed so epically that it actually caused physical pain. Then Leah entered the picture a few months back.

I could count on one hand the number of times Deacon and I had been in the same room together over the past year, and this was the first time we'd actually spoken.

I had been dreaming of this moment, craving it. Missing Deacon was like missing a crucial piece of myself. But now that the moment had actually arrived, I was so overcome with nerves that I couldn't manage to think of anything to say.

We stared at each other, the discomfort growing palpable. Thank God for Evie. She chose that very moment to let out a shrill scream, announcing to the room that she wasn't happy with the lack of attention on her, and smacked my cheek.

"Guess she's used to being the center of attention," Deacon joked, moving further into the room and extending a finger in her direction. Evie quickly latched on and tried her best to shove his finger into her mouth.

"Yeah, well can you blame her? She's so adorable she totally deserves it."

Deacon's eyes came back to me as he managed to extract his finger and take a few steps back. "Can't argue that."

The silence started to spread again, and I couldn't take it anymore. "So how have you been?" I asked, blurting out the first words that popped into my head.

"Good. I've been good. You?"

"Good. Yeah, me too. All good here."

Jeez, any moment now we were going to start talking about the weather or economy, or something equally boring and trite. I bounced Evie on my hip and started rocking side to side, to keep her calm and to give myself something to do.

"Leah seems really nice." I don't know why I said that, why I mentioned the woman. The words just poured out.

"She is."

Kill me.

I somehow managed to force supportive words out past the bitterness coating my tongue. "Great! That's great. I'm glad. Things seem really... great between you two." If I said great one more damn time I was going to kick my own ass.

"Yeah. She's great. We're great."

"Good," I croaked. "That's really good."

Well, at least I didn't say great again.

He didn't respond, and I started to fidget under the intensity of his stare. Once again, my mouth opened and words fell out of their own volition.

"This is weird. God, why is this so weird? I hate how weird this is. Does it feel weird for you too?" *For God's sake, Fiona, stop saying the word weird!* Squeezing my eyes closed, I gave my head a vicious shake. "Sorry, sorry. Shit. I'm sorry. I shouldn't have said that. I just...."

"Just what?"

My eyes shot open and I gave a small, startled jump at the close proximity of his voice.

He was so close that I could see the flecks of gold in his brown eyes, so close that I couldn't form a single thought. "Sorry?"

"Finish what you were saying, Fee. Just what?"

The golf ball–sized knot in my throat made it almost impossible to speak, but somehow I managed. "I just miss you," I stated on a hushed whisper. "I miss you, Deacon. You were the most important person in my life and I lost you... twice. I *hate* that. I *hate* how things are between us. And I know it's all my fault. I know I screwed up, Deacon—" He opened his mouth to cut me off, but I held up a hand to stop him and kept going, knowing I wouldn't have the nerve again to say what I'd been needing to say for over a year now.

"I want you to be happy. That's all I've ever wanted, and if Leah makes you happy and treats you how you deserve to be treated, then I'm thrilled for you. I lost my chance with you. That's on me, a hundred percent. I'll accept that and move on because I know, deep down in my gut, I *know* that you deserve the absolute best, Deacon. But I miss hanging out and having fun with you. I'd do anything to get that back. I know I don't have the right to ask, but if you could find it in you to one day forgive me, I'd be over the moon. Because not having you in my life at all is worse than any pain I've ever experienced."

By the time I finished my speech, tears burned the backs of my eyes. Thankfully I managed to blink them away. My throat was ravaged with emotion, but I'd finally garnered the courage to say what needed to be said.

Deacon's chest rose and fell with quick, heavy breaths. His eyes flashed and glinted with something I couldn't quite put my finger on, but whatever it was, my gut told me that it was important.

His hand came up. I thought he was reaching for the baby again, but his fingers landed on my cheek, tracing gently to my temple where he tucked a strand of my hair behind my ear. "There's nothing to forgive," he said in a soft yet gruff voice. "And I've missed you too."

The relief was overwhelming. I wasn't sure if I wanted to laugh or cry. Either way, I felt like a year's worth of weight had been lifted off my chest. My lips parted to speak when another voice pierced through our moment, shattering the familiar connection I felt forming between the two of us.

"Deacon?"

Damn. Damn, damn, damn, son of a bitch in heat.

Deacon cleared his throat and turned to his girlfriend. "Leah."

Leah's face was marred by a severe frown as she looked back and forth between the two of us. Her words were clipped as she asked, "Am I interrupting something?"

I could only imagine what it looked like: Deacon standing close, his fingers at my jaw as we stared into each other's eyes. We probably looked like something out of a chick flick. The relief I'd experienced just moments before was quickly replaced with a gnawing guilt. I'd already caused Deacon more grief than he deserved, the last thing I wanted was to create a rift between him and his girlfriend—whether I liked her or not. He cared about her and was happy. I couldn't ruin that.

"No," I answered quickly, taking two large steps back. "Evie tangled her fist up in my hair. Deac was just helping me before I was left with a massive bald spot." The smile I gave her felt forced and brittle.

Her eyes shone with suspicion and antipathy before she disregarded me completely and looked back to Deacon. "Baby, I'm starting to get a headache."

Fifty bucks said her head was perfectly fine.

"All right. Let's get you home."

My chest grew tighter and tighter with every step he took away from me, but I made sure the plastic smile stayed in place. The second Deacon made it to her, Leah threw an arm around his waist and cuddled into his side like she could no longer walk without his assistance.

She gazed up at him adoringly. "Thank you, honey. You always take such good care of me."

Gag.

I managed to hold back the puke and offered politely, "Oh no. I hope you feel better, Leah."

"Thanks," she replied in a saccharin-sweet tone that was as real as her tan. It was winter in Seattle, for god's sake. No one who lived here was *that* tan. Not naturally, anyway. "Have a good night."

Deacon looked at me over his shoulder and smiled as Leah started guiding him from the room. "See you soon, Fee."

"Yeah, Deac," I muttered at his back as he disappeared from my sight. Evie cooed, drawing my attention to her. "Well, at least that's something, right?"

"Boo. Gah!" A string of drool dribbled down her chin.

I decided to take that as her agreement.

"I'll eventually get used to seeing him with someone else, right?"

"Bah! Bah!"

I cuddled her against my chest and began swaying side to

side. "Learn from Aunt Fee, baby girl. When you meet the man of your dreams, hold tight and never let go. *Ever*."

In response, Evie reached up and gripped my hair tightly.

I grinned down at her cute face. "That's right, angel. Just like that."

CHAPTER FOUR

_____

FIONA

TEN YEARS old

THE FINAL BELL rang and I bolted from my desk, hooking my backpack over my shoulders in my hurry to escape. The kids in my class were jerks. And Katy Pierson was the biggest jerk of all. I didn't want to go to that stupid school and have to see any of their stupid faces anymore.

Instead of walking home like I was supposed to, I made my way to the Lockharts', rounding the side of their house to head into the woods beyond their backyard.

It had taken us all summer, but Deacon and I managed to build the most *awesome* tree house in history back in those woods. Nobody knew about it but us, and it was the only place I wanted to be right then.

The ground was layered with dead leaves that crunched under my Keds as I wound my way through the trees. I followed the path that Deacon and I had made by trudging back and forth to our secret hideout for the past several months. I knew the way by heart but still made sure to pay close attention to everything around me. Deacon had warned me that it was easy to get lost out here. He was always worrying about me like that. He was my best friend and looked out for me like nobody else could.

I dropped my backpack to the ground when our tree house came into view, then climbed the ladder up to my sanctuary. It wasn't until I was inside that I let myself cry over the hurtful words and laughs.

I didn't know how long I'd been up there by myself when the boards started to creak. With a sniffle, I swiped at the tears on my face and looked toward the opening just as Deacon came into view. His too-long hair hung down in his eyes, and his cheeks were pink from the chilly temperature.

"I've been lookin' for you. You were supposed to come to my house after school. Why're you up here all by yourself?" He settled in beside me and finally looked over to study my face. His forehead wrinkled with a frown as he leaned in closer. "Are you crying?"

Wiping under my nose with the back of my hand, I hugged my knees tight to my chest. "No."

"Liar."

Sometimes having Deacon as a best friend was a real pain in the butt. He knew me too well, so I could never get away with lying.

"I don't wanna talk about it."

"You have to talk about it," he demanded. "If you don't, I won't know who's butt to kick for hurting your feelings." Deacon bumped his shoulder with mine. "Come on, Fee. What happened?"

"It's...." More tears started to trail down my face. "It's stupid. The whole thing is stupid."

"It's not stupid if it made you sad."

God, I was lucky to have Deacon. Sometimes I forgot how

great he was, but then he acted all sweet and reminded me why he was my best friend. "It was Katy Pierson. She was makin' fun of me today."

Deacon's expression pinched with anger. "That girl's a bitch."

I let out a tiny giggle at the sound of that bad word coming from his mouth. "You know your mom's gonna wash your mouth out with soap again if she hears you sayin' stuff like that." I shouldn't have bothered with my warning. He'd eaten soap more times than I could count already, and it hadn't stopped him from cursing yet.

"Well it's true," he said with a shrug. "She's a spoiled little brat. What'd she say to you?"

Remembering what had happened made my skin burn with embarrassment, and I couldn't help but start crying all over again. "Sh-she said I was ugly. That all redheads were ugly, but that I was even uglier because I had bony chicken legs. She said it in front of the whole class, and everyone laughed like she was the funniest person in the world."

His arm came up and circled my shoulders, pulling me into his side as he spoke. "You're not ugly, Fee. You're the prettiest girl in that whole school. Katy Pierson's just stupid and jealous 'cause she knows she'll never be as pretty as you."

I sniffled and lifted my watery gaze to his. "You really think I'm pretty?"

He let out a loud snort that filled the entire tree house. "Are you for real? You're super pretty!"

My face stretched into a smile so big my cheeks started to hurt. "Thanks, Deac. You're awesome."

"I know," he teased, bumping me again before letting his arm fall away. "You're awesome too. I know that because you're my best friend, and I won't be friends with anyone who's not awesome."

I giggled and shoved at him playfully.

"I love you around the world and back again. You're my best friend."

He replied the same way he always did for as long as I could remember. It was our thing. "You're my best friend too, Fee. And I love you to Jupiter and back again. Now can we get the heck outta here? I'm freezing my balls off, and Mom's making cookies."

With a roll of my eyes, I headed for the ladder. Deacon liked to talk and act older than he really was, but he did it in a way that made him sound cool. All the other boys at school tried to copy everything Deac did, but none of them were able to pull it off like he was.

"You know, you shouldn't talk like that around girls," I scolded, repeating what I'd heard my mom say before, as I started climbing down. "My mom said that boys should be respectful and courteous whenever they're around a lad—"

My words were cut off when the board beneath my feet snapped. I hit the ground before I even realized I was falling. It knocked the air out of me, and I landed on my left arm in a really bad way. A pain worse than anything I'd ever felt shot from my wrist to my elbow.

"Crap. Fiona!" Deacon jumped from the ladder, landing like a ninja before rushing to my side. "Are you okay?"

"M-my arm," I croaked, holding my left arm to my chest protectively while a fresh wave of tears blurred my vision. "It hurts."

"Shh, I got you. It's okay. I'm here."

I'd never heard Deacon's voice sound like that before. It was soft, and full of worry, but I was in too much pain to process it. He carefully helped me from the ground and slung my good arm around his shoulders. "Come on, lean on me and I'll get you to the house."

I let him take most of my weight as he began guiding me through the woods. "The tree house," I stated once we were about halfway. "Your mom's gonna be so mad. She'll never let us hang out there again."

"Who cares about the stupid tree house, Fee. You got hurt."

"But... what if they tear it down? That's our secret hideout, Deac. Just yours and mine."

He looked at me from the corner of his eye. "We don't need a secret hideout. As long as we got each other, that's all that matters."

CHAPTER FIVE

FIONA

PUSHING through the door of the restaurant, I unwound my scarf and shook off the cold from outside while scanning the tables in search of my friends. We got together once a week for lunch, no kids or men, just the girls. It had become tradition, and it was the perfect time for me to lay into them for sticking their noses in my personal life.

The moment my eyes landed on them, I scowled, announcing my displeasure before skirting my way through the busy dining area.

I hit the table and heard Sophia say, "Told you she'd still be mad. You each owe me twenty bucks." She held her hand out to Daphne and Lola and wriggled her fingers. The two women rolled their eyes before slapping the bills into her palm.

"Of course I'm still mad!" I declared, removing my coat and hanging it on the back of my chair. "You pimped me out to an imaginary do-gooder with a heart the size of Mother Teresa who *doesn't exist.* And you did it in front of everybody, so backing out of this so-called blind date isn't even an option. It's only been two days and my mother's already called, beside herself with excitement. She's got it in her head that I'm going to be some fancy doctor's wife. So yes, I'm mad. No..." I paused to give it some more thought, then added, "I'm *pissed*."

"In our defense," Daphne started, holding her hands up in surrender, "the situation kind of got away from us."

I gave her a look of disbelief. "Got away from you? You *created* the whole mess!"

"We were only trying to help. You looked so...." Lola's bottom lip began to tremble. Pregnancy hormones had turned her into a raving lunatic. She cried at absolutely everything. Last week she split the seam of her favorite skirt trying to zip it up and lost her damn mind. She was inconsolable for hours. All because she kept trying to convince herself that she didn't need maternity clothes yet.

The woman was nearly five months pregnant and was naturally curvy as it was. She hadn't fit in her pre-pregnancy clothes for the past two months, but none of us had the lady balls to tell her. "They started in on you about marriage and babies, and Deacon is the love of your life, but *Leah* was there, and you looked so sad, and... and...." She choked on a sob and clamped a hand over her mouth.

"Here we go again," Sophia groaned.

Lola sniffled and waved her hands in front of her eyes. "Sorry, sorry. I'm stopping. Just give me a sec." We all waited for her to get her shit together. Finally she closed her eyes on an inhale, opening them as she blew it out calmly through her lips. "Okay. I'm good."

I bit my lip to keep from laughing at my friend's plight. When I was sure I had control, I finally spoke. "Look, I know you guys were just trying to help, but you really screwed me over here. I mean, can you imagine how heartbroken my mom will be when she finds out this guy isn't real? I'm sure she's already picking out china patterns and floral arrangements in her head!"

"Okay, yes, so this is a little bit of a mess," Daphne stated, a look of guilt on her face. "But just because we don't *know* a guy like we described doesn't mean he isn't out there. This is Seattle, for Christ's sake! If we put out some feelers, I'm sure we could line up a dude who has at least some of the qualifications we—"

"Made up?" I finished for her.

"Exactly!" Sophia cried. "Daphne's right! If there's anyone in this city who can track down a hot, sexy doctor who saves babies for a living, it's us."

I highly doubted that, but I couldn't bring myself to rain on their parade. Besides, despite my reservations, maybe this was just what I needed. I didn't hold out hope for a blind date to turn out well, but maybe this could be my way of dipping my toe back into the dating pool. My feelings for Deacon hadn't dwindled in the slightest, but he was getting on with his life. It was time for me to do the same.

Finally, I relented with a huff. "Fine. But it's your job to track this guy down and get the ball rolling. I'm not putting in any of the legwork, you hear me?"

Lola squeaked excitedly, clapping her hands. "Yay! This is going to be so great."

I highly doubted that.

I HATED GROCERY STORES. Like seriously hated them to the point that all that was in my fridge was a box of baking soda, half a case of soda, and something that might have been cheese at one time, but I wasn't a hundred percent certain on that.

Funny thing was, I used to love cooking, and I was damn good at it. But there was nothing enjoyable about cooking for one. I always ended up with leftovers that sat in my fridge until they inevitably spoiled. So I eventually moved to takeout or those sad meals for one you found in the freezer section. Thus began my disdain for the grocery store.

However, in my infinite wisdom, I'd decided that, since I was about to step back into the dating world, maybe it was time to implement changes in *every* aspect of my life. If I was going to get back on the horse again, so to speak, and start dating, then I figured why not just revamp everything?

I was going to be a whole new Fiona, one who stopped stress-eating snack cakes to fill the hole of loneliness inside of me. I was also going to implement a healthier diet and start working out.

It all sounded good, in hindsight. Then I signed up for one of those early-morning boot camps. I didn't even last half a session. I kind of lost my shit when the instructor yelled "*give me five more!*" while we were doing these god-awful things called burpees—an invention of the Devil, right along with bras and pantyhose. I'd done three and was already dying, so I told him to take his five more and shove them right up his clenched ass.

I got kicked out.

Then I tried Pilates and woke up the next day feeling like I'd pulled every muscle in my body. My third attempt at exercise was yoga. Thankfully that hadn't been so bad. I'd already gone three times and was actually starting to feel a little more zen. Sure, it probably wouldn't help with the little food baby I'd developed since Deacon started dating Leah and I'd decided to eat my feelings, but it kept me off the couch and away from the brain-rotting reality TV I'd started to become obsessed with.

And bonus: the instructor was hot. Granted, he was a vegan hippy who wore Birkenstocks and reeked like patchouli, so not my type at *all*, but the smell wasn't too over powering if I sat in the second row, and it provided me with nice weekly eye candy.

With dating on my horizon and fitness checked off my list, it was time to start the clean-eating portion of my New Fiona plan. Hence the trip to the supermarket after yoga.

I stood in the health food aisle, glaring down at the bag of kale chips in my hand like it had just insulted my mother. Little Debbie had just come out with their holiday cakes in the shape of Christmas trees, and they tasted a million times better than stupid kale chips.

My lip curled in disgust as I tossed the bag back onto the shelf. Maybe it would be best for me to start out slow, like a salad for one meal a day for a few months before expanding on that. I turned and started pushing my cart out of the aisle of tasteless, flavorless cardboard snacks only to come to a screeching halt at the sight of Deacon standing a few feet away.

"H-hi," I stuttered. Seeing him made my belly erupt with a million butterflies.

"Christ," he grunted in a deeply masculine, gravelly voice. "What the hell are you wearing?"

I looked down at my attire. Black yoga pants that hugged every inch they covered and a dark orange cami. I had a pale yellow jacket over my top, but it still clung to me from chest to waist, not that there was much to cling to. I was tall and thin, and while I had curves, they were nothing on par with Lola or my other friends. I had a happy handful of boobs and ass, but only *just* a handful.

I was covered from my neck all the way down to my feet, but the way Deacon was staring at me made me feel like I was standing in the center of the supermarket totally naked.

"Uh, yoga clothes? I just came from yoga."

His eyes left a burning trail up my body before meeting my own. I barely caught the heat in his gaze before it was snuffed out by curiosity and a bit of bewilderment. "You do yoga?"

I wanted to be offended that he'd be so surprised by my

doing anything even remotely active, but he'd known me all my life.

"It's a new thing," I said with a small shrug. "I decided I wanted to try and be healthier."

His lips quirked up in a smirk as he scanned the items in my cart. "Really? And mini donuts and Fruity Pebbles are part of your diet plan?"

I glared defensively, cocking my hip and crossing my arms over my chest. "I also got whole grain bread and baby spinach."

His smirk turned into a grin. "Oh, you're right, sorry. Those totally cancel out the breakfast cereal that's basically nothing but sugar."

"I'll have you know that cereal is perfectly healthy. It contains most of the basic food groups, and it's not like I'll eat the whole box in one sitting. And I'll have a salad for dinner to balance it."

He held up his hands in surrender and moved to the end of my cart, directly opposite me. "I'm sorry. I didn't mean any offense. I was just teasing."

His big hands wrapped around the thin metal prongs, and I couldn't help but notice how long and thick his fingers were. It made me think of something else of his that could possible be long and thick, and how badly I wanted to find out for myself.

Annnnd, I'm blushing again.

I smiled shyly. "It's cool. I know you were. I think... well, I think we're just finding our footing with each other again."

Deacon's face went soft, causing my insides to melt. "I'm thinking maybe you're right. But we'll get there."

We'll get there. At just those three simple words, the reality of just how badly I'd screwed up with Deacon hit me like a ton of bricks.

"Yeah," I whispered, my heart lodged in my throat. "We will."

We had to, because I'd been living a life without him in it for way too long.

After saying our goodbyes, I was left with a feeling of longing as I watched him walk away. Needless to say, I bought the damn Christmas tree snack cakes.

Two boxes of them.

CHAPTER SIX

DEACON

THOSE GODDAMNED YOGA pants were burned into my brain. Right along with her declaration on Thanksgiving.

"I miss you, Deacon. You were the most important person in my life and I lost you... twice. I hate that. I hate how things are between us."

It had been a week and I still couldn't remembered every single word like it had been yesterday. They were the very words I'd been dying to hear for so long. But fuck me if they didn't come at the worst possible time.

I couldn't go there, not again. That woman had crushed my heart one too many times, and despite the ever-present gnawing desire in my gut, I'd be a fool to go there again.

But everything she said rang true. Before I fell in love with Fiona, she'd been my best friend, the most important person to me. She was the one safe place I had to land when feeling like an outsider in my own home became too much to bear. Growing up, no matter how hard I tried, I'd always felt like I was the odd man out, the black sheep of the family.

My older brother Grayson could do no wrong. The smart one, the wunderkind, the son who was going to, one day, take over Bandwidth Communications from my father and carry on the Lockhart legacy.

I was the troublemaker. I was the one who got into fights at school, the one whose parents had to be called to the principal's office because I was failing a class or had back-talked a teacher.

I couldn't tell you how many time my father had looked at me with that gut-wrenching disapproval stamped on his face and muttered those words I'd always dreaded.

"Why can't you just behave, son? Why can't you be more like your brother?"

I didn't want to be anything like Grayson. I wanted to be my own person, not the carbon copy of my big brother—who was basically a mini Nolan Lockhart.

The funny thing was, if they had quit trying to turn me into something that I wasn't, I never would've gotten into those millions of scrapes as a kid.

Don't get me wrong, my family loved me—there was no question there—but I'd never been able to escape the underlying disappointment that weighed down the air in our house like a dense fog. So eventually I just stopped trying.

I turned my back on the family company, deciding to venture out and do something *I* wanted to do. It broke Dad's heart, but the thought of being stuck behind a desk day in and day out for the rest of my life was suffocating. I couldn't work like that. I needed to be free, not chained to an office.

When I decided to open my bar, my parents and brother thought it was just another way for me to rebel against the family. That couldn't have been further from the truth. All I'd ever wanted to be was my own boss. I wanted to own something that was solely *mine* and not tied to the Lockhart name. It had nothing to do with sticking it to my folks, and everything to do with me pursuing something that made me happy.

However, as the years had passed, I'd learned that trying to explain these feelings was pointless, so I'd given up. If they wanted to think everything I did was to spite them, then I'd let them.

I could deal with their displeasure because I had Fiona. She was mine. I never burdened her with my family drama because it was so easy to forget about anything and everything that wasn't *us* when she was around. There was a sense of peace when I was in her presence that didn't exist anywhere else.

And then she went and fell in love with my perfect brother. I knew I shouldn't have blamed her. I'd kept my feelings for her a secret for years, convinced that the timing of my confession had to be absolutely perfect. Then and only then would I tell her the truth; that I'd been in love with her all my life. She had no clue. But that didn't matter. My heart was broken nonetheless. I viewed her falling for Grayson as the ultimate betrayal.

Years passed, and I did my damnedest to move on. Eventually the pain began to fade. Like most young relationships, she and Gray hadn't lasted. He was now married to the only woman I'd ever met who had the balls to take him on head to head and give him a dose of his own medicine.

I'd finally started to heal. My relationship with my brother was still shaky, but it was getting better with each passing day. I had been knocked down by the woman I loved not once, but twice. The first time when she fell from my brother. The second when I finally told her the truth and she'd pushed me away. It had taken a lot to get myself to the place I was now, and hearing her confess how much she missed me on Thanksgiving had rocked me to my goddamned core.

Deep down, I knew I was probably better off letting her go completely. I just couldn't. No matter how hard I tried, no matter how many times I told myself that I was better off, I just couldn't let her go. She'd been mine for years. *Mine.*

Then I lost her.

That had been a pain unlike anything I'd ever felt. But I had learned my lesson. I was moving on and guarding my heart. I was older and wiser now, and maybe, just maybe enough time had passed and I could have my best friend back.

These were the thoughts rolling around in my head when I pulled into my driveway. It wasn't until I put my car in Park next to Leah's that I realized I'd left the goddamned grocery store without the items I'd stopped to get in the first place. "Shit."

Things with Leah had been tense since Thanksgiving, when she'd walked in on that moment I'd been having with Fee. Since then she'd been pushing to take our relationship to the next level, attempting to secure her spot as the woman in my life. Things grew even more tense when I told her, in no uncertain terms, that there was no way I was ready for us to move in together.

I wasn't sure how much longer the relationship was going to last. If I was being honest, I probably should've called in quits when I started questioning whether or not I saw her in my future, but she'd let the subject drop, and we were both working toward getting us back to that comfortable place we'd once been in.

She called earlier that day to tell me her plans to cook me dinner at my place. I'd just left the bar when I got a text from her asking me to stop and pick up a few ingredients she'd forgotten, but seeing Fiona in those fucking skintight leggings had rendered my brain useless.

I climbed from the car as my mind worked overtime to come up with a plausible excuse. I didn't feel like fighting tonight, and if I so much as mentioned Fiona's name, I knew I wouldn't hear the end of it.

"Hey, babe," Leah chirped as I pushed open the back door

that led straight into the kitchen. The place was a goddamned disaster. Pots and pans scattered everywhere. Dishes I hadn't even realized I owned lay filthy in the overflowing sink. The remnants of something I couldn't identify by look alone was splattered all over the countertop by the stove.

"Jesus, Leah. What the fuck?"

She looked around at the mess that took up my entire kitchen. "Don't worry, I'll clean up when I'm done. Did you get the oregano and cilantro?"

"Uh...." I scratched at the back of my neck. "They were out. Sorry."

Her eyebrows dipped into a deep V. "They were out? Of both?"

"Yeah." I felt like shit for lying. I felt like shit for a lot of things when it came to Leah. My head shouldn't be this fucked up over someone else when I was in a relationship.

"That's okay." She smiled brightly, and that ball of guilt in my gut grew even bigger. "It's not a big deal. I'm sure I can substitute them for something else. Or...." She scanned the chaos all around her. "Maybe just leave it out."

She sounded unsure, like she had no idea how the meal she was preparing was going to turn out.

I couldn't keep the uncertainty out of my voice as I asked, "Uh, so what is it you're making, exactly?" If the sight of the kitchen wasn't bad enough, the smell wasn't all that welcoming either. It was like a combination of dirty gym socks and rotten, burning garbage. I was actually scared to eat it.

"It's a surprise." She grinned excitedly, not bothered in the slightest that the stench of whatever she was concocting was actually burning the hairs in my nostrils. "You'll just have to wait and see," she finished playfully as she sauntered toward me and stood on her tiptoes to press a kiss to my lips.

I couldn't do it. I just couldn't. She looked so goddamn

happy to see me, and was busting her ass to try and be the perfect girlfriend... I couldn't keep up the charade any longer. That ball of guilt was going to grow and grow until it consumed me from the inside out.

"Leah, sweetheart, can you stop for a second?"

She set the spoon in her hand down and gave me her full attention. Her pretty face fell in a frown. She knew what was coming. Odds were she'd been expecting it, but that didn't mean it wasn't going to hurt.

"You know I care about you—"

Leah raised her hand to stop me before I could finish my sentence. "Don't," she said in a pained whisper. "Don't do that. Don't say shit like that to make yourself feel better. Just spit it out."

Jesus, I was such a fucking asshole. "I can't do this anymore. It has nothing to do with you, swear to God—"

A sarcastic bark of laughter erupted from Leah's throat. "'It's not you, it's me.' God, Deacon, could you be any more of a cliché? Just say it like it is. It's because of Fiona, isn't it? You have feelings for her."

"There's nothing going on between me and Fiona. Never will be."

Her head tilted to the side as her eyes narrowed suspiciously. "That wasn't a no, Deac. That was just a clever way of getting around the question. Do... you... have... *feelings...* for... her?"

My skin prickled, my hands clenched into tight fists. "Yes," I finally admitted on a ragged whisper. "But that doesn't mean anything. She and I will only ever be friends. There's too much water under the bridge there."

She shook her head, staring at me as if I were the most naïve person on the planet. "If you really believe that, then you're more clueless than I thought."

I opened my mouth to ask what the hell she was talking about, but it was too late. She stormed out of the kitchen, snatching her coat and purse from the couch. "For your sake, Deacon," she started as she jabbed her arms through the sleeves of her jacket, "I really hope you get your shit together before it's too late."

"What's that supposed to mean?"

"It means you either need to make it work with her or move the fuck on."

I gripped the edge of the counter separating us so tightly that it was a wonder the granite didn't snap off in my hands. "I *have* moved on."

Leah's deep chuckle grated at my skin. "Totally fucking clueless," she muttered.

She brushed past me on her way to the back door, and I came unfrozen from my spot just as she reached for the knob. "I didn't mean for it to be like this."

Leah looked at me over her shoulder and issued her parting shot. "I think *you* believe that. But the truth is it's always going to be her. Word to the wise, Deacon, don't start anything with another woman. Until you've *really* let go of the dream of the wonderful Fiona Prentice, you're just going to keep hurting people in your pathetic attempt to lie to yourself. Oh, and you can clean your own fucking kitchen."

Then she was gone, leaving me reeling.

CHAPTER SEVEN

FIONA

I WAS a nervous wreck as I parallel-parked outside Deacon's bar. With how my hands shook and my heart rattled against my rib cage, you'd have thought I barely knew the guy instead of him being one of my oldest friends.

Pulling in a fortifying breath, I killed the engine and grabbed the door handle as I quietly gave myself a pep talk.

"You can do this, Fee," I muttered as I pushed the car door open. The chill of the winter night air hit my face like a thousand tiny needles, making me suck in a quick breath. "You got this. The ball's in your court. Go in there and get your friend back."

God, I hated that word. *Friend.* As far as I was concerned, it was on par with *pap smear* or *gluten free* or *Lord Voldemort.* I didn't want to be Deacon's friend, but I had to accept what I could get, and having him as a friend was absolutely better than nothing at all. Besides, it was my own damn fault that I'd lost out on a chance at being more with him in the first place. I couldn't blame him for being unwilling to go there again. I'd hurt him twice already. I was lucky he wanted anything to do with me at all.

That was why I was currently standing outside his bar. I was the one who'd broken us, so I needed to be the one to take the first steps in healing our relationship.

Pushing the door of The Black Sheep open, I moved into the warm, bustling bar and out of the cold. I loved Deacon's bar. I'd been there as a friend of the family the day it opened, and a few times in passing after that, but with how strained our friendship had become after Grayson and I started dating, I hadn't felt welcome enough to show up regularly.

Things had shifted last year after I was part of a charity auction put on by Sophia, Daphne, and Lola for their radio show. I'd finally gotten my friend back after *years* of him keeping a distance, and I'd become a steady regular at The Black Sheep during that time.

Unfortunately it didn't last long, what with Deacon declaring his feelings for me and me pushing him away because I was scared. I'd been blindsided at the time, having only just gotten him back. I handled the situation poorly, and the result was losing him all over again.

This time I *couldn't* make the same mistakes.

I'd missed that bar almost as much as I'd missed him during our time apart. He'd taken what was once a hole in the wall and turned it into a thriving hot spot. It was one of the places to see and be seen in Seattle. Hence the reason it was nearly standing room only on a Thursday night.

I pushed my way through the crowd toward the massive U-shaped bar at the back, knowing that was where he'd be. If he wasn't in the back office doing paperwork, he was slinging drinks for thirsty customers. He loved being behind the bar. He thrived there—it was obvious to me from all the times I'd sat my ass on one of those stools and watched him in his zone.

The line of waiting patrons was three deep as I slowly advanced forward. It wasn't until I managed to find a break in the crowd to the far left that I caught sight of him. He and another guy worked in tandem to fill orders. His hands were a blur of motion as he made multiple cocktails at once and collected money from outstretched hands.

Resting my elbows on the bar top, I settled in and enjoyed the show of Deacon at work. I was totally content to bide my time until he made his way in my general direction, but it didn't take long to get his attention. As if sensing my presence, Deacon's head came up and turned. His eyes landed on me instantly, and the smirk on his lips sent a tremor through me.

"Hey!" I called loud enough for him to hear me over all the noise.

"Hey! What are you doing here?"

I leaned in closer so he could hear me better. "Just stopping by." I scanned the people around me and noticed the crowd had grown even thicker. "Jeez, it's a madhouse in here tonight."

Deacon lifted his arm to push his over-long hair back, causing his muscled bicep to strain the fabric of his shirt. "Yeah, tell me about it. And we had a waitress call in sick at the last minute, so we're short staffed. It's been a bitch of a night so far."

I stood from my hunched-over position and made my way behind the bar. "So put me to work," I demanded.

His chin jerked back in surprise. "What?"

I scanned the area and quickly found the aprons. Grabbing one, I tied it around my waist while looking back at Deacon. "Put me to work. You're short staffed, it's chaos, and I can help. So let me."

The sight of his warm smile did crazy things to my lady bits. "Fee, I'm not making you wait tables."

Slapping my hands on my hips, I scowled hard. "Why not? You know I have experience." And that was true. Despite my family being loaded, my folks had been pretty hardcore when it came to teaching me responsibility. They paid for my tuition and living expenses, but if I wanted money to go out or buy new clothes, I had to get a job. I didn't mind. I actually liked working for what I wanted, so I took jobs waitressing all throughout college.

"I know you do, sweetheart, but you aren't here to work for me. You're here to relax and have a drink, not serve them to other people. Besides"—he did a full body scan of me that made my skin burn—"you're in heels. You can't wait tables in heels, babe."

Ignoring the warm, gooey feeling in my belly I got from him calling me *sweetheart* and *babe*, I pushed forward. "Deac, I basically *grew up* in heels. I could run a marathon in these babies," I said, lifting one of my Alexander McQueen–clad feet. Okay, so that wasn't *totally* true. Yes, the shoes pinched toes a bit, but I'd manage. The studded booties were absolutely to *die* for, and cost a serious mint, but this opportunity was serendipitous. It gave me the chance to show Deacon I cared and wanted to be there for him. I wasn't going to let a stupid pair of shoes hinder my ability to help a friend in his time of need.

With a rich chuckle that shot warmth through my chest, he threw his hands up in surrender. "Okay, fine. You want to help, you can help. But don't say I didn't warn you."

I gave him a salute and a sarcastic "You got it boss. Now point me to my section."

He handed me a tray and guided me to the section of tables I'd be working for the next several hours. Then I was off.

"ONE JACK AND COKE. One seven and seven. And two cosmos." I finished calling off the orders I'd scribbled on my note pad and looked up at Deacon as he started on my drinks.

"You ready to admit defeat yet?" he asked with a smug grin.

"*Pfft*, please," I scoffed. "This is a cakewalk."

It wasn't. It really freaking wasn't. I'd been at it for four hours and I wanted to die. No, first I wanted to hunt down the asshole who designed my shoes and plant one up his ass—*then* I wanted to die. But I'd be damned if I let Deacon see any of that. I was determined to be the best damn friend that existed in the history of ever.

His lips quirked with a suppressed grin. "You sure about that? 'Cause you started limping pretty bad about an hour ago."

I glared at him across the bar top. "Just fill my damn order."

"Ma'am, yes, ma'am," he said with a laugh and a salute. I settled the drinks on my tray and carefully teetered toward my last table. It was late and only a few stragglers remained. I set the glasses down, smiled a friendly smile at the two couples who sat at the four-top, pocketed my tip, and headed back to the bar.

"Last call!" Deacon shouted just as my ass hit the empty barstool in front of him.

"Oh thank *God*," I mumbled before I could catch myself.

Deacon burst into laughter, and I got so caught up in watching his already handsome face get even *more* handsome that I forgot all about my poor aching feet. Humor dripped thick from his voice as he asked, "Still think this is a cakewalk?"

"Shut up," I grumbled.

He moved around behind the bar, pouring vodka into a glass over ice and squirting something into it with the well gun. He finished off with a squeeze of lime, then shoved another wedge onto the rim and slid it in my direction. "Vodka tonic. Drink and take a load off. Sherry can close out your last table before she clocks out," he said, talking about the other waitress who'd worked the floor tonight. She was a sweet girl waitressing her way through college, who seemed to be in a perpetually happy mood in spite of spending the entire night running her ass off, fetching drinks. It probably helped that she was wearing wait-ressing-friendly footwear.

"Thanks," I muttered across the rim of the glass before slug-ging some back. The cool, refreshing liquid slid down my throat, then settled into a soothing pool of warmth in my belly.

I'd finished my drink by the time Sherry made it to the bar, having finished up with the last customer who'd just headed out the door.

"You're a lifesaver, Fiona. I probably would've passed out halfway through my shift if it wasn't for you."

I smiled up at the bubbly blonde. "Happy to help. Oh, and here you go." I pulled the wad of cash that had been my tips for the night out of my pocket and extended it her way. "This should be yours."

"Oh no! I can't take that. You worked your butt off. You earned those tips, babe."

I pushed the bills into her hand and closed her fingers around them. "I just did it to help out a friend."

By the way she bit her lip and stared at the cash with hesi-tant yet hopeful eyes, I knew she needed it a lot more than I did. I could appreciate how important tips were when working your way through school.

"Seriously, babe. I'm good. I don't need it."

"You sure?"

"Absolutely," I answered with a resolute nod.

She let out a little squeal and jerked me into a hug. "You're totally the best, Fee! You feel like doing this again, make sure Deacon puts you on with me. I loved working with you."

I couldn't help but beam at the compliment. "You got it."

Sherry handed everything to Deacon so he could close her out, then took off shortly after with an exuberant wave as the door closed behind her, leaving Deacon and I totally alone for the first time in over a year. Thanksgiving hadn't counted since we had the buffer of Evie between us.

"So," I started, suddenly feeling all kinds of awkward. "I should probably head out and let you finish up for the night."

I pushed up from the stool just as Deacon spoke. "Nah, stay. Keep me company."

I wanted to do exactly that. I bit my cheek to prevent my over-excitement from shining through as I asked, "You sure? I don't want to get in your way."

Those deep chocolaty eyes of his hit me, and he winked. "I'm sure. After I'm done, maybe we can shoot some pool. Give you a chance to win back some of that money you lost to me growing up."

I shot daggers from my eyes and declared, "Oh, you're so on. And you only ever beat me because you're a cheat. I could totally kick your ass at pool now."

The whites of his perfectly straight teeth flashed as he smiled. "We'll just have to see, won't we?"

Oh yeah, we totally will.

CHAPTER EIGHT

FIONA

I WATCHED with a smile as the yellow ball fell into the corner pocket with a satisfying *clunk*.

Deacon let out an impressed whistle as I looked up at him with a cocky grin. "Wow. So you *have* gotten better."

It wasn't that so much as sheer luck, but I wasn't about to admit that to him. I lined up my next shot and missed by a mile.

"Or not," he stated with a deep chuckle. He took his turn, sinking one striped ball before speaking again as he lined up his next shot. "So, how's the world of fashion?"

I pulled in a breath as I leaned against the side of the pool table, sipping at the second vodka tonic Deacon had poured me. "It's... good."

He looked up after pocketing his second shot, lifting a skeptical brow. "Well don't sound too excited about it," he teased playfully.

Shame trickled down my spine. The very same shame I felt every time I thought about my career, and how I should've been more thankful for what I had.

"No, it's great," I lied. "Really. It's great."

Resting the butt of the pool cue on the ground, he studied

me closely, like I was a fascinating specimen under a micro-scope. "I know things have been rough between us the past...."

"Several years?" I finished for him.

"Yeah." He grinned. "Several years. But babe, you were never able to lie to me. That hasn't changed."

My lips puckered as I expelled a huge puff of air. I dragged a finger through the condensation on the drink glass I'd rested on the table ledge. "I have no business complaining," I finally admitted. "I have a great job that most women would kill for, a great pension, and excellent benefits, and I get to work closely with my dad. I mean, what right do I have to be unhappy?"

The cue let out a muffled clang as he dropped it onto the green felt tabletop. "You have every right if it doesn't make you happy. Fuck all that other shit. Just because it's someone else's dream job doesn't mean it has to be yours."

I rested my pool cue beside his and sucked back the remaining dregs of my drink. "I should be happy there. I know I should. It's just...."

"Just what?" he asked when I took too long to complete my thought.

"Just not what I thought I'd be doing," I answered with a shrug. "Don't get me wrong, I enjoy what I do. I appreciate all the chances my job gave me, but I guess I just always figured that I'd have something similar to what my parents have when I got older. My mom started working at Prentice Fashion after she married my dad. And not because she wanted to work in the fashion industry, but because she wanted to be close to him as much as possible. Dad wanted that too." I gave Deacon a small, slightly embarrassed smile as I admitted, "Maybe it sounds naïve, but I wanted that for myself, you know? I wanted to marry a guy I loved so much that I'd be working alongside him in whatever he did simply because I'd miss him too much when he was gone."

His expression grew soft as he murmured, "You always were a romantic."

"Yeah, I guess so. I just never really cared about building a career. I always dreamed of building a family."

The atmosphere had grown as heavy as the conversation. I needed to do something to change that, so I joked, "But don't tell Lola, Soph, or Daphne I said any of that. They'd strip me of my girl card and kick me out of the club."

When he didn't laugh, I tried something else, grasping at straws to move the conversation in a different direction.

"I kind of envy you, you know? You paved your own way, started this bar. I know it was expected for you to join Bandwidth with Grayson."

"That was never going to happen," he said in a growly, intense voice.

"Because it wasn't what you wanted?" I inquired, cocking my head to the side, giving him my full attention.

He looked from me to the table and picked up his pool cue. I followed suit when it became obvious that he was about to take another shot. "Something like that," he muttered as he sank another ball, officially taking the lead.

There was no missing the hostility in his words, but I couldn't understand it. Sure, I'd witnessed tension between him and his dad growing up, and he and Grayson had a competitive streak that never made any sense to me, but what I always saw most was a loving, supportive family unit.

I'd been a bit jealous of Deacon when I was a kid because he had a brother. As an only child, I'd always wished for a sibling, that built-in best friend I'd have all my life. I never got why those two were constantly trying to one-up each other.

"Well, no matter what, I know your folks are proud of you."

Deacon let out a noise between a scoff and a snort before

sucking back a swig of beer from the bottle he'd brought over to the table. "I wouldn't be so sure of that."

I lost interest in the game completely, too disturbed by the sudden frosty change in Deacon's demeanor. "What are you talking about? Of course they are. Deac, this place is amazing. Do you even know the statistics for new restaurants or bars closing within the first two years? I researched it when you opened The Black Sheep. I'll admit, I was a little worried for you at first, but when I saw this place? I instantly fell in love with what you created. You have no idea how amazing it is that you not only succeeded with this place but *thrived*. You're crazy if you think they aren't proud. They are. I know I am."

I'd been so lost in my tangent that I hadn't registered the massive shift in the atmosphere, at least not right away. Now that I was no longer talking, I found it difficult to breathe, the air so thick with whatever emotion was rolling off Deacon in waves.

His voice grew low and raspy. "You researched statistics?"

"Well... yeah. I know you and I weren't exactly close at the time, but all I ever wanted was for you to be happy, and The Black Sheep made you happy."

"You worried about me?" he asked, even lower and raspier.

"Of course I did, Deacon. Just because we weren't in each other's lives for a long time didn't mean I didn't still care about you. I missed you like crazy. I never stopped caring about you."

He closed his eyes, as if in pain. "Christ, sweetheart. You really are proud of me," he grunted before looking at me once more. I had no idea what was going on or why things felt like they were suddenly shifting. All I knew was that I meant every single word I'd said.

"Are you kidding?" I whispered. "I love this place. When you shut me out last year, I only *barely* missed The Black Sheep as much as I missed you. I'm over the freaking moon for you that you get to live your dream."

His pool cue clattered against the table as he tossed it down, sending the balls scattering along the felt as he rounded the pool table in my direction. My heart stuttered and my breathing escalated at the look in his eyes, like he was a caged animal just set free.

"Deacon, what—"

My cue crashed to the ground where he threw it. His fingers tangled in my hair and, using his hold on my head, he tipped it to the side for better access before his lips slammed against mine in a demanding, all-consuming kiss.

I gasped in surprise and he used the sudden parting of my lips to his advantage, thrusting his tongue into my mouth and tangling it with my own. I was instantly lost to the decadence of the kiss, to the taste of Deacon. It was so much better than I remembered our last and only kiss. He tasted like hops and mint. He was all man, and I melted into his hold, needing his support to stay upright.

A muffled moan crawled up my throat when his teeth clamped down on my bottom lip. My arms twisted around his neck to hold on for dear life as my tongue quickly got in the game, meeting his with every stroke.

I whimpered greedily with loss when his mouth broke from mine, but the noise quickly shifted into one of desire as Deacon's lips trailed along my jaw and down my neck. Never in my life had my skin been so sensitive, so responsive to a man's touch. I never wanted it to end. I wanted to drown in him.

"Deacon," I breathed, drawing his lips back to mine. I had no clue how long the kiss lasted. All I knew was that I'd die if he stopped.

"You're unsure of this, baby, you need to stop me now, because once we start there's no going back."

"Oh God," I groaned, throwing my head back as Deacon's

fingers found my rock-hard nipple beneath my top and began toying with it. "Don't stop. Please, *God*, don't stop."

That was all it took for him to snap completely. His hands on my ass, I was lifted off the floor and deposited on the edge of the pool table faster than I could suck in my next breath. Even through the denim of his jeans *and* mine, I could feel how hard he was, how *big* he was, and I wanted that. *God*, I wanted that.

Deacon's mouth was fused to mine as he rocked his hips against me, his thick erection rubbing against my most sensitive parts, causing shivers to rack my body.

"Need you," I mumbled into his mouth as I bit, and nipped, and licked, and kissed. "Deacon, please. I need you."

The man was a miracle worker. He somehow managed to get me out of my jeans *and* panties without breaking the kiss.

His words poured into my mouth as he asked, "You on the pill?" I was so delirious with desire that I barely registered the sound of his zipper coming down, or what that meant. My brain was focused on one singular goal: getting him inside me.

I couldn't fucking wait.

"Yes, yes. I'm covered. Please, now."

Then he was inside me.

CHAPTER NINE

DEACON

FIONA'S HEAD fell back on a sharp, keening cry as I buried my cock to the hilt.

Fuck me. God, I couldn't recall ever having a woman so tight, so goddamned wet and ready for me. I knew without a shadow of a doubt that the moment I sank into her warm, perfect pussy it was the closest I'd ever come to Heaven on Earth.

All that gorgeous, thick red hair tumbling around her shoulders and down her back was too tempting to ignore. Wrapping the heavy length around my fist, I pulled her head back up so I could look into Fiona's eyes as I fucked her. Pulling out slowly, I reveled in the sounds of her husky moan before thrusting back in.

"Open your eyes," I demanded, driving back into her. Her eyelids fluttered open as I moved. Her walls grip my cock like a goddamn glove as I powered in and out. Christ, it was sheer perfection the way she stretched and fit around me.

Fiona's beautiful eyes were dark with lust as she gazed into mine. Her lips were red and swollen from our kisses, and there was no missing the faint whisker burn along her jaw and neck from the stubble that coated my cheeks and chin.

I growled at the sight of it, feeling a primal need to mark her as mine in any way possible.

Her nails clawed at my shoulders and back as she fought to hold on, rolling her hips in time with mine. It was then that I realized my mistake. I shouldn't have done this here. I should've taken her back to my house so I could have her in my bed, all that hair spread out on my pillows, her scent coating my sheets. I should've waited so I had time to strip her completely naked and worship every inch of her creamy, soft skin.

"Harder," she panted, trailing her hands down my back to my ass. She dug her fingertips into my skin. "Deeper, Deacon. I need more."

She wasn't the only one. Now that I knew what it was like to be inside her, there was no way I'd ever be able to let her go. No fucking way in hell.

I pulled completely out, unable to mask my grin when she cried out a panicked "No!"

"Don't worry, baby," I gritted, yanking her off the table and spinning her around so her back was to my chest. "I'll give you what you need."

Then, with a hand between her shoulder blades, I pressed her chest down onto the soft felt of the pool table as I used a foot to kick her legs wider apart. Once I had her exactly where I wanted her, I drove back in, going deeper, so much fucking deeper.

"*Yes!*" Fiona shouted as she arched her back and tipped her ass up. "Just like that, baby."

When she looked at me over her shoulder, her eyes hooded and glassy, I nearly lost it. She pushed up, using her forearms on the table as leverage to drive herself back on my dick. Her gaze spoke the words she didn't need to say, demanding more, harder, faster.

She wasn't just taking what I gave. Oh no, not Fee. She participated in every goddamned second. Whereas some women were happy to lay there and let me do all the work—not that I ever cared as long as I was getting off—Fiona surprised the shit out of me by meeting me every step of the way.

"Who knew my Fee could go so wild," I grunted, holding on to her hips as the sound of skin slapping skin filled the otherwise quiet bar.

My words caused her pussy to clamp even tighter as she cried out, getting closer to that euphoric edge.

I couldn't get enough of her. No matter where I touched or kissed, no matter how deep I went, it wasn't enough. I fisted her hair and pulled her up straight, twisting her face so I could reach her mouth as my hips slammed against her. She instantly parted her lips, eager for my tongue. Fiona moaned down my throat at the same time one of her hands disappeared between her legs.

"Oh, fuck," she whimpered, thrusting her ass back into me as her fingers toyed with her clit.

I broke the kiss and rested my chin on her shoulder to get a better look at the show she was putting on for me. "Jesus Christ, baby. You're fucking killing me." I was losing my goddamn mind. My control snapped, and I took her even harder, ramming my cock so deep I was afraid we'd both have bruises the next day. But damn if I could stop. I grunted with every thrust as tingles started at the base of my spine.

"I'm close. Deac, God. *So close.*"

Batting her hand out of the way, I took over, rubbing quick, tight circles around that tiny bundle of nerves as my hips bucked almost violently against her lush ass.

I was about to lose it. Fortunately, she was already there.

With a cry so loud it echoed off the exposed brick walls, her pussy locked down on my dick like a vice. I felt each pulse, each contraction as her release rolled through her. I dragged it out as long as I possibly could before burying myself balls deep, dropping my forehead to her shoulder, and grunting low and long as I emptied myself inside her.

We both collapsed onto the pool table, sucking much-needed air into our lungs. After what felt like an eternity, I finally put my hands to the table and started pushing up. But Fiona's fingers wrapped around my wrists to stop me at the same time a rough sound dragged from the back of her throat.

"Just a second longer," she whispered.

I brushed the hair from her neck with my nose and planted a kiss against her skin, breathing in her scent. "I'm crushing you, baby."

"Mmm," she hummed contentedly, a dreamy smile tipping her lips as she twisted her neck and looked at me. "I like it though. You're so big and warm. I could fall asleep just like this."

I leaned in, giving her even more of my weight in an attempt to kiss that sinful mouth, when a voice suddenly broke through pleasant fog that surrounded us.

"Wow. Really, Deacon?"

FIONA

OH GOD. Oh shit. Oh fuck!

What had I done? How could I have forgotten? He had a girlfriend, for Christ's sake! And I'd just had *sex* with him!

I was a slut. *No!* I was worse than a slut. I was a home-wrecker. There was a special place in Hell for women like me.

I shot up so fast the back of my head nearly collided with Deacon's chin.

"What the fuck, Leah?" he growled near my ear, one of his arms going around my waist and holding tight as a steel band. "What are you doing here?"

Leah's gaze sliced through me, and I imagined she was currently wishing she had the mental capacity to melt my skin off. "I swung by to drop off your keys."

"At two in the goddamn morning?" Deacon asked, sounding bewilderingly put out by the sudden appearance of his girlfriend.

I pushed against his arm, wanting—no, *needing* to escape. The problem was the table was the only thing blocking my lower half from Leah's view. The *other* problem was the fact that Deacon was *still inside me!* I wanted to die.

"I was out with friends," she stated, like it was no big deal. "I saw the lights still on and figured now was as good a time as any."

Menace dripped from his words as he spoke, making me struggle against his arm even harder. "Well you thought wrong."

"Yeah, no shit," she snapped. "You're un-fucking-believable."

Deacon finally pulled out, and I had to bite my lip to keep from making a sound at the sensation of his still hard cock rubbing against my overly sensitive walls. Still holding onto my waist, he bent us both to the side, tagged my jeans and panties from the floor, and pulled us both to standing. "Get dressed, baby," he whispered in my ear before turning back to Leah. "Now really isn't a good time, Leah. Can we do this later? Maybe in private?"

Re-dressing the lower half of my body when Deacon *refused*

to release his grip on me was a lot harder than I imagined, but I somehow managed to do it. I wasn't sure where my shoes were, but I wisely decided I didn't care. Who needed them? I'd buy another pair. I just needed to get the hell out of there. Bare feet be damned.

"So much for nothing ever happening between you and Fiona. Looks to me like something pretty freaking big just happened!"

Now fully clothed, I resumed my fight against Deacon's arm, growing more and more frantic with each passing second.

"Leah, *Christ!*" he hissed. "Can we not fucking *do this right now?*"

"Deacon, let me go," I said in a hushed voice that he pretty much ignored.

"Tell you what, Deac. We don't have to do this now. As far as I'm concerned, we don't have to do this *ever*." She lifted her arms, and I noticed for the first time that a key ring dangled from her fingers. Leah made quick work of pulling a key off and threw it onto the floor before spinning on her heels and storming out through the back door, the same way she apparently entered —not that Deacon or I were in the mindset to have noticed at the time.

"Oh my God," I breathed as my body began to quake. "Let me go."

"Fiona, baby, calm down and listen to me."

I finally succeeded in breaking his hold and stepped side-ways, out from between him and the pool table. With Leah no longer there to witness, I took the time to locate my shoes and moved to put the table between Deacon and me. "I can't believe I did that," I whispered as I slipped one bootie on. "That was... I'm such a...." I stopped working my foot into the second shoe, my eyes going right to Deacon. "I can't believe I did that!" I cried, throwing my arms wide. "Oh God. Deacon, I'm so sorry. I'm so, so sorry,"

To hide the fact that tears were welling in my eyes, I quickly went back to work on my second bootie, barely managing to get the zipper up on the side and stand tall before he made it to me. I noticed then that he'd taken the time to stuff himself back into his pants, and zip up the fly, but the button was still undone, and his belt was hanging from his hips. It was a really fucking good look on him. But I let myself couldn't go there right then.

"Stop," I commanded, lifting my hand.

He thankfully did as I asked, but he didn't do it quietly. "Fee, if you'd just take a breath and let me explain—"

"What's to explain?" I asked on a hysterical shout. "I just had *sex* with another woman's *boyfriend*! All because I was so consumed with what *I* wanted that I totally forgot she existed! Who does that?"

"Baby, it's not what you think—"

I headed to the bar and snatched up my purse, spinning around to face him once more as I hooked the strap on my shoulder. "Really? Because what I think is that I just fucked up... *again*! Every time I get you back, I do something to screw with your life. No matter how hard I try *not* to hurt you, it seems like that's all I do!"

"That's not what that was," he insisted, taking several steps in my direction.

I quickly scurried backward toward the door. "Christ, Deacon, I just turned you into a cheater! That's *exactly* what that was."

I felt the cool metal of the door handle hit my back and blindly reached behind me for the deadbolt Deacon had turned before we started our pool game.

"Don't you walk out that door, Fiona," he warned in a voice

like granite. "Goddamn it, you need to stop freaking the fuck out and listen to me."

"I'm sorry," I whispered just as two fat tears broke free and slipped down my cheeks. "I never meant for this to happen, and I'm so sorry. I never should have put you in this position. Talk to Leah. Tell her it was all my fault. I'll take the blame, Deacon. Just put it all on me."

With that, I spun around, jerked the door open, and bolted.

CHAPTER TEN

FIONA

SEVENTEEN YEARS old

I SLAMMED my locker door shut and turned in the direction of my next class just as a long, muscled arm looped around my shoulders and pulled so my back crashed into a hard chest with an *oof*.

"Jeez, Deac. I'm not a rag doll," I grumbled as he shifted me to his side, arm still securely in place, and resumed walking. He always did that. Whenever he was near, he made sure to bring me close. It was sweet in an overly protective big brother kind of way, like he kept me within arm's reach to make sure he could intervene if trouble ever struck. It never did, of course, but it was just Deacon's way, had been all our lives. I'd gotten used to it, Deacon's behavior becoming second nature to me, but through the years I'd had a couple boyfriends who were less than thrilled with my best friend's touchy-feely nature.

Those relationships never lasted long. Other than my parents, Deacon was the single most important person in my life, my constant. Whenever a boy put his foot down, demanding *him or me*, I kicked them to the curb, informing them it would be Deacon. It would *always* be Deacon.

He looked down at me, the playful twinkle lighting his chocolaty eyes a contradiction to his fake innocent expression. "Can't a guy be affectionate with his BFF?"

"Oh yeah," I said sarcastically. "Because Bryan just *loves* it when you're affectionate." I was only teasing about my boyfriend Bryan having an issue with Deacon's and my friendship, but the way Deacon's head shot forward and his jaw hardened at the mention of it told me he didn't see the humor in my joke.

"Yeah, well Bryan can fuck off," he said with a low, menacing grunt.

I bumped my shoulder against his ribs to get his attention. When his eyes finally came back to me, I gave him a bright, beaming smile. "Lighten up, I was only joking. You know Bryan doesn't care. He gets that we're just friends."

He gave me his profile once more, and a grumbled "Freaking great."

His sudden mood changes was slowly starting to become second nature, but that didn't mean I liked it, or tolerated it. He'd been touchy about Bryan since we started dating at the beginning of our senior year. I always figured it was because Bryan was kind of a jerk the year before when Deacon made captain of the football team over him. Whatever the reason for Deacon and Bryan's animosity toward each other, I refused to be put in the middle of it.

Deciding a subject change was the way to go, I asked, "So have you decided who you're going to ask to prom?"

We were only a couple weeks away from the big night, and then graduation was just around the corner. After that it was on to college and the beginning of the rest of our lives. I couldn't freaking wait. I might have been nervous about what the future held if it hadn't been for Deacon and me deciding to attend the same college. At least with him at my back, I knew I had nothing to worry about.

A groan emitted from deep within his chest as he looked up at the ceiling of the hallway we were walking through. "Not this again. Jeez, Fee. I told you I don't even want to go."

He had. Multiple times. But I didn't care. "You *have* to go," I declared. "It's a teenager's rite of passage! And who knows, maybe you'll even have fun." I let out a mock surprised gasp. "Wouldn't that be something: Deacon Lockhart, the broody bad boy, having *fun* at his senior *prom*?"

I giggled as he skewered me with a look. "Broody bad boy?" he asked incredulously. "No one talks like that. You been sneaking your mom's romance novels again?"

I smacked his arm. He knew me so well.

"You know, you could've saved me the hassle of having to find a date by just going with me, but *nooo*. You have to ditch me for your preppy boyfriend."

If I was being honest, I would've much rather gone to something as important as prom with Deacon. If Bryan hadn't acted so excited about us going together, I totally would've bailed on him.

"Oh please," I scoffed. "Like you'd have a problem finding a date. All you have to do is crook your finger at one of your *many* admirers and they'd come crawling."

And wasn't that the damn truth. Deacon certainly wasn't lacking for female attention. He was tall and muscular, with a body that was cut and toned from years of playing any sport that held his interest. He dominated football and basketball. He was even part of a hockey league during the winters. He excelled at whatever he put his mind to, but it wasn't just that. It was the fact that he did all of that and still acted like he didn't give a damn whether people thought he was good or not that made him so intriguing to the other girls in our school.

I totally got the appeal. There was a mystery attached to Deacon Lockhart, and I was the only one who really and truly knew him. The knowledge that he'd kept everyone else at a distance, only allowing me into the inner sanctum, made me giddy. It was like being part of a secret club.

He didn't bother with a reply, so I pushed. "Please, Deac. Will you just ask someone? I don't want to go if you aren't there."

One corner of his mouth tipped up in a crooked smirk as we came to a stop outside our classroom door. "Don't let *Bryan* hear you say that."

I looked up at him and replied with complete honesty. "I don't care if he hears. It's the truth. I'm obligated to go with him because we're dating, but *you're* the only one I care about hanging out with. We've been together for every major milestone in our lives so far. There's no way I'm doing this without you."

Releasing my shoulders, he turned and faced me full on. His expression softened in that way I'd grown to love over the years as he reached up and twisted a lock of my hair around his finger. "Fine. I'll ask Marcy Danowitz. But I don't want to hear shit from you about being a crappy date when I ignore her and monopolize all your time."

"Deal," I squeaked excitedly. Prom was going to be epic— just as long as I had my best friend to enjoy it with.

THE FINAL BELL had rung no more than ten minutes before. I'd floated happily through the rest of the day after my conversation with Deacon, so running into Bryan in the student parking lot and having him break up with me in front of half the student body put a serious damper on my mood.

"Are you freaking *kidding* me?" I seethed, blinking back the tears that were burning the backs of my eyes as I glared up at Bryan. I couldn't think of another time in my life when I'd been this pissed off. No way in hell was I going to give that jerk the satisfaction of seeing me cry.

"Chase Wilcox saw you with Deacon Lockhart before Bio this morning," Bryan stated. His tone would've sounded almost bored had it not been for the thread of jealousy tangled around his words. "Said he was all over you, *again*. I'm sick of having everyone ask if my girlfriend's got the hots for another guy. You're supposed to be dating *me*, but you're always with that loser."

"He's not a loser!" I shouted, not giving a single shit that kids were starting to stop and stare. "He's my best friend. You knew that when we started dating, so what's the deal?"

"The deal is you pick him over me every time! I'm sick of it. I'm not going to waste the rest of my senior year on a chick who fawns over some asshole. Especially if she's not putting out."

My arm moved before I even realized what I was doing, and my palm cracked across Bryan's face. I'd never hit anyone in my life, but that jerk deserved it. And I had to admit, despite the vicious sting in my palm, it felt pretty damn good.

"You're an asshole," I hissed before turning for my car. Bryan spewed more hateful words in my direction, but I couldn't find it in me to care as I unlocked my door, climbed in, and took off. He didn't deserve another minute of my attention. If he wanted to dump me because he was threatened by my relationship with Deacon, that was his problem.

I was better off without him.

A WEEK HAD PASSED since the Smack Heard Around the Parking Lot, and despite my efforts to pretend everything was hunky-dory every day, word of my breakup with Bryan, and the nasty comments he'd been making behind my back, were spreading around the school like wildfire. I did my best to keep my head down and ignore the gossip, but that was damn near impossible when my ex-boyfriend—who just so happened to be the king of assholes—started flaunting the fact that he already had a new date to prom. Apparently, if the grapevine was correct, he'd started banging Zoe Sinclair before we'd even broken up.

Whatever. Better her than me. Or at least that's what I was telling myself.

It wasn't the breakup that upset me. The truth was I didn't really care that Bryan and I weren't a couple anymore. It was actually kind of a relief. But the humiliation that came with his spreading rumors and calling me a cock-tease while subsequently rubbing his cheating in my face was what hurt the most.

Deacon had been *pissed*, and was determined to do something about it. Luckily I'd managed to talk him down, or so I thought.

I closed my locker just as the bell for the next class rang. I'd been studiously ignoring the whispers as I turned and caught sight of Deacon coming down the senior hallway, that ever-prominent *I don't give a shit about anything or anyone* swagger that was *all him* drawing everyone's attention.

But it wasn't the vibe he was giving off that caught my attention. "Please tell me you didn't," I demanded on a furious whisper when he got close enough to hear. I lifted his right hand and began inspecting. It didn't take a genius to figure out why the skin of his knuckles was split and bruised.

He'd gotten his hands on Bryan.

"Fucker deserved it," he grumbled.

Damn it. Deacon had a nasty habit of getting into fights that led to one or both of his parents being pulled in. The last thing he needed was to get in trouble so close to graduation. "Deacon," I started on a warning, but stopped when the air all around us went electric. It took me a second to figure out why, but then the crowd parted and I got my first glimpse of *exactly* what Deac had done to my piece-of-shit ex.

Bryan looked like he'd gone eight full rounds with a professional boxer, but instead of putting up a fight, had spent the entire time as the guy's own personal punching bag.

I spun around and glared daggers at Deacon. "Have you lost your mind? You're going to get expelled!"

For reason's unknown to me, that made him smile. "Trust me, that fuck-stick isn't talking about what happened to *anyone.* And it didn't happen on school property, so you've got nothing to worry about."

"How can you say that? I just saw Bryan's face! Of course I'm going to worry."

He lowered his voice, his expression going soft. "Babe, like I said, he's not gonna say a word. Did you really think I was going to just stand there and let him talk shit about you? *You?* Come on, Fee. You knew I couldn't let that happen. You're my girl."

I glared again, holding it for several silent beats before I threw my hands in the air. "Gah! You're such a jerk. You make it impossible to stay mad at you when you say stuff like that!"

His smile turned cocky as he slung an arm around my shoulders, pulled me into his side, as per usual, and started walking us to class, acting like half the kids weren't staring at us with open curiosity and the other half weren't glaring because they'd bought into Bryan's lies.

"Of course you can't stay mad at me. You love me, remember?"

Grinning up at him, I replied, "I do. I love you around the world and back again."

With a wink, he responded, "And I love you to Jupiter and back again."

———

"FEE, HONEY! YOU'VE GOT COMPANY!"

At my mom's call, I stuffed the spoon laden with ice cream into my mouth, snagged the pint container, and started out of the kitchen. It was prom night, and I was going to eat as much ice cream as possible to help soothe the pain that came with knowing I'd be missing it. I could've gone by myself, but with what had happened with Bryan, I was too much of a coward to show alone.

"Who is it?" I yelled back, my words muffled by the combination of vanilla and fudgy chocolate packed into my mouth.

"Just get your behind out here."

I rolled my eyes to the ceiling and muttered, "Jeez, I'm coming." I'd just rounded the corner into the entry when I rocked to a stop at the sight of Deacon. Not regular Deacon, either. No, this was tricked-out-in-a-tux, looking-hotter-than-anything-I'd-ever-seen Deacon.

"Wha-what are you doing here?" I garbled through my ice cream.

Instead of answering, he smirked and asked, "You gonna get dressed or what? We don't have all night."

Mom beamed as she looked between the two of us, clearly in on whatever was happening. "Uh... Deac, I'm not going. I told you that."

He stepped through the door, shutting it behind him. Man, he looked cute. "You said you weren't going because you didn't want to go alone. Well"—he held his arms out at his sides—"now you're not going alone, so get a move on."

My nose stung and the backs of my eyes began to burn. Crap, I was going to cry, all because I had the sweetest, most thoughtful best friend on the *planet*. "But... what about Marcy?"

Deacon gave me a *don't ask stupid questions* look. "Let's just say I'm not her favorite person."

Omigod! Deacon had bailed on Marcy to take me! I couldn't believe it. "You didn't have to do that!" I cried.

"Yes I did," he answered simply. "Every milestone it's you and me, remember?"

God, I was lucky. With a squeal, I launched myself at him and wrapped him in a bone-crushing hug. "You're the best," I whispered in his ear.

"To Jupiter and back again, babe," he said softly.

"Around the world and back again," I replied.

I ran up the stairs the minute we pulled apart and got dressed in record time. When I was back downstairs, Deac and I did the obligatory picture thing for my parents, and I nearly burst into tears again when he pulled out a wrist corsage that matched my dress perfectly.

That night was one of the best nights of my life. And I knew down to my bones that as long as I had Deacon, there'd be a million more just like them.

CHAPTER ELEVEN

FIONA

FIGURING that Deacon would come looking for me after I'd blown out of The Black Sheep like a puff of smoke, I decided the best course of action was to avoid my house at all costs.

My parents' place was out, since all it would take was one look at my face and they'd know something was up. And my folks could be relentless in a loving, totally overbearing kind of way. I'd eventually cave to their nagging and tell them what happened, only to have to live through their crushing disappointment in me.

I couldn't run to any of my girls, seeing as they were all blissfully shacked up with their own guys. No doubt they'd see the sex hair and rumpled clothes and dig in like a dog with a bone. I loved those girls more than anything, but they had a knack for getting into business that wasn't theirs to get into. Hell, they'd proved that by making up *the surgeon* on Thanksgiving.

So a hotel was my only real option. I called into work sick the next day, then spent the rest of my weekend holed up in a cushy hotel room, trying to combat my muscle-straining guilt with spa treatments. It didn't work. After an hour-long massage, a detoxifying mud bath, and multiple trips to the steam room, I still felt like the shittiest human being on the planet, only with smooth, soft skin and looser limbs. No amount of scrubbing, buffing, or polishing was going to wash away my shame.

I was a terrible person.

Monday finally rolled around and, sick of my own company, I sucked it up and went home to get ready for work. My staff seemed oblivious to the turmoil swirling around inside of me, and I did my best to shove my discomfort to the back of my mind and buried myself in my job. Thankfully, taking the previous Friday off to lick my wounds meant there was a shit-ton of work piled on my desk, just waiting for me.

I worked until I lost track of everything happening around me. I was so consumed that I nearly jumped out of my seat when my cell phone rang, scaring the ever-loving hell out of me.

"Shit," I breathed, placing my hand on my chest to steady my rapidly beating heart. When I reached for my phone resting on my desk, I noticed that the sky outside my office window was completely dark. Spinning in my chair, I saw that the office had already been shut down for the night. Most of the lights were off, only a few lamps illuminating the cubicles and other offices outside my door. The clock in the corner of my laptop screen showed it was after nine. I'd worked over thirteen hours straight without much more than a bathroom break.

Snatching the phone up, I engaged the call and put it to my ear. "Hello?"

"Hey!" Daphne chirped through the line. "Where have you been? I've been trying to reach you all weekend."

Resting my elbow on the desk, I dropped my forehead into my hand and began rubbing at my dry, scratchy eyes. "Hey, sorry. I was... busy all weekend. Working."

"You okay?" she asked after a few seconds of silence.

I could've continued lying, but the weight of this... *thing* on my conscience was just too much to bear. "No. I'm not okay. I'm a terrible person. A terrible, awful person. I'm the scum of the earth."

"Whoa, whoa, slow down," she said, breaking through my self-flagellation. "What are you talking about? What's going on?"

"I slept with Deacon," I whispered, even going so far as to cover my mouth with my hand like there were people around who could hear me.

"You *what*?" she screeched, nearly bursting my eardrum. "Oh my God! *Oh my God! This is so great!* I knew you two were still circling each other. I *knew* it! I can't wait to tell the girls—"

"No!" I snapped. "No, you can't tell anyone. And it's not great, Daph. Have you forgotten about his *girlfriend*?"

More silence, then "Oh shit."

"Yeah. Oh shit's right," I grumbled. "It just... happened. We were hanging out, talking, and things just escalated. Leah totally slipped my mind. I wasn't thinking. Then she walked in—"

"*No!*" she gasped.

"*Yes*," I hissed. "Caught us with our pants down. Literally." I dropped my head into my hand again as my nose and eyes started to burn. "I'm the worst kind of person, Daphne. I helped Deacon cheat on his girlfriend."

"Wait. Hold on, this isn't all on you. I mean, Deacon was just as much a participant as you were. What did he have to say about it?"

Collapsing back in my chair, I stared up at the ceiling. "I don't know. I kind of ran out of there like my ass was on fire. Then I shut off my phone, avoided my house, and stayed in a hotel all weekend."

She was quiet for so long I thought the call might have dropped. "Daph? You there?"

"I'm here."

"Well?" I snapped when she didn't give me more than that.

"I just confessed to being a cheating hussy. Don't you have anything to say about that?"

"Sure I do. Firstly, you're not a hussy. And I don't think people even use the word hussy anymore."

I was going to lose my mind. "Can you be serious for one second?"

"I'm being dead serious. No one says that. Slut and skank, sure, but definitely not hussy."

Groaning into the phone, I said, "I'm hanging up now."

"Hold on! There's just one thing I need to know. It's super important."

Hesitantly, I asked, "What is it?"

"How was the sex? I always imagined Deacon was a take-charge kind of guy in the bedroom. Please tell me he lives up to my imagination."

"Ohmigod! Why are we even friends!" The faint ding of the elevators sounded after my shout, alerting me to someone else on the floor. I tuned out Daphne's rambling as a shadowy figure appeared through the wall of glass at the front of my office. A moment later his face came into view.

My lungs froze at the sight of Deacon coming my way. After all these years, he still had that relaxed swagger that drew everyone's attention, even in spite of the thunderous expression on his face.

"Oh shit," I whispered. I'd forgotten all about the phone at my ear until Daphne asked, "What's going on?"

"He's here," I continued in a hushed voice as a *very* pissed-off Deacon got closer.

"Who's there? *Deacon?*"

"Yes. Gotta go." I ended the call in the middle of Daphne's objection, placing the phone down just as my office door crashed open.

Oh shit.

His jaw might as well have been carved out of granite with how hard it was. "Hi."

"Hi?" he asked, the menacing growl of that one word sending a shiver down my spine. "You ran out on me four days ago, disappeared into thin fucking air, and all you have to say is *hi*?"

"Uh...." A trickle of fear shimmered through me, but even with Deacon practically breathing fire, I still couldn't help but notice how insanely hot he was.

He stalked to my desk, slamming his hands onto the glass surface. "You've got some serious fucking explaining to do," he barked. "What the fuck, Fiona?"

"What the fuck?" I was so taken aback at his sudden appearance that I couldn't get my brain to function.

"Yeah. What the fuck!" he repeated on a loud boom. "You bolted so goddamn fast that my cum was still dripping out of you. So what... the... *fuck*!"

I wasn't sure why that set me off, but the vulgarity and anger in his words made me snap. "Don't be crude!"

Deacon's chin jerked back in shock, his voice dropping ominously as he asked, "Are you kidding me?"

I stood up, mirroring his stance by putting my hands on the desk and leaning in closer. "No, I'm not kidding you. You want to be pissed at me, go for it. You want to tear into me, have at it—"

"Oh, I intend to!" he bellowed, cutting into my tirade. "Four days. Four *goddamn* days without a word from you. I've been by your house. I've talked to your folks. Where the hell have you been?"

Standing tall, I raked my hands through my hair in agitation. "I needed to think."

"You needed to think?"

"*Gah!* Will you stop repeating everything I say? Yes, I

needed to think!"

One corner of his mouth tipped in a vicious smirk as he straightened and crossed his arms over his chest. "Hate to break it to you, sweetheart, but the minute I sank my cock inside you, everything about our relationship changed. You no longer have the luxury of running away scared with your tail tucked between your legs."

I rocked back on one foot, the waves of anger rolling off Deacon and crashing right into me. "What's that supposed to mean?"

"It means you're mine," he growled. "After thirty fucking years, you're finally mine. You need to think, or breathe, or take the time to twist what happened between us in that head of yours and turn it into something fucked up, fine, but you do it *with me*. No more running away."

Good Lord, Daphne wasn't wrong about Deacon being a take-charge type of guy. And apparently it wasn't only in the bedroom. I'd never seen this domineering, alpha side to him before.

I should've been freaked out. Watching Deacon go all caveman should've pissed me right the hell off.

So why was it that instead of being angry, I was more turned on than I'd ever been in my life?

Pushing that thought from my mind, I planted my hands on my hips, throwing out as much attitude as I could possibly muster, and demanded, "*Excuse* me?"

"You heard me," he gritted. "And another thing, that bullshit blind date your girls made up? That's not happening. So you might as well go ahead and get them off whatever mission they're on to find you a man, because as of Thursday night, you already have one."

My jaw dropped, and I was pretty sure my brain just exploded all over the place.

CHAPTER TWELVE

DEACON

"HE'S NOT MADE UP!" she lied. "And I'm *so* going on that date, if for no other reason than you just pissed me off!"

Christ, even when she was lying through her teeth and making me so damn mad I thought my head might explode, she was still the sexiest woman I'd ever laid eyes on.

Putting my hands on my hips, I leaned across her desk. "The hell you will."

There were very few times in my life that I'd witnessed Fiona's anger. She'd always been sweet and mild-tempered, but that hadn't meant there wasn't a fire inside of her. When that redhead fury surfaced, it threatened to blow apart everything and everyone in its path. And from the look on her face, she was about to explode.

"I'm sorry," she started softly, but it wasn't her usual kind of soft. It was a soft that led up to a detonation. "But have you *lost your goddamn mind*?" she screamed, her temper flaring right on schedule. "Who the hell do you think you are? You can't tell me who I can or can't date! Especially considering the fact that *you're* the one with a girlfriend!"

"And if you'd have stuck around long enough to have

fucking listened, you'd have found out that I broke up with Leah days before I had you on my pool table!"

It was a damn good thing her offices had closed down for the night because we were making one hell of a scene, yelling the room down.

She continued to shout. "Well you should have —wait, what?"

"That's right. I broke up with Leah before anything happened between me and you. Christ, woman," I bit out, yanking my fingers through my hair. "Did you really think I'd do that to you? To another woman? You really think that goddamn low of me?"

"I...." She shook her head as if trying to clear it. Her brows dipped in the middle, showing just how upset my insinuation made her. "No," she whispered hoarsely. "God, Deacon, of course not. How could you ask me that?"

Fuck, she made it damn near impossible to stay mad when she looked at me like that.

"My freak-out wasn't about you," she continued, slaying me. "It was about me. I've already hurt you too many times, and when I thought I'd been responsible for doing it again, I just...."

I couldn't handle the space between us for another second. Rounding the desk, I wrapped my fingers around her arm and pulled her against me. My other hand came up to tilt her chin so I could look into her eyes. "I wish you'd stuck around so I could explain," I said, the anger disappearing from my voice. "You've spent the past several days beating yourself up for no damn reason. You didn't do anything wrong... except run away. Leah wasn't even in the picture."

I was so close I could hear and feel the way her chest stuttered on an inhale. Her voice was so hushed I almost couldn't hear it. "Why did you break up? I thought you said she made you happy."

The last thing I wanted to do was discuss an ex-girlfriend with the woman I'd spent my whole life wanting. But I could see it in her eyes, even though we were so close physically, she was still using Leah to keep herself at a distance. If I let her, she'd probably shoot out of the room so fast my head would spin. Unwilling to let that happen, I tightened my hold on her and answered, "It was never going to work out between us. I just didn't feel for her the way a man should feel about the woman he's dating."

Her body began to loosen, but then something else sparked across her face, making her go stiff as a board. "What was she talking about when she said 'So much for nothing ever happening between you and Fiona'?"

Shit. "Fiona—"

"Tell me, Deacon," she demanded, her words clipped. "What was she talking about?"

I could feel her attempting to rebuild those walls she kept around herself in order to keep me out. "She threw you in my face when I ended it, saying it was because of you that she didn't stand a chance."

Fiona's forehead wrinkled in confusion for just a second before the pieces finally began to fall into place. "And you told her nothing was ever going to happen between us." It wasn't a question, it was a statement, and each word out of her mouth dripped with the same pain that mirrored her expression. Seeing and hearing how that hurt her was like a sledgehammer right to the gut.

"Fee—"

A bitter laugh burst from her throat, and she began struggling against my hold. "Wow. You must've been just as surprised as Leah by what happened, then, huh?"

"Christ, Fiona. Will you just—"

"Or was that some sick way of getting back at me?"

It was my turn to go stiff. My blood went from a simmer to a rolling boil in half a second. "Are you fucking kidding me?" I whispered, letting Fiona go and taking a step back. "You think I fucked you to *get back* at you?"

She flinched like I just slapped her, but I couldn't find it in me to feel guilty, not just then.

That goddamned wall kept going up, brick by brick. "I.... No." She stepped away, raking her hands through that long, gorgeous, fiery hair, and began pacing agitatedly. "God, what are we doing here, Deacon?"

It wasn't until that very moment that I realized what she was wearing. I'd torn in there, so hell-bent on laying into her that I hadn't stopped to notice her dress. Skintight ivory that hugged her from shoulders to mid-thigh. It was sleeveless with a high neckline that didn't show a hint of cleavage, but the way it conformed to her body was sinful. And that was just the front. When she stomped away, mid-pace, and I caught sight of the slit that led dangerously close to where the material hugged her pert, round ass, I nearly came in my pants. And that wasn't to mention her stockings. From the front they just looked like a regular pair of stockings, but the back... *Christ*. They had a seam that ran from her fuck-me stilettos all the way up, disappearing beneath the short hemline of her skirt. They were the kind of stockings that made every man want to follow their trail to find out what treasure they led to.

"Jesus fucking Christ," I grunted, all the blood in my body traveling straight to my dick. "What the hell are you wearing?"

She stopped moving and spun to face me, her hands propped on her hips. "What?"

"You wear shit like that every day?"

Her eyes scanned down her body before returning to mine. "What's wrong with what I'm wearing?"

"It's indecent! Shit, Fee. You prance around in dresses like that every day, it's a wonder your male staff gets anything done!"

That redheaded fury of hers reared its head again, and damn if it didn't turn me on just as much as that dress. "And what the hell is *that* supposed to mean?"

"It means," I started slowly, my own anger and frustration on par with hers, "that most of the dudes in your office probably spend their lunch hour and every break before and after jacking off to the image of your ass in skirts like that because they're *burned into their brains*!"

She sucked in an affronted gasp before blowing her top. "You're *such* a pig!"

"That may be, baby, but I'm also a man currently sporting a hard-on strong enough to pound nails because of that goddamn dress."

She crossed her arms over her chest in indignation and continued to go toe-to-toe with me. "I'll have you know that this dress was part of our summer line last year, and it's *perfectly* respectable."

I let out a snort of disbelief even as my cock grew harder. "Perfectly respectable? So you're telling me it's *perfectly respectable* for me to know, just by looking at you, that you aren't wearing any goddamn panties right now?"

Her arms shot to her sides and her hands balled into tiny little fists that, had the blood flow to my brain not been diverted, I would've found adorable.

"I'm wearing panties!" she shrieked.

I don't know what came over me at that very second, but I suddenly lost all control and pounced.

I tagged her around the waist with one arm and pinned her to me, front to front, and used my other arm to swipe everything off her desk.

"Deacon! That's my—"

She didn't get another word out, because the next second my mouth was on hers. Fiona's lips parted on a startled gasp and I drove my tongue inside, desperate for a taste. The moment I gained entrance, she melted, and I knew I had her.

The kiss wasn't soft or sweet. It was demanding, almost punishing. It was brutal and hot, and I couldn't bring myself to slow down even if I'd wanted to.

One of my hands traveled to her hair, tangling the mass in my fingers, while the other moved down over that luscious ass. I yanked the dress up to her hips and moaned into her mouth when I discovered that she wasn't lying. She was wearing panties—if that was what you'd call the miniscule scrap of soaking wet fabric. But it wasn't only the underwear that had my dick threatening to bust through my zipper at any moment. Oh no, it was also the lacy tops of those stockings. Goddamned thigh-highs. *Fuck me.*

"*Shit,*" I wrenched my mouth away to get a better look, then groaned long and loud. That dress was nothing compared to what was beneath. *Nothing.*

"Lie back," I ordered. "Hands over your head. Grip the edge of the desk, baby. I can't be gentle right now."

Her chest rose and fell as she followed my instructions, stretching her perfect body out for my viewing pleasure.

"Deacon, please," she started to beg. It was almost enough to send me over the edge. I reached for my fly and was seconds away from freeing my throbbing cock when the elevator down the hall suddenly dinged and the sound of muffled music filled the air.

"Shit," Fiona hissed, tipping her head back toward the door. "The cleaning crew."

I wanted to cuss out the people who'd just unwittingly interrupted us, but with the time it allowed me to get myself under control, I realized it was actually a blessing in disguise.

Grabbing her hips, I pulled Fiona from the desk and held on until she was steady on her feet. Then I worked her skirt back down to cover the beauty I'd just discovered, and ordered, "Get your shit. We're going."

"What?" She stumbled on her heels but still managed to grab her phone and her purse as she asked, "Where?"

"My place." I took her hand in mine and started pulling her to the door.

"But Deacon. My car—"

I stopped and turned so quickly that she collided with me. "I'll bring you back tomorrow, but tonight you're coming home with me. I'm going to fuck you until you can't move. Then we're going to talk. This shit between us gets straightened out. *Tonight.*"

She sucked in a massive breath, but I wasn't finished.

"And Fee, just warning you now. If you try and run again, I'm tying your ass to my bed for as long as it takes. We clear?"

She didn't say a word, just nodded as her throat worked on a thick swallow.

CHAPTER THIRTEEN

FIONA

"*YES!*" My head flew back on a loud moan as one of my hands moved from the mattress to the headboard to brace against Deacon's brutal thrusts.

His fingers dug into my hips as he continued driving into me from behind. My orgasm washed over me just as Deacon's hips lost their rhythm and he started pounding into me so hard that I shouted his name as I came.

In the next breath, Deacon buried himself deep and groaned, his fingertips pressing in so hard I wondered if I'd have bruises the next day. He wasn't wrong. I was pretty sure I wasn't going to walk for at least twenty-four hours.

I fell to my belly with Deacon following me down. His heat stayed at my back as he twisted and pulled me to my side so we were spooning. I was still coming down from the highest high I'd ever experienced, so I hadn't properly guarded myself for my and Deacon's upcoming "talk." In fact, I'd been so wrapped up in what was happening that it had completely slipped my mind.

Until Deacon's lips brushed against the bare skin of my shoulder and his husky voice whispered in my ear, "We need to talk." My happy little bubble popped, bringing me back to the real world where things were uncertain and shaky. Feeling my body tense against his, Deacon's arm around my waist gave me a squeeze. "Relax," he whispered. The feel of his strong, warm frame and the gentle wisp of his breath along my skin sent a yummy tremble up my back.

I lost his heat, but only for as long as it took him to press his hand into my belly and roll me to my back so he could hover over me. Deacon stared down at me with sleepy, sex-drunk eyes that stole my breath. It was a look I'd never seen on him before, and knowing that this gorgeous man appeared so thoroughly and properly mussed *because of me* sent a new rush of arousal flooding between my legs.

Now that I'd experienced him like this, all warm and sated, I didn't think I could ever go back to what we had before. And just the thought of having to do that tore at my heart.

"What's running through that mind of yours?" Deacon asked, pulling me out of my head.

"Nothing," I said on a whisper, unsure of what to say or do. It seemed like everything that came out of my mouth was wrong and started a fight. Granted, those fights inevitably led to *exquisite* sex, but that wasn't something a relationship could be built on.

He continued to speak softly, even if his words packed a punch. "Bullshit. I just made you come so hard you damn near passed out, but somehow you're still managing to twist shit up in your head."

"I'm not twisting anything," I clipped with a glare. "You said we needed to talk, so talk."

He pressed more of his weight down on me. "First, tell me what you're thinking. Baby, this isn't going to work if we aren't honest with each other."

That sentence worked wonders to deflate my simmering anger. "And what exactly *is* this?" I asked hesitantly.

Deacon's chin jerked back at the same time his forehead creased in a frown. "Are you serious?"

Uh-oh. Once again, I'd said the wrong thing.

"Jesus, Fee. You're lying naked in my fucking bed right now. I just had my dick buried so deep inside you that I wasn't sure where I ended and you began, and you have to ask that?"

My belly twisted into a painful knot as he reared back, as if to pull away. I didn't know what came over me in that second, but the idea of him pulling away spurred me into action.

Placing my hands on his cheeks, I started speaking quickly. "Please don't. Don't pull away. Just give me a second to explain." When he remained motionless and silent, I continued. "I'm terrified, Deacon, because I keep screwing this up, and I don't know how to stop. I know you think I should get what's happening between us, but I'm going to need you to spell it out for me. Not because I'm twisting shit in my head, but because I want to *stop* screwing this up. I don't know how to take us from where we were to whatever we are now, because our relation-ship hasn't exactly been stable the past several years. I get that I'm the one who did that to us, and it's up to me to fix it. I want to do that, Deac, but I need you to cut me a little slack, okay? I'm just trying to find my footing, and I need you to help me do that."

His face instantly softened, his eyes melting into liquid as he looked down at me. The shift helped to unfurl that knot that was tangling up in my belly. "Okay, baby," he whispered, trailing his fingertips along my hairline. "I can help you with that."

My entire body sagged deeper into the mattress with relief. I'd managed to dodge a bullet. "Thank you," I whispered in return.

"First up, what's happening between us is that we're together. Label it however you want. I'm your boyfriend, or man, or partner. I don't really give a shit because it all means the same thing."

"But you told Leah—"

"I said that when shit was twisted in *my* head. I was still lying to myself about what I was willing to accept from you. I never should have started anything with Leah. I tried to make myself believe that I was finally ready to move on from you, but I wasn't, and in the end I ended up hurting a good woman because I wasn't being honest with myself. That's on me, not you. So don't hold on to any guilt over that."

"How can you tell me not to feel guilty? You broke up with her because of me."

"That's where you're wrong, babe. I didn't break up with her because of you. I broke up with her because it was the right thing to do. I knew there wasn't a future with Leah even before I knew I was going to pursue one with you. Whether or not I ended up with you in my bed, I still would've broken it off with her. I just lucked out and finally got you where I wanted you."

I liked the sound of that, but there was still one thing that nagged at me. I bit my lip and forced myself to summon the courage to ask a question I wasn't sure I wanted the answer to. "But what if we start this and you realize that I'm not worth the headache? Because I have to tell you, Deacon, I'm really not sure I am."

For some reason that made him grin. "I'm not going to pretend to know what the future has in store, Fee. All I can promise is that I want this now. I've wanted it for a really long fucking time, and as long as it's good, I'm going to do everything in my power to keep it that way. And I'll also promise that if it starts to go bad, I'll talk to you about it in the hopes that we can fix it and get us back to good."

Man, I liked that. "Okay," I continued to whisper.

"And I need you to make the same promise baby."

"I promise."

Deacon's mouth tilted into a full-blown smile, showing off his brilliant white teeth, taking him from handsome to downright sexy in a heartbeat. "This is going to take work," he continued. "You and I might've been in each other's lives as long as we can remember, but it was never like this. We're both on unfamiliar footing, but if we're honest with each other and put in the effort, I think this'll lead to something really fucking fantastic."

Okay, it was safe to say I *really* liked that. "Deacon Lockhart, you just have the answer to everything, don't you?"

His chest shook on a chuckle, causing his skin to brush against my sensitive nipples. "Glad you finally clued in on that, baby."

I faked a scowl and smacked his arm. "No need to be cocky about it."

He let out a deep belly laugh before leaning down and brushing a kiss against my lips. "Speaking of cocky...." I rolled my eyes. "Time for you to get cleaned up. I'm in the mood to see just how delicious that pussy of yours is, and I can't do that with my cum still inside you."

Ignoring the little shiver that shot straight between my thighs, I yelped. "Deacon! Don't be crass!"

His tongue snaked out of his mouth and ran along my bottom lip. "Don't lie, baby. You love how I talk to you. I bet it turns you on."

No way in hell I'd ever admit it to him, but it really did.

I WASN'T sure what woke me up, but when I opened my eyes to the darkness, it took me a few seconds to remember where I was and everything that had happened hours before. Then I felt Deacon all around me. His chest was flush with my back, his arm thrown over my stomach. Even his legs were tangled with mine, one over the top, the other nestled between my own.

Taking a moment to think back, I realized that this was the first time I'd ever actually cuddled with a guy in my sleep. There had been times with my exes that we'd start off in such a position, but one or both of us always ended up rolling away, and I woke each morning on my own side of the bed. Deacon was different. He was a full-contact sleeper in the sense that every single part of him was touching every part of me. And I had to admit I freaking *loved* that.

The unfortunate thing was that I was now wide awake, and I knew there was no getting back to sleep for me, at least not any time soon.

A glance at his bedside clock showed it was only a few minutes past four in the morning. Not wanting to disturb Deacon's sleep, I slowly unwound our limbs and scooted out of the bed, tucking the covers back around his body. I bent and grabbed my panties from the floor, sliding them into place before going back for the T-shirt Deacon had been wearing earlier and slipping it over my head.

It smelled like him, all spicy, musky man mixed faintly with laundry detergent. I slipped my arms through the sleeves and lifted the collar to my nose, inhaling deeply. The shirt was so big on me, hitting just above mid-thigh, that it was almost as good as being wrapped in Deacon's arms. *Almost.*

Once properly covered, I padded out of the bedroom quietly, pulling the door behind me so it was only cracked open.

When we first arrived earlier, we'd been so consumed with each other that I hadn't had a chance between the trip from the back door and the bedroom to get a look at Deacon's home. Now that I had a moment to myself, I used the moonlight filtering through the big windows to explore.

To say his house was unexpected was putting it mildly. I

knew he'd been there about three years, but he'd purchased it during a time when we weren't exactly speaking, so I'd never been inside. The décor was masculine without going overboard into frat-boy-bachelor territory. The large dark blue sofa in the living room had a matching love seat, chair, and ottoman. I took a seat to test it out and sank into the cushions like I was sitting on a cloud. Hell, the couch was so comfy it was better than some people's mattresses.

A huge flat-screen TV hung above a beautiful stone fireplace. The mantel looked like it was made of what used to be a big beam that had been cut down to size. It was awesome. On either side of the fireplace were massive built-ins painted white to match the crown molding throughout the room.

The house was open concept so, with the exception of the hallways that ran off the front and back of the living room, from where I was sitting I could see everything but the bedrooms and bathrooms. The kitchen had top-of-the-line, stainless steel appliances. The cabinets were all white except for the ones that ran along the back wall over the sink, which were glass-faced. The countertops were a dark stone, and the backsplash was a mixture of dark and white. It was a kitchen most women would die to cook in.

The dining area was just off to the left, with huge bay windows and an attractive dark wood oval table with cushy chairs in a light cream fabric. Deacon's place was the total opposite of mine.

Where mine had very limited personality, screaming *this place was a sound investment,* Deacon's said *come in, take a load off, and make yourself comfortable.* My place was a house. His was a home.

I stood to get a better look around and noticed the picture frames littered along the built-in bookshelves. Moving closer, I picked up the one closest to me and smiled at the picture inside.

Deacon and Grayson as little boys. They each had an arm flung over the other's shoulders in what looked like a hug, but I knew better. They were both hamming it up for the camera while most likely trying to put each other in a headlock. Their parents, Nolan and Cybil, stood behind them. Nolan was looking down at his boys with an expression that held only mild annoyance and a ton of love. Cybil was gazing down with a beaming smile like the two could do no wrong.

I set the frame back in place and reached for another, my heart lodging in my throat at what I saw. It was of me and Deacon, both of us in our gowns after our high school graduation. Deacon's cap sat lopsided on his head. Mine was in my hand. He'd picked me up just before the picture was taken, lifting me right off the ground and into his arms. My legs were kicked out, the hand holding my cap extended behind me. My head was thrown back on a laugh, and Deac was staring down at my face, smiling like he had the most valuable treasure in his arms at that very moment. That was a look I'd seen on his face a million times, but until right then I never understood the depth and importance behind it.

God, I was such a fool. I wanted to go back in time and scream at Younger Fiona, tell her to get her head out of her ass and see the precious gift that was right in front of her.

On that thought, I let out a frightened squeak as a pair of arms circled me from behind and wrapped around my waist. "Shit, you scared me. I didn't hear you."

Deacon let out a raspy hum as he used his chin to brush my hair off my shoulder. "Woke up and you weren't there. What're you doing, baby? It's the middle of the night."

I set the frame back on the shelf and turned, twining my arms around his neck. "Couldn't sleep," I answered, appreciating how adorable Sleepy Deacon looked. It was a close second to the Post-Sex Deacon look.

His eyes grew darker as his brow creased with concern. "Your head twisted again?"

I couldn't help but smile as I pushed up on my tiptoes and kissed his lips. "Nope. Head's totally sorted. I just woke up and wasn't tired anymore."

A sinful smirk tugged at his lips. He leaned in and nuzzled my neck, the bristles along his jaw scratching at my skin deliciously. "Well then, I'll just have to *make* you tired, won't I?"

"Hmm." I snuggled closer to his chest, loving the feel of being in his arms while I teased, "You up for the challenge?"

"Oh baby," he started, pulling back enough to look at my face. "I'm more than up for it."

Then, like the caveman he was, Deacon bent at the waist and tossed me over his shoulder like a sack of flour. Carrying me back to the bedroom, he commenced accepting my challenge.

And he did it *very* well.

CHAPTER FOURTEEN

FIONA

I WAS FLOATING ON A HAPPY, rainbow-colored cloud the next day at work. It was total chaos between meetings, conference calls, and drama with the design team, but none of it could touch me. With every step I took or movement I made, I could still feel Deacon between my thighs, and that wonderful ache made everything else disappear.

I finally had the man of my dreams. All the rest was inconsequential.

The trill of my cell phone cut into my work-addled brain. I reached for where it sat on my desk, a riot of butterflies in my belly at the thought that it might be Deacon. Once I saw the name on the screen and got over the initial disappointment that it wasn't him, I engaged the call and held the phone to my ear.

"Hello?"

"*What the effing hell!*" Daphne yelled so loud that I had to pull the cell away to keep from going deaf in one ear.

"What the effing hell what?" I finally asked once she was done shrieking.

"Oh, don't you even," she reprimanded. "When we talked last night, you were on the ledge about nailing your hottie when he had a girlfriend. Then he shows up out of nowhere, you hang up on me, and leave me hanging for hours? I don't *think* so! What's going on? What's happening? I want to know everything."

I didn't even bother to fight the smile tugging at my lips. "It's.... We're...."

"Spit it out! I'm dying here!"

"We're together," I answered in a quiet voice full of excitement.

She let out a scream so loud it was a wonder the windows didn't break. "*You're together*? How did that happen? And don't leave out a single detail!"

The riot of butterflies in my belly was back. It had been so long since I'd started a new relationship that I'd forgotten how much fun it was to share in the excitement with my girlfriends. And since this was Deacon, not just some guy, it was even more thrilling. "Well, he showed up last night because he was pissed that I took off on him after... well, you know."

"You mean after he gave you the business in his bar?"

"Yes, after that," I answered with a roll of my eyes. "Anyway, he was seriously pissed that I bailed without giving him a chance to explain—"

"Explain what?"

A giggle burst from my throat. "If you'd stop interrupting, I'd tell you!"

"Sorry, sorry. Continue. I'm all ears."

"He was mad that I didn't give him a chance to explain that he'd already broken up with Leah before anything even happened between us on that pool table."

Daphne sucked in a gasp. "Wait. The pool table? You're kidding! I knew that man was *all* man."

She had no idea.

"So, he'd already broken up with Leah. He nails you into a

pool table—which, babe, I have to tell you, that's flipping *hot*. Then he storms into your office all pissed off, and now you guys are together?"

It was ridiculous how giddy hearing someone else say that made me feel. "Yeah, pretty much."

She was silent for a beat, then "I'm pretty sure you're holding out on some major details." She wasn't wrong. "But that's okay, because I'll get the rest out of you tonight."

I shot up straight in my chair. "Tonight? What are you talking about?"

Just as she started to answer, there was a knock on my office door. I looked up and had to refrain from letting my annoyance show at the sight of Todd. I held up my finger in the universal gesture of *just a second*. Todd was a nice enough guy, but something about him had always rubbed me the wrong way. He was a few years younger than me, attractive, and totally knew it. But it wasn't his ego that set me on edge, it was that he clearly had a crush on me, and despite me never giving him a single signal, seemed oblivious to the fact that the attraction wasn't returned on my end.

Daphne kept chattering away in my ear. "We are *so* having a girls' night tonight. I'm telling Lola and Sophia everything. We'll expect the full scoop from you over drinks."

"Daphne, now really isn't a good time. Can I call you back?"

"Oh no you don't," she argued. "You aren't getting out of this. It's happening. Tonight. Seven. We'll meet you at Sapphire."

Once Daphne got something in her head, there was no talking her out of it. Those three were going to demand a command performance. As she talked, Todd just watched me in that slightly creepy way I'd come to expect from him.

"Okay, fine. Tonight at Sapphire. I'll meet you guys there."

"Don't be late."

"I won't, but babe, I have to go. Someone just walked in."

"All right, honey. See you later."

I disconnected and waved him in. He walked in with an air about him, like his shit didn't stink, when in fact the cologne he chose to bathe in regularly was already starting to give me a headache.

When he'd started at Prentice Fashion a few years before, I'd noticed him right away, even going so far as to toy with the idea of maybe asking him on a date. Then he opened his mouth and spoke, and all thoughts of Todd being handsome flew right out the window.

That hadn't stopped *him* from noticing *me*, however. The man was unrelenting, asking me out constantly in that first year. I'd made the mistake of using work as an excuse, claiming I didn't feel right about dating within the company. Apparently to him, that meant I'd totally be down for it if we didn't work together, when the truth was I'd rather get every hair on my body waxed off than spend more time than absolutely necessary in his presence. The dude was completely clueless.

"What can I do for you, Todd?"

Sitting in the chair across from me, uninvited, he started, "Just wanted to stop by and see how your morning's going so far," he said as his eyes scanned me lasciviously. "You're looking lovely, as usual."

Yep, totally freaking clueless.

Pasting on my own brittle smile, I replied, "Thanks. I'm fine this morning, but I'm a little busy right now, so...." I tried the best I could to clue him in without being too blunt. The last thing the founder of the company's daughter needed was a mark in her personnel file that she couldn't get along with her coworkers. "Is that what you stopped by for?"

"That, and because I wasn't sure if you're aware that the design department is in chaos. The fabric that came in for the

Spring line's maxi dress is the wrong shade of teal, and the designs for the Milan show still haven't been approved. With you being so busy and all, I just wanted to apprise you of the situation. I'm more than happy to contact our fabric supplier and finalize the designs if you're too busy."

I couldn't deny that, in spite of my personal feelings toward Todd, he'd always been a hard worker. He was good at his job and always offered to help. I wasn't naïve enough to believe that he did it simply to be a nice guy, but until he actually did something untoward, I was pretty much stuck having to remain pleasant with him.

Wanting to get him out of my office as quickly as possible, I said, "That's very kind of you, but I've already spoken with the fabric supplier. We'll have the correct material by the end of business today. And seeing as I signed off on everything for the Milan show this morning, we're all set. But I appreciate your concern."

He stood with a grin that might have made other women swoon, but had no effect on me. "Well, glad you have it all taken care of. I'll just leave you to it."

My cell phone rang just as Todd left. I easily turned my attention from the unfortunate encounter to my screen, and those butterflies took flight again.

"Hi," I answered, my voice sounding way breathier than I intended, but Deacon just did that to me.

"Christ, just you saying that one word makes me hard."

I choked on air as heat flooded my core. "I... uh... that's... wow."

Deacon chuckled through the line, warming me from the inside out. "You're even more adorable when you're a stuttering mess."

Finding my tongue, I frowned and snapped, "I'm not a stuttering mess!"

"There's my Fee."

Oh damn, he was good. "You know, you're pretty smooth, Lockhart. You make it almost impossible to get mad at you."

"Then my evil plan's working."

God, I felt like a teenager again, all giddy and excited to be talking to a boy on the phone. "You on your way to work?"

"Yep, heading to the bar now, but I wanted to call you first. You were gone when I woke up."

Leaving Deacon's bed was hard enough, but leaving it with a sleeping, shirtless, impressive Deacon still *in* it had been damn near impossible. "Yeah, sorry. I left a note."

"I know. I got it. That's the only reason I didn't call you the second I woke up, pissed as hell."

I giggled at the image of a fire-breathing Deacon waking up, ready to tear into me. "You were sleeping so peacefully, and I know how late your nights are. I didn't want to wake you."

"I appreciate it, baby, but from here on out, when you wake up, you get me up too. Especially when you're waking up to leave."

"Deac, I had to get up early to get to my car. Then I had to get home and get ready for work. The sun was barely up when I left this morning. That's way too early for you."

"Babe," he said in a hard, no-bullshit tone. "You wake up, you get me up. I don't give a shit if it's three in the morning."

Even when he was being a bossy pain in the ass, he still managed to make me melt for him. "Okay," I responded softly. "If I wake up, I'll force you to get up with me."

"Thanks, baby," he said just as softly. Man, I was gone for this guy. It wasn't the new honeymoon phase of a relationship that was making me feel like that, it was that he'd been my best friend through some of the most important years of my life and was now something so much more. I was seriously falling for him. And falling fast.

"You coming over tonight?" he asked as I pondered just how crazy about him I was.

Disappointment crashed over me at that question because I really, *really* wanted to go back to his place. "I'd love to, but Daphne's demanding a girls' night at Sapphire to get the full scoop on what's going on between you and me. She's already spilled the beans to Lola and Sophia, so if I don't go...."

"There'll be bloodshed."

I breathed a sigh of relief that he got it and didn't lay on a guilt trip. "Exactly."

"Tell you what, I'm at the bar until ten. When you're done with the three maniac musketeers, head over to my place. If you beat me, there's a hide-a-key in the front flowerbed closest to the door. I want you naked in my bed, waiting for me."

I fidgeted in my seat, aroused beyond words. "And if I don't beat you?"

Deacon's voice got low and husky. "Then I'll just have to do the honors of stripping you myself."

Oh, it was so on. "Then I'll see you later tonight."

"Oh, and Fee?"

"Yeah?"

"Pack a bag. For more than one night."

Yep, I was *definitely* gone for this guy.

CHAPTER FIFTEEN

FIONA

ONE DRINK at Sapphire quickly turned to multiple, and before I even realized it was happening, I'd spilled the full story, all the gritty details and everything. I could've blamed the booze for my loose tongue, but the truth was I loved being able to share what I was building with Deacon with my closest, bestest friends. What I was feeling for him was so much more intense and important than anything I'd felt for another man before, and I wanted to shout how I felt from the rooftops for everyone to hear.

After finishing my story, I lifted my margarita to my lips and took a long sip through the straw. When I finally glanced around the table, I noticed all three of them were watching me, their mouths hanging open in complete and utter shock.

"I...," Sophia started, but then immediately stopped, at a loss for words.

Lola picked up her water glass and started chugging. Once it was gone, she slammed it on the table. "I'm not going to lie, I just came a little bit."

Some of my margarita went down the wrong pipe and I began choking. By the time I got a hold of myself, Daphne was fanning her face with the drink menu. "That boy's all kinds of sexy caveman, isn't he?"

"Sweetheart, you have no clue," I teased.

They burst into laughter as our waiter dropped off the appetizers we'd ordered to share.

I picked up a crostini with basil pesto spread and shoved the whole thing in my mouth. When the alcohol flowed, manners be damned.

"He told me to pack a bag for more than one night," I told them through a mouthful of food.

Lola sniffled loudly from across the table, her dark eyes shiny with unshed tears.

"Oh God, not again," Sophia groaned.

"Sorry, sorry. I'm just so happy for you." She hiccupped and blinked rapidly to try and stop from bursting into tears thanks to her insane pregnancy hormones.

Unfortunately, I had already surpassed tipsy and was smack-dab in the middle of drunk, so I was feeling the love just a little too much, and started tearing up as well.

"Oh dear Lord, they're both about to burst," Daphne teased.

Ignoring her, I looked right at Lola and said, "I l-love you."

"I l-love you t-too," she blubbered.

"Sweet merciful Mother Mary. I need more booze to deal with this." Sophia waved at the waiter and ordered herself another glass of wine. By the time it was dropped off, Lola and I had gotten a handle on ourselves.

I downed the rest of my margarita before standing from my chair. "I have to hit the ladies' room. Will someone order me another drink while I'm gone?"

Sophia nodded. "Sure thing, babe."

It wasn't until I was on my feet, moving to the restroom, that I realized just how loose the tequila from my margaritas had made me. I did my business, washed my hands, and was busy reapplying my lip gloss in the mirror when I suddenly started thinking about all the benefits of drunk sex with Deacon.

Dropping the tube of gloss back into my handbag, I pulled out my phone and called up my text messages.

Me: *How do you feel about drunk sex?*

It took Deacon no time at all to reply.

Deacon: *Depends. Drunk enough to hurl is a no-go. Drunk enough to let me do anything I want to that sexy body of yours... I'm all for that.*

Oh man. A shiver coursed through me at his response.

I was just about to type that I was totally down for the latter as well when the bathroom door swung open and a svelte, exotic brunette came walking in.

She looked at my reflection in the mirror, and something about her expression immediately set me on edge. "Hi," she greeted, unexpectedly.

"Uh, hello."

I figured she would move to one of the stalls, so I was more than a little surprised when she hesitantly made her way to the sink beside mine. "I know this might sound weird since you have no clue who I am, but I couldn't help but overhear you talking to your friends."

"Okay," I dragged out, not having the first idea where this was going.

"By any chance, were you talking about Deacon Lockhart?"

With that, the bad feeling I had got even worse. I hadn't even noticed this woman, but she'd not only noticed me, she'd also eavesdropped on my conversation, and apparently felt she had a right to confront me in a restaurant bathroom.

"I'm sorry. Who are you?"

She gave her head a shake, sending her glossy hair swinging. "Sorry. I'm Deanna. I used to... well, Deacon and I... that is, we used to see each other." My stomach fell to the floor. "Well, what I guess I mean to say is that *I* thought we were seeing each other, but apparently he thought something different."

"What do you mean?" I couldn't help but ask, even though I *really* didn't want to know.

"Look, I know this isn't my place, but like I said, I overheard you and I just thought that maybe... I should warn you."

My forehead wrinkled as my brows scrunched into a severe V. "Warn me? Warn me about what?"

"He's not the type of guy you should get attached to. He's a total playboy. You might think you're in, that it's serious, but trust me, that man doesn't do commitment."

The happy alcohol-induced looseness I'd been experiencing disappeared in an instant. I was suddenly stone-cold sober, and every muscle in my body had locked up tight. "I think maybe you're talking about a different guy."

"I'm talking about Deacon Lockhart. That's who you're seeing, right? The guy who owns The Black Sheep?"

No longer able to form words, I simply nodded.

"Then it's the same guy. And it's not just me, believe me. That dude's run through most of the female population of the city, and as soon as he's done with them, he sends them packing. Women talk. None of us know the full reason, but word through the grapevine is that a chick did a serious number on him a long time ago, and because of that he refuses to commit."

Oh God. *Oh God!* I felt like crying again, but that time for a totally different, unhappy reason.

"I didn't mean to upset you," the unknown Deanna continued. "I just thought you should know." Then, after dropping a bomb that rocked my entire world, she walked out the bathroom door.

I stuffed my phone back into my purse, not bothering to open the texts from Deacon that came through while Deanna was giving me a verbal punch to the gut. My eyes scanned the dining room of their own accord, landing on Deanna and her pack of girlfriends. I caught her gaze and quickly averted mine, hustling on my high-heeled feet back to my own friends. The girls could see the upset written all over my face the second I made back to the table.

"What's the matter?" Daphne asked as soon as I sat down.

"Nothing," I lied as I lifted my newest margarita, put the straw to my lips, and sucked.

"I call bull," Sophia stated. "You look like you've just seen a ghost. And I saw you staring at that woman over there." She tipped her chin in the direction of Deanna's table. "What did she say to you?"

"Just... told me some unfortunate truths." Like the fact that it was my fault Deacon had slept with—and subsequently left brokenhearted—most of the women in the greater Seattle area. I'd done that to him. And I hated myself for it.

I shook off my morose thoughts and glued on a smile that didn't come close to reaching my eyes. "Let's just forget about her and get back to our girls' night."

They looked like they wanted to argue, but thankfully let the issue drop. Halfway through margarita number four, my cell phone began to ring from my purse.

I pulled it from my bag and sucked in a deep breath at the sight of Deacon's name on the screen before answering the call.

"Hi."

"Baby, you disappeared on me. You okay?"

God, I was the worst kind of person.

He was such a thoughtful guy. I could hear the noise from the bar behind him, but he'd still called to check on me when I went radio silent after starting a text conversation.

"Yeah, I'm good."

He didn't say anything for several seconds, then "What's wrong."

Damn it. Years of being a part of each other's lives meant the guy knew me way too well. "Nothing. Seriously. It's all good. I'm just having one last drink with the girls."

"Fiona," he said in a warning tone. "Remember that shit I said last night about honesty?"

I blew a frustrated puff of air through my lips since he couldn't see my scowl through the phone. "Deac, I'm fine," I stressed.

"Fee, you're lying."

"We can talk about it later," I tried.

But Deacon wouldn't be put off. He wanted answers, and he wanted them right then and there. "Or, seeing as I already have you on the phone, we can talk about it not. Not a big fan of giving you time to stew on shit, sweetheart."

"Fine," I snapped, my mood bouncing all over the place thanks to the booze and the bathroom bombshell. I'd fully intended to have this conversation with him when I got to his place later. The last thing I wanted was to do it over the phone, but when Deacon wanted something, he ran roughshod over anyone in his way in order to get it. "I ran into someone tonight, and let's just say the conversation was less than pleasant."

"Who was it?"

"I didn't get her last name, seeing as I was totally unprepared and blindsided by her, but do you recall a Deanna? Beautiful, dark hair, looks like she belongs on the pages of a magazine?"

"*Shit.*"

"From what she said, I'm surprised you'd remember. I mean, there were *so many women* I'm shocked you can keep their faces and names straight."

"Fee, it's not like that—"

"You know, I was going to talk to you about this later tonight because I was upset. Not because she made it sound like you've been with so many women that it would put a porn star to shame, but because the reason you refused to settle down was because you had your heart broken, and I *hated* hearing that. I fucking hated hearing that you behaved like that because of what *I* put you through. But you didn't want to give me the opportunity of talking to you on *my* time. Oh no, what Deacon wants, Deacon gets. So now I'm sitting here with my girls, and they're staring at me like I've lost my mind, which I kind of have seeing as I'm having a freaking meltdown on the *freaking* phone in the middle of a *freaking restaurant!*"

"Baby—"

"Now if you'll excuse me, I'm going to end this conversation and get back to my girls' night so Sophia, Daphne, and Lola can help me get my shit together. I'll meet you at your place later. After that, you and I will have a discussion about you being a bossy pain in the ass who pisses me off way too damn often. How's *that* for honest?"

"Sounds like we have a plan," he answered in a way that, I swear to God, sounded like he was trying hard not to laugh.

"Good. I'll see you later," I clipped before hanging up, because if I heard him laugh, my head might have exploded on the spot.

Jeez, I was losing my damn mind.

And it was all Deacon Lockhart's fault.

CHAPTER SIXTEEN

FIONA

BY THE TIME I left Sapphire a few hours later, I was sober enough to drive to Deacon's house. Unfortunately, that also meant I was sober enough to recall—in humiliating detail—my public outburst.

When I pulled my car into Deacon's driveway, I was on pins and needles. I had no clue how he'd react, and while that made me nervous, I held firm to everything I'd said to him over the phone.

Just as I shifted into Park and shut off the engine, Deacon's front door opened. My heart rate kicked up at the sight of him standing in the doorway. He wore a pair of jeans that hung on his body like they'd been tailor-made to perfectly show off the strength on his frame. His shirt was untucked, the sleeves rolled up to his elbows, highlighting his impressive forearms. Deacon's hands were shoved into his front pockets, and his bare feet were crossed at the ankle. Damn, he was a sight to see. Despite everything that had happened hours earlier, just seeing him standing there set my body on fire.

Blowing out a breath, I grabbed my overnight bag from the passenger seat and pushed my door open. Deacon's eyes were like penetrating lasers as I slowly made my way up the front walk.

He didn't move when I hit the front door, so I was forced to stop and look up. I couldn't read his mood from his expression, so feeling frazzled and still slightly embarrassed, I blurted the first thing that came to mind.

"You shouldn't be standing in the doorway with bare feet when it's this cold outside. You could get sick."

A weight lifted off my shoulders when his face cracked with a smile and he pulled his hands from his pockets in order to wrap me in a hug.

The embrace was short, but no less warm and comforting. Stepping from the doorway, Deacon led me into the house with an arm around my waist, using his free hand to take my bag and toss it onto the floor of the entryway.

Kicking the door closed behind us, he guided me into the living room, taking a seat on the couch and pulling me down next to him. He situated me so I was resting against one of the tall, squishy couch arms, then pulled my feet into his lap, plucking my heels off and dropping them to the floor.

I let out a contented sigh when Deacon's thumbs pressed into the bottom of my right foot and began massaging.

"Do you want to start or should I?"

Laying my head back against the arm, I closed my eyes and let myself feel the tension melt away. "You start. I'm too comfortable right now to pick another fight."

"Who said we're going to fight?"

I lifted my head just long enough to shoot him a sarcastic look before relaxing once more.

He chuckled. "That wasn't a fight. That was... a meeting of the minds."

Letting out an indelicate snort, I replied with a mature "Whatever."

"Baby, look at me," Deacon commanded in a gentle tone. When I lifted my head and opened my eyes, I saw his expression had gone from humorous to serious in a blink. "I want to talk about what you said on the phone."

My gut knew exactly what he was talking about. "I said a lot of things," I told him with a shrug.

One of his eyebrows quirked knowingly. "You know," he stated simply. With a sigh, I pushed up to sitting, pulling my legs from his lap as he continued. "Deanna had no business confronting you like that. It was fucked up. Especially considering she didn't know what the hell she was talking about."

A lump began to form in my throat, making it difficult to speak. "She seemed pretty well-informed to me, Deac."

"And I knew that was where your head was. That's why I pushed you on the phone to tell me what was wrong."

My face scrunched in a deep frown. "No, you pushed on the phone because that's what you do."

A muscle in his cheek began to tick, a telling sign of Deacon getting frustrated. But as if determined not to fight, he kept a tenuous hold on his anger. "Did you ever stop to think that I get like that with you because I know you so goddamn well? I knew you'd hold on to something like that until it tangled you up inside. What you consider pushy, I consider necessary. It's the only way I know I'll be able to get your head straight about us when you start twisting shit up again."

"Stop accusing me of twisting shit up in my head!" I snapped. I was really getting sick and tired of him throwing that back in my face.

"Then stop doing it!" he barked back. "You took what Deanna said and internalized it, making yourself feel guilty about something that wasn't yours to feel guilty about."

"How can you say that?" I cried. "It's spreading all over

Seattle that you'll never settle down because you've had your heart broken!"

"Jesus Christ! It has nothing to do with me having a broken heart, Fee! I wouldn't settle down with any of those women because they weren't you! Hate to break it to you, but I didn't spend my life as a goddamn monk. I'm a man. I like sex, and when the mood struck, I did something about it." I flinched, unable to hide how much I hated hearing that even though it was unreasonable. "But those relationships didn't end because of that bullshit Deanna fed you. They ended because I wasn't in love with any of them. I've only ever loved you."

My mouth opened to respond, but the words stuck in my throat when Deacon's words finally penetrated. "You.... Did you just say...?" I couldn't bring myself to finish the sentence for fear that I hadn't heard right.

"Are you really surprised?" he finally asked, putting me out of my misery.

I suddenly felt like Lola, prone to tears at the drop of a hat. "Maybe you should spell this out for me too," I giggled. "You know, just so I'm *totally* sure."

Deacon's face split in a huge smile, showing off his brilliant white teeth. "I love you, Fiona."

Giddy at Deacon's pronouncement of love, I launched myself across the couch and straddled his lap, peppering his face with kisses. Once my lips landed on his, he immediately wrapped one arm around my waist and tangled his other hand in my hair, holding me in place in order to deepen the kiss. When we finally broke apart, I was out of breath and unbelievably turned on.

"So I'm taking it that this means you love me too?" he joked.

"Around the world and back again," I whispered, every bit of the love I felt for him pouring from those words.

His hand in my hair clenched uncontrollably. "Say it," he insisted on a gruff whisper. "I need the words, baby."

Cupping Deacon's cheeks, I rested my forehead against his, looking him right in the eye. "I love you, Deacon."

Deacon's eyes slammed closed. It was like hearing me say that lifted a weight from him. "To Jupiter and back, sweetheart," he said, his voice gruff with emotion.

A GROWL EMITTED from deep within Deacon's chest, drawing my eyes up from what I was doing. The heat in his gaze as he watched me take his cock down my throat sent a rush of arousal between my legs.

"Oh *fuck*," he gritted, dropping his head back against the headboard where he sat propped on the pillows as I worked between his spread legs. His jaw clenched and his fingers fisted in my hair as his hips began to pump up, shoving him deeper down my throat. "Yeah, baby. Just like that. Take me deep."

I moaned at his dirty words, loving what they did to me, but loving what I was doing to him right then more even. The sheer power of pushing Deacon to the edge like I was currently doing was exhilarating. I couldn't get enough. I was so close to coming simply from sucking him off.

One of my hands wrapped around the base of him while the other snaked between his thighs to cup his balls. I gave them a gentle squeeze at the same time I swallowed, pulling a grunt and a rumbly "S*hit!*" from his throat. Deacon's defined abs tensed and convulsed beneath his skin, his cock swelled, and his balls tightened.

"Fee, climb on and ride me."

That caused another gush of arousal, but I was too far gone with what I was doing to follow direction. I wanted to watch him blow, wanted to experience the thrill that came with having a front row seat to Deacon's orgasm. My head started bobbing fast, my fingers on both hands squeezing to apply more pressure.

"Baby, now."

He fell from my mouth with a pop, and I started jacking him as I looked up at his face. "I want to watch."

"You can watch later. I want to come inside you. Get up here and ride me."

"But—" My objection was cut off with a yelp as he grabbed my hips and yanked me up to straddle him. I felt the head of him press against my entrance just as he thrust up and pulled me down, filling me completely.

I had already been on the edge, so when he lifted me and shoved me down one more time, I started coming. Throwing my head back on a long moan, I started riding him with abandon as my release washed over me. "Oh God. Deacon, baby." I moved faster and faster. My orgasm seemed to last forever as he pulled on my hair to lower my face to his.

"You wanted to watch, sweetheart." Just as he finished speaking, every muscle in his body tightened. He pumped up once, twice, three times before planting me in place and letting out a long, loud roar as his head fell back.

Watching him come was absolutely spectacular, and the sight was so sexy it set me off again. My second climax had just begun to fade at the same time as Deacon's.

When we finished, I collapsed against him in a heap, pressing my face to the crook of his neck.

Deacon's fingertips skated along the skin of my back in soft, featherlight touches.

"I love you around the world and back again," I whispered.

"And I love you to Jupiter and back."

CHAPTER SEVENTEEN

FIONA

TWENTY YEARS old

IT WAS OFFICIALLY SUMMER BREAK. But while most of my friends were celebrating the end of our second year of college, I was spending my time interning for my father at his fashion company. I didn't consider it my dream job, but at least the work was interesting and kept me entertained. Every free moment I had was spent with Deacon, either over at the Lockharts' or at my place.

That day, I was heading over to his place to hang out by the pool and relax. Bypassing the front door, I went around to the back and found Deacon already in his swim trunks, lounging on one of the long cushy chairs that sat around the pool.

"Hey."

His head lifted at the sound of my voice, his aviator-covered eyes homing in on me at the same time a big smile stretched across his face. He always smiled at me like that, like he hadn't seen me in years when the truth was we hung out all the time.

We even went to the same college, and made an effort to have at least one meal together every day.

"Hey, yourself," he said, sitting up and swinging his legs over the cushion so his feet were on the ground. "Why aren't you in your suit?"

The perfect view of his abs struck me momentarily speechless. The changes to Deacon's body over the past few years weren't lost on me at all. Hell, they weren't lost on any female in a three-mile radius. That was why he always had a girl on his arm the past two years of college. He'd always been cute. Hell, he's always been one of the best looking guys I'd known, but it was no longer in that boy-next-door kind of way. Deacon had grown into a man. He was taller, broader. He had taken to working out and running, and the effort he put into his body definitely showed. The muscles beneath his smooth, tanned skin stood out everywhere, from his biceps, to his chest and stomach, to his thick thighs.

I shook off my stupor and did my best to stop gawking. "Uh, I left it here last time we went swimming. I just need to change in the pool house real quick and I'll be ready."

But even as I spoke, I couldn't make my feet move or keep my eyes from trailing back down to those abs. *Damn, those abs.*

Deacon cocked his head to the side in curiosity. "You gonna change or keep standing there looking at me all weird?"

I jerked out of my fog. "Change. Definitely change." I wandered over to the pool house and entered, closing the door behind me without looking at Deacon in the hopes of hiding the way my cheeks were burning with embarrassment. By the time I got my bathing suit on and headed back outside, I'd managed to get myself under control.

When I came back out, everything between Deacon and me was back to the way it had always been. But I couldn't help but notice every move he made, and the way tiny beads of sweat were starting to trickle through the valleys of those *freaking* abs. Good Lord, when had Deacon gotten so hot?

I took the lounger next to his and laid back, ready to soak up some rays when I heard the hiss of a bottle being opened. Lifting the sunglasses I'd slid onto my face, I looked as Deacon extended a beer my way.

"Thanks." I grabbed the bottle and took a sip, the cold liquid refreshing on such a hot day. "So where's Rory?" I asked about Deacon's latest fling in the hopes of getting my mind out of the gutter when it came to my best friend. I had no business noticing him the way I was, and if he knew what I was thinking, he'd probably freak right the hell out.

He laid back, resting his arms behind his head. "No idea," he answered nonchalantly.

I let out a snort and flipped to my stomach, aiming my sunglasses his way. "You don't sound like you give a damn about where your girlfriend is," I pointed out.

With a snort of his own, he replied, "Rory was never my girl-friend. She was just someone I hooked up with for a while."

I rolled my eyes behind my lenses. "You're such a playboy," I teased playfully. "Deacon Lockhart, the ultimate heartbreaker."

Deacon didn't say anything for a while, and when he finally did, I couldn't help but feel there was something meaningful behind his words that I didn't quite understand.

"I'm not a heartbreaker. It's just that none of them were the right ones. When I finally have her, I'll treat her like a queen."

He sounded so damn certain. I hoped with all my heart that someday he'd find the girl to treat like a queen. I wanted nothing but happiness for my best friend.

I BROKE through the surface and sucked in a lungful of air. "I totally beat you!" I shouted just as Deacon resurfaced. Brushing the hair out of my face, I grinned triumphantly as he scowled. "Suck on that, loser."

"You know, there's such a thing as a poor winner," he grumbled.

Laughing brightly, I started climbing the stairs. "Says the *loser*. I'm getting a soda from inside. You want anything?"

"Grab me one too."

Wrapping a towel around my waist, I gave Deacon a salute and headed into the house. I pulled two cans from the fridge and slammed the door shut, letting out a startled shriek at the sudden appearance of Grayson, Deacon's big brother. "Damn it, Gray, you scared the crap out of me."

I'd grown up with both Lockhart brothers, but seeing as Grayson was a few years older, Deacon was the one I had a closer bond with. Also, there was the little fact that I'd had a teeny crush on Grayson for years that made it a hard to get closer to him, seeing as I couldn't help but behave awkwardly. It was one of those unrequited, childish crushes that I never thought would go anywhere. I had relegated myself to appreciating Gray from afar until I eventually got over him, but that didn't mean I wasn't a stuttering, blushing mess whenever he was around.

And it was only made worse by the fact that he didn't seem to notice my existence beyond me being his little brother's annoying friend.

"Sorry, didn't mean to frighten you. I thought you heard me come in." He smiled at me, his eyes trailing from my face down my body. It was only at his unusual gaze that I remembered I was only wearing a tiny bikini with a towel wrapped around my waist. I was suddenly very aware of how much skin I was showing, and the fact that it was much chillier in the kitchen than I'd realized.

Crossing my arms over my chest to hide the evidence of the temperature, I cleared my throat and did my best not to stutter. "No, it-it's cool. I mean, it's your house, right? I just... didn't realize you were here. I mean home. I didn't realize you were home."

Gray had recently graduated from college, and word was he planned to spend the summer in Europe before coming back to start his new position at his father's company.

He came farther into the kitchen, which brought him only a foot away from me. Leaning against the closed fridge, he crossed his arms over his chest, giving me his complete attention. "I'm not leaving until next week."

"Oh, well...." I was forced to uncross my arms so I could set the cold-ass soda cans on the counter. "That's... fun." *Jeez, I'm such an idiot.*

"Wow, Fee, how long has it been since we've seen each other? Months?"

It was an odd question for him to ask. "Uh, I guess?" I had to give it some thought. "I think it was... wow, it has been a while. I didn't realize. I think it was around Christmas."

Grayson did another full-body scan before declaring, "You've changed. Or maybe I'm just seeing you as a grown-up for the first time, I don't know. But you look good, Fee. Real good."

I was pretty sure every inch of my skin was burning with a furious blush. "Um, I... well th-thank you."

The back door opened and Deacon came waltzing through.

What's taking so lo—" He jerked to a stop at the sight of Grayson and me. "What's going on in here?"

"Uh...." I wasn't sure how to answer because I honestly didn't have the first clue *what* was happening at that moment.

"I was just telling Fiona that she's grown up really well. Why didn't you tell me, bro?"

His gaze went back and forth between me and his brother. "Didn't realize I was keeping it a secret."

"Hmm," Grayson hummed thoughtfully. "Then I guess I'm an idiot for not noticing sooner."

Oh. My. Wow.

I went from crushing on Grayson to immediately smitten in the blink of an eye. And when he asked me out shortly after, I didn't hesitate to say yes. I wouldn't realize it right away, but that was the moment when everything in my life changed, and not necessarily for the better. And it would be years before I got back everything I lost with that one simple *yes*.

CHAPTER EIGHTEEN

DEACON

WHILE FIONA WAS CLEANING up in my bathroom, I headed into the kitchen for a beer. I popped the top and was standing at the sink, staring out into the darkness of my back-yard when her arms slid around me. Fiona's tits pressed against my back made my dick respond beneath my sweats. When I turned to face her, leaning against the counter, I couldn't help but notice how beautifully mussed she was. She'd slipped on the shirt I'd taken off earlier, only doing up a few of the buttons in the middle, so I had a perfect view of her sexy lace panties beneath.

I'd have been happy with Fee wearing nothing but my shirts every day for the rest of my life. The only downfall for her was that she'd never be able to leave the house. Not as long as there were other men out there to admire her mile-long legs and all that silky hair and skin.

She pulled the beer from my fingers and took a sip before passing it back and hopping onto the island in front of me. The childlike way she crossed her ankles and began swinging her legs back and forth, while also looking like a walking wet dream, only made her that much more endearing to me.

I moved in her direction, setting my beer down beside her and placing my palms on her knees to spread her thighs wide so I could fit between them. I couldn't get enough of her. If she was within sight, my hands constantly itched to touch or caress her. Finally having her how I'd wanted her all my life didn't lessen my desire. If anything, knowing just how amazingly she fit me only made it that much stronger. I felt like I was finally whole.

That was why I had a tendency to be pushy. I wouldn't admit it to her, but I still had that niggling voice in the back of my head that this wasn't going to last. When you spend so long craving a person, finally being with them is almost too good to be true.

The feeling ate at me, but I couldn't bring myself to discuss it with Fiona. I was too scared that she'd use my deeply rooted concerns to put that goddamned wall back up between us.

But I had to admit, hearing her tell me she loved me went a long way in soothing my worry.

Once more, she picked up my beer and took a healthy drink. I laughed and asked, "You want one of your own?"

"Nope," she responded with a huge grin. "Yours are better."

My chest instantly warmed. "Yeah? How's that?"

"Don't know," she answered with a shrug. "They just are."

She wrapped her arms around my neck, pulling me closer. The playfulness melted from her face as she said, "I'm sorry for earlier tonight, when I got mad at you on the phone. I just... I was overwhelmed, and you were right. What that woman said really bothered me."

I slid my fingers up her bare legs and tensed. I hated the blame she laid on herself. Fiona was usually such a confident, caring person, but the shit that had gone down with us had dented her self-confidence. And I was to blame for that. If I'd been more of a man and hadn't cut her from my life, not just once but twice, she wouldn't question every one of her actions when it came to me.

"First off, stop apologizing. Especially for being yourself," I demanded. "If you ever feel like I'm running over you, I expect you to lay into me about it because that's who you are, Fee. You stand up for yourself. I don't want you to ever change that. If you change yourself because you think it'll make me happy, I'll be pissed."

I felt some of the tension seep from her body, and a sense of relief washed over me. "So does this mean you're giving me permission to bitch you out?" she teased with a small smile.

I returned her grin and answered, "Hell yeah. If it means I get to see that fire in you more often, then have at it, baby." My top lip quirked in that smirk I knew turned her on.

It was easy to tell that she was getting riled up again, and I had every intention to act on that when my cell phone suddenly rang from the bedroom, interrupting the moment.

"The hell?" I muttered, looking in that direction.

Fiona followed my gaze. "Who could that be? It's really freaking late."

I disengaged from Fee and started down the hall to the room. By the time I reached the door, the sound had stopped and started again. The hair on my arms stood on end at the persistent ringing. Pulling the phone from the pocket of the jeans I'd discarded earlier, I looked at the screen and my entire body locked tight. Two calls back-to-back from my brother.

Sliding my thumb across the screen, I lifted it to my ear. "Gray? What's going on, man?"

"Deac," he choked. "Fuck. Deacon."

My blood ran cold at the sound of his agonized voice. "Talk to me, brother. What's wrong?"

"It-it's Lola. We're at the hospital. She... she went into labor."

Oh shit. Oh no. It was too early.

I raced through the room, grabbing whatever clothes I could find as I spoke, "Where are you? Tell me where to go." From the corner of my eye, I saw Fiona rushing around, grabbing pants from her bag and quickly yanking them on.

"Northwest. Just... Christ, I don't know.... Just get here. I need you."

I couldn't recall ever hearing my confident, fearless big brother tell me he needed me. "I'm coming now. Just hold on, brother. I'm coming."

Fiona whipped off my shirt and tossed it to me as I disconnected the call. "What's happening?" she asked as she slipped on her bra and a T-shirt.

"Lola went into labor," I answered, frantically searching the floor for my socks and shoes. "Grayson's losing his mind. Fuck! Where are my goddamn boots?" I shouted, losing hold of my calm as my brother's tortured voice echoed in my skull.

Fiona was suddenly in front of me, her hands on my cheeks, forcing my face to hers. "Breathe, honey," she instructed calmly. "It's going to be okay."

I shook my head as best as her grip would let me, worry clenching my gut painfully. "It's too soon," I whispered. "She's barely six months along.

"And Lola's a fighter," she stated in a decisive tone. "There's no way in hell that she's going to let anything happen to her or that baby. And the doctors will take care of her. I promise, baby, it's all going to be okay."

She let me go, bent to the floor, and retrieved my socks and boots that I'd kicked off after coming home hours before. I put them on, and we were out the door in a matter of minutes. She insisted on driving, knowing I was too racked with concern for Grayson and Lola to be careful on the icy roads.

I kept her hand firmly in mine, needing the connection with

her to keep me grounded while we made our way through the hospital to the waiting room we'd been directed to. When we stepped in, Grayson was there, pacing the floor like a caged lion while our parents stood in a tight huddle with Sophia and Dominic. All eyes came to us the minute we walked through the waiting room door, Grayson's entire frame deflating in relief at the sight of me. Seeing that moved me in a way I'd never experienced. I let go of Fiona's hand and, after a brief greeting with my folks, moved to my brother, slapping him on the back before pulling him into a brief hug that was no less meaningful despite it being short.

When he finally pulled back, he looked ravaged. He shifted to Fiona and gave her an embrace before looking at me again. "Have you spoken to the doctor yet?"

Grayson shook his head. "No, not yet. They kicked me out of the room because I was losing my goddamn mind and making everything worse."

I didn't think there was ever a time in my life when I'd seen him at such a loss. Even though my relationship with Grayson had gotten better the past couple of years, it still wasn't what I'd consider to be great. But at that very moment, I'd have given anything to take his pain away.

"It's going to be all right," Fiona told him gently, giving him another hug. He held on to her like she was the only thing keeping him on his feet. In the past, seeing something like that would've set me off. Each familiar embrace, even when they were no longer together, was like a dagger to my heart. But just then I saw it for what it truly was: two friends comforting each other.

Feeling utterly helpless once they broke apart, I asked him, "Is there anything I can do? What do you need? Just name it."

"Just...." He shook his head, struggling to find the words. "Can you just stay here?"

Christ, he was killing me. "Absolutely." I clapped him on the shoulder. "Anything you need, I'm here."

Fiona glanced between us, and I noticed her eyes growing glassy with unshed tears. I was just about to ask if she was okay when she offered, "How about I get everyone coffee?"

Grayson, still in a fog, simply nodded and turned his gaze to the window that led to the parking lot. I moved a few feet away with her, still making sure to keep my brother in my line of sight. "You need me to get anything else?" she asked in a quiet voice. Even with her obvious concern for Grayson and her fear for her friend, Fiona was trying to take care of the rest of us around her.

I held her arms so she was facing me. "Are you okay?"

She sniffled and cleared her throat. "I'm fine. It's just that seeing him like that... it's really hard."

"I know. I just...." I shook my head and squeezed my eyes closed as tightly as possibly. Finally opening them, I admitted on a whisper, "I don't know what to do. Fee, how do I help him?"

Her face crumpled as if she could feel my agony. Fiona wrapped her arms around my waist, pressing her cheek to my chest. "Just be here for him, baby. That's all you can do."

"He's never—" I choked as I tried to speak. "He's never needed me before. I don't know what to do."

She pulled back, holding my face in her hands and smiled up at me. "He's your brother, Deac. He's always needed you. And you need him. You've got this, honey."

I pulled her back in and held her tightly. "I love you."

"And I love you," she exclaimed softly. "Around the world and back again."

CHAPTER NINETEEN

FIONA

I WALKED BACK into the waiting room, my hands laden with two coffee trays. Lola's mom and her husband, Maury, had arrived while I was gone, and were standing with the Lockharts, Dominic, and Sophia. Deacon was still off to the side with Grayson, his hand resting on his brother's back. Their heads were close, Grayson's drooped in exhaustion and worry as Deacon spoke quietly to him.

I didn't want to interrupt, so I moved over to Sophia when she broke away to join me. "Hey." I handed out coffees to anyone who wanted them and set the rest aside. "Any word?" I asked, turning my attention back to Soph.

She shook her head. "No, but I hope we hear something soon. Grayson looks like he's about to rip this place apart with his bare hands."

Glancing back over in that direction, I mumbled, "Yeah."

As if sensing my attention, Deacon looked back at me and offered a small grin before turning back to his brother.

"So...," Sophia hedged. "Things good between you two? You know, after your little thing at Sapphire?"

It wasn't the time or place, but I couldn't stop from smiling.

"Yeah, they're pretty terrific. I love him," I admitted. Saying it out loud to someone other than Deacon made it feel even more real.

"I'm happy for you, honey. You deserve it."

Daphne and Caleb blew into the room a few minutes later. Caleb moved to the guys while Daphne came to us girls. "Shit, sorry we took so long. We had to wait for Caleb's mom to get to our place to watch Evie. Has there been any update?"

Sophia had just opened her mouth to reply when a man in a white coat stepped through the doorway and asked, "Are you the family of Lola Lockhart?"

Grayson immediately detached from Deacon and rushed to the doctor. "Yeah, I'm her husband. Is she okay? Is the baby all right?"

The rest of us gathered behind him and waited for the news. My heart had lodged itself in my throat when Deacon stepped beside me and took my hand. My fingers clenched his as the doctor started talking.

"They're just fine." A collective sigh swept through the room. "The baby is a stubborn little thing and wanted to come early, but Mom is just as stubborn about keeping the little one in there longer."

"That's the Abbatelli genetics running strong," Dominic joked, making most everyone around us laugh.

"We managed to stop the contractions, but we're going to keep her for a day or two to make sure they don't start up again. Once she leaves here, I'm writing her a prescription for Terbutaline. It'll keep her from going back into preterm labor. I'm also recommending bed rest until it looks like we've gotten things under control. She can get up and move around, but nothing strenuous, and not for more than an hour or two total each day. With the medication and rest, I'm confident we can keep the little one where it belongs for the next few months."

"Can I see her?" Grayson asked.

"Yes. Since you're the husband, you'll be allowed to stay over with her, but visiting hours are over for tonight, so we're asking everyone else to wait until tomorrow."

Deacon's fingers tightened for a few seconds before his grip loosened again. Grayson barely managed a wave over his shoulder as he hurried after the doctor, desperate to get to his wife. After a few minutes, everyone started out, but Deacon and I were stopped by his parents before we made it out of the waiting room.

Cybil stood on her tiptoes and kissed Deacon's cheek before doing the same to me. "I'm so glad this night turned out okay."

"We are too," Deacon replied, swinging an arm around my shoulders and pulling me close to his side.

The claiming gesture wasn't lost on Cybil, and her lips stretched into a huge grin. "So, I take it this means it didn't work out with the pediatric surgeon?"

I went stiff at her question. I'd completely forgotten about that particular lie until that very moment. When Deacon's body started to shake, I glanced up and saw he was trying to hide his chuckle. We hadn't talked about it since that night he brought it up in my office.

"Yep. You could take it that way," he answered for me.

Jabbing my elbow in his side, I glared up at him when he looked down at me.

"Well, I just have to say this makes me so happy," Cybil continued, unable to hide her elation. Her eyes flitted back to her son as she asked him, "Does this mean you'll actually attend our Christmas Eve party next week?"

Deacon let out a groan and stared up at the ceiling, as though searching for divine intervention.

I attended the Lockharts' annual Christmas Eve party every year I was able, and for the past few years Deacon had been visibly absent. Apparently Cybil wasn't above using our relationship to get what she wanted from her son. And from what Nolan said next, it was clear that he wasn't above it either.

"Of course he will, honey. Fiona attends every year, and now that they're together, he'll be her date."

A giggle erupted from my throat at the frustrated look on Deacon's face.

"Yeah, Mom. We'll be there," he finally relented, unable to deny his mother something she so badly wanted. Even though I didn't really understand the distance between him and his father, he was still loyal to a fault. It was just one of the many reasons why I loved him.

Cybil clapped, her expression like she'd just been told that she won the lottery. "That's just marvelous! Oh I can't wait. This is so wonderful. Sweetheart, just wait until I call your mother."

Ah hell. Sometimes my mom being best friends with Cybil Lockhart was a major pain in my ass.

"You can call Evelyn and gossip like a bunch of hens later, but right now I need to get Fee home. It's the middle of the night, and she's got work in only a few hours."

He was back to being bossy Deacon, but instead of annoying the shit out of me, it made me feel nice and floaty because I knew that was just his way of trying to take care of me. And the truth was I was pretty freaking exhausted. It was already after three in the morning, and the past several hours had been insanely intense. I leaned into him, burrowing into the warm comfort of his body while thinking that there was no other place I'd rather be than by him side.

"Of course, of course," Cybil chirped. "We won't keep you two a second longer."

I gave her another hug, then embraced Nolan. Deacon said his goodbyes and we were on our way out.

As soon as we climbed into his car, I let out a sleepy yawn and rested my head against the passenger window. "I can't wait to get home. I'm beat."

Feeling his eyes on me and noticing that he hadn't started the car, I lifted my head and looked his way. He was watching me closely, his eyes shining with pleasure through the darkness in the cab. "What?"

"You said '*home*.'"

"Huh?"

"You just said you couldn't wait to get home. Not that you couldn't wait to get back to *my house*."

My brow furrowed in confusion because that seemed to mean something to him, I just didn't understand why. "Okay...?"

He turned his whole upper body my way. "Baby, I'm seeing that you don't get why this is so important, so let me lay it out. You just called my place home. To me that means you're not only comfortable there, but it's a place you *want* to be. Can you see why that'd mean so fucking much to me?"

When he explained it like that, I totally got it, and I absolutely *loved* that. "I'm guessing you like that?"

Deacon leaned in, placing a hand behind my head to pull me closer. With his forehead against mine, he whispered meaningfully, "Yeah, baby. I like that a whole fucking lot."

I smiled wide, staring him right in the eyes as I breathed, "Good."

His hand in my hair clenched. "Christ," he grunted. "I didn't think it was possible to love you any goddamn more than I already do, but you just keep proving me wrong."

My breath caught in my chest. "I *really* like that."

One corner of his mouth quirked up in a smirk as he replied, "Good."

"And I love you too, honey."

He finally pulled back and straightened in his seat, a shit-eating grin on his face. "Well thank God for that. At least I know I won't have to compete with that fake doctor to win your affections."

My face immediately fell into a severe frown. "Jerk. How did you even know?"

Deacon twisted the key in the ignition and started the car up as he answered. "You forget, I know you better than you know yourself. It was written all over your face when your girls made that whole thing up on the fly."

Slumping back in the seat, I crossed my arms over my chest and faced the windshield to pout. "Sometimes you knowing me so well is a real pain in the ass, you know that?"

His deep, rich laughter filled the car as he put it in gear and started out of the parking lot. "Maybe for you. For me, it's pretty damn handy."

I rolled my eyes at the windshield and grumbled, "Will you shut up and take me home already?"

Deacon's laugh shrank to a soft chuckle that was no less attractive than his full laugh. Then he proceeded to make me all melty by saying, "Anything for you, sweetheart."

CHAPTER TWENTY

FIONA

THINGS AT WORK were crazy thanks to the fact that our offices were closing for the upcoming holiday. We were all in a mad dash to get everything finished in time so we could enjoy the break without any stress. Unfortunately that meant our stress the two weeks before was at an all-time high.

I'd been pulling so many late nights that I couldn't keep my hours straight. Each night I left, drove to Deacon's, and then proceeded to crash wherever I lay my head down. The only thing that had kept me going the past week was the fact that I had the world's best boyfriend. He rubbed my feet when I complained about them aching. He had dinner prepared and waiting for me each night when I got home, because he knew I'd been so wrapped up that I'd completely forgotten to eat. Even on the nights that he was still at the bar when I got home, he'd made sure to leave a note telling me where he'd stashed the left-overs. There was even one night when Deacon led me into the master bathroom after lighting a bunch of candles and filling the tub with a nice, hit bubble bath. He ordered me to strip and climb in, and then he disappeared. When he returned, it was with a glass of wine.

The bath was so relaxing, so heavenly, that I ended up falling asleep in the tub. Deacon found me like that before the water had a chance to go cold. He got me out and ready for bed. A few minutes later, I was out like a light, curled snuggly against him in bed.

I couldn't remember a time in my life where I'd ever been so content. Even my relationship with Grayson hadn't been this blissful, because there was still the underlying pain of having lost Deacon. Now I felt like I had everything. It used to be that I'd wake up each morning with my mind intent on nothing but work, so consumed with my job that it was all that mattered. This past week I'd found myself doing something I hadn't done once since starting at Prentice Fashion: counting the hours until I could leave and go home to my man.

"Fiona, you still with me?"

Todd's voice yanked me out of my daydream about how well Deacon wore a pair of jeans. "Sorry. Spaced for a second." Picking up my pen, I quickly scribbled my signature on the order forms Todd had brought in ten minutes before. Once finished, I pressed my fingertips into my temples to alleviate the dull ache building in my skull.

Todd had been standing next to the chair I was sitting in, leaning over my desk, so the overwhelming stench of his cologne was only making my growing headache worse. At the feel of his hand on my back, my head shot up and turned his way to find that he had moved his attention from the documents he was going over to me. "You okay? You're looking a little tense."

I shifted to remove his hand and offered a bland smile. "I'm fine. Just tired. It's been a madhouse around here. I'm ready for a vacation."

He stood from his hunched position, and I briefly hoped that meant he'd gotten everything he needed and was going to leave. Todd, however, seemed to have other ideas. Instead of moving to the door, he turned, resting his back end on the edge of my desk and crossing his ankles like he was getting comfortable. It was obvious that he was settling in to stay a while, something I did *not* need. Especially considering he'd sat close enough to encroach on my personal space. "You and me both. You got any big plans for Christmas vacation?"

As discreetly as possible, I scooted my chair a few inches to the side as I answered, "Oh, you know, typical family stuff. I'm basically just hoping to relax for a few days."

Todd crossed him arms over his chest as he smiled down at me with that *I-know-I'm-good-looking-and-you-should-want-a-piece-of-this* grin. "I know what you mean. You know, if you find yourself without plans one night, I'd really love to take you out for a drink. I've been hearing about this new place that's supposed to be awesome—"

I was saved from having to shoot him down *again* by a knock on my office door.

"Come in," I called out a little too enthusiastically. The door opened, and I instantly smiled at the sight of Deacon. That was, until I caught him looking between me and Todd with a dark, unhappy expression on his face.

"Hey, honey," I chirped, standing quickly in an effort to put some space between me and Todd, and his Axe body spray. "This is a surprise," I continued as I rounded my desk and headed his way. Once there, I placed my hands on his chest and lifted to my tiptoes for a quick kiss. It wasn't nearly enough, but just seeing him worked wonders on easing some of my stress.

He looped a claiming arm around my waist and pulled me closer, the caveman in action for Todd's benefit. "I figured you probably skipped lunch again, so I stopped by with a sub on my way to the bar."

My stomach let out an embarrassingly loud growl at the

mention of food, but I was suddenly too hungry to care. "Crap, is it after lunch already?"

Deacon shot me a crooked smirk. "Babe, it's after three."

"Damn," I muttered, snatching the plastic bag from his hands and peeking inside. "Ooh! Turkey and swiss! Did you—"

"I told them easy on the lettuce, heavy on the mayo," he answered, already knowing exactly what I was going to ask.

"God, you're such a lifesaver. I saw two sandwiches. Does that mean you get to stay for a bit?"

"Just a little while. Then I've got to get to work."

Willing to take however much time with him I could get, I gave him another peck and turned back for my desk, only to jerk to a stop since I'd momentarily forgotten that Deacon and I had company. "Oh, Todd. This is my boyfriend, Deacon. Deac, this is Todd. A coworker of mine," I added, hoping to drive the point home to Todd that nothing was ever going to happen between us.

Deacon stood there, staring blankly as Todd sized him up. And being the arrogant ass he was, from the look on Todd's face I could tell he was under the mistaken impression that he was better. He couldn't have been more wrong.

I spoke to get his attention back on me, and hopefully hurry him out the door. "Is there anything else you needed, Todd?"

He picked up the documents I'd just signed and turned back to me with a slimy smile. "No, Fiona. That's it. For now." He began to leave, but not before stopping just beside Deacon and glancing back at me over his shoulder. "And let me know about that drink. You've got my number."

Then he was gone, closing the door behind him.

The asshole.

Deacon's eyes went from the door to me. One brow quirked up as he asked, "You've got his number?"

With a roll of my eyes, I started pulling the food out and

setting it on the desk. "Everyone here has each other's numbers. They're all listed on the employee database." I took a seat on the desk to face him as he sat in the plush chair in front of me. I passed him his sandwich and began unwrapping my own.

"There something with that guy I should know about?" Deacon asked before taking a bite of his own lunch.

"Nope," I replied after swallowing a mouthful of the best sandwich in Seattle. "Like I said, he's just a coworker."

I shoved another huge bite in my mouth, my stomach thankful for the sustenance. Lately, all I'd been eating at work was whatever shitty, several-days-stale junk I could get from the break room vending machine. If I had to eat one more PowerBar or bag of pretzels, I was likely to stab someone in the eye.

"You know he wants to fuck you, right?"

I choked on a piece of turkey I'd just swallowed and had to cough to clear the way for air. Once I could breathe normally, I told him, "He's harmless, Deac. He's just a bit clueless is all. You've got nothing to be jealous about," I added with a teasing wink.

He snorted disdainfully. "You think I'd be jealous of him? That dickless wonder wears enough cologne to choke a horse."

A giggle burst past my lips as I set my partially eaten sandwich down and kicked off one of my high heels. Running my foot up Deacon's calf to his thigh, I lowered my voice and said, "Sure sounds like you're jealous to me."

My toes encountered the bulge behind his fly, and my breath hitched as I rubbed against his erection, earning myself a ferocious growl from him.

"I see my girl's in the mood to play."

"Mmm," I moaned, pressing harder against his thickening cock. "I can't help it. You're just so damn sexy."

Tossing his lunch to the side, he stood from the chair, dislodging my foot, and came closer, pressing his palms against the desk on either side of my hips. "You want me to fuck you, baby?"

"Always," I said on a whoosh of air.

He smiled that delicious smile that spoke to all the naughty things he wanted to do to me. "Tell me, Fee. Are you already wet just thinking about it?"

My lips parted to inhale deeply as I nodded, so turned on I was unable to form words. One of his hands moved, coming to rest on the inside of me left thigh. His fingers slowly started trailing up beneath my skirt as he leaned in and whispered, "Let me see."

I spread my thighs as wide as the tight material would allow and dropped my head back on a gasp as his fingertips whispered across the soaked material. He pressed down, putting pressure on my clit as he hummed appreciatively. "Oh yeah, you're ready for me. Think you can keep quiet while I take you fast and hard on your desk?"

I smiled wickedly and said, "If I can't, I'm sure you'll come up with a creative way to silence me."

At my challenge, Deacon shoved aside my panties and plunged two fingers inside me. When my lips parted to let out a loud moan, Deacon's mouth crashed down on mine, swallowing the sound with a searing kiss as he continued to fingerfuck me, pushing me closer and closer to release before I was ready.

He ripped his mouth from mine and stated with a cocky grin, "Oh yeah, I'm sure I can come up with something."

CHAPTER TWENTY-ONE

DEACON

I WAS in a perpetual state of arousal when it came to Fiona. It was bad enough that I couldn't control my hard-on, but now that Fee was letting her guard down and her inner vixen was coming out, it was so much worse. My dick hadn't been this out of control since right after I hit puberty.

Her wet heat surrounding my fingers was driving me out of my mind. I couldn't wait any longer. And from the frantic way she writhed her hips, neither could she.

"Fuck," I growled. "Do you have any idea how hot you are?"

Her breath hitched as her pussy clenched. "God, Deac. Now. I need you now. Please."

Christ, I'd never get tired of hearing those words. But I wasn't done toying with her just yet. Pulling my hand from between her thighs, I put my fingers in my mouth and sucked them clean. "Take me out," I ordered as I started undoing the buttons of her fancy blouse.

Fiona's eager hands fumbled at first, but moments later my cock was free. She wrapped her fingers around it, and I had to bite my cheek to stifle my groan as she began jacking me. With her shirt completely undone, I ripped it from her skirt and pushed it open, revealing her perfect tits covered by sexy peach lace. My dick twitched in her hand at the sight of her tight, puckered nipples peeking through the flimsy material.

My eyes traveled back to her face. Fee's cheeks were pink, her eyes glazed with lust. Her tongue darted out of her mouth to lick her bottom lip as she stared at my hard-on like it was an ice cream cone she couldn't wait to devour.

"You like my cock, baby?"

"Mmm," she hummed in affirmative, giving it another stroke.

I was so turned on that I could barely see straight. The hold I had on my control was slipping. "Lie back," I demanded.

She complied so perfectly. When her back was flat against the desk, I yanked the cups of her bra down and sucked one nipple between my lips. Fiona took in a harsh breath at the sensation. Her back arched and her hands came to my head. The slight scrape of her nails against my scalp sent tingles of pleasure down my spine as I sucked and licked the turgid peak before giving it a gentle bite.

I moved to the other, giving it the same attention while Fee moaned beneath me, circling her hips in need. When I was done, I pulled back to view my handiwork. Her nipples, usually a creamy peach color, were now a deep rosy pink from my ministrations.

From the corner of my eye, I spotted Fiona's cell phone from her desk and was struck with a brilliant idea. Picking it up, I swiped the screen, bringing it to life, and engaged the camera function so I could take a picture of her luscious tits. Her hazy eyes opened, her lids only half-mast as she looked up at me.

"What are you doing?"

"This sight's too good not to photograph."

She giggled. "With *my* phone?"

I ran the pad of my thumb across one of the puckered

nipples and took another photo when her lips parted and she gasped. "Your phone was closest. I'll text them to mine when I'm done with you."

Before she had a chance to say anything else, I jerked her skirt all the way up past her hips and whipped her panties down her legs, stuffing them in the pocket of my jeans as soon as they cleared her sky-high heels.

Then I held the phone in place and clicked as I slowly sank into her, making sure the shot of her pussy taking me was absolutely perfect. The second I was buried as deep as I could get, all thoughts of the camera phone were forgotten. I snapped, lust and desire sending me over the edge.

Dropping the phone onto the desk with a clatter, I pulled out and thrust back in so roughly that Fiona's body slid up the desk. Her lips parted on an uncontrollable cry, so I put a hand over her mouth as I moved again, pulling out and pushing in brutal and fast.

"I'll give you slow and sweet later. Right now I need to fuck you so hard you'll feel me for a week."

Fiona's eyes rolled back and she began to buck her hips, taking me even harder. Her arms extended above her head to grip the edge of the desk for leverage. I kept one palm over her mouth while the other held on to her waist to keep her in place.

"Fuck, sweetheart. *Fuck.* You're so perfect. So. God. Damn. Perfect." I punctuated each word by driving into her tight pussy.

Uncovering her mouth, I leaned over her, continuing to fuck her as I swallowed her moans and whimpers with a hungry kiss. Lack of oxygen eventually required that I pull back a few inches.

Staring down into her eyes, I asked, "You like how I fuck you?"

"Love it," she breathed. "God, I love it."

"You love my cock?"

Her legs came up and circled my waist. "Yes," she whispered, locking her gaze with mine.

"You love me?"

She pulled in a stuttered breath and answered, "With all my heart."

My heart swelled so big I wasn't sure there was enough room for it in my chest. I stood tall, continuing to pump in and out of my girl with everything I had. Sweat beaded along my forehead and started trickling down my spine as I told Fiona, "I love you too, Fee. With all my heart." I reached between us and pressed my thumb against her clit as I ordered, "Hands over your mouth."

Once she'd done as I'd told her, I picked up the pace and pinched her clit until the walls of her pussy trembled and convulsed around me. A second later, her entire body arched as she came, her cries muffled by her own hands. I dragged it out as long as I possibly could before the tingle at the base of my spine swelled and burst, creating an explosion of stars behind my eyes as I poured myself into her with muted grunts and groans.

I didn't know how it was possible, but every time with my Fiona was better than the last.

"YOU KNOW, it's kind of uncomfortable walking around with no underwear," she grumbled once she'd finished cleaning up and getting her clothes and hair back in order.

With a huge grin, I lifted my head from her cell after texting myself the fucking *amazing* pictures I'd taken. I closed it out and dropped it back on the desk. "You'll get used to it."

She rolled her eyes but walked the few feet between us, tipping her head for a kiss. After I gave her what she was silently asking for, she muttered, "Pain in the ass."

"Yeah. But you love me anyway," I said with a chuckle.

"I do," she replied with a teasing huff. Moving back around her desk, she took a seat. "So, you're working late tonight?"

Resting my hip on the edge of the desk, I crossed my arms over my chest. "Yeah, I'm on until close."

The pout on her face told me she wasn't thrilled that we wouldn't be going to bed together again. With our work schedules this past week, there had been more nights like that than I was happy with.

"What if I come by the bar when I get out of here later this evening? Maybe I could help out again like I did last time."

My chin jerked back at her suggestion. "Baby, you've been working your ass off all week. You're exhausted. Don't you remember how beat you were last time you offered to help?"

"Well...." She stopped to think. "I wouldn't have to wait tables. I could wash dirty glasses or something."

My face went hard. The thought of her scrubbing dirty dishes set my teeth on edge. She was too good for that. No way in hell. "You aren't washing dishes, Fee.

"I'm perfectly capable of washing a damn glass, Deacon," she argued with a roll of her eyes.

"Don't doubt that. But you're still not doing it. It's beneath you."

She shot to standing, planting her hands on her hips in a pissed-off stance. "You're being a caveman again. Remember what you told me I should do when you tried to run over me to get your way? Well, I'm about to rip you a new asshole."

That redheaded fury making a sudden appearance made me smile. "Baby, I'm not trying to run over you to get my way. I'm just telling you how it is. You don't wash dishes."

"I wash the dishes at home all the time!" she cried, throwing her arms out in exasperation. "What's the difference?"

"Let me amend my statement. You don't wash dishes *in my*

bar. And you seem to be forgetting the fact that when we're together, I always help out. And technically you *don't* wash. You dry. *I* wash."

Fiona knew damn good and well that I was right, which was why her face started getting red with anger. If it was just the two of us, she never did shit like that—I did.

"Jeez, Deacon, are we seriously fighting about me washing a few stupid glasses? What's the big deal?"

I circled the desk and pulled her into my arms, loving how her body felt against mine, like it belonged, like it was made to lean on mine for support. "The big deal is you work hard every single day at this company. You do your part here every day, so when you're off work, that's your time to rest. I'll take the load off as much as I can. That isn't me trying to be a caveman, baby. That's me trying to take care of what's important to me. And in case you haven't noticed yet, you're the most important person in my life."

I knew I had her when her body pressed deeper into me. "It's really not fair that you get to win this argument by being sweet and awesome."

Her face lit up at the same time I chuckled and gave her waist a squeeze. "I know!" she exclaimed, smacking her hands on my chest. "I can come and do your books!" Before I could object, which I was about to do, she kept going. "You're always bitching about all the paperwork that comes with owning The Black Sheep. You hate doing it, so you put it off as long as possible. I'm good with numbers. I'm good with all that stuff, and I actually enjoy doing it. It's the perfect solution!"

Part of me wanted to tell her no, but she sounded so excited at the thought of doing administrative shit. And she wasn't wrong. I fucking *hated* paperwork. So I finally relented. "Fine. You can come by tonight and do my books. Happy?"

She let out a little squeal of delight and clapped. "Very happy."

Damn, this woman was something else. "Good. Now give me a kiss. I need to get to work."

Fiona tilted her face back once more, her expression growing soft and warm. When I broke the kiss, the last thing I wanted to do was leave her, but if I wanted to keep my bar in the black and provide for my woman, I had no choice.

"To Jupiter and back again, baby."

"Around the world and back again, Deacon."

CHAPTER TWENTY-TWO

FIONA

IT WAS the night of the Lockharts' Christmas Eve party, and I was a nervous wreck. It was mine and Deacon's first time as a couple in front of all our friends and family. Sure, they already knew and said they were happy for us, but this felt different.

For the past few weeks, it had been like Deacon and I were living in our own personal little bubble where nothing from the outside could eek in and infect our private world. It was irrational, but I felt like attending this party together was a huge deal, like it was my time to prove that I really did deserve him after everything I'd put him through.

I spun in a half circle to try and see what the dress I was wearing looked like from behind. "Is this dress too much? It's too much, isn't it? Why the hell did I pick red? I should've known better. Redheads don't wear red!"

What the hell had I been thinking? Not only was the dress red, but it was covered in sequins. The neckline dipped in a V that revealed more than a bit of cleavage, and the V at the back was even deeper, making it impossible to wear a bra. The hemline barely hit mid-thigh, making me wonder how I'd be able to sit without flashing my goods to the entire room. The black, round-toed platform Louboutin stilettos on my feet added several inches to my frame. I looked like a club chick who was trying way too damn hard.

"Jesus Christ, Fee. I've told you a million times already that you look gorgeous. I feel like I've been talking to my damn self."

I whipped around to where Deacon stood propped in the bathroom doorway and shot him a glare. "You aren't being a very supportive boyfriend right now."

Uncrossing his arms to throw them wide, he asked exasperatedly, "How many different times do I have to tell you that you look hot?"

"At least three more," I snapped.

He rolled his eyes and let out an annoyed sigh. "You've been bitching about that dress for twenty minutes now. We're already late, baby. Either change or get your sexy ass in my car."

I shot daggers at him. "You're a pain in my ass."

Deacon gave me that cocky half smirk. "Says the woman who's already made us twenty minutes late."

"Fine!" I relented with a frustrated huff, and started stomping out of the bathroom. When he didn't immediately move out of my way, I stopped and crossed my arms over my chest. "*Excuse* me," I snarked. "Are you going to let me by so we can go or not?"

His smirk remained in place. "As soon as you give me a kiss. You know how much I love it when you get all fiery."

Pretending to still be annoyed to mask the fact that I was a little bit turned on, I gave my head a frustrated shake before tipping it back so his lips could reach mine. The kiss was quick, but no less effective.

"Now we can go," he stated after making my knees wobble.

"OH MY GOODNESS! Look how pretty that dress is!"

The moment Deacon and I walked in, his parents had descended.

Cybil gripped my upper arms and gave me an overly excited shake, her exuberance so great my teeth clacked together. I bit back my wince and discreetly extracted myself from her hold with a smile.

"Thanks, Cybil." I leaned in and kissed her cheek. "You look beautiful yourself, as usual."

"Oh, well." She waved me off with a bashful blush. "You're too kind. And look at you!" she declared loudly to Deacon. "My boy cleans up so well!" Cybil grabbed him by the cheeks and yanked him down to plant a kiss on one. "So handsome," she continued. "I've always loved you in a suit."

She wasn't wrong about that. My man looked *hot*. When he'd walked into the bathroom earlier while I was applying my makeup, I'd almost stabbed myself in the eye with my mascara wand. Deacon's typical style was faded jeans and a T-shirt, or faded jeans and a button-down with the cuffs rolled up, and a pair of boots.

I nearly drooled on myself at the sight of him in a black suit and charcoal shirt with black pinstripes. He skipped the tie, but even without it the outcome was still *dayum*!

"Mom, for fuck's sake," Deacon grunted in the typical annoyance you'd see from a son when it came to his mother's affections.

"Language, Deac!" she hissed.

"Well can you blame the boy?" Deacon's father, Nolan, chided. "You're treating him like he's still twelve." He placed his hands on her shoulders and pulled her back before going in himself. "Hey, son."

"Dad," Deacon greeted. They gave each other the man version of a hug with one-arm back smacks.

They disengaged and Nolan moved to me. "Fiona, darling. Welcome."

After I returned Nolan's hug, Deacon wrapped his arm around my waist and pulled me backward into him.

"Oh, Nolan. Don't they look so great together?"

I stifled a laugh as Nolan discreetly rolled his eyes behind his wife's back. "Yes, sweetheart, they look good. Now can we please let them into the house, or do you intend to spent the entire party in the entryway?"

A big grin stretched across my face as I looked up at Deacon. He quickly glanced at the ceiling as if he were searching for patience before leading me into the house where the party was currently underway.

The instant we walking into the sprawling family room where all the partygoers were gathered, my parents saw us and swooped in.

"Hey, Mom and Dad."

"Oh my goodness gracious! Calvin, just look at them." My mother, Evelyn, exclaimed, and sweet Mother Mary, it looked like her eyes were glassy with unshed tears of happiness. "They're so lovely."

If Cybil Lockhart seemed dramatic, Evelyn Prentice topped her by at least ten percent.

My father looked just as damn happy as Mom did. I'd gotten my red hair and pale complexion from my dad, so it was obvious to me that the pink in his cheeks was due to excitement.

Dad had always been slight, thin, and short at only five-foot-eight inches. Adding the red hair that had been falling out for as long as I could remember and the paper-white skin was a terrible combination. All my life I'd heard people question what my tall, lithe mother—who just so happened to look like a woman who belonged on the runway modeling for Prentice Fashion's designs—saw in such a plain, nerdy-looking man as my father. I never had to question it. He'd treated her like a queen, giving her whatever her heart desired, but at the same time, he wasn't weak. He had a backbone and had never been afraid to stand up for himself if he felt he was being taken advantage of. Dad didn't spoil my mom because he was scared of losing her. He spoiled her because he knew she was worth it. And she'd paid back that admiration with her own ten times over.

"Yes, Evelyn, dear. Absolutely lovely."

"Dear God," I muttered, glancing back up to find Deacon biting his lip to keep from laughing. "Let's just make a run for it. I can totally run in these shoes, I promise. And if I trip, you can just throw me over your shoulder and keep going. You're strong enough."

A snort-laugh vibrated from his chest, and he lowered his head to whisper in my ear. "Just breathe, baby. No need to freak out."

"No need? Seriously?" I whisper-yelled. "My mom's about to cry out of sheer joy, which means *your* mom will join right in. And from the looks of Dad, he won't be too far behind. I haven't seen our moms this giddy since they got drunk on champagne while watching the royal wedding. Do you really want a repeat of *that* event? 'Cause it's coming. I promise you that."

No one wanted to see that again. You'd have thought the two of them had close, personal friendships with Kate and Prince William with how they'd behaved.

Deacon's lips pressed against mine in a quick kiss. "Breathe," he repeated quietly against my lips. "I love you."

I scowled as best I could, considering we were still lip to lip. "I love you too."

A loud squeal shattered our moment. When I turned my head, Mom was watching us. She looked like she was about to explode and splatter her joy all over the room. "Calvin, did you hear that? They said 'I love you.' Oh, this is so wonderful. *So wonderful!*"

My laser-like gaze jerked back to Deacon and I mouthed, "I told you so."

Mom reached forward and yanked me into a hug so tight my ribs creaked. "I'm so happy for you! Best friends as children, now in love," Mom cried. "Aren't you so happy for them, Calvin?"

"So happy," Dad answered, still beaming.

Someone kill me.

Something from the corner of my eye caught my attention, and I glanced to the side just as Deacon began slinking backward, like he was trying to make an escape *without me.*

That shady son of a bitch!

"You know what, Mom? I think Deacon would like a hug too."

Deacon's face fell at being busted. A shit-eating grin stretched across my lips at his severe frown. He was about to abandon me to save himself. *Screw that.*

"Of course, of course!" Mom let me go and wrapped her arms around Deacon's neck. Even with as tall as she was, Deacon still towered over her, so he was forced to bend deep at her awkward hold.

"Honey." Dad's soft-spoken word called my attention away from my mom and boyfriend. Dad was grinning at me as he looped an arm across my shoulders. I rested against his side as he continued speaking quietly. "Are you happy?"

I returned his gentle smile and answered honestly. "Blissfully."

His chest heaved with a deep inhale. A look of relieved contentment slipped across his face. "Good. That's really good, my sweet girl."

Mom had finally released Deacon from her death grip but

hadn't let him go completely. When his gaze finally met mine, he must have seen something in my expression he liked because his face went all warm and soft. It was a fantastic look. It was a look of love. It was the exact same look my father wore every time he looked at my mom, the very look I'd always dreamed of getting from a man.

"Fee!" Daphne's voice broke through my euphoric fog. She and Sophia stopped beside me. "Damn, girl." Sophia whistled. "That dress is fabulous."

Deacon caught my attention once more and mouthed, "I told you so," just like I had minutes before.

Pain in the ass.

But I loved him anyway.

CHAPTER TWENTY-THREE

DEACON

"SHE'S LESS than thirty feet away, brother. She isn't going anywhere. You don't have to watch her like she's about to evaporate into thin air."

I flipped Grayson off with one hand and used the other to lift my beer to my lips. He, Dominic, and Caleb all laughed. I was going to need a lot more than beer if I was going to make it out of my folks' house without my head exploding. It had already been two hours, and I could feel the twitch in my left eyelid. There was a reason why I hadn't attended many of these events in the past few years, and it wasn't only because I was trying to avoid Fiona. I loved my family and friends, but fuck me, sometimes they drove me insane.

"I'm not worried that she's going to evaporate. I just like watching her ass."

"Hmm," Dominic hummed. "She does have a pretty... watchable ass."

If I hadn't already known Dom was so enamored with Sophia, I might have broken his nose. Lucky for him, I knew he was just giving me shit like the rest of the guys, so his nose was safe. For the time being.

"I can't fault him for that," Caleb chimed in. "I can't keep my eyes off Daph's ass. And it's only gotten better since she had Evie." He looked to where Fiona was gathered around the sofa with the rest of the girls. Lola was camped out on the couch, tricked out in a fancy dress and heels, but unable to get up and walk around for more than a few minutes per doctor's orders. Caleb's eyes did a full-body scan of Daphne. "Damn, my wife's got it going on."

"They all have it going on," Grayson grumbled. "Unfortunately the four of them together is a whole lot of batshit crazy."

I couldn't help but laugh at how right he was.

"Tell me about it," Caleb added. "Remember when Fiona was so sweet and unassuming? Those three totally corrupted her."

Dominic snorted. "I've known those girls all their lives. If there's one thing they're good at, it's corrupting the innocent."

Shaking my head, I turned to the guys and spoke up. "Nah, that wasn't their fault. Fiona's always had that fiery streak in her. She's just kept it buried deep beneath the surface. Those women just made her comfortable enough to let it come out."

And for that I'd be eternally grateful. That fiery side had only ever come out with me in the past, and it was sexy as fuck. I thanked Christ every day that she'd found friends she was comfortable enough with to let it all hang out like that. That meant I got to reap the benefits every time she lit up.

"Really?" The surprise in Grayson's voice as he asked that made me roar with pleasure inside. She'd never given him that. That fire was mine. It had only ever been mine.

"Son, you got a minute?" All heads turned toward my father, who'd just joined our little huddle. At first I thought he'd been talking to Grayson—it wasn't uncommon for those two to go off to discuss business—but when I saw his focus on me, my skin started to prickle for some reason.

"Uh, yeah. Sure."

"My office. I promise it'll only take a second, and then you can get back to the party."

Gray's expression told me he was just as clueless as to what Dad wanted to talk about as I was. But whatever it was, I couldn't imagine it'd be good. My father asking to talk in private had never ended well for me in the past. It usually led to us fighting—usually about his disappointment in my life choices and shit like that. And that fight would typically lead to us not talking until my mother had enough and ripped us both new assholes or burst into tears while laying the guilt on nice and thick.

Dad's office smelled the same as it had when I was growing up, like leather and old books. The wood-paneled walls and heavy oak furniture created a warmth in the room that was at total conflict with the feeling in my sinking gut.

"So, what's up?" I asked as soon as the door closed behind us.

Dad walked behind his desk, pointing to one of the over-sized leather chairs across from it. "Have a seat."

I stayed on guard as I slowly sat, resting my elbows on the arms of the chair, trying to look as comfortable as possible even though I didn't feel that way. "This is starting to feel like a business meeting, Dad."

"How serious are you about Fiona?"

My back shot straight. "Excuse me?"

He held his hands up in surrender. "I only ask because... well, I know your reputation, son. You aren't exactly known for settling down. And this is Fee. She's practically family. I just don't want to see you—"

"Are you kidding me?" I snarled, moving to the edge of my seat. "Did you really just say that? Christ, Dad. I *know* it's Fee. I know better than *any* of you."

"Son, I mean no offense—"

"Then don't ask me shit like that." I ran a hand through my hair in frustration. "Jesus, Dad. You really think I'd do something like that? To *her*?"

"Look. I'm sorry. I just...." He shook his head. "I'm sorry."

I tried my best to let go of the anger that was starting to simmer in my veins. Resting my hands on the chair arms, I began to push up. "Okay, well, is that all you wanted?"

"Actually, no." Dad waved me back down before I'd even had a chance to fully rise. I sat back down, letting out a frustrated breath. "Now that I know where you stand with Fiona, I thought that now would be a good time to revisit the subject of you coming to work at Bandwidth."

Collapsing back, I let out a bark of humorless laughter. That simmer turned into a full boil. "Dad. Don't," I said in a low warning tone. This wasn't the first time he'd tried having this conversation with me. But he hadn't attempted in years. I thought he'd finally gotten past his bullshit of thinking The Black Sheep was just a childish phase. Guess I was wrong. "We aren't doing this." I stood to leave as he kept talking.

"For God's sake, Deacon. You're a grown man entering into a serious relationship with a woman who's important to the entire family. It's time to stop playing around with that bar of yours and grow up."

I jerked to a stop and spun back around. "Playing around? Fucking seriously? Is that what you think I'm doing?"

Dad shot up and threw his arms wide. "Well what the hell would you call it? You're a Lockhart, Deacon! You're supposed to work in the family business. You should be working alongside your brother and me. I'm going to retire. Grayson'll take over, and you should be the second in command."

"Christ, Dad, I'm not Grayson!" I shouted, losing hold on my calm completely. "When are you finally going to fucking accept that? You got your golden boy already. You don't need another one."

"It has nothing to do with that! But you need a career where you can take care of a family. You really think you can support yourself, Fiona, and the children you might have one day with that *bar*?"

"Newsflash, Dad, it's not the fucking fifties anymore. Fiona has a job all of her own. She doesn't need me to take care of her. But even if she did, that *bar* you think is nothing but a joke is flush. I've been well into the black the past six years. If, and that's a big goddamn *if*, Fiona wanted to quit her job and pop out a shitload of kids, I'd be more than capable of taking care of all of them for a good long while."

His face grew red as he continued to argue. "You belong with your family. When are you going to get over this... this need of yours to rebel against me?"

The door shot open and Grayson came rushing through, quickly shutting it behind him. "What the hell's going on in here? I could hear you shouting from down the hall."

My stomach hit the floor. It felt like I'd just taken a wrecking ball to the chest. Ignoring my brother, I stared directly into my father's eyes. "Wow," I hissed sarcastically. "So glad to know my own father's got such a high opinion of me."

"Deacon—"

"Hate to break it to you, but my bar has not one fucking thing to do with you. It wasn't an act of rebellion, or a way to stick it to you."

"Jesus Christ, Dad. Did you really say that to him?" Grayson asked in bewilderment.

"Gray, just stay out of it," our father warned.

"Dad, this isn't the time or the place—" my brother pushed, but I spoke over him.

"This conversation is over. For good. And just so you know,

me opening The Black Sheep had absolutely *nothing* to do with you. If you'd ever paid attention to a single goddamn word I said to you, you'd know I opened that bar because it was what I always wanted to do. That was my dream, not being a pencil pusher. If you knew me, you'd know that sitting behind a desk for the rest of my life would be a nightmare. Despite what you think of me, I did what I did because it made me happy. Not that you'd give a shit."

I turned and started for the door again. Just as I reached for the doorknob, Grayson's hand landed on my shoulder.

"Wait. Just wait, Deac. Let's just talk all this out. We can fix this."

"Nothing to fix, brother. He wants a carbon copy of his perfect son, and that's just not something I can do. I have to go."

I was officially over this party. I just hoped I could get Fiona out without making a scene.

CHAPTER TWENTY-FOUR

FIONA

I DIDN'T HAVE the first clue what was going on with Deacon, but the more time that passed, the more I started to worry. Something wasn't right. However, every time I tried to talk to him about it, he shut down on me.

He'd been acting strange since practically dragging me out of his parents' party. Christmas Day, he'd acted normal, but that was exactly what it was—an act. As the week progressed and my concern grew, I started asking what was going on. Deacon insisted that there was nothing bothering him, but I could tell when he was lying just as well as he could with me. I let the subject drop for New Year's Eve, putting on an act of my own while we celebrated at the bar with Sophia, Daphne, Dominic, and Caleb.

Lola couldn't attend thanks to her mandated bed rest, so she and Grayson celebrated alone at their house.

Other than worrying, I'd spent the majority of my vacation from Prentice Fashion helping out at Deacon's bar, updating his accounting and scheduling systems so they ran more efficiently. Shockingly enough, I really enjoyed it—not because I liked bookkeeping, but because I felt like I was a part of something bigger, more important. Working at The Black Sheep alongside Deacon made me feel like I was finally doing what I was *meant* to be doing. I was working with my man, helping him build and nurture his dream. Just like my mom had done with my father.

It was exactly where I wanted to be. And because of that, I was kind of dreading the offices opening in two days. It meant I'd be too busy with my own work to go to The Black Sheep and help out.

For the time being, I decided to push that thought to the back of my mind and live in the now. And in the "now" I'd just been struck with a genius idea that I couldn't wait to share with Deacon. Jumping up from the desk I'd been sitting at in Deacon's cramped, messy office, I rushed down the hall and into the main part of the bar.

I spotted Deacon sling drinks behind the bar and made my way to him. "Deac, honey. You got a minute?"

He gave me the universal sign for *one second*, then drained the contents of the silver shaker into a tumbler before topping it with an orange slice. Once finished, he came my way and leaned in close to me. "You bored out of your mind and want to call it quits yet?" he asked, a crooked smirk on his face.

I returned the grin, trailing a finger along the back of Deacon's hand. "Not at all. I actually love it. And I'm done for tonight, but that's not what I want to talk to you about."

Deacon stood and came around to me, taking my hand in his. "Let's go in the back where it's quieter."

I let him lead me back to the office, following eagerly as the idea swimming around in my head made me more and more excited the longer I thought about it. He pulled me into the office and shut the door, but before I could get a word out, Deacon pinned me against the wall and started laying wet, toe-curling kisses down my neck.

"Mm, Deacon. Deac. Wait." I laughed, suddenly breathless

and wobbly-legged as he pulled back. "You know I'm always down for an office quickie, but I *really* want to talk to you about something first. Then we can get back to that," I added with a wink.

That sexy grin returned to his face and he lifted his head, but he didn't move away. "All right, shoot."

Resting my hands on his chest, I started exuberantly, "Okay, so I had a brilliant idea while I was going through the finances. The Black Sheep is doing well, *really* well actually, but I think I've come up with an idea to make it even more profitable."

Deacon's smile fell and his expression went blank, but I was too far gone in my story to really notice. "I was thinking, what if you had an open mic night? You've got more than enough space to put a stage in. All it would take is reorganizing the tables, and—"

"Whoa, whoa. Just hold on for a second." Deacon's hands went up to stop me as he took a step back. "Fee, this place isn't a tacky karaoke bar."

"No, of course not. I'm not talking about a karaoke bar. The Black Sheep is too classy to do something like that. An open mic night is completely different. And this is the perfect place for it. Just think about it, Deac. Seattle has some of the most talented unsigned bands in the country. You could have them sign up, then come in during off hours to audition so you could be certain they were good before giving them a spot. You've got plenty of money to cover the upfront cost of any construction needed to put in the stage and lighting and all that stuff. And the acoustics in this place are *amazing*.

"Once this gets off the ground, I was thinking we could try to expand to bigger acts. Not full-blown concerts, but maybe private shows. Have you heard of Civil Corruption? They're one of the most popular bands on the planet. And they're local, Deac! If they agreed to do a small show, we could sell tickets and close the doors to the public for events like that. The price of the tickets and implementing a two-drink minimum would more than cover the cost of closing down to the public and losing on potential sales. Plus it would take the Black Sheep's reputation to the next level. Just imagine how much you could make with only a few private concerts a year. The bar would explode! The Black Sheep would be *the* go-to place for fantastic live music!" I ended on a gleeful squeal.

It wasn't until I was finished speaking that I noticed Deacon's stony demeanor. He didn't seem nearly as excited as I was. "What's the matter?"

"What's the matter?" Deacon mimicked sarcastically.

My head jerked back while my stomach twisted into a violent knot of tension. I was dumbfounded by his reaction. "Are you... I'm sorry, are you mad at me?"

He jerked his hands through his hair as he started pacing. Deacon's voice dripped with bitterness when he spoke. "Mad? Why would I be mad? I mean, it's not like I have a right to be upset that my girlfriend thinks my bar's a goddamn joke, right?"

The hostility coming off him in waves crashed into me so hard that I had to take a step back. "What?" I whispered in utter disbelief.

Deacon stopped and skewered me with a vicious look. "That's what you're saying, right? You're obviously not happy with the amount coming in already. What, worried you'll be hitching yourself to a broke loser who can't take care of his family if you stick with me?"

"Of course not!" I cried as I desperately tried to keep up with the conversation so I could hopefully figure out what the hell was going on. "What are you talking about?"

"I'm talking about the fact that you think I'm a failure."

"I do not!" I shouted, confusion mixing with anger and anxiety, a very toxic combination. "I never said that! I love this bar. I just want to help you succeed. They were only ideas, Deacon."

"Christ, you sound just like my father."

Tears started to sting my nose and burn the backs of my eyes as I shouted, "*What?*"

"Yeah." A bark of brittle, humorless laughter burst from his throat. "The old man thinks everything I've tried to build here is nothing more than a childish act of rebellion that's doomed for failure. And apparently so do you."

My hands went up, arms extended in front of me. "Wait, just... hold on a second. That's not true. I don't think you're going to fail. I've *never* thought you'd fail at this. I don't know what you're talking about with your dad, but that's not how I feel at all. Is that what's been bugging you all week? Did you and he get in a fight or something?"

"I don't want to talk about it."

Was he kidding? "I'm sorry, but you're going to have to. Something happened between you and your dad, and whatever it was, you're taking your anger out on me. I'm not going to be your punching bag, Deac. If something's upset you, I want you to talk to me about it."

He clasped his fingers together at the back of his neck as he looked up at the ceiling. I watched for several seconds as his chest rose and fell with deep breaths. The whole time I watched on silently, dread coiled in the pit of my stomach.

Finally, Deacon dropped his arms and blew out a loud exhale while shifting his gaze to his feet. "Look, I'm sorry. I just... I have a lot of shit on my mind right now, and I need to get it straight on my own. Maybe it would be best if you stayed at your house tonight."

My heart splintered into a thousand pieces and crashed to the floor. "I—what? No. No, I'm not doing that."

"Jesus, Fee," he barked, making me jump. "Can you just give me some space. I need time to think."

I wasn't going to cry. I *refused* to break down and fucking cry. "If I recall correctly, the last time I told you I needed some time to think, you told me I could have it as long as I did it *with you*." *Goddamn it*, my voice cracked on those last two words, and I had to sniff against the threatening tears.

Deacon finally looked up, his jaw ticking as he took in my pale, stricken face. "That doesn't work for me. Please try and understand—"

"Understand?" I snapped. "What exactly is it that you want me to understand, Deacon? That you're a hypocrite who refuses to make the same compromises you demand of me? Or is it that you want me to understand why you're putting bullshit words in my mouth and picking a fight for reasons totally unknown to me? Or maybe you want me to understand that when something's bothering you, like whatever you've been dealing with for the past freaking *week*, you'll shut me out instead of confiding in me."

"Fee—"

"Sorry to break it to you, Deac, but *that's* not going to work for *me*. You got pissed and stormed into my office when I tried doing the same thing. I'll be damned if I let you push me away."

"Goddamn it, Fiona," he snarled.

"What's going on with you and your dad?"

"I'm not doing this with you."

I repeated, "What's going on with you and your dad?"

"I don't have time for this shit. I've got a bar full of people out there."

With that, I snapped and shouted, *"What's going on with you and your dad?"*

"He wants me to be just like Grayson!" he yelled in return, stunning me into silence. "He's always wanted me to be just like

Grayson. His perfect son. The goddamn golden boy. I've never been good enough, and as far as he's concerned, my bar's nothing more than a fucking joke."

The fury and pain in his voice hit me like a sledgehammer, forcing me to take a step back. "Deacon," I whispered brokenly. "Honey, your dad loves you. He's proud of—"

"Really?" he interrupted. "Is that why he pulled me into his office during the party and told me it was time to grow up and join him and Grayson at Bandwidth? Is that why he claimed that this place, everything I've worked my ass off to build, was nothing more than an act of rebellion?"

"That...." I was in total shock. "He said that?"

"I might have paraphrased, but that sums it up, yeah," he answered, his expression like thunder.

I shook my head and looked away, unable to comprehend the Nolan Lockhart I knew speaking so callously to his own son. "I can't believe that."

"Hard for you to believe that the wonderful Nolan and Grayson aren't as perfect as you expected, huh?" he chided, storming past me to the door.

"Deacon, wait. Please—"

"Tell you what. You take that time to wrap your head around the truth. I need to get back to work. I'll call you tomorrow."

Then he stormed out, leaving me reeling and heartbroken.

CHAPTER TWENTY-FIVE

I WAS AN ASSHOLE.

And a coward.

I'd taken all my issues with my own family out on Fiona, and she hadn't deserved any of it. My head was completely fucked up. My father's words twisted in my mind until I convinced myself that I wasn't good enough for a woman like Fee. That thought was what kept me from reaching out to her, even though I knew, deep in my gut, that it was the right thing to do.

That was why I was currently holed up in my house, alone and miserable, with nothing but a bottle of Jack for company.

I was a quarter of a way through when someone started pounding on my front door. Knowing Fee wasn't strong enough to nearly beat my door down, I chose to ignore the persistent knocking—that was, until my brother's loud, booming voice joined in.

"Deac, open up. I know you're in there! Your car's in the driveway!"

"Son of a bitch," I grumbled under my breath as I pushed up from the couch and shuffled toward the door.

"Deacon!"

"Jesus, I'm coming!" I boomed in return to get him to stop his hammering. As soon as I got the door open Grayson shoved his way inside. "Sure, yeah. Come on in," I huffed. "After all, I love uninvited company."

He stormed into the living room and came to a sudden stop, spinning around to take in the trash that had been piling up the past two days. Empty pizza boxes and beer bottles were littered around the coffee table and floor, day-old Chinese food containers scattered on the side table.

"Christ, Deac. This place is a pit. And what's that smell?" His face scrunched up in disgust after he sniffed, moving closer to me. "Good God," he uttered, jerking back. "When the hell was the last time you showered? You're fucking ripe."

Dipping my head, I gave my underarm a sniff, wincing at the stench. "I've been off work. Excuse me for wanting to spend the past couple days relaxing."

Gray spotted the Jack Daniels. "Yeah? Is that also your excuse for downing hard liquor before three in the afternoon on a Wednesday?"

I flopped back down on the couch, my head at one end, feet on the other, and turned back to the TV. "Yup. And you're interrupting my relaxation, so do me a favor and spit out why you're here so you can go and let me get back to it."

He smacked my feet off the couch, forcing me to sit up to look at him. "I'm here, asshole, because you're fucking up. Daphne talked to Fiona yesterday. She wouldn't go into detail with what was happening, but she admitted that you two got in a fight, and now you're totally shutting her out. That means Daphne got upset and called Sophia, who then called Lola, and now they're *all* upset. And you might not have experienced that yet, but the full force of those women all pissed off at the same time has detrimental outcomes for the men in their lives. Which means now *I'm* upset, because I'm not a big fan of my wife giving me the fucking silent treatment and kicking me out of our bedroom at night to sleep on the couch because, and this is a direct quote, 'I share DNA with a dickhead!' So tell me, little brother, what the hell is going on with you?"

I rested my elbows on my knees and dropped my head into my hands, digging the heels of my palms into my eye sockets. "I'm an asshole," I finally admitted on a groan. "God, Gray, I'm such a fucking asshole."

He sat on the coffee table across from me and started talking. "Look, I know you and I have had our issues in the past. To be honest, I'm not even completely sure why we haven't been closer until recently, but you're my brother, Deac. Whatever's going on with you, I'm here."

I'd spent my childhood resenting Grayson because I felt my dad had him on a pedestal I'd never be able to climb. Then our adult life was tarnished because of my animosity over him and Fiona. I never talked about it with anyone, but there was a part of me that wanted to hate my brother for always having it all. He was the honor student, the class president, the most popular guy in school. And because I'd always blamed him on some level, I'd spent my life striving to go in the opposite direction.

The sad truth was I'd let the rift between us last far too long, allowing it to bleed into every aspect of my life. Looking up at him, I finally opened up and admitted to all the childish bullshit I'd let stand between me and him all our lives.

"You know, Dad used to ride my ass growing up. About grades, getting into fights, the girls I hung out with, anything he thought I was doing wrong. He was always on my case. 'Why can't you be more like Grayson?' 'Grayson has a 4.0 GPA. If you'd apply yourself like your brother, you could do just as well.' 'Why can't you just meet a nice girl and settle down like Grayson has with Fiona?' It was always a fucking comparison.

No matter what I did, it was never as good as how you'd have done it, so eventually I just stopped trying."

Grayson's eye widened in shock. "Shit, Deacon. I had no idea."

"I know. I mean, how could you? It wasn't like I told you about any of it. Honestly, I don't even know if Dad realized what he was doing. It just got to the point where eventually, I was done. Then you started dating Fee."

Blowing out a sigh, he combed his fingers through his hair while looking off to the side. "I didn't know about that, man. I swear. I had no idea you had feelings for her. I just thought you guys were friends. I never would have—"

I held my hand up to stop him. "I know. I should've said something. That's on me. Unfortunately, it took me too damn long to realize that. I blamed you for being the good son, and I blamed you for taking Fee from me, but the truth was you didn't do anything wrong."

"If you'd just talked to me about Dad, maybe I could've said something, and I don't know... gotten him to back off or something."

A self-deprecating chuckle worked its way past my lips. "There were a lot of things I should've talked to you about. Hindsight's a real bitch sometimes."

"So tell me what happened with Fee."

Just thinking about it made my chest squeeze so tight that it hurt to breathe. I'd fucked up, but all I could do was pray the damage wasn't irreparable. My stomach twisted and roiled at the thought of losing her. The anxiety settled in my gut like rancid food.

"I let the fight with Dad at the party get to me. I stewed on it instead of talking to her, and eventually just blew up."

"Wow. That's so unlike you," Grayson chided sardonically.

Flipping him off, I continued, "She had an idea for the bar

that she was really excited about, and I twisted it up, turning it into something bad. I accused her of thinking I was a failure just like Dad."

"Jesus," he hissed. "You screwed up worse than I thought. God, you're an idiot!"

"No need to be a prick about it. I feel bad enough as it is. I'm well aware of my tendency to overreact when I'm pissed off."

He stood from the coffee table and crossed his arms, staring me down in that condescending way only older brothers could pull off. "Okay, so the question now is what are you going to do about it? It's been two days, Deac. That's one day and twenty-three hours too long."

I scrubbed at my face, frustration over my behavior and bull-shit pride setting in. "I don't know."

"Well you need to come up with something!"

"You think I don't know that?" I snapped back. "I know! I just need to figure out what to do, okay?"

Grayson watched me closely, like a specimen beneath a microscope. "How about you shower while you think?" he suggested sarcastically. "You smell like hot garbage."

Glaring, I asked, "You taking all your bossiness out on me because your wife's the one with the balls in your household?"

His shit-eating grin told me my insult didn't affect him in the slightest. "Keep being a pain in the ass and I'll make a few calls. I'm pretty sure the girls would be more than willing to load up and come over to rip you a new asshole for hurting their friend's feelings."

The threat actually made me shiver. Those three were a force to be reckoned with on a good day. I figured they'd be more than happy to rip me more than a new asshole. I'd be lucky if I still had my manhood by the time they were done with me.

Grunting several choice words, and calling him every name

I could come up with, I stood and headed for the bathroom to do as suggested, because I knew for a fact that he wasn't bluffing.

I CAME out of the bathroom in a pair of clean gray sweatpants and a navy T-shirt while scrubbing at my damp hair with a towel.

"There, happy now?" I asked, stopping at my kitchen counter and holding my arms out to show my new level of cleanliness.

Grayson slid a mug of fresh coffee my way. "It's an improvement to the stench coming off you when I first arrived, that's for damn sure."

"What's the coffee for?" I asked, even as I lifted the mug to my lips and took an invigorating drink. "It's the middle of the day."

Gray rested his palms on the countertop, his arms stretched wide as he leaned in. "It's to sober your ass up. You've got some groveling to do later today. But first." He lifted a hand and waved in the direction of my living room. "Clean this cesspool you call a house. Just in case you somehow manage to get her to hear you out, you don't want to bring her back to this pit."

I was starting to regret healing that rift between my brother and me. He was quickly becoming a serious pain in my ass.

It seemed that was a hereditary trait for the Lockhart men.

CHAPTER TWENTY-SIX

FIONA

MY JOB SUCKED.

Okay, so maybe it wasn't my job that sucked so much as my mood, but because of that, I'd hated everything and everyone the past two days.

I took my shitty attitude out on anyone who crossed my path. Hell, my poor assistant, Sarah, was walking around on eggshells after I bit her head off the day before because the coffee she'd brought me wasn't hot enough. The truth was the coffee was just fine, but I was in the mood to snap, so I snapped.

It was like I was PMSing times a thousand, and no one was safe.

Sometimes being at the boss level was a bitch. If I didn't have so much responsibility at the company, I would've called in sick these past couple of days. Unfortunately that wasn't an option. I still had at least three hours' worth of work to finish before I could leave for the evening.

Turning my attention from my computer screen, I glanced at the cell phone sitting facedown next to my keyboard. Like I had a gazillion times in the past forty-eight hours, I picked it up, turned it over, scrolled to my text thread with Deacon, and sighed heavily at what I already knew I'd find—nothing.

With a huff, I blacked the screen once more and dropped it back on my desk. My heart ached at the same time that anger started simmering in my veins. That prideful, stubborn jerk hadn't reached out to me once since that fight in the back of The Black Sheep, and the more time that passed without hearing from him, the more pissed off I got. I'd screwed up countless times, but I always owned up to my mistakes and worked my ass off to apologize. He owed me the same.

Two quick knocks sounded, followed by Todd peeking his head around my partially open office door, saying, "Knock, knock." God, I hated that. If a person was already knocking, then why the hell did they feel the need to *say* it as well? "How're you doing?"

Barely able to restrain myself from rolling my eyes, I looked back at my computer as I spoke flatly. "Everything's fine, Todd. Do you need something?"

He stepped all the way inside my office, uninvited, and closed the door behind him. "I don't mean to be intrusive, but I'm concerned about you. You haven't been yourself since we got back from the holidays. Is everything all right?"

"Like I said," I started, speaking to my monitor, "everything is fine."

I sensed Todd moving closer to me and shifted my attention from the computer to him just as the stench of his cologne hit me. "Look. I know we don't know each other that well, but I've always considered you a friend, Fee. I care about you, and it's obvious there's something bothering you. Talk to me. I'm here to help."

The stress of the past few days settled in my stomach like week-old pizza, and I'd finally reached my breaking point. "Deacon and I are having some... issues," I admitted, unable to keep the words from flowing. It wasn't Todd's concern that had me blurting something so personal. It was just that I'd been teetering on the edge for two days, and finally slipped and fell over. It was as if I had no control over what I was saying and to whom.

"That's tough. I'm so sorry."

His sincerity, or lack thereof, didn't even register. It was like the floodgates had been opened and I just couldn't stop. "We got into a fight a few nights ago and haven't talked since."

"He hasn't called you? Are you serious?"

"I know!" I shouted, throwing my arms up. "What's the deal with guys not calling when they screw up? I mean, *I'm* not going to make the first move! It's not my place. *He's* the one who messed up."

He moved around my desk, coming to a stop behind my chair, placing his hands on my shoulders and massaging gently as he said, "You're absolutely right. You aren't a doormat. You shouldn't be the one to back down. God, honey. I'm so sorry." The unwanted familiarity of his caress, and the way he called me *honey*, as if I were more to him than just a work colleague, snapped me back into reality and sent an unpleasant shiver down my spine. I couldn't believe I had just let all of that out. It was as if I'd been having an out-of-body experience.

I shot up and put several feet of distance between us. "I'm sorry. I shouldn't have just said all of that. It was unprofessional and inappropriate. Just...." I waved my hands in front of me. "Just forget it."

"You have nothing to apologize for. It's obvious all of this has been weighing on your mind, and you needed to get it out."

I shook my head, angry with myself for not only losing my cool, but also losing it in front of Todd, of all people. The guy's boundary issues were bad enough already; I shouldn't have done anything to give him any more ammunition.

The atmosphere of the room had suddenly changed, making me extremely uncomfortable. "No, actually, I don't want to talk about it anymore. No offense."

He held up his hands in surrender. "None taken. I'm just glad that you felt comfortable enough with me to open up."

God, I'm such an idiot. "Look, Todd, I let my emotions get the best of me, that's all this was. Nothing more than that. Now, if you don't mind, I have a lot of work to get done."

He continued to push. "Why don't you let me take you to dinner? I can get you out of here, take your mind off things."

"No, thank you."

"Listen, Fee. Maybe it's not my place to say this, but you deserve so much better than that guy."

"Todd," I clipped warningly. "You're right, it's not your place. At all. And as I've said, this conversation is over."

Closing the distance between us, Todd placed his hands on my hips, causing my entire body to lock up tight. "If you were with me, I'd never ignore you for days at a time."

Professionalism went out the window. "Todd, I'm going to say this one time, and one time only. You don't know me well enough to touch *or* talk to me in such a personal way. We're coworkers, and as coworkers, what you've just done crosses all kinds of professional boundaries."

Despite having laid it out for him in a way that he couldn't possibly misunderstand, Todd smiled, his fingers pressing deeper. "Come on, Fiona. I know you want me. We've been tiptoeing around each other for years. You can't possibly tell me what I feel is one-sided. I know better."

Smacking his hands away from me, I took a big step back. "That's *absolutely* what I'm telling you. There isn't the slightest romantic inclination for you in my mind, and the fact that you could come in here, ignore my first warning, and keep pushing your boss to the point of harassment blows my mind."

Todd's entire demeanor changed, like a switch had been flipped. "Are you serious? I came in here to check on you, and you basically poured your heart out. Talk about leading a guy on."

"Oh my God!" I cried. "Todd, I'm sorry to burst your bubble, but I didn't pour my heart out to lead you on. Call it momentary insanity or whatever you want, but I would've snapped no matter who walked through my door. It had nothing to do with you."

"You've got to be kidding me," he snarled, showing his true colors. I knew they'd be bad. I just had no clue *how* bad until right at that moment. "You know, it's no wonder that loser you were with ghosted you. You're nothing more than a cock-tease."

My back went straight. I lifted my chin and turned my back on him to stomp to the door. "I'll remind you *again* that I'm your superior in this company. I'm willing to chock this episode up to a one-time misunderstanding, but let me make myself perfectly clear. If you ever speak to me or anyone else in this office in that manner again, if you so much as step a *toe* out of line, you'll no longer be employed at Prentice Fashion. Do I make myself perfectly clear?"

His lips curled up in an unpleasant sneer. "Crystal."

"That's good to hear." Grabbing the knob, I yanked the door open and continued, "Now, please leave. And unless it's something directly related to your job here, do not set foot past this door again."

After he left, I walked back to my desk on wobbly legs. The adrenaline pumping through my system left me shaky, and my heart was threatening to burst from my chest. Bracing my hands on the cold surface, I glanced at my computer screen and noticed the time in the top right corner. I had a department meeting in five minutes, which meant I had no time to freak the hell out like I desperately wanted to.

It would have to wait.

I MADE the turn onto my street, dreading the idea of going home to my colorless, sterile house. After spending so much time at Deacon's warm, inviting place, mine felt sad and lonely. If I was being honest, I kind of hated it. There was no life or personality. It was simply a glaring reminder of everything I didn't have.

Daphne had invited me to come over to her and Caleb's place for dinner, thinking that spending some time with their baby would cheer me up, but I politely turned down the offer. I loved all of them, especially Evie, but being around a loving couple and their precious daughter would've only made me feel worse.

My plan was to drink my way through a bottle of wine while binging on whatever Netflix show held my interest, but when I pulled into my driveway, the headlights of my car illuminated Deacon sitting on the top step of my front porch.

My heart started pounding against my ribs at the sight of him, and my breath stuttered as I turned off the car and climbed out. Hooking my purse over my shoulder and wrapping my coat snuggly around me, I slowly started up my front walk and stopped just shy of the first step.

"What are you doing here?" I asked, crossing my arms defensively.

I wasn't sure whether or not he was ready to apologize, but if that was the case, I wasn't going to make it easy on him. That jackass had his work cut out for him.

CHAPTER TWENTY-SEVEN

DEACON

I PUSHED TO STANDING, taking one step down toward Fiona, the need to touch her driving me mad. "Sorry to just show up. I tried calling you."

Reaching up with one hand, she rubbed at the space between her eyebrows with two fingers, like the weight of her stress was starting to affect her physically. I could understand that all too well. "I lost my phone back at the office. It's probably in the conference room or something."

"Oh, well...." I shrugged with discomfort. "I guess that's why you didn't answer or return any of my texts."

Fiona started shifting on her feet, the cold obviously getting to her. The way her nose and cheeks were burning a bright shade of pink made me want to grab her and pull her into my arms in an effort to warm her up.

"Look," she sighed a few seconds later, "I'm not sure why you're here, but I've had a really bad day, and I just want to get inside and crash." Starting up the stairs, she was careful to keep a distance as she went around me.

I spun quickly, desperation thickening my words as I all but begged, "Fiona, please. I'm so sorry. Please, can we just talk?"

Even with her back to me, I could see the defeat in her body as she dropped her head on a deep exhale. After what felt like a miserable eternity, she finally spoke. "Fine. Let's go inside. I'm freezing out here."

Even as I breathed a sigh of relief, in the back of my mind I knew my battle was far from over. Walking into her house, I was hit with a shock. Before we started dating, I'd never made it past her front stoop, seeing as we were barely even friends back then. Since getting together, Fiona had insisted on staying at my house every night, claiming it felt more like a home than hers. And she hadn't been wrong.

The place didn't have a single ounce of Fiona's personality anywhere. It was all undecorated white walls and monochromatic furniture in different shades of beige. It was like walking into the front lobby of a doctor's office, uninspiring and drab. The only thing missing were the two-year-old editions of magazines no one had any interest in reading.

"So," she said, breaking into my thoughts. "What do you want to talk about?" I watched her ass move beneath her skirt as she removed her coat and scarf, hanging them on a hook by the front door. My gaze stayed transfixed as Fiona wandered through the living space and into the less-than-appealing kitchen. It wasn't until she looked back and snapped, "Deacon!" after catching me leering that I lifted my eyes to her face. Even seeing the fury sparking behind her eyes, I couldn't bring myself to feel guilty for checking her out. My hands had been all over that ass, and my mouth had tasted her everywhere just a few days before. I'd fucked up, but until she said otherwise, her body was mine to gawk at.

"You wanted to talk, so either talk or leave so I can go to sleep."

Fuck me. She wasn't going to make this easy. "I screwed up, baby. I never should have piled my shit on you a few days ago. I was an asshole for sending you away like I did, and then I made it worse by going days without making it right. I'm sorry. I'm so fucking sorry, Fee."

After staring silently at me for several seconds, she reached out and pulled the cork from an already open bottle of wine, pouring it into a glass she retrieved from a cabinet. Once finished with that, Fiona went to the fridge, pulled out a beer, and uncapped it, sliding it toward me.

It was only after she was done with our drinks that she spoke again. "We had this conversation when I was the one with my head up my own ass. But I'll give you a refresher, seeing as this time you're the one who was twisting shit up." She took a sip of her wine and placed it on the counter, resting her hands on either side of it before diving in, her tone serious as a heart attack. "We don't shut each other out. We don't play games. We're honest with each other always. If you need to think, you do it *with me*. If you've got something that's weighing on your mind so heavily that you're in a perpetual state of grumpiness, you don't take that out on me. If you don't want to talk right then, that's fine. Say so, but don't push me away while you're stewing over your problems. I'm not your doormat, and I never will be."

Christ, there was that fire again. And damn, if it didn't make me hard as hell.

"I'll give you time to process whatever's bothering you as long as you promise to eventually open up to me. If this is something you can't agree with, then we need to stop this right now, because this is something I can't compromise on any further."

I watched, completely enraptured by her, as I lifted my beer and took a huge gulp to help alleviate the dryness in my throat. "That's a promise I can make." Her entire body sagged in relief. "Anything else?"

At my question, her chin tilted up and she crossed her arms, exuding an air of haughtiness. "Yes, as a matter of fact, there is. Your thinking time has officially expired. I want to know about you and your dad. *Everything*, Deacon."

"Okay."

My immediate compliance shocked her, and her body gave a surprised jolt. "Oh. Okay. Well, that's... good."

However, I had a stipulation of my own before giving *her* what she wanted. "But first I need you to come around here."

Fiona's head tipped in bewilderment. "Why?"

"Because I've needed to kiss you since you climbed out of your car, and I'm done waiting. You want answers, and I'll give you everything you want, just as long as you let me touch you while I'm doing it."

She didn't make me wait, coming as fast as her fuck-me heels would allow. By the time she rounded the white marble counter separating us, she was nearly at a run. I braced just in time for her to launch herself at me, wrapping her arms around my neck in a death grip. I returned the gesture, holding on to her waist and lifting her off her feet.

"I missed you." Her voice was like gravel, emotion making her words thick.

Hearing that was a solid punch to the gut, leaving me breathless. "Missed you too, baby," I replied, my words rough and jagged. "I'm so goddamn sorry."

She pulled back quickly, taking my face in her hands as she scowled up at me. "Never do that again. Ever. If we fight, we go to bed together. Even if we're on separate sides and not talking, I don't care."

Wrapping my fingers around her wrists, I removed her hands from my cheeks and leaned in closer. "Never again. I swear. I've been fucking miserable without you."

Her eyes grew glassy and bright with unshed tears. "Me too."

"Now kiss me."

She might have been the one to initiate the kiss, but the instant her lips touched mine I took control, tangling one of my hands in her hair and grabbing her lush, perfect ass with the other. When she opened her mouth on a moan to give me access, I nearly lost control. I growled and deepened the kiss, thrusting my tongue into her mouth and stroking it against hers. Pulling her tighter against me, I groaned into Fiona's mouth when her tits pressed against my chest. I felt like I'd been missing this, missing *us*, for a goddamned lifetime, not just a few days. It wasn't until I felt her against me again that I realized how essential she was. It was as if I'd been missing a limb without her, and now I was whole once more.

We were both breathing hard when I finally pulled back, but I didn't let her go. With one arm still firmly around her waist, I grabbed her wine and handed it to her before getting my beer and leading us into the living room. Fiona's sofa didn't look nearly as comfortable as mine, but it would do for now. At least until I got her back *home*.

I took a seat, pulling her down right beside me so that most of her chest was pressing into my side, then propped my feet on the coffee table. "Okay, so you wanted to know the deal with my dad."

When she tried to pull away, I squeezed her waist tighter.

"Uh, Deac? Is this really the best position for this talk?"

Her face was barely two inches away when I looked down at her and smiled. "Feels pretty perfect to me."

She scrunched her face adorably. "It's kind of awkward. Your face is *really* close."

I tipped my head down a bit farther and pressed my lips against hers in a hard, quick kiss. "I know. That's the point."

"Fine," she said with a roll of her eyes and a little sigh.

Facing forward, she lifted her wineglass and sipped. "So tell me what's going on with you and Nolan."

At her request, I dove in and opened myself up, showing her absolutely everything. I told her everything I'd told Grayson earlier that day, how I always felt second best, how I resented my father and brother, how it crushed me when she and Grayson started seeing each other. From the way her cheeks turned pink and her eyes teared up, I knew it was almost as painful for her to hear as it was for me to say.

"Deacon," she breathed when I finally reached the end. "I'm so sorry."

"Not your fault, sweetheart," I said softly, winding a strand of her deep red hair around my finger. "It is what it is."

"But it shouldn't be," she declared forcefully. "What you've done with The Black Sheep... how can he not see how amazing it is?"

That was a question I'd asked myself a million times. "I've given up trying to figure that out. I shouldn't have let him get under my skin at the party, and I really shouldn't have taken it out on you. I don't know if things between me and Dad will ever be better than they are now, but I promise you, I'll never take it out on your again. You have my word."

She went silent and dropped her cheek to my chest, deep in thought. After about a minute, she snapped, "I don't accept that."

I leaned back and put a finger under her chin to lift her face to mine. "Don't accept what?"

Her expression was one of fierce determination. "That your relationship with your dad is what it's always going to be. I don't accept that. I know you guys. I know how much Nolan loves you and Grayson, and how much you love them. It doesn't have to be this way. If you'd just talk instead of fight, maybe you two could fix things."

Everything she said sounded good—in theory. But I wasn't going to hold my breath. "I don't want you to get your hopes up, baby. You'll just end up disappointed."

Her gaze drifted to the side, going unfocused. "Maybe," she mumbled a while later. "But it's worth the risk."

"Hey," I called, wanting her attention back on me. "Why's this so important to you?"

She looked at me like I'd just said something stupid. "Because *you're* important to me. When you hurt, I hurt. And I'll do whatever I can to make it better for you. That's what you do when you love someone."

Jesus, she was killing me. "I love you too, baby."

She smiled up at me with that bright, gorgeous smile, and I knew down to my bones that we were back to us. And I'd never been more thankful for anything in my life.

"Around the world and back again," she said softly.

"To Jupiter and back again."

That time, she was the one to lift up and give me a kiss. "Good. Now take me home."

I didn't have to be told twice.

CHAPTER TWENTY-EIGHT

IT WAS the Sunday after mine and Deacon's heart-to-heart, and things couldn't have possibly been any better. After telling him to take me home, he'd promptly shot off the couch and headed to my bedroom. By the time I caught up with him, all of my luggage was laying open on my bed, and Deacon was leaning over the top drawer of my dresser. In one go, he scooped the entire contents into his arms and dumped the load into one of the suitcases. Then he did the same with the second drawer. And the third.

It wasn't until the dresser was empty and he moved to the closet, haphazardly throwing all my expensive dresses and blouses on top of the growing pile, hangers and all, that he looked at me and stated, "Baby, you handle all the bathroom shit. I got this. Anything that doesn't fit in these bags, we'll come back for later."

His order went in one ear and out the other as I stood frozen, watching in complete shock. "Uh, honey? What's happening right now?"

Deacon's response wasn't exactly an answer, even though it kind of was. "When we have free time, we'll go through everything else. If there's something you're really attached to, we'll find a place for it at home. If not, we'll have a yard sale. You like your furniture better than mine, then we'll talk and come up with a compromise. But just a heads up, I'm pretty sure my shit's more comfortable. I don't mind trading out, but I'm not down with redecorating every two or three years just because you get a wild hair. Make sure you pick the set you can live with for the long haul."

My mouth had been hanging open the entire time he spoke. Once he was finished, I managed to find my voice and asked, "So... are you saying that I'm moving in with you?"

He tossed another armful of designer clothes into a bag and turned to face me, his hands on his hips. "Is this place home?"

"Huh?"

One hand shot out, waving to encompass the room around us. "This place. Does it feel like home to you?"

"Well...."

"Baby, there isn't a single ounce of *you* anywhere in these four walls. This place is sterile. You're not. So my question is, does this house feel like home for you?"

Gah! Sometimes he was too damn intuitive for his own good. "It was an investment," I found myself answering honestly. "I figured, at my age and with my income, the smart thing to do was own property."

Deacon's face went soft. "Does my place feel like an investment?"

"Of course not," I declared. "I *love* your house. It's inviting and cozy and warm. It's homey. This"—I looked around at my white walls—"isn't homey."

He smiled so big it took up his whole face. "Then you're moving in with me. It's settled."

And it was. All of my clothing, toiletries, and about half my shoes went back to his place—now *our* place—that night. True to his word, he'd taken me back the next evening, and the one after. I had everything I needed to be fully moved in with Deacon. All that was left was selling off everything I didn't want —which was most of it—and putting my house on the market. I couldn't believe how easy it had been.

This time around, coming home to him every night felt different. We might not have slept apart before, but having all of my belongings mingled with his under one roof, and *knowing* his home was also mine, made it even better.

I'd been walking on air all week. Everything was absolutely freaking perfect. There wasn't anything that could get me down —well, except for the teeny fact that I'd put together a family dinner and had failed to mention it to my boyfriend.

Whoops.

And there was less than an hour before our families started arriving.

Deacon had spent his day off camped out in front of the TV watching whatever game he could find, so occupied that he didn't notice me running around the house like a madwoman, cleaning up, prepping, and then cooking dinner before finally getting myself all dolled up. Unless he needed another beer, or needed to pee, he hadn't even left the couch.

I opted for comfortable yet fashionable when I picked my outfit for the evening: my favorite pair of faded skinny jeans, a loose-weave cream-colored sweater threaded through with a tiny bit of gold that drooped off one shoulder, a gold camisole under-neath, and a pair of tan suede booties with a fat three-inch heel.

Walking out of the bedroom and down the hall, I decided it was time to bite the bullet. The pork tenderloin I'd put in the slow cooker earlier that morning was almost done. The green beans had been blanched, seasoned, and almondine-d—which I was pretty sure wasn't a word, but whatever. The timer had just gone off on the oven for the potatoes, so all that was left to do was inform Deacon. The one thing I'd been dreading so much I quite literally waited until the last minute.

"Honey?" I said softly once I reached the living room.

Deacon's beer came to his lips, his eyes never leaving the TV, as he asked, "Yeah, baby?"

"Well... dinner's almost ready."

"Awesome," he returned, still entranced by the game. "I'm starving. Whatever you made smells delicious."

"It's pork tenderloin, green beans almondine, and au gratin potatoes."

"Wow, sweetheart. You really went all out," he said, still talking to the television.

"Thanks. Oh, and there's just one last thing."

That finally got his attention, and he shifted his gaze to me. His eyes traveled the length of my body, shining with approval at my clothing choice. "Yeah? What's that? And why're you all dressed up?"

"It's nothing, really. No big deal. It's just that our parents are coming to dinner," I blurted, then spun around and bolted to the kitchen, calling over my shoulder, "I'll just let you get back to your game."

"Whoa, whoa, whoa!" The noises of the ball game went silent, and his footsteps echoed behind me as I leaned over and pulled the casserole dish from the oven. "What the hell do you mean, our parents are coming to dinner?"

Setting the dish on a pad, I tossed the potholders aside and started preparing the salad I was going to serve with our meal. "I mean I invited everyone for dinner."

"You invited them," he said incredulously.

"Yep."

"To dinner."

"Uh-huh."

"Your parents *and* mine."

"That's typically what *our parents* means, honey."

"Fee," he growled in a warning tone. "Put the goddamn croutons on the counter and look at me."

Well, damn. With a hard exhale, I dropped the bag of croutons and lifted my gaze to his, pulling my lips between my teeth.

"Why did you invite our parents to dinner?"

I gave him a look that said it all, but just in case he didn't get the message, I told him, "You know why, Deacon."

With a sigh, he asked, "When did you set this thing up?"

"Um...." I bit down on my bottom lip, hesitant to answer. "Thursday?"

The muscle in Deacon's cheek jumped. "Are you kidding me? The day after you moved in with me? You just couldn't help yourself, could you?"

"Look, Deac, I know I should've told you earlier, but this needs to happen. The issues between you and Nolan have been going on for too long." I attempted a smile, hoping it would soften him up. It didn't work very well. "And if it helps, it's not just our parents. Grayson and Lola are coming too, and I think your folks are bringing your nana. It's a family dinner," I chirped happily.

"*Nana's* coming?" he barked. I couldn't really blame him for his reaction to that. His nana was kind of a nut. Looking up at the ceiling, Deacon muttered, "Fucking Christ. There goes the neighborhood," toward the heavens before tipping his head back down. "And when exactly is this *family* dinner supposed to happen?" The doorbell chimed at that very moment. "Ah, fuck me," he grunted.

"Hey." I closed the distance between us and placed my hands on his chest. "It's going to be okay. No matter what happens, no matter what's said, I'm here. Okay? I'm right here, and I'm not going anywhere. I'll have your back no matter what, because I love you, and I believe in you. That's all that matter, Deacon. You and me, what we have, that's all that matters."

The doorbell rang again, but Deacon ignored it and wrapped his arms around me, bringing his forehead down to rest against mine. "I love you," he said fiercely. "I love you so damn much."

"Good." I smiled. "Now answer the door, and I'll finish the salad."

He pressed a quick kiss against my lips and let me go. I'd gone back to finishing the salad when I heard Grayson's voice.

"For God's sake. How long were you planning on making us wait out here? It's cold as hell. I think my balls just burrowed up into my stomach for warmth."

I smiled down at the tomato I was slicing as Deacon replied, "And how's that's different from where they normally are?"

"You two can stand here having your pissing match for as long as you want, but can you at least let me inside first?" I heard Lola snark. A few seconds later, she came waddling around the corner. "Thank God," she breathed once she caught sight of the spread all around the counters. "I haven't eaten in about three hours. I'm seriously hangry right now, and if I don't eat soon, I can't be held responsible for what I do to my husband. Or his brother, for that matter."

She lifted herself onto a barstool—*not* an easy feat with that baby belly in the way—while I giggled and pushed the bruschetta I'd made as an appetizer across the counter to her.

"How are you feeling?"

She let out a sigh of relief and pounced on the bruschetta like a lion on a wounded gazelle, talking with her mouth full. "The doctor loosened up on my bed rest. I'm allowed to get up and around for a little longer, but I have to take it easy, which means no work until I deliver. So basically I'm going out of my mind. And Grayson's been hovering twenty-four/seven. I love the guy, but at this point I don't think there's a jury in this country that would convict me for murdering him hard."

My head fell back on a long laugh. "You don't have much longer, honey."

"I hope not. I'm going stir-crazy, and I'm bored out of my mind. You know I love you, and I'd do anything for you, but to be honest, I mainly came tonight because there's a 99 percent chance for some drama happening, and I need a little entertainment."

I gave my friend a fierce scowl. "There isn't going to be any drama. Sorry to disappoint, but tonight's just going to be a nice, quiet family dinner."

Another knock came at the door. A moment later I heard Deacon's grandmother, clear as day. "Heard our sweet little Fiona's moved in with you. I'm all for living in sin, my boy, but don't knock her up before you put a ring on it. Take my word, the pullout method is a crock. You're father here's living proof of that."

Lola snorted.

I rolled my eyes skyward.

Apparently I'd spoken too soon.

CHAPTER TWENTY-NINE

DEACON

WE HADN'T MADE it farther than the front entrance and I was already I was praying for this family dinner to be over.

From Nana's introduction, it was obvious that she was in the mood to stir shit up, something she was unbelievably good at.

"Hey, Nana. Good to see you." I leaned down and kissed her papery cheek.

"Good to be seen. Means I haven't kicked the bucket in my sleep yet."

"Mom," my father said in a chastising tone.

Nana's head jerked in his direction. "Don't you use that tone with me. I could take you when you were a kid, and I can still take you now. I might be old, but I'm spry. I won't hesitate to put you over my knee."

I bit the inside of my cheek to keep from busting up. Grayson and my mother barely managed to suppress their snorts of laughter as Dad muttered a quiet curse. "Lord, deliver me."

"Oh, I'll deliver you, all right. Keep pushing," Nana warned before looking back at me. "Boy, you'd think I didn't raise you with any manners, keeping an old woman like me standing inside the doorway."

"So sorry," I said. "Come on in. Can I get you anything, Nan? Champagne? Maybe a palm frond to fan you with?"

She shot me a killing look. "Such a smartass. Where's that girlfriend of yours? I like her better than you."

My lips twitched as I fought my grin. "The kitchen."

She and my mother went to join Fee and Lola in the kitchen, leaving me with Grayson and my dad. Gray gave me a look that spoke volumes. He was there to have my back.

"Son," my father spoke, drawing my gaze to him. He cleared his throat uncomfortably. "Look, about what happened at the party—"

"Dad," I interrupted. "It's not necessary. Water under the bridge and all that."

"Yes... well, good. That's good." He pulled at the neck of his shirt as if the material was squeezing too tight for comfort. "So, is it true? Fiona's moved in here?"

"That's right." My chest swelled with pride at knowing she was all mine and under my roof. For good.

"Good. I'm glad. You two make a great couple." To most people, that wouldn't have seemed like much, but hearing my dad say that meant everything to me.

Dad clapped me on the shoulder and headed off to the kitchen. When it was just the two of us, Grayson asked, "You good?"

I was. No matter what happened, no matter what was said later, I had my brother and my woman at my back. "I'm great."

The front door pushed open and Calvin came walking through with Evelyn on heels, calling out, "Hello! We're here, we're here. Sorry for being late."

I took their coats and hung them by the door. "You aren't

late at all," I replied, kissing Evelyn's cheek and shaking Calvin's hand. "Fee's just about finished with dinner, and my family only just arrived. And just a heads-up, Nana's feeling feisty this evening."

Evelyn's giggle sounded much like her daughter's. Calvin chortled and patted me on the back as they started past. "Isn't she always?"

"You can say that again," Grayson grumbled under his breath as we followed behind them.

When we cleared the front hall and headed into the living area, I stopped and watched as Fiona greeted her mom and dad with excitement. Everyone was drawn to her, huddled around the bar that separated the kitchen and living area, wanting that light of hers to shine down on them. And as I stood silently, several feet away, I watched it happen. I watched the love of my life pour her beautiful bright light out onto everyone she cared about. And when her eyes found mine and she winked, I felt it pour over me as well.

Oh yeah. I was more than good.

FIONA

SO FAR, dinner was going smoothly. With the exception of Nana periodically spouting off something that wasn't appropriate for mixed company, there hadn't been the slightest bit of tension. We'd made it through the main course and had just set on the chocolate cake I made for dessert when Grayson asked, "So, Deac, how's the bar?"

My lungs seized for a second, but when I looked to the head

of the table and saw that Deacon was as calm as could be, I started to relax. "It's great. Actually, I'm starting construction next week to put in a stage. Once a week, The Black Sheep will host an open mic night."

The fork in my hand clattered to the plate and my head shot up. "You are?" I asked on a surprised whisper.

"That's an amazing idea," my dad exclaimed.

Deacon gave me a tiny wink before looking down the table at my father. "Thanks, Calvin, but it was all your daughter's idea."

Tears stung the inside of my nose, but I refused to let them fall. He'd listened to what I had to say. Despite the huge fight, he'd really listened. And he'd taken action because he thought it was a good idea. My God, I loved this man. Smiling brightly down the table, I mouthed those very words to him, and when he winked, I swooned a bit.

"Like a karaoke bar?" Nolan asked derisively, shattering the blissfully happy moment. "Is that really the kind of reputation you want for your bar?"

"Nolan," Cybil bit out warningly, but it was too late. The mood in the room went stagnant.

"No, Dad. Not like a karaoke bar. It's open mic. I'll audition local musicians, and if they're any good, they'll get a spot in the lineup. I haven't worked out all the logistics yet, but it was a brilliant idea Fiona came up with to increase revenue. We're even toying with the idea of hosting small private concerts every few months."

Nolan watched his son quietly for several seconds. "So you're having an issue with money? Is that why you're doing this?"

Uh-oh.

"Dad, not cool," Grayson growled.

"What? I was only asking a question. I worry. I just want my son to be stable and secure for the future."

"And who says he isn't?" Grayson retorted.

"Nolan, this is neither the time nor the place," Cybil chided.

"As a father, am I not allowed to be concerned for my own son's well-being?"

Deacon and everyone else remained silent as those three went at each other.

"Not if your concern is a mask for you trying to tear him down. Jesus, Dad," Grayson boomed.

For the first time, I finally saw exactly what Deacon was talking about. It wasn't that his father wanted to bring him down. Nolan's concerns were genuine, he was just going about voicing them in a very wrong way. All of a sudden, I saw just how much Deacon and his father were alike. Two strong-willed, stubborn men who weren't sure how to handle being in the wrong.

"I'm not tearing him down! In case you forgot, I know a little about running a business. I'm just worried about my child. It's something you won't understand until Lola brings your little one into the world. If he'd have just joined us at Bandwidth—"

"It's not what he wanted!" Grayson cut in.

Things were deteriorating quickly. Especially considering the Lockhart men were all hot-headed. I'd promised to have my man's back, and that was exactly what I intended to do.

"Nolan." At the sound of my voice, the argument stopped and everyone turned to look at me. "I understand your concern. I know you're worried about Deacon because you love him, but have you actually sat down and talked to him about the bar?"

He blinked. "I.... No."

I offered him a gentle smile as I continued. "If there's one thing I've learned after a lifetime around the Lockhart men, it's that you're all incredibly strong-willed."

"Darling, why do I get the feeling that's your polite way of calling me stubborn?" he joked.

Breathing a sigh of relief that I hadn't pushed him too far—at least yet—I said, "Because I kind of am." Nana burst into laughter, but I chose to ignore it and kept going. "You built Bandwidth from the ground up, so you know how stressful it is. But what you don't understand is that Deacon isn't going to fail. He's already succeeded."

"Fee, it's fine," Deacon said in an attempt to stop me.

"No it's not," I told him. "You two have been fighting instead of communicating." I looked back to Nolan. "What your son's built is amazing. If you'd just let go of the animosity you have with Deacon for not coming to work for you, you'd be able to see that. I love you and your whole family. You know that. I grew up considering you and Cybil my second parents, but you're in the wrong here. Be proud that you raised a man strong enough to know what he wants and to work his ass off to get it. He's that strong because you raised him to be. That's something you should be celebrating, not worrying over."

By the time I finished, the room was so silent you could hear a pin drop. It was as if everyone was holding their breaths, waiting for Nolan's reaction.

He stared at me from across the table for so long that I started to grow anxious, fearing I'd crossed a line. But I didn't regret speaking up. Everything I said was the God's honest truth, and needed to be said. I'd handle the fallout if it came.

Then he spoke. "I think, darling, that you may very well be the best thing that's ever happened to my son."

My body sagged and I smiled in relief. "Well I'm glad, because I know for certain that he's the best thing that's ever happened to me."

Nolan returned my grin.

We both jumped in our seats when Nana banged her cane

on the floor with a loud clack. "*Finally!* I love these boys, but their heads have been planted so far up their own asses I feared they'd have to be surgically removed. I can't tell you how relieved I am to know it won't come to that. I'm too damn old to be dealing with idiots."

CHAPTER THIRTY

FIONA

MY FINGERS WRAPPED around the top of the headboard in a death grip as Deacon lay beneath me, holding my hips so tight I'd probably have bruises the next day. The sensation of his tongue and teeth devouring my pussy was almost too much to bear, but when I tried to lift up, he'd jerk me back down, his ministrations relentless.

One of Deacon's hands traveled down my quaking thigh, causing the trembles to grow more pronounced as I drew closer and closer to an out-of-this-world orgasm.

The moment he stopped flicking his tongue against my clit and drove it inside my opening, stars burst behind my eyes. I'd never had a man give me so much pleasure just from going down on me. He feasted like he was positively starving and my body was the only thing that could sustain him.

His growl sent vibrations through my core, and I sucked in a choked gasp as the pleasure overwhelmed me.

When I looked down between my spread thighs, the sight of Deacon's face buried in my pussy caused my entire body to tremble. It was the most beautifully erotic thing I'd ever seen.

"Oh God, honey," I panted, grinding myself against his face.

"I'm gonna—" My words cut off with a low moan as I came, writhing and squirming, riding his tongue as I exploded.

I hadn't even finished when he pushed me down his body. One hand went to his cock and he lined it up with my entrance just a moment before he shifted his hips and filled me.

"Take yourself there again," he commanded.

Putting my hands on his chest, I did as ordered and began moving up and down on his rock-hard erection. His hands came up to cup my breasts, his thumbs dragging across my tight nipples. I dropped my head back as the intensity of his touch sent sparks from my breasts to my clit. I moved faster, harder, riding him with everything I had, desperate for another release.

"Fee," he grunted, pinching my nipple and sending bolts of lighting throughout my body. "Eyes on me when you get off."

Tilting my head back down, I let my hair drape over my shoulders as I opened my eyes and met his. Digging my nails into his chest, I sucked in a breath at the desire glinting in his gaze as he watched me. "Deacon," I panted. "God, I love you." Then I came again, unable to keep my eyes from rolling back in my head.

He flipped me to my back and took over, pounding into me again and again. Hooking his arm behind my knee, he pushed it toward my chest so he could go so deep there wasn't a single part of me that his cock didn't touch.

I turned my focus to him as I started coming down, lifting my free leg and wrapping it around his hips as he powered in and out.

"Fuck me, *Fiona*," he growled. Sweat glistened on his brow as he stared directly into my eyes. "Love you so much. So *goddamn* much." His cock swelled thicker, stretching me so perfectly.

Deacon pulled almost all the way out and paused for just a

second before slamming back inside. He did it again and again, taking me hard but slow at the same time.

"Christ, baby. You light up for me every fucking time."

He wasn't wrong about that. I couldn't get enough. Each time was more spectacular, more consuming than the last. I couldn't get enough of Deacon Lockhart. "Always, Deac. I'll always light up for you."

A feral growl rumbled up his throat. "Goddamn, you're perfect for me. *Fucking. Perfect.*" He punctuated those last two words with brutal thrusts. "Never get enough of you. Never stop loving you."

I let out a whimper as pleasure washed over me. Happy tears filled my eyes. I couldn't drag my gaze from his as he buried himself inside me, the muscles in his neck and jaw growing tense right before he groaned out his orgasm between gritted teeth.

Deacon collapsed on top of me once it left him, releasing my leg so I could wrap my limbs around him and hold on tight. After a few minutes, he pulled out, rolled us to our sides, and brushed the hair from my face.

"My girl had my back tonight," he murmured with a gentle smile on his face.

I returned his grin. "I told you I would."

His chuckle shook my body, pressed close to his. "Yeah. I just didn't know you'd do it so damn well. I think you might have actually gotten through to my old man."

Reaching up, I traced the length of his jaw with my fingertips. "Whether I did or not, it doesn't matter. As long as it's you and me, everything else is pie."

His bright white teeth flashed on a grin. "Pie, huh?"

"Yep, pie. As in *easy as pie.*" I was content to just lie there and stare at his beautiful face until I fell asleep. But then I remembered what he said at dinner. "Are you really starting an open mic night?"

"Yep."

"*Omigod!*" I squealed. Sitting up quickly, I sent my loose hair flying in all directions. "Deacon, this is so great! We need to come up with a marketing campaign," I started rambling. "I'm thinking we blast this on social media. We'll put the signup for musicians on the home page of your website. Do you have a newsletter? If not, we need to get on that, like, now. Word of mouth will probably be our biggest draw, so I'm thinking maybe we make up some fliers. Oh, and a banner! The Black Sheep is packed every night, so we'll put up a banner announcing that open mic night is coming soon, and we'll include the web address for your site so bands know where to go to sign up for auditions. This is going to be *amazing*!"

"Whoa, whoa." Deacon sat up on a laugh. "Slow down, baby. All this is good, but I barely followed what you just rambled, seeing as you didn't even take a breath."

Grabbing his face, I pulled him closer, unable to keep the huge shit-eating grin off my face. "That's okay. I already have a plan. I want to help with this."

"Sweetheart, you're forgetting the little fact that you have a career of your own. This is going to be a ton of work."

"I don't care!" I chirped. "I'll make it work somehow. It might seem boring as hell to you, but I loved coming to the bar and doing the books for you. I like the idea of us working side by side. And I *want* to help with this."

He examined my face for several seconds, like he was searching for something before pulling back, my hands dropping to my lap. "I hesitate to ask this, since you're such a fan of calling me a caveman, but have you thought about working at the bar full time?"

My upper body tipped back in surprise. I knew I loved

working at the bar, not just because I was working alongside Deacon but because I actually enjoyed the work. I hadn't once given thought to leaving behind Prentice Fashion to do it full time. But now that he'd mentioned it, I wasn't sure I could *stop* thinking about it.

When I didn't reply, his expression turned skeptical. "You're not about to lay into me for being sexist or misogynistic or some shit like that, are you?"

"No... I... No. I'm not."

"But?" he asked hesitantly.

"But...." I shook my head to try an organize my thoughts. "I can't actually think of a *but*."

His back went straight and he leaned in closer. "Is this something you'd actually want? To work with me at a bar? I think you already know this, but it's not exactly a glamorous job."

I looked at him with a vicious glare. "Are you trying to talk me out of it? Because that's what it's sounding like. If you don't want me to work for you—"

Deacon's hand came up and clamped over my mouth. "Calm down, crazy. I wasn't saying that at all. First off, you wouldn't be working *for* me. You'd be working *with* me. We haven't had this conversation yet, but just so you know, I fully intend on marrying you one day in the very near future. When that happens, what's mine becomes yours. That means the bar. So if you decide that working there is something you want, it'll be as my partner, not an employee."

I smacked his hand away and my jaw dropped. My eyes bugged out as I began sputtering, "I—you—but.... Are you serious?"

"You surprised? I remember you telling me that you always wanted what your folks had. You watched your mom work alongside your dad and help him build the company up to what it is today. Is that still what you want?"

A golf ball–sized lump of emotion formed in my throat. I struggled to swallow it down and croaked past it. "Y-yes."

He leaned in farther, so close I had no choice but to fall to the mattress. Deacon hovered over me, his biceps bulging as he held his weight up on his arms. "I want to give you everything you want, baby. If you think working at The Black Sheep will make you happy, then I want you there. I'm not trying to pressure you. I just want you to know how I feel."

With a watery smile, I lifted my hand and stroked his cheek. "Stop being so awesome. You're going to make me cry."

He chuckled and bent his elbows to plant a kiss against my lips. "Just think about it, baby. The offer's on the table indefinitely. There's plenty of time."

I sniffled and batted at my watery eyes. "Okay. I'll think about it."

"Good." One of his hands snaked between our bodies and down between my legs. "Now, how tired are you?"

My blood began to heat with arousal even though I'd just come more than once. "You know, I'm suddenly feeling wide awake."

"Hmm," he hummed. His fingers skated through the slickness between my thighs. "Then how about you show me how awesome you think I am?"

Suddenly, that was exactly what I wanted to do. Licking my lips, I rested my hands on his chest and applied pressure, taking him to his back. I slid between his legs and shimmied down his body, placing wet kisses along his defined abs on my way down.

"Is this what you want?" I asked playfully, my tongue peeking out to lick at the muscular indentations of his hips.

"Yeah, baby," he hissed between gritted teeth. "You know it is."

I was so turned on that I was dripping as I hummed and bent my head, opening my mouth to take him as far as I could. Deacon's grunted curse the instant my lips wrapped around his shaft set my entire body on fire and encouraged me to make this the best blowjob he'd ever have. And that was exactly what I set out to do.

And just a few minutes later, after he came down my throat and flipped me to my back, Deacon returned the favor.

CHAPTER THIRTY-ONE

FIONA

AS I WALKED into the office Monday morning, I felt so happy that I was sure there was nothing in the world that could bring me down. I was so deeply entrenched in my euphoria that I didn't realize the atmosphere in the building was uncomfortably heavy as I walked the halls to my own office.

Ignorant to everything but my own bliss, I greeted my coworkers as I passed without registering the quiet whispers and lingering stares all pointed in my direction.

It wasn't until I reached my assistant's desk that reality set in. She shot up from her chair, eyes big as saucers when she saw me. "Oh my God. Fiona. You're here."

I gave Sarah a funny look and tilted my head to the side. "Of course I'm here. It's Monday morning. Where else would I be?"

Her mouth opened and closed in shock several times before she finally whispered, "Oh shit!"

"Sarah, what's going on?"

"Oh God. Oh *shit*! You don't know."

The hairs on the back of my neck stood on end as dread seeped into my bones. "I don't know what?"

Instead of answering, Sarah bolted from behind her desk,

grabbed my hand, and hauled me into my office, slamming the door shut behind us. "I'm so sorry. God, Fee, I'm so, so sorry this happened. I thought someone would've called you."

"Called me about what? Sarah, you're starting to freak me out here. What's going on?"

She chewed on her bottom lip and twisted her fingers for several seconds, as if trying to come up with the right way to word whatever bomb she was about to drop.

"Uh... well, you see... late last night, a company-wide email was sent out. There were some... uh... pictures attached."

My stomach dropped as bile crept up my throat, burning like acid. Dropping my purse to the floor, I rushed around my desk and turned on my laptop. I chanted, "Nonononono," over and over as I logged into my company email and began scrolling. When I came to the subject line that read '*What she does during company time,*' my coffee threatened to make a reappearance.

The last thing I wanted to do was open the email. But I had to. I had to see if it was what I feared.

I clicked the first attachment and tears immediately welled in my eyes. "No," I breathed, my heart falling to the floor. Right there, clear as day, were my naked breasts for the entire office to see. There wasn't even a chance at denying it was me since my face was front and center in the photo.

There were four pictures in total, each worse than the last. When I got to the picture Deacon had taken of his cock entering me while I was spread out on my desk, I finally lost it, bending at the waist to heave into the trash bin beside my desk. I vaguely recalled Sarah darting to me and holding my hair back as I emptied the contents of my stomach.

Those pictures were private. The only ones who knew about them were me and Deacon. How had this happened? Who had sent those photos? I racked my brain, trying to figure it out, but each time I thought about everyone in the office seeing me so exposed, I heaved again until finally there was nothing left.

Once I finished and sat up, tears trailing down my face, Sarah snatched a handful of tissues out of the box on my desk and handed them to me. "Who sent them?" I croaked, my voice ravaged from throwing up. "Who did this?"

Her face was awash with sympathy as she answered, "Human Resources has launched an investigation, but no one knows yet."

I dropped my head into my hands and let out a groan. "Oh God." Human Resources was investigating. That meant *everyone* knew. Then something hit me like a Mac truck. I shot up straight and sucked in a breath. "My dad. Has he...? Has...?" I couldn't even finish the thought.

"I don't know," Sarah replied.

When I burst into gut-wrenching sobs, she leaned in and wrapped her arms around me, humming soothing words in a failed attempt to calm me down. The whole office had seen me naked—or at least mostly naked. They'd seen me having sex, for Christ's sake. Calm was out the window. All I could do was freak the fuck out.

"This is bad. This is so, *so* bad. What am I going to do?"

Before she had a chance to answer, my office phone rang. Jumping into her duties as my assistant, Sarah snatched the phone up and brought it to her ear. "Fiona Prentice's office. This is Sarah, how may I help you?"

I couldn't hear who was on the other end, and there was no way in hell that I was looking at the caller ID.

Sarah listened to the person through the line, mumbling, "Uh-huh. Okay. Yes, she is. Uh-huh. Uh-huh. I'll let her know," before hanging up and looking at me with fear in her eyes. "Um, that was Anthony in HR. He and your father are waiting for you in Mr. Prentice's office."

It felt like I was preparing for the firing squad as I stood and stared at the door, the only thing keeping me safely cocooned in privacy. As soon as I walked out that door, I'd be taking the most humiliating walk of shame ever imagined.

I was going to be sick again.

I SAT in complete silence as Anthony and my father discussed those horrible pictures and what would happen to me as if I wasn't even in the room. Keeping my gaze cast down, unable to meet my father's eyes, I listened as the two of them went back and forth.

"The IT department is currently tracking down the IP address that email was sent from. I'm confident that we'll have answers by the end of business. In the meantime, I suggest Fiona take a personal day until we can decide what measures to take."

What measures to take. I was going to lose my job. There was no way my father would be able to keep me on, let alone hand the company over to me one day, after a scandal like this.

My father, normally so carefree and jovial, sounded positively irate as he fired back. "What I want to know is what's being done to ensure these images don't leave this building. So help me God, Anthony, if I find out naked images of my daughter are being splashed all over the internet there will be hell to pay. I want the name of the person who sent that email, and I want it now."

"I assure you, Calvin, we're doing everything possible to remove those images. The email seems to have been sent to the employees of this office only. I've been in contact with the heads of HR in all the other offices in the states, as well as Paris and Italy, and no one there received these images, so we have that on our side. And a memo is already being drafted that anyone caught forwarding that email will be terminated immediately."

Oh God. A memo's going out. About me. And my filthy pictures. This was so humiliating.

"Okay. Thank you, Anthony. Keep me abreast of the situation."

Anthony left just moments later, leaving me and my father alone in his office.

Finally finding the nerve to glance up, I saw my father collapse in his chair, looking as crestfallen as I felt. I hated that I was the reason my dad's joy had been sniffed out.

"Daddy," I whispered in a small, pathetic voice. "I'm so sorry."

He let out a sigh so heavy it sounded like the weight of the world was resting squarely on his shoulders. And it was all my fault. "Fiona...." That was all he said, just my name, but it was impossible not to hear the heartbreak in his voice.

"Did you...?" I swallowed down the acid crawling up my throat. "Did you see the pic—"

"No," he answered quickly, sparing me from having to ask the full question. "I was warned before I had the chance. Thank Christ," he grunted, running a hand through his thinning red hair. "But I was told enough about them to get the gist. How did this happen, Fee?"

"I don't know," I cried, a new wave of tears rushing down my cheeks. "The only ones who even knew about those pictures were me and Deacon. I don't even know how someone got ahold of them. They were taken with my phone, and I always have it on me...." *Holy shit.* I trailed off as my blood turned to ice in my veins.

"What? Sweetheart, what is it?"

"I misplaced my phone last week. I figured I left it in the conference room or something, but when I got in the next day, it was on my desk so I didn't give it a second thought. I just thought I'd been a bit scatterbrained."

Dad sat up straight. "You think someone broke into your phone and took those pictures?"

A massive headache was threatening, and I began massaging my temples as I answered, "It's the only logical explanation." He grew quiet for so long that the tension in my muscles grew tighter. "I'm sorry I put you in this position," I said, batting at the tears trickling down my cheeks. "I'm sorry I disappointed you."

"Oh, honey." Dad shot out of his chair and came my way, pulling me up and into his arms. The comfort of his embrace proved to be my undoing and I broke down for the second time, crying into my father's chest as he held me tightly.

"I'm not disappointed in you," he said quietly. "You've done nothing to be ashamed of. Do I wish those pictures didn't exist? Of course. But none of this falls on your shoulders. I promise you, I'll fix this."

I pulled back, rubbing my hands over my face as stress ate away at me. "I don't think this is something that can be fixed," I admitted, my heart breaking into a million pieces. "I don't know how I can stay on here. Not after everyone's seen... I just can't."

"We'll figure it out, sweetheart," he whispered. "We'll figure everything out."

I wasn't sure how he figured we'd do that, but I didn't voice that particular concern. I'd already caused enough trouble to last a lifetime.

I left my father's office shortly after and made my way back to mine at a quick pace. I kept my eyes cast down to the carpeted floor and let my hair provide a curtain between me and my coworkers. But even then I could feel the penetrating stares coming at me from all directions. I'd never been so humiliated, so ashamed in all my life.

Bypassing Sarah at her desk, I rushed into my office, grabbed my purse, and bailed out. It wasn't until the elevator doors opened in the parking garage that I was able to breathe somewhat normally again. I had no idea what was going to happen, or what my future was going to hold.

The only thing I wanted to do was go home, curl up in bed, and pretend the rest of the world didn't exist.

CHAPTER THIRTY-TWO

DEACON

"YO, boss man. You got someone out front asking for you."

I looked from the inventory sheet I'd been scribbling on to Sherry standing in the open doorway of the stock room. I went back to making notations for what needed to be ordered as I spoke. "Kind of in the middle of something here, Sher. Can you take care of it for me?"

"I would, but he specifically asked for you. And he's got a vibe to him like he's a high-ranking political figure, or that he's got the kind of connections to squash me like a bug, so I didn't want to push my luck." My head shot up in confusion at her curious description. She gave me a shit-eating grin as she continued, "Oh, and he looks *exactly* like you, and introduced himself as Nolan Lockhart. I'm guessing you'll need to handle this one on your own. If it helps, I'll take over in here."

Dropping the clipboard with the stock inventory sheet onto the shelf in front of me, I glared at Sherry as I started toward the door. "You couldn't have just opened with 'Hey, Deacon, your dad's out front asking for you?'"

She shrugged and skipped into the stock room. "Eh, where's the fun in that?"

I moved past her and down the hall to the front of the bar. We were in the middle of the lunch rush, so the place was busy, but nowhere near as chaotic as it would get later that evening. Construction was set to happen in just a few days, and I'd have to close down until it finished, but I was actually looking forward to a little time off and had been thinking of ways to convince Fiona to ask for a few personal days so we could take a little mid-week vacation together. I was thinking somewhere private with no cell reception so there wouldn't be a chance of any interruptions.

But before I could put that plan into motion, I had to deal with whatever shit my father had come to lay on me.

As soon as I pushed through the swinging door that led out front, I spotted him standing by the bar with a thoughtful expression on his face while he looked around. I couldn't tell if his sudden surprise visit was good or bad, so I steeled myself for anything as I headed toward him.

"Hey, Dad."

He gave a surprised jolt and spun around to face me. "Oh, hey there, son. Sorry to drop by unexpectedly. I thought...." He glanced around the crowded room. "Well, I didn't realize you were open for lunch. I thought it would be a good time. If I'm keeping you from anything—"

"No, it's fine. This is actually our slow time, so I've got a few minutes."

Dad's head jerked back and his eyes went wide. "This is what you consider slow?"

"Compared to what it's like in the evenings, yeah."

"I had no idea," he muttered in awe.

I wasn't sure how to take his reaction, but if there was one thing I'd learned growing up, it was not to get my hopes up when it came to pleasing my old man. "So what brings you by?"

He tugged at his tie in discomfort before answering. "Well,

what Fiona said last night really hit home. It's rather painful to realize I've spent years voicing my concerns as your parent the wrong way. I owe you an apology, Deacon. All these years I've been making you feel like you were less than your brother in my eyes, and that couldn't possibly be further from the truth."

"Dad, you don't have to—"

His hand came up to stop me. "I do, son. And it's been a long time coming. It was never my intention to make you feel like you couldn't live up to my expectations. The truth is, from the moment you learned to walk, I've lived in a perpetual state of fear. You've had an iron will since the moment you were born. Nothing ever scared you. You treated every day like it could be your last, squeezing every ounce of enjoyment from life. I always admired that about you, even if some of the shit you pulled put gray hair on my head."

I couldn't help but laugh at that. My father had been blaming me and Grayson for the salt liberally sprinkled through his pepper hair for years.

"I envy your zest for life, Deacon. You have more courage than I ever could've hoped for at your age. You never let other peoples' opinions stop you from doing what you wanted, even mine. There hasn't been a single day that's passed since you entered the world that I haven't been proud to call you my son."

My throat suddenly burned as a lump swelled so big that it was a struggle to breathe. I had to clear it in order to speak, and when I finally did, my voice was hoarse with emotion. "Thank you." It was a lame response to everything my father had just said, but it was all I could come up with in that moment. When the shock of hearing my father tell me he was proud to call me his son finally wore off, maybe I'd be able to fully express how much those words meant to me. But I had a feeling that, for now, a simple thank you would do just fine.

Dad clapped me on the shoulder in a show of support.

"Good. I'm glad we've finally cleared the air. Now, I'm starving. I don't suppose you'd have time to join me for a quick bite before you get back to work?"

Even if I'd been swamped, I would've pushed everything else to the back burner to have lunch with my old man. "Got all the time in the world, Dad. Let's grab a table."

COLLAPSING BACK IN THE BOOTH, Dad tossed his napkin onto the table and patted his stomach in contentment. "Have to say, Deacon, that was the best burger I've ever had."

I let out a low chuckle and lifted my water glass to my lips. I had to agree with him on that. The Black Sheep served the best burgers on the West Coast. "Glad you approve."

"I more than approve. I think I'm probably going to lapse into a food coma when I get back to the office. Speaking of...." He lifted his arm and took a look at the Rolex on his wrist. "I should probably be getting back. What's the damage?" Dad asked, shifting to reach for the wallet in his back pocket.

"On the house." He gave me a look like he was about to argue, but I cut him off at the pass. "You come in for lunch again, I'll charge you. First one's free. Friends and family discount."

Dad looked at me with a smile full of pride. "I'll take you up on that."

We both stood from the booth, and I walked with him to the door. "I'll look forward to it."

He stopped to slide his coat over his arms before turning to me once more. "This visit was actually a way for me to kill two birds with one stone. Your mom's been on my case since yesterday. If you and Fee don't come over for dinner soon to show we're good, this might be the last time you see me breathing."

My head fell back in full-blown laughter. "Wouldn't want that, would we? I'll talk to her and see when we can set something up."

"Good. Enjoy the rest of your day, son. And... this place is amazing. I'm proud of you."

My chest constricted, squeezing so tight it was almost painful to take a breath. But damn if it wasn't the best feeling in the world. "Means everything, Dad. I'll see you later."

Dad left a moment later, and I watched as he walked down the sidewalk until he was out of sight, thinking that, for the first time in my life, everything was absolutely fucking perfect. I finally had the woman I'd loved all my life. I had my dad's approval. And I was succeeding at doing what I loved. I was sure there wasn't a damn thing that could get me down.

Unfortunately, as life had proven more often than not, happiness wasn't guaranteed. And when you let your guard down long enough, bad shit usually came creeping in.

My cell phone rang and I pulled if from my back pocket, frowning at the unfamiliar number on the screen.

I swiped to engage the call and lifted the phone to my ear. "Hello?"

"Deacon? It's Calvin. Is Fiona with you? I've been trying to reach her, but she's not answering her phone."

Something in his tone set me immediately on edge. "No, I'm at the bar. She's not at work?"

There was a long pause that made my gut churn painfully. "You haven't talked to her." It was a statement, not a question, and it did nothing to make me feel any better.

"I haven't. What's going on, Calvin? Did something happen?"

Another pause. "Maybe I should let her tell you."

A sick, sinking sensation hit me like a sledgehammer. "I'm

thinking you need to tell me what the hell's going on before I think the worst and lose my mind."

Calvin sighed through the line, causing the hairs on my arms to stand on end. Finally, after what felt like an agonizing lifetime, he started talking. "Something happened at the office this morning. There was... an email that was sent out." He stopped to let out a choked cough. "Look, I *really* think Fiona should be the one to tell you what happened. If she knew you heard it from me, she might get upset—"

"Look, Cal, no disrespect, but you called me and started dropping hints that something happened almost immediately. Now, if you don't start talking, *I'm* going to be the one who gets upset."

That time he didn't make me wait. "Last night there was an email circulated to all the employees in the Seattle office. The email contained explicit pictures of Fiona in some rather, uh... compromising positions." My vision was suddenly coated with red as fury set in. "I think you probably know the pictures I'm referring to."

"How the fuck did that happen?" I barked through the line as my hands clenched into tight fists. "How the hell did someone even get ahold of those pictures?"

"The who is what we're currently working to find out. As for the how, it seems that Fiona misplaced her phone one evening. She thinks, and I'm inclined to agree, that what really happened was someone took it and found the pictures."

I had no words as worry for Fiona flooded my system. "Where is she?" I snapped, the need to get to her as soon as possible overriding everything else.

"I honestly don't know, Deac. I thought she might have gone to you when she left here earlier. Maybe she's at home?"

Suddenly a memory from our childhood came flashing into my head, and instinct told me I already knew exactly where to find her. "I know where she is," I said to Calvin. "I'm going to her now."

"Thank God," he breathed into the speaker, his relief palpable. "Deacon, just do one thing for me. Take care of my little girl. She needs it now more than ever."

As long as I was alive, I'd spend my every waking minute taking care of Fiona. It was the most important job I'd ever have, and one I had no intention of ever failing at. "Always, Cal. You have my word."

I knew I had his trust and his approval when his only reply was "Go get her, son."

CHAPTER THIRTY-THREE

FIONA

THE TREE HOUSE was long gone, age and weather having turned it into a dilapidated wreck. Most of the wood had rotted and fallen away, leaving behind a skeleton of what it used to be. I remembered thinking it was glorious as a child, a hidden treasure Deacon and I had built with our own two hands. I hadn't thought about our tree house in years, but for whatever reason, I found myself drawn to our secret hideout when I left work earlier that day.

I sat on an old fallen tree, staring up at the remaining pile of rubble for hours. The clothes I'd picked for work earlier that morning weren't suited for hanging in the woods behind Deacon's childhood home in the middle of winter, but at least there wasn't any rain. I pulled my knees to my chest, wrapping my wool coat around them for warmth as I tried hard not to think about the fact that countless people now knew exactly what my breasts...and other parts of me looked like.

The crunch of leaves and the snapping of twigs alerted me to someone's presence, and I wasn't the least bit surprised to find Deacon coming my way when I turned to look over my shoulder. Sometimes I wondered if he knew me better than I knew myself.

"Hey," I said, my quiet voice resonating in the silence of the woods.

"Hey, baby. Had a feeling I'd find you out here. Also had a feeling that you wouldn't be properly dressed to be hanging outside, so I brought you this." He held up the huge fleece blanket he'd been carrying under his arm, and I could've cried with relief. I'd lost feeling in my legs too long ago to recall.

"Thanks," I muttered as he sat on the log beside me, pulled me flush against his side, and wrapped the blanket around the both of us. "So I'm taking it you heard?"

Because this day couldn't possibly get any worse.

Deacon nodded in confirmation. "Your dad called me when he couldn't get ahold of you. In his defense, he wanted you to be the one to tell me. I kind of forced it out of him."

I managed a small smile in spite of everything. "Why am I not surprised," I said as I laid my head against his shoulder. He held me to him and I did my best to absorb the warmth and safety I always felt whenever he was close.

After several minutes of silent contemplation, he asked, "You want to talk about it?"

I heaved a sigh, and instead of answering, I asked, "Do you ever think about this place?"

I felt his chin shift my hair, and as he spoke, his lips brushed against the top of my head. "You mean the tree house?"

"Yeah." I continued to talk on a whisper. "Our special secret hideout. Do you ever think about it?"

"Yes." He spoke just as softly. "I used to think about it all the time. After you and Grayson...." He stopped and I felt him swallow. "After I lost you, I used to come out here and sit just like you were when I found you. No matter what was going on between us, when I came out here I felt like I still had a piece of you with me."

I pulled back to face him, tears stinging my eyes as I said, "You always had me, Deacon. Even when you wanted nothing to do with me, you always had me."

Deacon's hand came up and stroked my cheekbone. "Yeah. Just maybe not in the way I wanted back then."

Squeezing my eyes closed, I turned away while pain lanced through my heart. "After everything happened, when I left the office, this was the first place I thought of. It was like instinct brought me here. I remembered feeling safe every time I climbed into that tree house because I knew you'd eventually show up."

Deacon's quiet laughter shook my body. "That's ironic since the damn thing was a death trap. If it was such a safe place, you never would've broken your arm."

I thought back to that day, and it wasn't the pain I remembered. It was Deacon carrying me back to his house and taking care of me like he always did. I swallowed down the swell of emotion clogging my throat. "I think I loved you, even back then. I was just too young and stupid to realize it."

His eyebrows drew together in a concerned frown. "Baby, you don't need to say stuff like that. We agreed that the past was the past. Nothing that happened before matters. We're together now."

Shaking my head, I pressed more of my weight against his side. "I'm not saying that to try and make up for the past. I've been sitting out here for hours, and that's a lot of time alone to think. I came here because this place holds memories of you. Every good childhood memory I have is because of you. Even when you weren't in my life, if something happened, you were always the first person I wanted to call. You're right. That damn tree house should've been condemned the moment we finished it, but I'll only ever remember loving it because it was *ours*. I know we said the past is the past, but I was in love with you back then, Deacon, and I never stopped. It was always you. No matter what, it's always been you. I just hate that I didn't realize it sooner. We could've had so much more time togeth—"

He silenced me with a kiss so brutal my lips felt bruised when he pulled away and cupped my jaw. "The time wasn't right for us back then, sweetheart, but it's the right time now, and that's all that matters."

"But—"

His thumb rested against my lips to cut off my words. "And when we have our kids, we get to tell them how Mommy and Daddy grew up as best friends before that grew into something even better. How many people get to say that?"

I released a watery laugh, one tear breaking free. "You're being awesome again. I'm going to need you to stop. I've already bawled my eyes out like five times today."

Deacon smiled, and for the first time in hours I felt like everything might be okay. "Can't make any promises, sweetheart. I'm just an awesome guy."

A giggle erupted from deep within my chest. Feeling lighter than I had since that morning, I laid my head back on his shoulder and looked at the ramshackle tree house.

I don't know how long we stayed like that before I finally got the nerve to talk about what had happened earlier. "I think I know who stole my phone," I said, admitting it out loud for the first time. Deacon's entire body grew tight but he didn't say a word, giving me a chance to continue uninterrupted. "The day I lost my phone, Todd had come into my office. He crossed a line and I kind of lost it on him. He got pissed." The shiver that worked its way up my spine had nothing to do with the temperature. "Like *seriously* pissed. We exchanged some words, and things got kind of ugly. I kicked him out of my office after he called me a cock-tease. I don't remember seeing my phone again after that until it turned up back on my desk the next morning."

Anger radiated from every pore, every molecule of Deacon's body. "He called you *what?*" he snarled so ferociously that it scared me a little.

"Deacon—"

He roared over me. "That motherfucker called you a cock-tease? Are you *fucking kidding me?*"

"I... no." I don't think I'd ever seen Deacon so angry in all my life. If I didn't know him so well, I'd have been terrified.

"What happened before that?"

"Deac, it doesn't—"

"Swear to fuckin' Christ, Fiona, if you tell me it doesn't matter, I'm going to lose my goddamn *mind*. Now what happened. Before. That?" he clipped.

"He came in acting like himself at first, trying to be charming. But then he... well, he grabbed me by my hips and—"

Deacon shot off the log so fast I nearly fell backward. "I'm going to fuckin' *kill* that asshole!"

All of a sudden I was terrified for an altogether different reason.

"You are not!" I shouted, jumping to my feet, the blanket around my shoulders keeping me warm all but forgotten. "Deacon, you're not going near that guy. Especially not when you're this upset."

"Upset? Got news for you, baby. I'm not *upset*. I'm fucking *pissed!*"

"Exactly! And if you do something like oh, I don't know, *beat the shit out of him*, you'll be the one who ends up in trouble. I know this guy, Deac. He's a snake. You lay a finger on him and he'll press charges."

His jaw ticked furiously as he growled, "It'll be worth it."

"And what about me?" I cried. "What am *I* supposed to do while you're locked up for assault?" I started to grow more and more frantic as I ranted. "I only just got you, Deacon! I'm not going to lose you after all this time!"

As if sensing I was on the verge of a nervous breakdown, the rage seeped from his muscles. What he said next shocked the hell out of me. "Okay, baby, okay. Just calm down. I'm not going to do anything that could take me away from you."

That wasn't quite good enough, so I demanded, "Promise me."

His arms shot out and wrapped around me, pulling me into an embrace. "I promise."

Those two words were all I needed to hear to relax, because I knew, to my soul, that Deacon would never break a promise to me. My forehead fell to his chest and I sighed, "Thank you."

"Don't thank me yet." When I tried to pull back to look at his face, his arms tightened around me like steel bands, keeping me in place. "I promise I won't do anything that could take me away from you, but I don't promise to sit back and do nothing. As soon as I get you home, I'm going to your office to talk to Calvin."

My entire body drooped in defeat. *Oh well, I guess it could be worse.* "I don't suppose I can talk you out of getting involved?"

I could hear the humor clear as day in his voice as he answered, "Not a chance in hell."

But I wasn't done trying. I still had one card to play. "Not even for a blowjob?"

"Not even for that," he laughed.

Putting as much attitude in my voice as I could muster, I threatened, "Then I guess you can kiss your blowjobs goodbye."

His fingertips stroked up and down along my spine in a soothing gesture. "Sweetheart, you can lie to me all you want.

With how soaked you get every damn time, I know you love sucking me off almost as much as I love having those pretty plump lips of yours wrapped around my cock."

Damn it.

He was *such* a pain in the ass sometimes.

CHAPTER THIRTY-FOUR

DEACON

I GOT Fiona home and into a nice warm bubble bath so she could thaw out after spending hours in the cold. When I felt she was settled and there was no risk of her losing it, I jumped back in my car and headed for Prentice Fashion. A minute after the receptionist called to tell him I was there, Calvin appeared in the lobby.

"Deacon, I'm surprised to see you here."

"Calvin," I greeted with a chin lift. "You got a minute to talk?"

He hesitated for a split second before tentatively waving me through the glass doors and into the main offices. I followed behind, scanning every face I passed until my gaze landed on the fucker I was searching for. I knew when all the color drained from his face the second he saw me that he was the one who emailed those private, naked pictures of my woman for everyone to see. And he was going to pay.

Her body was mine. No one had a right to see what lay beneath her clothes but me. *Especially* if she didn't give them permission. I was going to make that prick regret the day he was born.

Calvin led me into his office, closing the door behind him. "Is everything okay?" he asked, rounding his desk. "Is Fiona all right?"

"She's fine," I assured him. "I found her back by our old tree house. We talked and I think I got her calmed down, but she admitted something that I didn't want to wait to tell you."

He took his seat and waved to the one across from him for me to sit in. "I'm all ears. Anything to find this asshole. Our IT department thinks they're close to some answers, but it's not moving fast enough for my liking."

I relaxed back in the chair, propping an ankle on the opposite knee. "That guy sitting three doors down from here. You know who he is? Dude who dresses like a Tiger Woods reject and reeks like cheap drugstore cologne?"

Calvin's face pinched in confusion. "Um, you mean Todd Walden?"

"Yeah, that's the guy. Seems he didn't take Fiona shooting him down too well. Put his hands on her when she made it clear that she didn't want him to touch her, and called her a cock-tease when she made it even more clear that she'd never go there with him."

Calvin's face burned as red as the small amount of hair he still had on his head. "Tell me you're joking."

"Wish I was. Fee told me she noticed her phone missing shortly after that exchange, but didn't really think anything of it when it appeared back on her desk the next morning. A guy like that, incapable of taking a hit to his ego, I'm thinking he'd take a woman's rejection as a personal slight and do whatever he could to get back at the chick for not returning his affections."

"I've heard rumors," he said, his focus sliding beyond me to the closed door. "But that was all they were, just rumors. No one's ever come forward, and we haven't had any definitive proof in order to take action."

I tapped my index fingers on the arms of the chair. "My guess, you have your IT guys dig into this Todd asshole, you'll find where the email came from."

Calvin's eyes flashed with fire as his body grew stiff. "You know, I'm beginning to think you're right. If you wouldn't mind, I need to make a quick phone call. It shouldn't take but a minute."

"Do what you need to do."

Calvin picked up his phone and made a call. Things moved surprisingly fast after that. With Todd's name, the computer guys were no longer searching for a needle in a haystack. They were able to confirm that the email came from his personal account, but that the dumb fucker had sent it from his company laptop.

A few minutes after that, a guy named Anthony came into the office. I left him and Calvin to their business of preparing to fire the motherfucker, but I wasn't about to let the asshole off that easy. Instead of heading home to Fiona, I took the elevator down to the parking garage and waited.

Thirty minutes later, douchebag Todd came storming out of the elevator to a ragtop convertible that screamed *my dick's so small I have to overcompensate with my ride, but I'm too broke for anything better than a Miata*. His face was so red it was starting to turn purple, and he carried a box of all his personal shit in his hands.

"Yo. Asshole."

He stopped and spun around, momentarily startled at the sight of me before he slipped his *my shit doesn't stink* mask into place. "Get the hell out of my face. I've got nothing to say to you."

"That's good, because you've got nothing to say that I want to hear. I'll do the talking. You'll keep your mouth shut and listen if you're smart. But since I already know you're a dumb fuck, I'm not counting on that."

"Fuck you," he hissed, dropping the box on the trunk of his car. "It's not enough that that slutty bitch of yours got me fired, she had to go crying to her daddy so he'd blackball me. I worked my ass off for this bullshit company, and what do I have to show for it? I'll be lucky if I can get a job anywhere in Washington now, motherfucker."

Keeping from plowing my fist into his face took more self-control than I thought I had. "See? Now that's exactly what I meant about you being a dumb fuck. Call my woman a bitch or a slut one more time. I dare you."

The cock-sucker sneered, convinced he was untouchable. "What're you going to do, huh? You touch me and I'll press charges."

I grinned as I took a step closer. "Oh, but I don't think you will."

He tried to hide it, but I could see his confidence waver when he sized me up and realized he lacked the height and muscle needed to take me in a fight. It was all bravado as he squared his shoulders and tipped his chin up, asking, "Oh yeah? And why's that?"

I took another step. "Because if you press charges, then you'll have to admit to the cops that the reason you got your ass beat was because you purposefully broke into a woman's phone, stole her private photos, and distributed them for purposes of revenge. Now, I might be a little behind on the legislature, but last I checked, laws against revenge porn can range anywhere from a misdemeanor to a class C felony." His entire face blanched, but I wasn't finished just yet. "And considering that I have close familial connections with several of the men who wear robes in this state, I'm sure that after Fiona presses *her* charges, they'll be inclined to lean toward a felony. And make no mistake, she *will* press charges.

"You think you're blackballed now? Just wait until the judge presiding over your case finds out that the only reason you spread personal, intimate photos of a woman from a well-known and respected family was because she rebuffed your advances. They don't take too kindly to women with outstanding reputations being harassed and assaulted. Which is what the state of Washington considers your little stunt."

Proving that Todd Walden was as stupid as I already knew him to be, he gritted his teeth and hissed, "Fuck you, and fuck that bitch."

"Don't say I didn't warn you," I said, right before slamming my fist into his jaw. His head flew to the side, blood and what looked like a tooth flying from his mouth at the impact. I landed one last blow, and the sound of his nose breaking was so much more satisfying than I would've imagined. Then I walked away, leaving Todd a crying, writhing mess on the dirty cement floor of the garage. I'd done what I set out to do, stripping the jackass of the only thing he had left: his pride.

Now it was time to get back home to my girl.

CHAPTER THIRTY-FIVE

FIONA

I RESTED BACK on the huge plush couch, sinking deep into the fluffy cushions as I watched Deacon add a few logs to the fire. It had been a week since the incident with those photos, and I still hadn't gone back to the office. Honestly, I wasn't sure if I was ever going to feel comfortable going back.

When Deacon told me The Black Sheep had to be shut down for a few days due to construction and suggested an extended weekend away with just the two of us, I'd jumped at the chance.

We packed up and headed to my parents' cabin in the mountains. It had been four days of private bliss with the love of my life. We hiked through the snow, we talked, we made love by the fire. It had been perfect in every way. But our time alone in our cabin hideaway in the woods was drawing to a close, and we were heading back to the real world tomorrow.

I was sad for it to end.

"Hey," Deacon said, pulling me from my morose thoughts. "What's on your mind, sweetheart?"

"I was just thinking that I'm going to miss this when we head home tomorrow," I answered as I lifted my knees so he could sit on the cushion next to me. Once he was situated, he pulled my legs across his lap and began idly massaging my feet.

"Yeah, I know what you mean. This weekend has been pretty great."

I studied his profile in the firelight as he concentrated on my feet, and I suddenly saw everything I wanted with such clarity. It was like a veil had been lifted, revealing my picture-perfect future, and it was right in front of me, just waiting for me to grab it. All I needed to do was reach out. It was that simple.

"Deacon?"

He kept his focus on his ministrations as he replied, "Yeah, baby?"

"Can you look at me, honey?"

Reading the meaning in my voice, his head shot up, his brow furrowed when his eyes came to me. "What's wrong?"

"Nothing's wrong," I giggled, suddenly overwhelmingly giddy. "As a matter of fact, it feels pretty freaking right."

He released my feet, placing one arm on the back of the sofa and the other on the outside of my legs as he shifted closer. "What feels right?"

Unable to control my growing excitement, I began to ramble. "My future. Well, our future. That is, if it's still what you want."

Deacon's blinding grin warmed my chest. "Baby, slow down so I can follow what you're saying."

I pulled in a deep breath through my nose and exhaled through my lips before diving in. "I talked to my father before we left to come up here. Nothing was set in stone, but after this weekend, I know it's the right decision."

"What's the right decision?"

A huge grin split my face as I admitted, "I don't want to go back to Prentice Fashion. And before you say it, it's not because of what happened with Todd. I mean, I'm not thrilled that everyone saw those pictures, but the real reason I don't want to go back because I want to work at the bar. With you."

His chest swelled just before he asked, "Sweetheart, are you sure that's what you want?"

"I've never felt more sure about anything," I replied with a resolute nod. "Just the thought of working alongside you makes me happy. Helping you build and maintain your dream is more important than anything else I could ever do. I think my father understands that, because that was all my mom wanted after she fell in love with him."

"Fuck," he muttered, dropping his forehead against mine. "Just when I thought I couldn't possibly love you any more than I already do, you go and prove me wrong."

"Does that mean you still want me working for you?"

"*With* me," he quickly corrected. "And hell yes. I can never get enough of you. Maybe having you beside me every day will start to alleviate some of that need."

I let out a happy laugh and caressed his cheek, loving the feel of the short beard he'd let grow during our trip rubbing against my palm. "Good, that leads me to my second thing."

Deacon pressed deeper into my touch. "There's a second thing?"

"There is. Deacon, I want to marry you." He drew in a sharp breath and held it, his eyes flickering wildly at my declaration. "I've loved you since I was a little girl. You were my best friend, and now you're the love of my life. I want to build a family with you. I want to give our kids what my parents gave me, a childhood where they see their folks so blissfully in love that they know what's waiting out there for them is beyond anything they could imagine. It's always been you, Deac, and I don't want to wait a second longer than absolutely necessary to start our lives together."

He hooked his hand behind my head and pulled me

forward, pressing his lips against mine in a kiss so full of love it stole my breath. "I'm glad to hear you say that, sweetheart." He shifted to reach into the pocket of his jeans as he said, "This thing's been burning a hole in my pocket for weeks. I can't tell you how thrilled I am to finally put it where it belongs."

Grabbing my left hand, he slid a gorgeous diamond solitaire on my ring finger. Tears spilled down my cheeks at the sight of it. "How long—"

"Since the day after you told me you loved me. I've just been biding my time, baby, because it's always been you."

With a cry, I threw myself at him and wrapped my arms around his neck, peppering his face with kisses. "I want a short engagement," I insisted.

"You got it."

"And a small, intimate wedding."

"Works for me."

"And I want to get married to you at our special hideout. Under where our tree house used to be."

Deacon let out a loud belly laugh. "But if we get married there, it won't be our secret place anymore."

"I don't care," I replied vehemently. "That place is special, and it's where I want to celebrate the most important day of my life."

He clenched his fingers in my hair as he gave me that sexy, crooked smirk. "Whatever you want, I'll give it to you."

I already knew that to be true. Deacon had proven it over and over again, with actions as well as words. "I want you. For the rest of our lives."

"Then that's exactly what you'll get."

EPILOGUE

DEACON

A YEAR and a half later

"REMIND me the next time you ask for my help to tell you to go to hell."

I slid the hammer back into my tool belt and glanced over at Caleb. "Will you quit your bitching already? We're almost finished."

"Well thank God for that," he grumbled. "My blisters have splinters, for Christ's sake."

"Aw, poor baby Caleb. Never had to work a day of manual labor in his life," Dominic laughed. "Is real men's work too tough for you?"

Caleb shot the bird in Dominic's direction. "Says the man who gets manicures."

"It was one time!" Dominic shouted. "Sophia dragged me along. What was I going to do, just sit there bored out of my mind?"

Grayson wiped the sweat from his brow and shifted his gaze between our pain-in-the-ass friends before rolling his eyes. "You two think you can get your shit together long enough for us to get this done? I'd like to have dinner with my family tonight, not be stuck out in the middle of the goddamn woods, watching you two bicker like little girls."

Caleb and Dominic stopped fighting and got back to work. Without the distractions, we managed to finish an hour later and headed back to my parents' house. It was the Fourth of July, and everybody had gathered at the Lockhart house to celebrate the holiday with beer, barbeque, and family.

Dad was manning the grill on the back porch with Calvin and Maury gathered around, getting in some guy time well away from all the womenfolk. Nana was lying on a lounger in typical Nana style, with a pair of giant sunglasses on her face, a big floppy hat on her head to block out the sun, and a margarita in her hand that spelled trouble. My mom ran around with Evelyn and Elise, setting up huge spreads of food on the outside tables while Caleb's mother flitted around the yard chasing after Evie and Liam, Grayson and Lola's little boy, while somehow managing to hold Sophia and Dominic's three-month-old daughter, Annabelle, on her hip with surprising ease.

I scanned the area until my gaze landed on the one person I was looking for. Fiona sat near the pool with Lola, Sophia, and Daphne. The four of them were in a tight huddle, talking and laughing without a care in the world, and just like it had all my life, my heart flipped at the sight of her gorgeous smile.

I broke off from the guys and made my way to my wife, stopping about five feet away. When her attention turned to me, I lifted my hand and crooked my finger, chuckling under my breath as she rolled her eyes at my caveman antics. She said something to her girls before standing and heading in my direction. I watched in fascination as she moved, the swell of her belly prominent beneath her filmy sundress. There was nothing more attractive in the world than the sight of my wife heavy with my child. When she held that stick up seven months before, the two pink lines clear as day, I finally understood what my father was talking about when he described the pride he felt when it came to his children.

"You summoned?" she teased once she made it to me.

"There's something I want to show you. Can you spare a few minutes away from the band of merry misfits?"

Her face scrunched with curiosity as she examined my sweaty T-shirt and dirt-covered jeans. "I think I can make a little time for you."

My lips quirked in a grin as I took her hand and started leading her toward the tree line past my parents' backyard.

"Ooh," she cooed playfully, tugging on my hand as we got farther and farther away from the party. "Are we sneaking off for a quickie? Why, Deacon Lockhart, you're so naughty."

My head fell back on a burst of laughter as I continued leading her deeper into the woods. "As enticing as that sounds, that's not why I'm bringing you out here." I hooked my arm over her shoulder and pulled her into my side, kissing her temple. "At least not yet, anyway," I added, because her idea definitely held merit. But first....

Fiona jerked to a stop with a loud gasp. "Oh my God. Deacon." She looked from the tree house to me, tears welling in her beautiful eyes. "You... oh my God, you built me a tree house."

"Well, we can't keep calling it our secret hideout if there's nowhere to actually hide out in, now can we?"

"It's... it's...." She let out a hiccuped sob and reached up with her free hand to cover her mouth. "This is the most perfect tree house ever." Spinning into me, she wrapped her arms around my waist as best she could with our baby growing between us and burrowed into my chest. "I'd go inside"—she let me go to look down and rub her belly—"but this little guy's throwing off my center of gravity. I don't think I could make it up the ladder."

I placed my hands over hers and tangled our fingers together right above where our son grew healthy and strong. "It's not going anywhere. Unlike the last one, this tree house has been built to last. It's a gift for you as well as this little guy right here."

She sniffled and looked back to the tree house. "I can't believe you did this for me, Deacon," she whispered, giving me her eyes once more. "It's amazing."

Moving my hands from her belly, I lifted them and tangled my fingers in her thick, fiery red hair. "When our son is old enough, we'll bring him here and tell him stories about his parents' friendship growing into something so much more. We'll teach him what real, unconditional love is, and maybe one day, when he finds the girl he knows, down to his bones, he's going to spend the rest of his life with, he'll bring her here and make it their own special, secret hideout. Just like his dad did with his mother."

A tear slipped free and made a track down her cheek. I caught it with my thumb and leaned in to kiss her rosy pink lips.

"You're being awesome again, Deacon," she said in a mock scolding tone.

"Better get used to it, baby. This is only the beginning."

Her sigh was filled with contentment as she leaned into me and gave me a hug. "I love you, Deacon. Around the world and back again."

I breathed in the scent of her hair, relishing the fact that this amazing woman was mine for the rest of my life, and responded the same way I always did. The same way I always would. Forever.

"And I love you to Jupiter and back again."

The End

*I hope you enjoyed reading about the Fiona, the other ladies of Girl Talk, and the men who won them. For more laugh-out-loud romance keep reading for a sneak peek at **Fire & Ice**, the first in my **Locklaine Boys series***

FIRE & ICE EXCERPT

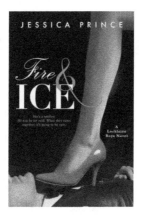

Prologue

PEPPER

I'D SEEN the love of my life approximately four times in the span of nearly a decade. And every single time I laid eyes on that picture of male perfection my heart rioted in my chest, my skin grew clammy, and my stomach flip-flopped so many times it could give a gold-medal gymnast a run for her money.

The first time I met Griffin Locklaine I was only twelve years old. He was friends with my older brother, Dexter. He and his cousin, Rowan, had come home with my brother for Thanksgiving break. It was love at first sight. My tiny, pre-teen heart went all a-flutter the moment he walked through our front door. He was everything a girl could ask for in her dream man. Tall, muscular, with a face so beautiful it belonged on a magazine. His brown hair was so dark it looked almost black, and the unruly waves flopped over his forehead, making him look almost innocent. And I knew he had to be intelligent if he was going to NYU with Dex. They didn't let just anybody in there, after all. Or at least that's what my mom loved to say every time she bragged about my big brother.

But it was his eyes that drew me in the most. From the moment his icy blue gaze hit me I knew that was it. He was *The One*—capital letter worthy—and in my little girl imagination I was already planning our wedding, complete with a horse-drawn carriage and doves releasing the moment we kissed. It was all grotesquely romantic, completely unrealistic, and kind of nauseating whenever I thought back on those particular fantasies.

Unfortunately for me, there wasn't much a twelve-year old girl could do to hold the attention of a twenty-one year old *man*. I was still in a *training bra* for God's sake! So there I was, suffering in silence for an entire *week*, holding my love deep inside so no one could have possibly guessed how I felt.

Oh, and just an FYI, if you hadn't yet figured out that I was an overly dramatic kid, let me just clear up any misconceptions.

I totally was.

Anyway, back to the topic at hand.

I was in love. And the object of the slightly obsessive, somewhat misguided fantasies barely even knew I existed. The only words he spoke to me the entire week were, '*What's up, red?*' causing my pale skin to glow as brightly as the fiery hair I'd inherited from my father's Irish side. It was in moments such as those that I cursed my handsome brother for getting everything from our mom's side while I was stuck with hair that shined like a glowing beacon under any and all florescent lighting.

I wanted to run and hide in my room—which was basically what I did most of the time, only coming out when my mother practically dragged me down the stairs, insisting I *socialize*.

It should also be said, that at that point in my life, I kinda hated my mother. But I digress.

I did the best I could to avoid being in Griffin's presence for the rest of their stay, only finding comfort in the rare times I was able to watch him, unknowingly, from afar.

Like a total creeper, but whatever. Unrequited love would do that to a young girl, after all.

THE SECOND TIME I saw Griffin I was fourteen, having my first period while experiencing the worst breakout in history. and wearing braces with neon colored rubber bands.

It was a travesty the likes of which Humanity had never seen before.

He was twenty-three, fresh out of the police academy, even better looking than the last time I saw him, and with his girlfriend.

With.

His.

Girlfriend.

Her name was Heather. I hated Heather. I wanted to throw her out in the frigid Buffalo winter and watch her slowly freeze into a ditzy, blonde dumbsicle. I hadn't thought it was possible, but watching him kiss her or lean in and whisper in her ear, or hell, even *smile* at her, hurt like tens of thousands of tiny paper cuts. My heart was broken. My melodramatic, hormonal teenaged world had come to an abrupt end. There was nothing in life worth living for if Griffin Locklaine didn't know I existed.

Okay, yes, so I was a teensy bit overemotional. But I was a young girl, premenstrual for the first time in *my life*. Add raging hormones and a whopping dose of adolescent angst together and the combination was catastrophic.

THE THIRD TIME I saw Griffin was pure happenstance... or fate, depending on how you looked at it.

Just a heads-up, I totally saw it as fate.

I'd moved to New York City shortly after graduating high school, determined to fulfill my dream of opening my very own high-end clothing boutique, so I was going to school for business and fashion merchandising, living in the same city as my brother and my forbidden crush.

I might have changed substantially over time, physically and maturity wise, but that didn't mean I wasn't reduced to a bumbling idiot when I just so happened to stumble into him and his *date* on a random sidewalk after seeing a movie with a few friends.

"Pepper? Is that you?" I nearly choked on my tongue as his familiar voice broke through the laughter of me and my friends as we made our way home from a late show. "Holy shit! Is that really you?"

I didn't know whether or not to be offended or flattered by the bewildered look on his face. Yes, I looked different. Gone were the knobby knees and pointy elbows, and in their place were curves that rivaled one's I'd seen in women in magazines. I'd discovered a smoothing cream that managed to tame my wild, frizzy hair that no longer glowed neon orange, thanks to the deeper red and brown lowlights I added. I wore makeup—correctly. I dressed in clothes that fit my frame. I'd come out of my shell, grown up. I'd developed my own style and personality. I wasn't that same shy, nerdy little girl I used to be.

That was, until I crossed paths with my unobtainable crush after almost five years...while his arm was wrapped securely around a blonde that barely deemed me worthy of acknowledgement.

"H-hey, Griff," I stuttered as my two girlfriends gawked at him with undisguised longing.

"No fuckin' way!" he laughed excitedly, and nearly dropped dead right there on the sidewalk as he released his life sized Barbie doll and wrapped me in a tight hug. "Look at you, red. All grown up." He grinned affectionately as he placed his hands on my shoulders and held me away from him so he could get a better look. My heart tripped over in my chest at the gleam I caught in his frosty blue eyes. If I squinted *juuuuuuuust* right, it looked a teeny-tiny bit like lust. I was sure of it.

"Come on, babe," the blowup doll behind him whined in a nasally voice. "We're going to be late for the movie. You know how much I like watching the previews."

It took everything in me to suppress the urge to lunge for her and snatch the extensions from her hair as Griffin let go and stepped back.

He shot me a friendly grin as he pulled the blonde against him. "It was good seeing you again."

I wanted to die as I forced a smile of my own. "Yeah, you too."

"Well, see you around, kid."

With that, he was God.

Kid?

Kid!

Yep, I was most definitely dying inside.

THE FOURTH TIME I saw Griffin was the night everything would change. I was twenty-one years old and in the middle of the grand-opening celebration for my boutique, Fire & Ice. I'd done it. I was living my dream. I had my own shop where I sold some of the finest clothes in the city. I was on cloud nine, so euphoric that I didn't even cringe at the sight of Griffin walking in just behind Dex. I was totally blissed out and slightly buzzed from the glasses of champagne to even care about the whole *kid* incident from three years earlier.

That night was nothing short of magical. As the hours ticked by the party grew livelier to my ecstatic surprise, Griffin actually seemed to *notice* me. I couldn't have imagined feeling happier than I was right then, standing in the shop of my dreams with the man I'd loved for nearly a decade by my side. I was convinced that this was as good as it could get.

I'd been wrong.

It got even better later that night when I gave my virginity to Griffin, knowing, deep down in my bones that it was the start of something epic between us. I finally had everything I'd ever wanted.

So imagine my surprise when I woke with the sun the next morning and rolled over, wanting nothing more than to snuggle against my man, only to find the sheets cold and empty and myself completely alone.

Read More Now

MORE FROM THE LOCKLAINE BOYS

Opposites Attract

JESSICA PRINCE

DELILAH NORTHCUTT HAS BEEN DESCRIBED as weird, nerdy. But her favorite term is quirky. The eccentric flower shop owner definitely marches to the beat of her own drum. On the rebound from a cheating ex, she's not looking to open her heart to someone else any time soon. On a whim, her best friend convinces her that one night with a stranger she'll never see again is just what she needs to pull herself out of the funk she's been living in.

Overly serious, workaholic Richard Locklaine was always described as the twin determined to do the right thing. Even if it was at the cost of his own well-being. But after years in a love-less, manipulative marriage, he's finally free and ready to build a life of his choosing. And nowhere in that life is there room for another woman—unless it's for just one night, of course.

They are complete opposites in every single way. But for some reason, fate has decided to force the two of them together. Despite the chemistry, they're determined to fight the attraction growing between them. Besides, what could a florist with horrible taste in music and an attorney from Connecticut ever really have in common? Only one thing is certain. When they finally come together, it's going to be epic.

Almost Perfect

DEVON   MCMILLON   WASN'T LOOKING for a knight in shining armor. She didn't need a man to rescue her or take care of her. She just wanted someone who would treat her as an equal and love her for who she was. Unfortunately, even in a city as big as Manhattan, finding a guy who wasn't intimidated by a strong-minded,   slightly   outspoken woman   was   proving   harder   than expected.

Having fallen in love at the age of fifteen Collin Locklaine was convinced he'd already found the woman he was destined to spend the rest of his life with. That was, until she pulled the rug out from under him and ended their relationship. He'd taken care of her, been her protector. And now he was forced to start over again.

A man with a hero complex and a woman with a fierce independent streak should never work. However, fate has other ideas. Besides, sex that good can't be a fluke, right? With an attraction like theirs, Devon and Collin have no other choice but to dive in and see where it leads them. Only one thing is certain. When they finally come together, it's going to be epic.

DISCOVER OTHER BOOKS BY JESSICA

THE PICKING UP THE PIECES SERIES:

Picking up the Pieces

Rising from the Ashes

Pushing the Boundaries

Worth the Wait

THE COLORS NOVELS:

Scattered Colors

Shrinking Violet

Love Hate Relationship

Wildflower

THE LOCKLAINE BOYS (a LOVE HATE RELATIONSHIP spinoff):

Fire & Ice

Opposites Attract

Almost Perfect

THE PEMBROOKE SERIES (a WILDFLOWER spinoff):

Sweet Sunshine

Coming Full Circle

A Broken Soul

CIVIL CORRUPTION SERIES

Corrupt

Defile (Declan and Tatum's story – coming 2018)

GIRL TALK SERIES:

Seducing Lola

Tempting Sophia

Enticing Daphne

Charming Fiona

STANDALONE TITLES:

Chance Encounters

Nightmares from Within

DEADLY LOVE SERIES:

Destructive

Addictive

CO-WRITTEN BOOKS:

Hustler – with Meghan Quinn

ABOUT THE AUTHOR

Born and raised around Houston, Jessica is a self proclaimed caffeine addict, connoisseur of inexpensive wine, and the worst driver in the state of Texas. In addition to being all of these things, she's first and foremost a wife and mom.

Growing up, she shared her mom and grandmother's love of reading. But where they leaned toward murder mysteries, Jessica was obsessed with all things romance.

When she's not nose deep in her next manuscript, you can usually find her with her kindle in hand.

Connect with Jessica now
Website: www.authorjessicaprince.com
Jessica's Princesses Reader Group
Newsletter
Facebook
Twitter
Instagram
authorjessicaprince@gmail.com

CPSIA information can be obtained
at www.ICGtesting.com
Printed in the USA
LVHW111103200920
666576LV00001B/100